DAMASK ROSE

"[Smith constructs] strong, complex characters, and this dark tale of vengeance and redemption is splendidly told!"
—*Publishers Weekly*

"Haywood Smith crafts a tale that grips you and never lets go. You'll be mesmerized by the magical and mystical qualities of the story and left spellbound . . . A tale for the discriminating reader searching for the ideal mix of history, mysticism, dreams and romance." —*Romantic Times*

"A beautifully woven tale . . . Ms. Smith delivers a rich fascinating plot. Splendid!"
—*Bell, Book, and Candle* (4½ Bells)

"DAMASK ROSE proves that with faith and love, all things are possible. Once every year or so I read a story so compelling, so moving, that the characters stick with me for months afterwards. Such is the case with DAMASK ROSE. Add this keeper to your personal library."
—*The Old Book Barn Gazette*

"Don't miss this first class read!"
—*Belles and Beaux of Romance*

SECRETS IN SATIN

"Will appeal to readers who love characters that show faith, strength, and courage while learning to build a lasting relationship." —*CompuServe Romance Reviews*

"A beautiful tale . . . entrancing and amazing. Just sit back and let Haywood Smith draw the world of 17th century England around you." —*The Literary Times*

ST. MARTIN'S PAPERBACKS TITLES
BY HAYWOOD SMITH

Shadows in Velvet
Secrets in Satin
Damask Rose
Dangerous Gifts
Highland Princess
Border Lord

BORDER LORD

Haywood Smith

St. Martin's Paperbacks

BORDER LORD

Copyright © 2001 by Haywood Smith.

ISBN: 0-312-97859-6

Printed in the United States of America

St. Martin's Paperbacks edition / April 2001

St. Martin's Paperbacks are published by St. Martin's Press, 175 Fifth Avenue, New York, NY 10010.

10 9 8 7 6 5 4 3 2 1

ACKNOWLEDGMENTS

Just when you think you know where life's taking you, things can take an alarming turn. I've been on some pretty wild detours in the past two years, and I would like to thank publicly some of the people who have helped me make lemonade out of lemons. God has blessed me with so many wonderful friends and family that I cannot name them all here, but there are a few I must.

First, kudos to associate publisher and editor Jennifer Enderlin for her unfailing support and patience—and her brilliant editorial instincts. Also to her and publisher Matthew Shear for believing in me enough to support my leap into an exciting new fiction adventure.

Next, to my precious support-group friends who have helped me learn to find peace and happiness even amid chaos. Thanks to their caring, wisdom, and experience, I'm growing daily and rediscovering the joy I'd lost.

My deepest gratitude to my precious sisters, whose unqualified love is always there. What a blessing from God y'all are. Betsy, I'm sorry I wrecked all your stuff when I was little. Susan, I'm sorry you got caught doing everything I got away with. Lisa, I'm sorry I woke you up to do the dishes so Daddy wouldn't find out I was tipsy that night when you were only ten.

Last, I thank a gracious Creator for blue skies, a roof over my head, sweet breezes, hot baths, second chances, and hope.

Chapter
ONE

Catherine Armstrong clung to the rail of the merchantman *Dere* and lifted her face toward the tempest. "You're God," she shouted heavenward, more frightened now than ill. "You should know I didn't mean it when I asked You to kill me! And it's not very godlike to take everyone else down with me!"

The frantic sailors paid no heed to her rantings; they were too busy trying to save the ship from the freak summer storm. But the God of Abraham, Isaac, and Jacob was not amused. He responded to her insolence with a huge wave that blasted Catherine halfway across the deck.

Brilliant! She frantically grappled for a handhold. *First you ask Him to kill you, then when He tries to do it, you question His methods! And insult Him!*

"I'm sorry," she gasped as she was swept between the mainmast and the center hatch. "I take it all back."

She struck something pliable and grabbed hold for dear life. It turned out to be a sailor, but instead of anchoring her, he tumbled onto her, head to hind, in a drenched tangle of arms and legs, sliding across the deck in the rush of seawater.

"Let go!" he bellowed in coarse northern accents that were muffled by the sodden fabric of her dress. "Or we'll both end up overboard!"

At last, they slammed against the side. She landed atop him with her head between his knees and her skirts washed up completely, leaving her arse exposed to the wind and rain.

Flesh no man had ever seen lay exposed to the commonest sailor's idle glance.

Humiliated, Catherine scrambled to cover herself, but her efforts were hampered by the ship's heaving and the seaman's struggle to escape the drenched folds of her skirt. He wrestled like a monkey in a sack, making it difficult to tug down her clothes.

"Be still, man," she shouted, "and I'll have you free in a moment."

"Get off me, woman!" He gripped her bare thigh with his coarse hand. "Off, I say!"

Catherine stiffened in outrage at such a violation of her person. "I cannot unless you let go of me!" She managed to free her own hand and whacked at the rough grip on her leg. "*You* . . . let . . . *me* . . . go . . . this *instant*!"

"Stop hittin' me, ye bilious wench!" he howled. But he did let go, only to resume thrashing against her soaked skirts and petticoats.

Finally, she managed to right herself and roll free of him. "Insolent knave!" Soaked and chilled, she lurched to the fittings around the mainmast and held on. "Touch me again, and I'll report you to your captain!"

The seaman staggered to his feet. "And I'll report ye for bein' here! All passengers belowdecks," he roared above the storm. "Captain's orders!" Then he stomped away to attend his business.

The mere mention of returning to the stench of her cramped cabin was enough to set Catherine's stomach roiling. She gagged, turning her face into the wind in a futile effort to calm her innards. The stink below was why she'd braved the elements in the first place—that, and Charles's endless complaints.

A fine protector he'd turned out to be.

He hadn't stopped whining and demanding attention since his own seasickness had struck. Never mind that she was ill, too. To listen to him, one would think he were six instead of sixteen. But then again, he was always whining and demanding attention.

Catherine sighed. Prodded by guilt over her intense dislike for her stepbrother, she decided she ought to go down to check on him at least.

Handhold to handhold, she lurched across the deck toward the cabin entrance. As she neared it, another grim-faced sailor emerged, bringing with him the odor of sickness, tar, waste, and unwashed bodies from below.

One whiff was all it took to change her mind. Charles could cling to his berth in the stinking darkness with his head in a bucket if he wished. She would take her chances in the storm, even if the Almighty punished her insolence by airing her arse again.

The deck rose abruptly, then dropped away beneath her feet, taking her stomach with it. Catherine staggered to the open rail and retched.

The devil's own irony, that she could be so ill with her stomach long since empty!

The gale and sideways rain plastered her wet clothes to her as she held on to the rail and willed herself through second after miserable second. She had no idea how much time had crawled by before she heard a desperate cry from the rigging. "Land! Avast! Land ho!"

Catherine looked ahead and saw explosive sheets of spray as storm and sea met the low cliffs of the coastline.

Nausea gave way to a harsh twist of fear, abruptly replacing her wretchedness with a tingling surge that set her heart slamming against her ribs like a wild hawk trapped in a cage.

Dear heaven, the storm was driving them straight to destruction.

She heard more shouts and turned to see the captain at the wheel with two helmsmen, their faces distorted by effort as they fought to turn the ship.

"Full astarboard!" the captain shouted. "Lend a hand, here!"

Two more men fought their way to the helm and added their weight to the battle.

The ship groaned from deep within. Slowly, it began to turn.

Perhaps God did not mean to kill them, after all.

Then a ragged, moaning shudder belowdecks was followed by a sharp concussion Catherine felt in the soles of her feet, and all five men at the helm went flying.

The wheel spun crazily in one direction, then the other.

The rudder! Had they lost the rudder?

Catherine was no sailor, but even she knew that without a rudder they would end up on the cliffs.

Where was the captain? He would know what to do. Her mouth dry as ash, she scanned the deck and saw him lying crumpled at an odd angle against a hatch.

The helmsmen rushed to his aid.

Please, God, don't let him be dead. Without a captain . . .

To her relief, he stirred, then grasped the front of the helmsman's coarse shirt and shouted something. The helmsman nodded. While his companion raced below, the helmsman stood and cupped his hands to his mouth. "All hands on deck!"

Crewmen poured from the bowels of the ship, shouting frantic orders and scattering to their tasks.

Catherine turned back to the rail, her eyes drawn to the looming disaster ahead. The wind caught her hood and blew it back, exposing her prim coiffure, but she paid no heed, spellbound by looming destruction.

The ship was doomed. She knew it with the same certainty she'd known her mother was dead that night fourteen long years ago.

Where they were, she could not guess. They'd set sail for Cornwall from Morecambe Bay yester noon, but the vicious storm had borne down on them in the night and blown them God knows where.

Rage and frustration boiled inside her as she peered into the distance at the deadly obstacle in their path. She could not end this way! Not after surviving thirty years of border wars and pestilence so firmly rooted to the land.

Was this God's final paradox, a last celestial joke?

Well, Catherine had no intention of taking it lying down. *I'm only here out of obedience, for the good of the family,* she directed heavenward. *For this, You kill me? Not to mention the others on the ship!* Her stepbrother Charles among them.

Not that that would be so great a loss for the world.

I didn't mean that about Charles, God, she promptly retracted. *Forgive me.* It would not do to die with such a hateful thought unshriven. Her sins were great enough as it was, her lack of humility chief among them.

But before she could form another prayer, two strong hands closed on her throat from behind and throttled her. Sheer surprise immobilized her.

Who? *Why?*

Not a crewman; he was cloaked.

Whoever it was, he was powerful, for Catherine was a strong woman, but when she broke through her shock and began to struggle, the assailant lifted her as if she were a child and tossed her over the side. Gulping in a precious lungful of air as she fell, she caught one brief glimpse of a broad-shouldered silhouette before the heaving waves claimed her.

The sea swallowed her into the cold and quiet, her clothes enveloping her like a fatal flower. Time seemed to slow in the dim and deadly calm below the storm. She flailed back her cloak and skirts. So cold, even in summer, the chilling waters sucked her deeper, her eyes stinging, unable to make out anything but the faint light of the surface. Frantic heartbeat by heartbeat, she struggled toward it as her clothing dragged her down.

Why? Who had done this? The dark questions gripped her frantic heart, but imminent peril forced her to focus on her predicament. She had to swim. Find the surface. She didn't seem to be making any progress, but the will to survive was as much a part of her as her substantial bones and sinew. She could no more surrender her life than she could breathe the harsh gray waters that were trying to take it.

Devil or God—whoever had caused this—she would not die without a fight! A fierce denial overtook her, distilled into a single desperate purpose that fixed her vision on the light above and gave her superhuman strength.

She kicked off her shoes, propelling herself upward as she shed her heavy cloak, ripped loose her heavy skirts, petticoats, and furbelow, tore away her elaborate sleeves and ruffed collar, then clawed to pieces the bodice that bound her now-burning lungs.

As she did, she thought of nothing—no farewells, no regrets. Her life did not flash before her eyes. She did not see her beloved mother beckon from Eternity, nor her sire, though she would not have known him if he had.

Up was all that mattered. Up to air, and life.

Clad now only in her precious shift, she kicked her cold-numbed legs with every ounce of strength her rage could muster. The edges of her vision began to sparkle, and just as she had begun to fear she'd fought in vain, she broke through the surface at last.

Her desperate gulp of air was cut short by a wave, choking her. Coughing frantically, she searched with stinging, salt-blurred eyes for the ship, but was unable to find it for the roiling sea. Then she heard a distant rending, splintering roar as the ship was driven against the shallow cliffs.

Charles. All those men . . .

You cannot help them, an inner voice chided, but you can help yourself. Swim!

But swimming through this tempest was a far cry from her sedate outings into the pond back home. Catherine fought down the paralyzing terror that threatened to overtake her, and tried to get her bearings.

Still coughing sporadically, she caught sight of a narrow strand in the distance and struck out for land through the terrifying troughs and peaks.

At first, it seemed she was getting nowhere, but she kept on going.

Please, God, she prayed as her nose and throat burned and her muscles began to quiver. *Give me strength and direction. Keep me moving toward the strand. You've preserved me thus far* . . . Though why He had was a mystery, since He'd allowed her to be thrown overboard in the first place.

Who had done it? And why?

Again, she ignored the questions in favor of more immediate matters. *Just keep me till the shore, and I'll ask nothing more of You. Truly.*

And I really didn't mean that about Charles, she added, knowing it was a lie. *Please spare his life. He's Papa's firstborn, and Papa loves him.* Despite her difficulties with Charles, she truly did not wish her beloved stepfather the grief of losing a son.

After what seemed like hours, she reached the limits of her failing strength. So cold and weary she could scarcely move, she sensed an easing in the storm and took advantage of the lull to float upon her back for a brief respite. Her arms and legs felt heavy as stone. Closing her eyes to the rain, she was tempted to give up.

That was when she heard it: the sound of breakers on sand.

A shriek of thanks rose from her soul. Catherine rolled over and swam with renewed energy toward the blessed sound until she was so breathless she had to stop. She dropped her legs, but could not touch bottom. Yet the shore was close. She could hear it, even though she couldn't see it for the waves. Just a few yards away, she told herself.

Then she felt an ominous backward tug and heard the eerie sough of the huge wave rearing behind her.

She turned to see it arch above her, green and greedy and flecked with seaweed.

No! Not now! Not so close to deliverance!

The wall of water crested overhead and came crashing

down, leaving her time only to wonder if she would
waken next in hell.

THE NEXT MORNING AT NEARBY ANNANLEA, HOME OF
DUNCAN MAXWELL

"Duncan!" Michael Graham called as he strode through
the doorway with the vigor of a man half his age. "We've
got trouble!" Duncan's foster father and trusted com-
mander was ominously terse for a man who usually made
much of little, loudly and with vehement conviction. Michael's grim expression underscored the fact that this was
serious, indeed.

Closing his worn copy of Homer's *Iliad,* Duncan
nudged his mastiff out of the way. "Move, Clyde, ye great
lazy beast." The huge dog lumbered to his feet so Duncan
could stand.

Hot on Michael's heels, Thurlow Ridley and Darby
Carlisle engaged in a heated exchange as they approached
the open doorway. Thurlow was bleeding from the head,
and both looked as if they'd suffered a drubbing.

A sharp thrust of foreboding landed heavy in his chest.
They'd been guarding the salt cache. He was no stranger
to trouble—no one who battled out an existence in these
wild border regions was—but the survival of all at Annanlea hinged on their salt cache. If something had happened to it . . .

A cold shudder rippled through him, punctuated by a
stab of panic that no one must ever suspect. He braced
himself for the worst.

The two men tried to shove inside at the same time,
tangling them both in the jamb.

" 'Twas the divil, I tell ye!" Darby said as he wiggled
free of Thurlow's large frame and popped inside. He hob-
bled forward as fast as his twisted leg would allow, dripping a rusty trail of blood across the floor and onto Aunt
Brigit's precious Persian carpet. "There was nae sound!"

he exclaimed to Duncan. "One minute, I'm mindin' ma post, and the next, the sun is up and I'm lyin' in me own blood! It had ta be the divil, or I'da heard 'em comin'! I may have a bad leg, but I've the best ears at Annanlea, and none can dispute it. An' I heard nothin'! 'Twas the divil, I tell ye."

"Divil, me arse," Thurlow countered in the rough accents of his English origins. " 'Twas flesh and bone that laid me low, and not without a fight. Musta been at least five of 'em." He glared at his wounded compatriot. "If Darby had done his job on lookout, I'd at least've had some warnin'."

The nucleus of panic tingled larger deep inside Duncan.

Through the open door behind the errant guards, Duncan saw the rest of his men gathering outside in the courtyard, their faces agitated. "Bid the men come inside," he said to Michael. "Better to have them hear it straight than feed on rumors later." They were all in this together.

Listing on his lame side, Darby inadvertently shifted against Thurlow, and the two men started shoving each other like wayward children fighting over the last oatcake.

" 'Tis a lucky thing they hit ye in the head," Thurlow railed. "Yer skull's as thick as a papist's missal."

"Stop that," Duncan commanded the warring parties. "It does nae good to fight each other." He glanced at the rug where Darby was standing. "Step back, Darby, you're bleedin' on Aunt Brigit's rug. We've trouble enough without runnin' afoul of her."

Both men quailed at the mention of the tiny woman who was the scourge—and heart—of Annanlea. Thurlow made sure his skinned knees weren't dripping while Darby hastily retreated to bare wood. Meanwhile, eight of Duncan's ten other men finished filing silently into the far end of the parlor, all ears. The only two missing were the ones who'd relieved Thurlow and Darby.

"Tell me what happened," Duncan said to the two injured guards.

True to form, Thurlow and Darby spoke atop each other.

"The divil himself, or the ghost of a Johnstone takin' his revenge," Darby declared.

"There must've been five of 'em, at least. Seven!" Thurlow said emphatically.

"One at a time," Duncan instructed, to no avail.

Darby did his best to drown Thurlow out. "Like I said, I never saw 'em, 'cause there was nothin' to see."

"There were hoofprints everywhere," Thurlow said even louder in an effort to add weight to his own position. "The divil doesna ride a horse," he said to Darby. "Men ride horses, and 'twas men what did us in, ye acorn-balled clod-pate!"

Duncan's legendary self-control threatened to give way to his even more legendary temper. "Stop arguin' *who* did it," he roared, "and tell me *what* they did!"

He knew full well what they were about to say, but he had to hear it for himself.

"They got the salt," the two men blurted as one, dropping their heads in shame. "All of it."

His worst fear, realized. The hard knot of panic in Duncan's chest opened up into a tingling void. His men stood watching him, expecting him to know what to do. Duncan felt ancient, far beyond his thirty years. What would they say if they knew that he was just as stricken and confused as they? But they would never know. He was their leader, their protector. He had to act the part, even when he did not feel it.

Do the next right thing, he told himself, as he had through so many crises before. Just do the next right thing. "Nae sense guardin' what's gone," he said with a quiet calm that was only skin deep. He turned to Michael. "Have one of the lads call Quinn and Rory back in."

Michael nodded and strode for the courtyard.

Nine months' worth of salt harvest, gone. It was all they had to trade for provisions to carry them through the winter. Without it, his own family, and those of his dozen men and score of cottagers, might very well starve. For unlike other reivers—the wild outlaws of the marches, called Steel Bonnets for the close helmets they wore—Duncan refused to feed his people at the expense of others with brutal raids and cattle theft. He and his men rode the moors only in defense of his own.

"What'll we do now?" Thurlow asked. "I'd rather have died than give it up, Duncan."

"Nae salt is worth a man of mine," Duncan snapped.

He meant it, but he had no idea how they would manage. The salt was the only security Annanlea had. Demand peaked at harvesttime, but it would take them far longer to amass enough to trade. By then, cold weather would be hard upon them, and demand would have fallen sharply, with only root crops and spirits left to trade for.

Every one of the men who had found refuge under his protection knew that. Mining and guarding the salt was their most sacred charge—keeping it, and its location, safe and secret. Of the women, only Aunt Brigit knew the whereabouts of the cache.

None but the most trusted of his men were allowed to harvest the hidden salt pans and protect the yield, and death—swift and certain—was the penalty for breaking that trust.

Yet Annanlea had been betrayed. It was the only explanation.

The very thought of it loosed a pain in his gut as sharp as the stab of a Steel Bonnet's pike.

Duncan had moved his salt cache every few weeks within the extensive network of tunnels and underground safe-rooms, and he shifted his guards' positions often, changing watches with great stealth only under cover of darkness. Even so, the raiders appeared to have found Darby and Thurlow easily enough. And the salt. Only one of his own men would have been privy to its well-hidden location.

"Was anything clse taken?" he asked as Michael returned and stood beside him. "Kine? Sheep?"

"Nay," Thurlow answered. "We checked the near pastures on our way back. Nae a single head was missin'."

Odd. More than odd.

But Duncan didn't pursue the idea for wondering which of his men had betrayed him and everyone else at Annanlea.

He considered the possibility that Darby or Thurlow or both had concocted the scheme, but quickly dismissed it. Darby was devoted to his children and had a baffling attachment to his wife. He would never risk their security. And he wasn't clever enough for such subterfuge. He'd have given himself away by now.

Thurlow? The Englishman was all bluster, but no traitor. His methods were more direct. On hot trod to reclaim stolen cattle ten years ago, Duncan had won the man's loyalty by rescuing him from an English gallows, then secured it by bringing Thurlow's family to Annanlea. If Thurlow ever came to cross-purposes, he would challenge Duncan outright, but he'd never betray him.

If not Thurlow and Darby, though, who?

Duncan scanned the waiting men, then exchanged a pointed gaze with Michael, who echoed his unspoken question with a scowl and a sigh.

"You two, join the others," he said to the chastened sentries. The seed of an alarming possibility was forming in his mind. "Michael, we must talk." He nodded to the rest of the men. "Bide here. We'll be back."

Michael followed as he strode across the sunny courtyard to the ancient walls that had protected Annanlea's inhabitants over the centuries. Washed clean by yesterday's storm, the Annan River valley stretched fresh and green and tranquil below them, but its beauty was lost on Duncan as he asked the question neither of them could answer. "Who?"

"Nae Thurlow or Darby," Michael was quick to say. "They're—"

"I've already ruled them out."

"All the others were accounted for last night," Michael said. "I had the late watch maself."

"So our traitor is working with someone from the outside."

"Aye. Someone either verra foolhardy or verra powerful, to risk a blood feud with the Black Bastard."

Duncan planted his fists on the thick leather belt that secured his scabbard. He paced as he always did to help him think. In the past fourteen years, he'd dealt swiftly and brutally with anyone foolish enough to steal from him or threaten his people, making the Black Bastard a name to be reckoned with even among the most savage border reivers. Without reserve or hesitation, he'd consigned all who dared abuse him to hell. But nothing was ever safe or certain in the marches, where new enemies materialized every day.

He shook his head. "There's much amiss, here. They didna kill Thurlow or Darby, yet didna take them hostage, either. And nae so much as a sheep is missin'." He faced the grizzled warrior who'd taught him everything he knew of war and survival in the marches. "Why? Everything has a reason. Find the reason, and you find the culprit. Ye taught me that."

"Aye." As he always did when faced with a dilemma, Michael absently raked his stubby fingers through his once-red beard that had paled to ruddy gold with age. After a pensive pause, he said, "It almost seems as if whoever was behind this didna want ta tread too heavy on yer pride or put the red hand between ye."

No killing. No burning. No theft, besides the salt. "Could be," Duncan conceded. "But why?"

Even Auld Wat Scott followed the unwritten code of the marches: strike fast, hard, and openly, then deal immediately with retaliation. Yet this raid had none of the characteristics of a reiver's strike.

And if there was a traitor in their midst, nothing and no one at Annanlea was safe.

Michael broke through Duncan's troubled musings.

"You're assumin' there *is* some sinister plot afoot," his foster father said. "What if they simply wanted the salt? It was worth at least a hundred pounds, and easy enough to make away with." He exhaled with a snort. "Could be halfway to Evil Bess's table by now."

"Nay. I doona think the English did it," Duncan reasoned. "They'd have killed ma men, and couldna pass up takin' at least a sheep or two."

"You have a point." Michael hefted his belt. "Shall we rally fer the trod, then?" he asked, his face reflecting the same reservation Duncan felt.

"Nay." All of Duncan's instincts told him he should not leave Annanlea thinly protected.

Michael tucked his chin in surprise. "The trail's at least five hours cold by Thurlow and Darby's reckonin', but the salt'll slow 'em down. Fifty-seven barrels are nae small matter. We could still catch 'em."

"Only a fool would flee by land," Duncan reasoned. "Send Logan and Ander to the deputy warden to claim hot trod. But I doubt it'll do any good. Ma guess is, the thieves left by sea and are long gone." Even a heavily loaded wagon could reach the firth in three hours. Mounted men, far quicker. "We'll track them straightaway, but I fear 'tis too late already."

"Blast!" Michael whacked his thigh with a fist, staring out in frustration over the valley.

"Even so, this stinks of a diversion to me." The possibility seemed more than logical. "The minute we go on trod, they could move in and take everything at their leisure—our women, our children, our kine, and all our goods."

"Unlikely, for there's nae a sign of anyone aboot. But it is a possibility." Michael eyed Duncan askance. "I've never known ye to shrink from a fight, though, lad."

"And I'm nae doin' it now," Duncan snapped. "I'll find whoever did this and deal with them. But ma gut tells me we should stick close to home." He granted his mentor a mirthless grin. " 'Twas ye who taught me to trust ma instincts."

"So I did." Michael tugged at his beard. "Shall I send Quinn and Carlin to mark their trail and follow after?" A seasoned poacher and a fallen warden's man, the two were Duncan's best trackers.

"Aye." What then? he couldn't help wondering.

As if he'd read Duncan's thoughts, Michael asked, "And if one of 'em's the traitor?"

A sickening swell of revulsion twisted Duncan's innards. "He'll kill the other, then come back with word alone and put us off the scent."

"A wretched business, this." Michael clapped the shoulder of Duncan's black leather doublet. "We'd better go back and tell the others. They'll be chafin' fer a trod."

"Mark their reactions when I tell them," Duncan instructed as they made their way back to the once-majestic brick structure that hugged the ancient castle's steepest curtain wall.

"Aye." Michael lifted his face briefly to the morning sun, then followed him inside.

Back in the parlor, Duncan searched the taut expressions of his men, every line and fold and subtle shift more familiar than his own. He recognized the tightened postures and sharp odor of readiness in their bodies, and wondered if fear would smell or look the same. "Do any of ye ken anything about this?"

"Nay," they all responded, visibly shaken that he would question the loyalty that bound them to him and each other.

One by one, he looked into their eyes, but saw no shadow of betrayal. "There'll be nae trod," he announced bluntly, surprising them further.

He singled out his trackers. "You, Quinn . . . and Carlin." The two men shouldered forward. "Provision yourselves, then find out how many there were, where they came from, and where they're headed. Take Thurlow's lad with ye to send back with word afore ye go after 'em."

He leveled a warning look at each of them. "If ye find those responsible, note all ye can, but come straight back. Doona get yourselves caught or swap swords with 'em. Is that clear?"

The poacher and ex-soldier nodded.

"Off with ye, then."

No sooner had they made for the door, though, than a clatter of wooden shoes and cries of alarm preceded Darby's lad Gareth into the hall.

"Master!" The gangly boy clamored straight for Duncan, leaving a trail of barn filth in his wake. "Master! Ainsel the fisherman's son Will has come! He ran all the way from the firth, with scarce enough breath left to tell me his da must see ye straightaway, most urgent, at their home."

The salt. Had Ainsel seen something? Or was this another effort to draw Duncan away from Annanlea?

Darby, too mortified by his son's bad manners to heed the content of the message, limped forward and collared the boy. "Have ye nae respect for yer master, stone-pate, bargin' in here without permission? And in yer barn shoes, trackin' goose shite everywhere!" he railed. "Ye've nae only shamed me and yer master, ye've ruined Miss Brigit's rug!" By far the greater sin.

Duncan pointed to Gareth, who now had the good sense to tremble before him. "Bring Will to me." As Gareth clattered away, Duncan turned to the others who were waiting for their orders. "Darby and Rory, bide here with me." In choosing Darby to ride with him, he thus redeemed the man for lapse of duty as well as his son's affront. "The rest of ye," he continued, "tell the women to prepare for an attack. Then bring the lads and all the kine in from the fields. Report anything suspicious, nae matter how slight, directly to me or Michael. Once it's safely dark, hide the families and supplies and kine. Ye ken the routine." He dismissed them with a nod. "Quick to it, now." Darby and Rory stayed behind in anxious silence.

He did not have to ask Michael to stay. In times of crisis, it took a direct command to drive the old man from his side.

As if sensing Duncan's inner turmoil, his mastiff Clyde trotted over and sat alert at heel. Long minutes passed before Gareth returned with the exhausted fisherman's son in tow.

At Duncan's nod, Michael dragged up a chair facing them and motioned the messenger to sit. "Rest yourself, lad." The boy obeyed with gratitude and fear in equal measure.

Duncan turned his attention to Gareth. "Now make amends for yourself by readyin' ma horse and Rory's, and yer sire's."

Michael's eyebrows lifted in alarm. He leaned close and murmured, "It could be a trap. Surely ye doona mean to go yerself?"

"We'll see," Duncan answered calmly. He addressed the fisherman's son. "Will, is it?"

"Aye, sir," the boy panted out, wringing his woolen cap.

"What's happened, then, lad," he asked quietly, "that ye should come with such an urgent summons?"

"There's been a shipwreck. In the storm yester eve. Da saw 'er driven hard ashore, so we set out after, but by the time we got there, there was naught we could do. She went aground full force, and we stood helpless as the storm beat 'er to bits." Will's words grew faster and more anxious by the sentence. "There wasna even any decent salvage—just bodies, scraps o' canvas, and shards of wood, and nae reachin' those fer the tempest still a-ragin'."

He shot Michael a nervous look. "Nae sense standin' in the storm, Da said, so we headed back home, but on the way Da tarried, lookin' fer whatever mighta washed ashore along the way." The boy dropped his head. " 'Twas dark and still blowin', and I was wore out, so I asked to go ahead. Da didna like it, I could tell, but he let me." He paused to catch his breath.

Impatient though he was, Duncan knew better than to order the boy to get to the point. People told their tales each in his own way, and there was much to be learned from the telling. "And?" he prodded gently.

"I ran home, ate, then fell asleep waitin'. Woke deep in the night, and he still wasna back. I feared some mischance. When he finally came at last, he ordered me to run and fetch ye."

Duncan had hoped for answers, but had garnered only more disturbing questions. Yet still he held out hope Ainsel had seen something of the salt. "Ye doona ken why he sent for me?"

"Nae, master." The lad straightened. "He didna vouchsafe ta tell me, but ma da is nae an idle man. If he says he must see ye, and ye alone, then there's damned good reason fer it!"

"Watch yer mouth, lad," Michael growled in warning. "Yer speakin' to yer master."

"He's defending his father," Duncan corrected without rancor, "who's as good and honest a man as has ever worked ma lands and waters." He paced slowly before the boy. "Did ye notice anything untoward in his manner? Anything atall?" he asked, careful to observe the boy's reaction.

"Nae." No subtle gestures betrayed a lie. "He was wet through, and cross, but only as cross as befit the hour and the situation."

"Did he seem frightened?"

"Nae," the lad said swiftly. "Just hell-bent that I get upon ma way with the message."

Duncan laid a reassuring hand on the boy's shoulder. "Ye've done well, lad." He pointed to the kitchen door, where he knew his aunt was listening even now. "There's the kitchen. Tell Aunt Brigit I said to give ye food and drink and a warm place to sleep."

Will rose, bobbed three times in exaggerated deference, then hurried away.

Duncan turned to Darby and Rory. "We ride for Ainsel's as soon as it's dark."

"Duncan!" Michael's voice resonated rebuke. "Is that wise? Let me go instead."

Duncan bristled. There were limits, even for his foster father, and Michael had just crossed one. "Ye would question my orders in front of ma men?" he asked with deadly softness.

"Nae," Michael hastened to amend. "But ye said yerself that ye shouldn't leave Annanlea. I was only—"

"I *said*," he corrected in a more conciliatory tone, "that we shouldna leave Annanlea thinly protected, which is why I'm putting ye in charge until I'm back."

"As ye wish, of course," Michael conceded, but his face said otherwise.

"We'll be back before sunrise," Duncan reassured him, wishing to bring the brief conflict to an end.

Michael's barrel chest inflated. "And if yer not?"

"Send Ander, but none other, and dig in for whatever comes." Duncan grinned. "Doona worry, auld man. We'll go wary and find out soon enough if it's a false lure." He slid his smallsword into its scabbard then added an extra dagger to the high cuff of his boot before retrieving his broadsword from its mounting on the wall. A brace of pistols and bag of shot and powder completed his kit. Well armed, he tossed weapons from the arsenal to Darby and silent Rory, wondering briefly if he was arming a traitor.

Poison, such suspicions, but a poison he had not unleashed.

"Come, men," he said with an optimism he did not feel. "We'll join young Will at table for a hearty meal, then scout the area until dark."

Whether they would find answers to any of the mounting questions remained to be seen.

It was well past midnight before they crested the last knoll overlooking Solway Firth. Duncan dismounted, as did his men, reassured that Clyde and the horses remained easy. By the faint silvery illumination from the northern horizon, he located Ainsel's humble thatched dwelling with its surrounding clutter of fish racks and nets. A gust from the firth carried the strong odor of drying fish and offal up the swale.

Everything seemed ordinary enough. He didn't sense an ambush, but under the circumstances, he wasn't about to take any chances, despite the fact that Clyde remained tense and alert, but showed nae signs of alarm. He turned to Darby and Rory, who now stood beside him. "Hide your horses separately, then meet back here straightaway."

If one of them was the traitor, he didn't want them to know where his mount was hidden. After securing his Percheron, Rogue, in a sheltered depression behind a tangle of stunted larches, he crept back to his men. "The two of ye stay together." Duncan's departure from his usual methods clearly struck them as odd, but both men nodded. "I'll keep watch while ye go down and make certain all is well. Then come back together." If only one returned, he'd have his traitor.

He watched as the pair crept down to the fisherman's hut, circled it, then disappeared behind the flap of hide that served as door. Long tense seconds passed before the two exited together and made their way back up the hill.

" 'Tis a woman," Darby panted out.

Blast. Not the salt.

"Ainsel found her half-dead on the shore in only her shift," Rory said in a rare departure from silence.

"Half-dead?" Darby snorted. "I'd say three pecks toward the bushel, more like it. She's cold as a flounder, and just as limp."

"Aye," Rory conceded, "but she's breathin'. A lady. Her shift's all padded and embroidered at the hem, and there are pearls in her hair."

A hostage, especially one near death, was the last thing Duncan needed. But if she were Scottish and a lady, saving her might secure a useful alliance. "Come." He loped down to the hut with his men close behind.

Once safely in the deep shadow of the thatch, he murmured, "Rory, ye keep watch outside, but stay well hidden." He nodded to Darby. "Ye guard the door inside." Duncan disturbed the thick flap of leather as little as possible upon entering so as not to reveal himself by the dim light within.

All seemed well inside the soot-blackened interior. Scarlet embers glowed in the fire pit, and an anxious Ainsel waited beside the figure bundled in threadbare blankets on a crude bed of salt grass.

Clyde went straight for her, sniffing her all over with alacrity. Then, to Duncan's surprise, he flopped down beside her and laid his massive head across her body. Clyde, who barely tolerated anyone save Duncan and his children.

Disconcerted, Duncan nodded to the fisherman. "You've done well, Ainsel."

Looking down on the woman in the frail light, he noted her strong, plain features, lanky frame, and broad shoulders. An orderly embellishment of pearls still decorated her tightly dressed coiffure. Shipwrecked, yet not a hair out of place.

She was not comely, but wasn't ugly, either. Yet even unconscious, she projected a silent strength. How, he couldn't imagine.

He drew down the covers to pick up her right hand. The flesh was cold, but he felt none of the roughness or calluses that marked Aunt Brigit's. Only a faint thickening at the ends of her first two long, spatulate fingers—the result, no doubt, of hours of embroidery.

Ainsel had rightly guessed her to be a woman of leisure.

A half-dead lady. Just what he needed. He'd stood by and watched five women die already—his gentle mother and four wives, lost to pestilence, childbirth, and . . . mischance. If this one died, too, it would only add fuel to the foolish rumors that he was hexed.

"What of the shipwreck?" he asked Ainsel.

" 'Twas an Englisher," the fisherman responded, his eyes darting nervously. "A merchant ship."

Damn. That meant the woman was almost certainly an Englisher. The same irrational hatred rose within him that always did whenever he dealt with anything English, a vitriol born of his English father's desertion and fueled by his Scottish grandsire's scorn for the British blood that tainted Duncan.

"The storm drove 'er aground five mile hence," Ainsel said, still far too agitated for Duncan's liking.

Clearly, Ainsel was concealing something, but what? Duncan's senses sharpened. If this was a trap, why hadn't they been overtaken already?

Exquisitely aware of every tiny sound and movement around him, he lifted the woman's hands into the light and studied them. Then he stood to his full height, towering over Ainsel. "It seems odd she has nae rings. Were her hands bare when ye found her?"

Ainsel's features went slack with terror. "Ah . . . nay, sir, nay." He fumbled in the woven belt that bound his coarse plaid. "I was merely holdin' 'em fer safekeepin'," he stammered, producing two magnificent rings, one of pearl and the other a large rectangular ruby, both set in gold. "I meant ta give 'em to ye straightaway, but what with all that's happened, I pure forgot."

Little wonder the humble fisherman had been tempted beyond his means to resist.

If worst came to worst, Duncan could sell the rings at

least. Fine as they were, though, the proceeds wouldn't compensate for the loss of his salt. Still, they'd fill Annanlea's—and Ainsel's—larders for a time, anyway.

Duncan stashed the treasure safely inside his leathern jacket, relieved that Ainsel's theft, not betrayal, was the secret he had hidden. Duncan decided to be merciful. " 'Tis well enough ye've given 'em to me now," he announced. "But if such a lapse should e'er occur again, your lad will find himself an orphan."

"Never, master. Nevermore." Ainsel dropped to his knees and groveled. "God bless ye, sir."

Appalled, Duncan tugged him to his feet. "Stop it, man. I want your loyalty, nae your pride." Embarrassed, he turned his attention back to the pallid woman.

Odd, that this lone survivor had washed ashore so far from the wreck. But who could fathom the sea's caprices? "Any other survivors?" Perhaps he could learn the woman's identity.

"Wilbern gave a haloo as he rowed by on his way home from the wreck," Ainsel said. "He said two common hands had survived, but nae other was found alive."

Nae luck there, then. Duncan briefly considered leaving the woman in Ainsel's care and sending food, fuel, and blankets back with Will. He'd do her no favor taking her back to Annanlea and all the trouble.

But if she survived, he had little doubt she'd ransom well, perhaps bringing enough, along with the sale of her rings, to offset the rest of his losses and feed his people. "I'll take her with me. Tell no one, on pain of your life. We'll keep Will with us until this matter is settled."

Ainsel's wizened face fell. "Aye, master."

It was a common practice, securing someone's silence by holding family as surety, yet Duncan did not do so lightly. Life in the marches was an endless series of hard choices. This was just one more.

He uncovered the hostage, then removed his cloak and scooped her up into its folds. "Oof. She must have bones of lead." She weighed a good two stone more than he'd expected. When he heaved her over his shoulder, a slurred, "Stop that this instant!" escaped her in cultured English tones.

Blast. An Englisher, just as he'd suspected. And a bossy one, to boot.

He drew her back into his arms and found her barely conscious, murmuring unintelligibly. Only then did he notice the dark bruises on her neck.

She'd been throttled.

And washed ashore miles before the shipwreck.

"Doona die on me, woman," he said as he carried her toward the door. "Ye'll do me nae good that way."

He had trouble enough without that, but something told him he'd have even more if she lived.

The sun was not yet up when Duncan came upon his aunt in the kitchen. He'd deposited the hostage in a spare bed, then consoled his weary mind and heart with a visit to his seven sleeping children before coming down for food. He found his aunt already in the kitchen.

Though it was barely light outside, fresh charcoal glowed hot in the fireplace, and he crouched to warm his hands. Lucas wouldn't be in to start the day's cooking for at least another hour. "You're up early, Bink," he said, surprising himself with the nickname he hadn't used since childhood when "Aunt Brigit" had been too much of a mouthful to manage.

"I heard ye come in," she grumbled, scowling at him in accusation. "Saw ye carryin' some woman upstairs. Is she a wastrel, or have ye taken ta kidnappin' now?" Faith, she acted as if he'd stolen an innocent wean from its crib instead of rescuing an unconscious English aristocrat.

"I kidnapped nae one," he answered, rising to his full height beside the fire. "And I doona ken if she's a wastrel. She's an Englisher, a lady. Washed up on ma own shore, so by ma way of thinkin', the good Lord's presented us with a hostage. And a treasure with 'er." He produced the rings for his aunt's perusal.

She studied them with her usual thoroughness. "These should bring a goodly price in Glasgow. Let Michael take them; he haggles well." She handed them back. "And the woman?"

"Clearly a person of means." Duncan smiled at her with a humor dimmed only slightly by his hard night without sleep. " 'Twould be most ungrateful nae to accept such generous blessin'."

"That's one way o' lookin' at it," she said dryly. "Blasted Englishers. Nothin' but trouble, as well ye ken." She waggled a stern finger at him. "Mark me, lad, she'll bring trouble with her."

Duncan suppressed a yawn. "Bring trouble? Faith, Bink, we've so much mischief of our own already, even trouble would run the other way."

"Hmph." Aunt Brigit headed for the larder. "I'll warm ye some scones and beer."

Duncan dropped his weary bones to the bench beside the worktable. "If she lives, she'll ransom well, and we can use the money to feed our people. 'Tis an answer to prayer."

Aunt Brigit remained skeptical. She set a bowl of left-over scones, some butter, and a pitcher of beer on the table "If she lives," she repeated crossly. "Meanin', if I can nurse her back to life." She fetched a knife to cut the scones, then buttered them and laid them facedown on a griddle. "As if I hadna' enough to do. I'm toilin' maself to a nubbin as 'tis." She poured a hearty measure of beer into a kettle and hung that low over the coals. The griddle went directly on the glowing embers.

Two years had passed since his last wife's death, and Bink was constantly reminding him he was derelict in his duty for nae finding another wife to help her with his seven children. Duncan regretted adding to her labors, but he had neither the means nor the inclination to search out a suitable wife. It was too soon after Aselma's tragic death and the hateful rumors that had followed, saying she had leapt instead of fallen from the peel.

Even if Duncan did marry again, she'd only die like the others anyway. Though he was loath to believe the rumors, something in him wondered if they were true. His wives always died, which was reason enough not to be in such a hurry to remarry. Why condemn some poor innocent woman? "I'm sorry things have been so hard lately, Bink. Truly I am."

The rich, pungent aromas of browning scones and hearty malt began to fill the kitchen, making Duncan realize just how hollow he was, but he was more concerned with Bink than his stomach. In the lean years since his mother's death and the loss of his last two wives, Bink had done her best to fill the gap, bearing the work of many on her narrow shoulders. Her endless wry complaints had become the music all who loved her lived by.

Were it in his power, he'd have honored her with a life of leisure, but Annanlea was no grand estate where the master and his family lived idle on the labors of others. It was and always had been a working estate where everyone—himself included—labored long and hard to survive.

He rose, circled behind his aunt, and bent to wrap her in an affectionate bear hug, taking comfort from the brief contact and her familiar scent. Her tiny frame felt far too fragile in his arms. "You're the soul and sinew of Annanlea, auld woman, and we couldna manage without ye." He dropped a brief peck on the gray halo of braids she always wore.

"Fie!" She whacked him with her hand, but the blow lacked conviction. "Doona try ta get around me."

"I never could," he said, smiling as he released her. No one got around Aunt Brigit.

Everything he did, he did for her and the children. If he were to lose her or one of his children—even rebellious Amber—nothing could fill the void.

He said a silent proof against evil at the very thought. If the phantom raiders came back, would his family be next?

Shutting away the terrible question, Duncan returned to sit on the bench. "How's ma brood? I've scarce seen a blink of 'em awake since the raid."

Bink softened, as he'd kent she would. "Fit, loud, and hungry, as usual. I've kept 'em hard by, as ye asked." She retrieved the scones, flipped them deftly onto a wooden charger, then poured him a steaming mug of beer. "Erinn's lost another tooth and found another cat." She set the food before him. "I swear, I doona ken where all the creatures come from."

"Word has spread among the cats o'er all the Western March." Duncan chuckled. "Perhaps because she loves 'em so. They sense it." Some children had dolls. Eight-year-old Erinn had a collection of cats that she dressed and played with. The miracle was, the usually haughty creatures were docile as rabbits in her hands. They followed her like a pack of pilgrims in the wake of a prophet. " 'Tis well enough to indulge the lass. Her kittens keep us free of rats."

"And the house adrift with fur. Nae to mention the cat shite in the corners," his aunt complained for the hundredth time.

She sobered, eyeing him askance. "I had ta beat Amber. Again. Caught her tryin' to creep away in the middle of the night."

"Saint Columba's kneecaps!" Duncan exploded. "Has she so soon forgotten the last canin' she earned that way?" Turning thirteen had transformed his docile daughter into a rebellious, headstrong chit almost overnight. Duncan leaned into his palms and massaged his temples with his thumbs. "What's got into her? She was such a good lass, then suddenly, she's all mouth, and we canna keep her in the house."

"I've told ye," Bink chided, pouring a bucket of spring water into a kettle. She tossed several chunks of charcoal onto the fire. "She's come into her womanhood. A husband is what she's needin'—her own hearth and weans to tether down those fanciful notions of hers."

Duncan bristled, just as he had the last time she'd broached the subject. "She's still a child," he argued, appalled by the idea of handing his innocent daughter into the clutches of any man, much less some gangling, spotty-faced lad. "She still plays house with Erinn's cats, fer glory's sake!"

"Nae longer, Duncan," his aunt said with uncharacteristic gravity. "Amber dreams a woman's dreams now. Ye'd best to settle a match for her before those dreams get out of hand and she runs away for good." She added salt and rolled haver to the kettle for porrich.

Duncan rose and carried it to the fire and hung it.

"Ye might consider Wat's lad, Ethan," Bink suggested. "He's comely, fit, and seems a serious fellow for his years. I caught Amber eyeing him when last Wat came. 'Twould be a prudent alliance."

"Nae Wat's lad," Duncan said more harshly than he intended. "None of Wat's." He didn't think Auld Wat was behind the salt raid, but he couldn't be certain. Until he was, such a betrothal was out of the question.

Aunt Brigit pinned him with that look of hers that stripped him to his soul. "So there's trouble there, then?"

Duncan was far too tired for this, but he knew better than to try to put her off. "Nae."

Unconvinced, she scowled at him in reproach.

"Mayhap . . . I doona ken."

"The salt . . ." she murmured wisely, then let out a deep sigh. "Trouble with Wat is trouble, indeed."

"Aye." Duncan had worn himself out with wondering ever since the raid. Weary as he was, it took all his energy to plan the day ahead. He blinked heavily and tried to pretend he'd slept all night and just gotten up.

His aunt eyed him critically as she refilled his mug. "Ye'll need some meat to get ye through this day with nae a wink o' sleep."

Duncan picked up another scone and took a bite. "Ye didna beat Amber too hard, did ye'?"

"If ye ask her, nigh unto death," she answered dryly,

settling at last to the bench opposite him. "Nae near hard enough, if ye ask me." She stretched, then pinned him with a piercing gray gaze. "Get her a man, Duncan, afore she comes to mischief."

"*You've* done well enough without one," he shot back crossly.

His aunt went still as stone. "And how would ye ken how I've done, ye, ye *man,* ye?" she said in a voice pregnant with hurt. "Ye've nae idea what it's like to live at sufferance in this house as a spinster, denied ma birthright as a woman by ma own sire because he was too stingy to give me a dowry. Ye ken nothing, Duncan, of how hard it was to watch as yer blessed mother gave ye life then loved ye in spite of everything, and all the while, achin' that nae child would ever grow inside of me." Angry tears brightened her gray eyes, and he caught a glimpse of the proud woman she might once have been. "Or to see the sad devotion in yer blessed mother's face when she thought of yer father, even after he'd abandoned her, and ken that I would never feel such love." Her voice broke, but her posture remained rigid. "To witness the grief ye bore when we lost her, and ken that ne'er a child would grieve for me that way."

He was a stone-pate. Stricken, Duncan strode to her side and circled her thin, rigid shoulders, planting a kiss on her withered cheek. "I shall grieve that deep when ye are gone."

She leaned ever so slightly into his embrace. "I wasna jealous, mind ye," she said quietly. "I loved yer mother to ma soul, just as I love ye." She pulled away and faced him squarely, her vinegar returning. "But I willna have ye do to poor Amber what ma own father did to me. Make her a suitable match, Duncan, or I'll leave this place without a backward look and take the veil."

"Ye canna take the veil, old woman," he said affectionately. "You're not a Roman."

She drew back, rigid. "Then I'll become one," she snapped, and he believed it.

"But ye have nae dowry."

"I'll steal those rings and get one."

He believed that, too. "Aye, then," he conceded. "Ye win, as usual. I'll start lookin' for a match."

"Start, nothing. Do it, and soon."

Just what he needed right now—another problem to deal with.

Catherine was shivering when she woke.

She tried to speak, but her gullet was raw from the saltwater she'd swallowed, and the muscles in her throat throbbed in agony.

She curled deeper under the covers. Phew! The bed-clothes stank of must, and the sour odor of neglect tainted the air around her. Dusty cobwebs draped the coffered ceiling overhead.

Where was she?

She tried to sit up, but her body was strangely un-cooperative.

"Ach! So Her Majesty's awake at last," a coarse-looking, ropy old woman said in alarming accents as she loomed over Catherine with a look of disdain. "Welcome to Annanlea, Yer Highness."

A Scot!

Dear God, was she in Scotland?

The old woman's expression shifted to suspicion. "What's wrong? Canna ye speak?" She arched an eye-brow over piercing gray bird-eyes. "Little wonder, with those bruises on yer throat. Looks like ye cheated the gibbet." Seeing Catherine's fear, the unpleasant creature grumbled, "Lie still. I'll fetch some food." She left abruptly.

Catherine closed her eyes, trying desperately to think.

Flashes of memory winked through her mind: heart-breaking goodbyes to Hal and her stepfather; Charles retching helplessly in their cabin; the overwhelming odors of illness, pitch, and men's bodies that had driven her abovedecks into the purging fury of the storm. The cold silence of the sea. And last, her endless struggle to reach the shore.

So she hadn't drowned, after all. She'd wakened here instead of hell.

But Scotland . . .

Lord, I thank you for preserving my life, truly I do, but why have You handed me over to the Philistines? She wondered sincerely if hell would have been any worse.

The Scots were a barbarous race. They'd left her fatherless when she was but a babe and visited their savagery across the borders more often than she could count.

And now here she was, at their mercy.

A chilling thought burned through her brain. If the brutes were to discover she was English . . . She'd heard the whispered stories of rape, torture, and worse.

Thank heaven for her sore throat. If she'd spoken, she'd have given herself away to her enemies as an Englishwoman. She resolved on the spot to act a mute, at least until she was strong enough to—

The thought was interrupted by several soft plunks onto her bed and the pressure of small feet everywhere. She opened her eyes to find herself covered in cats, with more arriving by the second. Too weak to swipe them off, she lay there watching helplessly as they swarmed over her.

"Nay, ye wicked beasties," a musically childish voice protested from beyond the chamber's open door. "Doona devil the poor auld thing. Papa said she's verra ill."

The poor *old* thing?

A fair, delicate little girl of six or seven hurried inside, dragging behind her a smiling, stocky, odd-looking toddler with almond-shaped eyes. Both of them wore threadbare clothes and had dirty hands and faces, but even so, the little girl radiated a special light. Which promptly faded when she saw that Catherine was awake and covered in cats.

The child shot an anxious glance toward the hallway. "Aunt Brigit's sure ta cane me if she catches us here, but ma kitties saw the door open, and I couldna stop 'em."

Despite Catherine's frown, the faerie child hastened to the bed, her silent charge in tow. She took one of Catherine's large, cold hands into her own tiny warm one. "Doona fear, hostage lady."

Hostage lady!

She was a hostage?

"Yer safe now," the child assured her, roughly grating her *r*'s. "Ma kitties willna harm ye." She relinquished her hold to shoo the plague of felines from the quilt, but those she banished were immediately replaced by others.

Catherine glanced to the floor and was startled to see at least two dozen cats milling around the little girl more like devoted dogs than indifferent felines.

" 'Tis their nature to be curious," the child explained. "Once they've snooped about a bit, they'll leave ye be."

Catherine endured the cats' inspection with as much dignity as she could manage. She liked cats—they were useful animals and not nearly as smelly or demanding as dogs—but being covered by so many made her skin crawl.

A pithy comment rose to her lips, but she remembered just in time to stifle it. This wasn't going to be easy, keeping silent after a lifetime of freely speaking her mind.

Most of the cats merely padded around a bit then went their way, but one stuck its cold little nose in her ear while two others swatted playfully at the pearls her hair. Yet another climbed her chest, kneaded its paws into her breasts and sniffed her breath, then turned its backside to her, tail upright, arching on tiptoe before it strolled to the edge of the bed and jumped off.

All the while, the boy child grinned at her like a clown with lockjaw. Seeing him standing there gaping at her, Catherine felt her ears grow hot with outrage. But when she looked into his eyes, she realized he wasn't making sport of her. The child was simple.

What sort of place *was* this, where servants spoke so

froward to their betters, and cats and children roamed un-
attended through the house?

"I'd tell ye ma name," the little girl volunteered cheer-
ily, "but as yer a stranger, Papa willna permit it. 'Tis
perilous, y'see." She draped a long-haired gray cat over
her shoulder and stroked it. "Nae one must ken we're the
Black Bastard's children, or there'd be hell to pay," she
confided innocently.

The Black Bastard?

Catherine had heard many a colorful tale of the Black
Bastard. He was one of the most notorious reivers on the
wild side of the border, a man of legendary ruthlessness,
retaliation, and handsomeness.

Her hands went even colder than they were. Dear God,
she'd fallen into the clutches of a desperate, lawless brig-
and.

"There, now," the faerie girl said brightly as the last
of her cats lost interest. " 'Twasna so bad, then, was't?"

Catherine eyed her skeptically, wondering if the cats
had anything to do with the pagan traditions everyone
knew the Scots still practiced despite their claims of faith.

With supreme effort, she managed to lift her head and
look about. Never in all her life had she lain in such a
dank, neglected place. Dust and cobwebs were everywhere. Great patches of mold stained the low ceiling and
cracked daub-and-wattle walls, and the grimy window-
panes scarcely admitted any light.

And the coarse shift she was wearing—

Not her shift!

Panic gripped her and brought her bolt upright. She
looked at her bare hands. Her rings! She barely managed
to stifle a cry of alarm.

Her shift gone, her mother's jewels with it! Had the
outlaws found them sewn into the padded embroidery? Or
had the sea stripped her naked before it spit her out?

She must know what had happened. But how could
she find out if she couldn't speak?

"What's the matter?" The little girl took a step backward, pulling the lad behind her protectively. "Have ye seen a fetch?"

Catherine tugged at the musty garment she was wearing and pointed to it, desperate question in her eyes.

"Canna ye talk?" the child whispered, clearly afraid.

"Canna talk, canna talk," the little boy repeated in singsong.

Catherine shook her head, which was pounding now with every heartbeat. Again, she pointed at the coarse garment and looked frantically about for some sign of her shift.

"Ye had nae clothes when Papa found ye," the girl explained, "save yer shift."

So it hadn't washed away. Catherine motioned to the room, willing the question she dared not speak into her eyes and gesture.

"Ach! Yer wonderin' where yer shift is, then?" the perceptive child said.

Catherine nodded in affirmation, tears of fear and gratitude spilling down her cheeks.

"Doona trouble yerself. Ye'll have it back." The little girl picked up a small orange tabby that promptly climbed onto her shoulders and balanced there. "Aunt Brigit said 'twas so stiff with sea salt, it had rubbed yer poor skin raw, so she washed it in rainwater. 'Tis hangin' in the kitchen now." She smiled. "Such a fine thing. We've all felt of it, even Baran."

Catherine's most intimate apparel, on display for all these ruffians to see . . . and *touch*! She shuddered. Her sense of violation prompted her to wonder if her person might have been subjected to even more intimate abuse while she'd been insensible, but she banished the thought as too horrid to consider.

"Your shift is dreamy soft," the child went on. "Another day, and it'll be dry." She pointed to the one Catherine was wearing. "That one's from the wives' chest. Aunt Brigit said it belonged to Nevin's mam, Aselma, God rest her soul."

The wives' chest? Catherine was wearing a dead woman's shift, trapped among a tribe of filthy heathen thieves who were probably touching her undergarments even now.

At the sound of a distant clank, the little girl straightened in alarm. "Aunt Brigit!" She grabbed the boy and dragged him toward the door. "Quick, Nevin. Quick." The cats followed en masse, and the room was safely clear long before the insolent crone returned.

When the brisk, closely spaced footsteps grew close, Catherine slid deeper under the covers and pretended to be asleep.

She heard someone enter and caught a faint whiff of food. "Sit up. I'll bring ye food if I must," the old woman's voice declared, "but I draw the line at feedin' ye when ye can do it yerself."

She felt a thunk and cracked her eye the tiniest slit to see a tray bearing a steaming bowl and tankard on the bed, and above it the sour-faced serving woman glaring down at her.

She closed her eye.

A rough hand shook her shoulder. "Up, I say."

Catherine moaned and curled into a ball on her side in what she hoped was a convincing imitation of insensibility.

The old woman grunted. "Play tortoise if ye wish. Ye can eat it cold, then." She gave Catherine one last poke. "I havna time to waste with the likes of ye." She left amid a cloud of grumbled complaints.

As Catherine lay there in the bed, questions flooded her mind. Where was she? How long had she been here? How far from England had the ship strayed?

Was Charles still alive? Would everyone think her drowned?

She still couldn't remember how she'd ended up in the water.

Her questions ended abruptly with the sound of scratching claws and heavy footsteps approaching. The claws grew louder as the odor of dog assailed her. Then she heard a juicy slurp and felt a blast of moist doggy breath in her face. She peeked through her lashes to find an enormous mastiff nose to nose with her, his massive head plopped onto the pillow. Ugh!

When she looked at him, he whined and put a huge paw on the bed, jostling the tray, but made no move for her food.

The footsteps halted at the doorway, drawing her attention from the unwelcome canine to the formidable male figure obscuring the entire open doorway.

The Black Bastard?

A thrill of terror tightened every muscle in her body.

Stooping low, her visitor ducked inside, then straightened to stand peering down on her with silent intensity, his fierce mane of ebon hair brushing against the beams of the ceiling.

He fit the tales of the Black Bastard: strikingly tall and handsome despite his unkempt appearance, hard as a standing stone, and clad in black leather from head to toe.

Whoever he was, he did not enter the room, he overtook it, radiating raw male intensity. Steeped in command and dark purpose, he had to be her captor.

Catherine's aching throat tingled in alarm. Through the smallest possible crack in her eyelid, she scanned her captor from his powerful legs to his broad shoulders to his classic features carved in plane and shadow. But it was his eyes that frightened her most. Blue as sapphires, they glittered just as cold with grim resolution and chilling calculation.

What did he mean to do?

Suddenly conscious of her nakedness under the brief shift, she clamped her eyes shut. *God, surely you did not spare my life only to have me suffer degradation at the hands of a brigand. Save me!*

The dog chose just that moment to swipe his tongue up the side of her face. Catherine gasped, her eyes opening in outrage, but she managed to bite back the rebuke that flew to her tongue.

The Black Bastard regarded her with a lazy sensuality that stirred an alarming warmth in her own body, his gaze stroking her like a caress. "Ah. So Aunt Brigit was right," he said in a baritone as rich as hot butter. "Ye were playin' tortoise." He bowed only slightly in the manner of a man accustomed to power. "I am Duncan Maxwell, and ye are ma hostage."

Catherine couldn't have spoken, even if she wanted to. This Scottish outlaw made all the men she'd ever met seem like mere boys.

Duncan Maxwell, he had called himself.

Without another word to her, he turned and ambled toward the door. "Clyde, heel." The deep command was soft and smooth as black velvet, sending another betraying shiver down her spine.

She watched, every muscle tense, as man and dog retreated. Only when she was certain she was alone did she allow herself to take a deep breath, as if to purge herself of the spell he had worked on her.

Catherine forced herself to stop obsessing about the Black Bastard himself and consider her predicament. Handsome or not, Duncan Maxwell was one of the most notorious outlaws in the borders, and she was his hostage. Her stepfather had no means to ransom her. All his assets were currently tied up in shipments, and the conditions of her mother's will forbade selling River House or its lands. Even to save her life.

She had already relinquished control of her inheritance to Papa, everything but her mother's jewels. She'd left behind everything—and everyone—she loved for the good of her stepfamily. The corrosive strife that had come between her and her elder stepbrother Charles had poisoned the whole family. It had broken her heart, but she had realized that there could be no peace at River House as long as she and Charles were both there. So she had taken a position as companion for an elderly relative in

Cornwall as her sacrifice for the only father she'd ever known, and for her precious younger stepbrother, Hal.

And now this.

Had Charles survived?

Poor Papa. He'd had his differences with Charles, but he loved him. What must he be feeling, now?

Did he think she was dead? Catherine knew Papa loved her as his own, despite the fact that they shared no blood, just as Hal loved her.

A nagging shadow tugged at the edges of her memory. There was something about the shipwreck, something she couldn't quite remember . . .

Catherine put her face into her hands and rocked.

Dear Father, show me the way out of this. She would not let the Black Bastard extort Papa and rob Hal of what would one day be his.

The jewels.

A sliver of hope illuminated her pit of fear. Assuming she got them back—which was a huge assumption—she could try to ransom herself with some of them. But if the outlaws discovered she had treasure, what was to keep them from taking all she had and still demanding a ransom from her stepfather? Nothing.

Nay. If by some miracle her mother's legacy was restored to her, Catherine realized she must keep it secret.

Then what? She could not pretend to be asleep every time anyone came to her. What was she going to do?

And what was going to be done to her?

Duncan Maxwell hadn't ravaged her this time, but that was no assurance he might not yet.

Chapter

THREE

Robert Storey did his best to concentrate on his reading. He sat in a patch of summer sunlight that warmed the richly polished floors of the library, but his efforts to lose himself in John Napier's fascinating mathematical treatise were fruitless. He hadn't had an easy moment in the four days since he'd watched the merchant ship *Dere* disappear on the horizon.

His sight-hound's tail thumped against the floor as Robert stared unseeing at the bright motes of dust drifting in the slash of amber light. Usually, this room was his private retreat, a peaceful island of repose in the bustling estate he managed for his beloved stepdaughter, but since she'd gone, he'd found no surcease in the waiting quiet that permeated the cozy, cluttered space.

Too quiet. The house seemed like a tomb without Catherine's reassuring, industrious presence and Charles's incessant bids for attention.

He should never have let her leave. It was weakness, pure and simple, to permit her to take that position as companion in Cornwall. River House was her home, her heritage; he and his family had no right to it. *They* should have left, not Catherine, when the friction between her and Charles had become unbearable.

Now, alone in the unnatural quiet, Robert faced the fact that he had allowed her to go because this was the only home Willa and their boys had ever known. With all his funds tied up in shipments, he couldn't even have rented suitable accommodations elsewhere. He'd been selfish, not wanting to uproot his family. Weak.

That was his curse, his inability to do what was right in the face of painful consequences.

Catherine was just the opposite. It was one of the reasons he loved her so much. With typical stubbornness, self-sacrifice, and practicality, she had accepted her distant cousin's plea for a companion and packed herself off to Cornwall—ironically, with Charles as escort for her journey. And Robert had taken the path of least resistance, as he had too many times in his life, and let her go.

He shifted in his perfectly comfortable chair and adjusted the bound treatise in his lap.

She had been so determined, as she was about everything she decided to do. Yet both of them had known she didn't really want to go. She'd done it only to bring peace to the household. And Willa had backed her up.

Wrong. It was all wrong. He missed Catherine sorely already.

Charles, though . . . Robert only hoped a brief respite from each other would improve the tension that had grown between him and his selfish, petulant firstborn. Yet he could hardly condemn Charles. He had been just that selfish and demanding in his youth, before the suffering he'd caused himself and others had made a man of him at last.

A long-buried image of innocent beauty rose up to tear at his heart, an image so painful he could scarcely bear it.

If only he had had the courage at eighteen to defy his father . . .

But life had its compensations, and Catherine was one. She and Hal were the children of his heart, despite the fact that Catherine bore neither his blood nor his name. Still, she was his in every good and gracious way that mattered.

And Charles was his penance.

Robert sighed. He'd known, deep down, that Charles's open jealousy was Catherine's real reason for leaving, and he regretted it profoundly.

It would join the long list of regrets he'd forged in his lifetime.

Forcing his attention back to the treatise, he finally managed to lose himself for a blessed interval. He wasn't sure how much time had passed when an urgent knock summoned his attention to the doorway.

"Sirrah?" His secretary, John Walker, opened the door slightly and leaned forward wearing a troubled frown. "Pray forgive me for disturbing you, but a messenger has arrived with an urgent communication from Lord Carleton."

Carleton? Robert knew of the border lord whose holding lay near Carlisle, but they'd had no dealings. What matter of urgency could there be between them?

A shard of disquiet struck him as he rose in deference to the sender's rank. "Show the messenger in."

Moments later, John ushered in a small man weary and begrimed by his fifty-mile journey. Eyes properly downcast, the courier bowed and extended a sealed message with a flourish.

Robert accepted the letter. "See that he's fed and rested," he instructed his secretary. As John and the courier retreated to the kitchens, he broke the seal and scanned past the opening amenities to the meat of the message:

I write with a heavy heart because the manifest of my merchant ship Dere *indicates that your son and step-daughter were passengers on that ill-fated vessel.*

Robert's heart went cold within his chest, and the fingers holding the message numbed. He sank into his chair.

It is my sad duty to inform you that shortly after its departure, the Dere *was driven off course by a fierce storm into Solway Firth. She ran aground and broke up in Scottish territory near Annan with overwhelming loss of life.*

Catherine! Charles . . .

At this writing, only two survivors—common seamen—
have been located, but every effort is being made to
ascertain the whereabouts of your family. As their bod-
ies have not been recovered, we may hope that God in
His infinite Mercy has seen fit to spare them. Our
search is hampered by the lawlessness and hostilities
of the region, but I have sent emissaries to Her Majesty
requesting permission to petition King James for as-
sistance in this matter. I shall notify you immediately
of further developments.

An anguish such as he had not known in almost thirty
years threatened to devour Robert.

The image of Catherine's strong, lively features sprang
full and lifelike in his mind. She couldn't be dead.

And Charles . . . No image came, prompting a wave of
guilt that his first thought had been for his stepdaughter
instead of his own eldest son.

They couldn't be dead. Surely he would have felt
something if they were dead, sensed it somehow.

And there were no bodies. There was hope. There had
to be.

Robert dropped the letter to his lap and stared without
seeing at his wife who now stood in the open doorway,
her usually benign expression arranged in an artful man-
ifestation of concern. "Robert?" Willa glided forward several steps. "I heard there was a message. What's
happened? You're pale as whey."

For a fleeting instant, he had the oddest feeling her
words had been rehearsed, like lines from a play, and that
she'd been expecting this, but he rejected the baseless
notion as hideously unworthy.

Dear God, he would have to tell her.

This could destroy his patient, kindly wife. She doted
so on Charles and had done her best to be a loving mother
to Catherine, despite the scant years that separated her and

her stepdaughter. Not to mention Catherine's froward ways.

Poor Willa.

"The Dere . . ." he choked out. "There was a storm . . . She ran aground in Scotland." Forcing out each word felt like wrenching great chunks from his own flesh. "Catherine . . . Charles . . . they're missing."

"No!" Willa's plump body went rigid, and her wide, placid face flushed. "That's not the right message!" Anger and denial contorted her features, making some distant part of Robert wonder fleetingly why she'd put it that way. "There's some mistake," she argued, her voice tight with desperation. "They can't have gone aground in Scotland. They were bound for Cornwall. It's a mistake, Robert. A mistake!"

Her panic jolted Robert from the deadly inertia that had claimed him. He stood and strode across the room to envelop his wife. "A storm blew them north, deep into Solway Firth. They wrecked near Annan, in hostile territory."

"No! It cannot be," she said fiercely. He tried to guide her to the chair, but she fought him like a she-wolf. She clawed at his arms and twisted in his embrace. "Not Charles! Catherine, but not Charles. He can't be gone. Not Charles!"

"They are in God's hands, Willa," Robert soothed. He held her fast, his heart breaking even further for his docile, devoted wife. "And there is hope yet. Catherine and Charles could still be alive. No one has found their bodies. We shall pray together that God has spared them."

She shoved him away so hard he almost lost his breath. *"Them! Them?"* Her green eyes blazed bright with hatred. "Even when you speak of this horrid thing, you put her first!" She glared up at him. "Shame, Robert! Charles is your son, your own flesh and blood, yet you put her first! You should be praying for our son, Robert! Our *son!*"

Robert understood that her rage and frustration had deflected into this unexpected accusation, but there was enough truth in the indictment to wound him deeply.

"Hush, dearest." He hugged her to him. "You are distraught. Do not say things you will later regret." To his relief, he felt her sag into his embrace. "We'll find them," he said, knowing it was a promise only God could keep. "We'll find them. Alive."

She stiffened again, and when she spoke, it was with the voice of a stranger—eerily thick and resonant against his shoulder. "Find him, Robert. Alive. Hal is too soft to inherit, too much like you. Charles must be alive. He *must*."

Robert stilled . . . *Too soft to inherit, too much like you.*

She was making no sense, for Robert had precious little to leave his sons. But it stung to hear her speak such contempt for shy, quiet Hal, every bit as much their son as Charles.

Defensive, he remembered that it had been Willa who'd insisted Charles accompany Catherine to her destination. But Robert's better instincts reminded him that Willa was beyond herself with grief, for Charles was the child of her heart, and Charles alone.

How could he condemn her, when he was guilty of the same sin, twice over? In his heart of hearts, Robert loved Catherine and Hal far more than poor selfish, difficult Charles.

"Willa, I would to God it had been I instead of Charles," he said. "But we cannot change what providence has brought us, no matter how hard it is bear."

Radiating hostility, she seemed to fold inward as she struggled to escape the comfort he offered.

All of a sudden, Robert felt too weary to fight her any longer. He let her go, then watched as she lurched toward her room.

Hal intercepted her in the hallway. "Mother, are you all right?" He reached out to steady her. "I heard—" Willa glared at the twelve-year-old with such hatred Hal stopped short and recoiled.

"Don't touch me," she said in that same throaty, chill-

ing tone. "Do not touch me. I cannot bear to look on you."
With that, she skirted him as if he had the plague and fled
to her room.

Baffled by his mother's rejection, Hal turned to his
father. "Why did she say that, Father? What's happened?"

Robert sank into the empty chair. "Your brother . . . the
ship he and Catherine were on ran aground." Tears welled
in his eyes. "They're missing."

"Catherine?" The color drained from Hal's face, leaving his ruddy cheeks and dark brows in stark contrast. He
adored his stepsister and thrived on her fierce, gruff devotion. He looked to Robert in anguish. "When? Where?"

"Shortly after they sailed." Robert leaned forward and
dropped his head into his hands, letting the tears come.
"A freak storm blew them north into Solway Firth. The
ship broke up near Annan."

"Scotland . . ." Hal sank to the floor beside him, gathering the sight-hound into his arms in a futile bid for
solace. "Charles . . ." Grief and guilt battled in his handsome young face, settling at last to resolution. "We must
search for them." He looked up to Robert. "Send me,
Papa. I'll find them. I know I can."

Robert hadn't stroked his son's curly chestnut locks
since the boy was six, but now the need to touch overwhelmed propriety. The texture of those curls had thickened somewhat, but he drew unspeakable comfort from
the brief contact. "Nay," he told his son. "You must stay
and comfort your mother. I shall go. And I shall not rest
until I've found them." His voice cracked. "One way or
another."

The shadow deepened in Hal's large hazel eyes. "I
don't think Mother wants me to be the one to comfort
her." His sad frown communicated the truth they both
knew but never discussed.

"Your mother is distraught, Hal," Robert replied, per-
petuating the illusion of impartiality they'd all so carefully
maintained. "She doesn't know what she's saying. Remind yourself of that when she lashes out. She doesn't

know what she's saying." They both knew she did, but Willa merited their compassion. "Your mother needs all our understanding now." Robert stood, and Hal stood with him. "I'm counting on you to watch over her while I'm gone."

Already, the lad was taller than he, all knees and ears and elbows. Soon Hal would be a man, and a good one. Far better than his father. Hal was the son Robert had hoped for; Charles, the one he deserved.

"Come." He put his arm around Hal's lanky shoulders. "You can help me supervise my packing."

THAT SAME DAY—ANNANLEA, SCOTTISH WEST MARCH

One of Erinn's cats crossed Duncan's path as he took the dusty stairs two at a time on his way to check his hostage. He scooped the fluffy white creature into his hands and curled it to his chest, meeting the animal's wide, clear green gaze with his own troubled one. "I'd give up ten years' worth of salt to trade places with ye, ye prissy little beast."

Tongue bobbing, Clyde loped along beside him, oblivious as ever to Erinn's pets.

The cat blinked, purring loudly, then burrowed its forehead into the patched leather of his jacket.

Aunt Brigit had told him the Englisher was improving, so he felt compelled to see for himself how she was faring. Yet he had no idea what to say to her should she be awake.

Idiot, he chided himself. *What are ye afraid of? She's just a woman, and an ordinary one at that.* The woman hadn't been born who could get the best of Duncan Maxwell—nor the man, for that matter.

So why in blazes was he suddenly at odds and evens?

Perhaps it was Clyde's strange behavior that had raised his guard. He wasn't jealous, of course, but it troubled him to see his dog spend his devotion on anyone outside the family, much less a perfect stranger—and an Englisher at that.

Englisher. He recoiled at the very thought. The same craven breed as the father who had deserted him and his mother, leaving him a bastard.

Duncan halted just short of the open doorway to the hostage's room and peered cautiously inside. To his vast relief, she seemed to be asleep.

Careful not to step on any of the abandoned toys and clutter that littered the floor, he picked his way past the broken spinning wheel and baskets of uncarded wool to stand beside the bed.

Another loud purr from the cat reminded him he was still clutching the creature, so he hastily set it to the floor. He couldn't very well instill terror into his captive with a kitten in his arms.

He scowled down at the sleeping woman. As before, she struck him as a wiry creature, not an ounce of pleasing fullness to her, and overlarge for her sex, but her bones were strong and true.

He sensed a certain prim stubbornness about her. Mayhap it was the way he found her lying straight as a corpse, her hands neatly folded over the covers at her waist. Or mayhap it was her tightly dressed coiffeur, still not so much as a hair out of place, the pearls that adorned it firmly embedded in her dark, anchored locks despite catastrophe and convalescence.

The pearls looked real, but he wasn't certain about her hair. The English often wore wigs in imitation of their unnatural queen. If this were a wig, though, surely she would have lost it. Unless it was glued down tight. Locking his forearms behind his waist, he bent close to inspect her hairline.

As if she sensed his nearness, the sleeping woman opened her eyes, surprising them both.

Duncan popped erect, bumping his head on the rafters.

The Englisher jerked the covers high to her chin and opened her mouth in alarm as if to speak, then clamped it shut, glaring at him as if she were Evil Bess herself and he a common churl who had invaded the royal bedchamber.

"Peace, woman," he blustered, furious at himself for the defensive tone in his words. "Nae harm'll come to ye. Just tell me your name, so I might make arrangements with your kinsmen to redeem ye."

Her large, intelligent brown eyes flashed fear and indignation, but she remained inexplicably mute.

"I asked ye a simple question," he said forcefully, in response to her haughty glare. "Tell me who ye are, so ye might be reunited with your kin. Speak up, I say."

A canny expression hardened her ordinary features, but she said not a word.

Duncan knew she could speak. He'd heard her that first night at Ainsel's hovel.

When she saw that they were alone, her eyes widened in terror. She shrank deeper into the bed, her dark brown gaze darting in agitation to the door, then the window, then to him.

Duncan checked his rising temper. "I told ye," he reassured her as calmly as he could, "nae one will harm ye, but we must have your name, to let your people ken that ye did not perish in the shipwreck."

At the mention of the shipwreck, a shadow crossed her anxious features, and it occurred to him that she had not been traveling alone. No decent woman would. And this woman's stiff posture and appearance were proof positive that she was nothing if not a decent woman. "There must have been others with ye," he ventured. "We canna find out what happened to them unless ye tell us your name." Surely she would appreciate the logic in that.

But still, the Englisher said nothing.

That's what came of having such a froward, unnatural female on England's throne for all these years. A scandalous example for the women of that realm. Little wonder that England's women held their men by the short hairs and meddled in everything. Their menfolk had bowed too long to the conniving Tudor bitch who'd killed Scotland's own lawful queen.

Duncan felt it his duty to let this particular English-woman know that things were different here. Scotland's men were men, and their women served them as properly they should.

Bink chose just that moment to make her entrance with a tray bearing beer, bread, plums, and cheese.

"Nae food," Duncan said calmly, staying the tray with his hand. "Nae until she speaks."

His aunt reared back and looked at him as if he'd lost his mind. "I've spent the last four days coaxin' the lass back from the brink of the grave, and now ye want me to starve her? I think nae." She shoved past him and handed the tray to the woman, who arched an eyebrow at him with a smug smile.

"Beelzebub's balls, woman!" he railed at Bink. "I am laird here, and if I say nae food, nae food it is until she speaks!" How in blazes could he be expected to maintain order if his own kinswoman contradicted him? In front of the hostage!

He could have sworn he'd seen a flash of gratitude, even admiration, in the look the silent Englisher granted his aunt as she accepted the tray.

"After she's eaten, Duncan, please take her out for some sun," Aunt Brigit directed briskly, further disgracing him in front of this stranger. " 'Tis such a fine day that I had a chair set by the wall for her to warm herself."

His wounded dignity athrob, Duncan thrust a crooked finger at his mother's sister. "I shall speak with ye later."

"But ye canna speak with the lass," Bink had the temerity to say. Her expression softened. "Nae yet, anyway. Look at her throat, Duncan. Little wonder she canna make a sound."

In silent confirmation, the hostage stretched her long

neck to better reveal the vivid welts of purple and yellow
that ringed it. "So?" She'd been able to speak well enough
at Ainsel's—*after* she'd been throttled—but he didn't
care to discuss that in front of her.

The hostage met his frown with a look of undeniable
defiance.

Duncan clenched his fists, his temperature rising. No
one, man or woman, dared to look at him thus.

He cared not why she had chosen to feign muteness;
he was in no mood to tolerate her foolish game of silence.
The sooner she acknowledged him as master—out loud—
the better for everyone. "She will talk," he rumbled, determined to bring this harpy to heel. He owed it to the
men of the world. "And she'll talk to me." To her obvious
chagrin, Duncan wrested the tray of food from his hostage's grasp.

Good. He wanted her angry.

"Leave us," he said brusquely to his aunt, shoving the
tray onto the cabinet under the window. Duncan paid no
attention to his aunt's huff of disapproval, just returned to
the foot of the bed and pinned his hostage with a chal-
lenging stare.

From the corner of his eye, he saw Aunt Brigit
straighten, hesitate, then reclaim the tray. "Doona forget
to take her outside," she said in a parting sally as she
stomped from the room. She'd be bashing the pots
about and sulking for days, but Duncan would gladly
weather her disapproval. Discipline must be maintained,
after all.

He waited until he was certain his aunt was out of
earshot to bend close and inspect his hostage with a crit-
ical eye.

She met his gaze head-on, but one hand fluttered to
her hair to reassure herself that her cast-iron coif was still
intact.

Ah. There was a weakness he could exploit. All
women—even ones as plain as she—were vulnerable
when it came to their appearance, so he decided to pro-

voke her to speech by attacking her vanity. "Rather dried up, aren't ye?" he mused aloud, eliciting a fresh spark of outrage in her unrelenting glare.

Duncan smiled. Women were so predictable. "An old maid?" She wore no wedding ring, and the third finger of her large, capable left hand had no telltale indications that she ever had. And the breasts beneath her fine woolen shift were high and firm for a woman of her advanced years, a good indication she'd neither borne nor suckled any bairns. "Pity. But then again, ye are a bit tall and scrawny. And stubborn, judgin' from that hateful grimace you're wearin'." He shook his head in censure. "Whew! What man could bear to look at *that* expression every day of the world?"

Clearly, he'd hit a nerve. Despite her weakened condition, she summoned up the strength to lob a pillow at him, sending feathers flying. Yet she did not utter so much as a gasp.

Smiling even wider, he plucked a feather from the air. "Nae man worth the hair on his cuddy would wed himself to such a sour, uppity creature."

Her cheeks still flushed, she remained silent, hiding behind a haughty look that branded her as an aristocrat. Just his luck, to end up with a spinster of her advanced years to ransom. Not good. Spinsters rarely ransomed well.

He tried another tack. Swiftly, he tugged back the patched covers from the bottom corner of the bed and captured her left foot, lifting it up for his perusal. "Ach. Just as I suspected. A true trencher, that."

Twisting so he could not see up her shift, she tried her best to wriggle free of his grasp, but Duncan easily held her foot fast.

"Let's see if you're ticklish." He scraped his fingernail up her instep, causing her toes to curl, and watched with satisfaction as her face contorted in an effort not to laugh.

Duncan was beginning to enjoy this, despite her continuing silence. Rawboned though she was, the curve of her calf and feel of her fine, creamy skin in his hand were surprisingly distracting.

How long had it been since he'd had a woman? His manhood twitched at the thought, but he couldn't remember the last time he'd dallied with a willing wench.

A few months after Aselma's death, he reckoned, and then only for solace. But his partner had been more than willing. Unlike this haughty prune.

Employing the feather, he traced a torturous path up his hostage's instep. Her face folded inward and her eyes watered in response, but still, not a sound.

A small part of him granted her grudging admiration for holding out so well against him. But the last thing he needed was another bossy woman in his life. Aunt Brigit was bad enough, and lately Amber showed alarming signs of following in her great-aunt's footsteps. He could not tolerate any further rebellion at his own hearth, especially from a stranger.

He stroked the feather up her instep again. At the subtle torture her breathing grew labored, her plain face contorted even further, and tears traced down her cheeks, but she did not utter a sound.

Duncan recognized her fierce stubbornness as one that would not break so easily. He'd seen that same mettle in men who'd held out under far more grievous testing. That meant she could only be broken by threatening someone or something she cared about.

He would have to find that someone or something. Duncan dropped her foot to the mattress. "Ye shall speak, and speak to me," he said with quiet resolution.

She would tell him who she was, and he would gladly be rid of her—for whatever price he could get.

The hostage pulled her feet back up into her elaborate shift, drawing his eye to the padded embroidery that circled the elegant garment's hem. Aunt Brigit had told him the woman had been distraught when she'd awakened in a strange shift, and hadn't eased until her own had been returned.

He glanced to her face just in time to see a spark of raw fear flash in her eyes before her expression hardened to one as cold as a tidal pool in January. With calculated slowness, she drew the covers over her shift, silently daring him to torment her further or touch her again.

A formidable woman, this. She had the same steel as Aunt Brigit, but hers was tainted by her English blood.

Just as he was tainted by the English blood that constituted half his own.

Duncan considered leaving her alone, then remembered Aunt Brigit's less-than-deferential request to take the woman outside. He did not have to comply, of course. But he'd already crossed his aunt once this day. To do so again would guarantee retaliation. The last time he'd crossed her twice in one day, she'd put a powerful physic in his stew, and he hadn't been able to get more than twenty paces from the chamber pot for days.

Weighing the risks, he decided it suited him well enough to do as Aunt Brigit wished. He plucked the dressing gown from its peg beside the clothes Aunt Brigit had scrounged from his late wives' belongings. "Here." He tossed the robe at his hostage. "Cover yourself. I'm taking ye outside."

Relieved that the handsome savage of a Scotsman had been distracted from the padded embroidery that concealed her mother's jewels, Catherine did her best to keep up a brave front. But she still trembled from the way he'd looked at her shift—his startling blue eyes narrow with conjecture.

But now those eyes had moved from her shift to the woman inside it.

Suddenly Catherine was all too conscious of being almost naked before him, unchaperoned, and in a bed.

She'd heard the whispered tales of the reivers' rape

and cruelty, and seen with her own eyes the wretched aftermath in broken souls and lost repute.

She wanted to cover herself, but instead she held out the coarse, musty robe for inspection, wondering if its owner smelled as gamy as her captor, and whether lice infested it.

The question must have been patent on her face, for her captor muttered, "It belonged to one of ma wives," as if the explanation had sprung forth against his will.

One of his wives? Was he a polygamist, as well as raider and kidnapper? *The wives' chest,* the faerie child had said.

Again, he responded to her unspoken question, unnerving her. "Ma late wives," he rumbled in the barbaric accents of his race. A hard glint of intelligence brightened those compelling blue eyes. "The tall one . . . was that Peggy, or Beth? I never could keep 'em straight."

Catherine glared at him in shock and disapproval. What sort of brute was he, that he couldn't even rightly remember the name of the woman who had worn this robe and shared his bed?

How many wives had he *had*? she wondered. Was he merely so callous, it did not matter what their names were?

She did not flinch under his piercing scrutiny as he met her reproof with maddening smugness. "I've been unlucky in ma wives," he volunteered coolly, "all four of 'em, God rest their souls."

Four! It wasn't unusual for a man to survive two, even three wives, but four? Why, he scarce had any gray in his unkempt black hair. Had he murdered them, then?

Far from being intimidated, her captor seemed amused by her hostility. "Aye," he mused aloud. "Most unsatisfactory, ma wives. I wed them, bed them, and beget with them, then just when I've begun to get accustomed to their ways, they up and die on me." He shook his head with a frown. "Most unsatisfactory. A *good* wife doesna die on a man at the drop of a hat."

So much for murder. Suicide seemed a definite possibility, though, in light of his boorish pronouncement.

This was a brute, not a man, to speak so callously of the women who'd had the misfortune to be his wives. Catherine would have loved nothing better than to tell him so, but she managed to keep her sentiments locked behind clamped teeth and compressed lips.

Then it occurred to her that he might be deliberately baiting her in an effort to get her to speak. Well, if he was, he would lose. Old Bess would run naked through Westminster Abbey before Catherine would grant him the satisfaction of speaking, much less revealing her beleaguered stepfamily's identity so he could extort a ransom from them.

She couldn't help shying away, though, when he strode up close beside her and planted his fists on the thick leather belt that girded the tapered waist of his leathern jacket. Why didn't he wear the customary plaid of his countrymen? she wondered. His black leathern breeches . . . Catherine did her best not to look at his muscular calves and thighs and generous codpiece, but they weren't easy to ignore as he stood so close beside her.

Despite the odors of smoke and horseflesh and hard labor, he radiated a powerful, inexplicably affecting male presence. Catherine found herself wondering what he would look like after a good scrubbing and grooming.

Not that she still didn't want to slap him soundly. She held back simply because she had no desire to soil her hand.

Oblivious to her silent reproof, he cracked a grin revealing strong, even teeth as he openly leered at her bare arms. "If ye doona wish to wear the robe, so be it." He arched a dark brow. "But there's a stiff breeze outside. Ye'll rue goin' out like that. Then again . . . Though you're plain, ma men will nae doubt relish havin' such an ample look at ye."

Horrified, Catherine shoved her arms into the robe

and hastily fumbled with the ties, but before she could arrange herself properly, he scooped her into his arms as if she weighed no more than a bannock. She reached down just in time to snatch the coverlet to hide her bare legs.

The result was ludicrous. The robe was twisted about her, its ties unevenly matched and its sleeves too short by inches for her long arms.

It took all her willpower not to demand that he put her down long enough to arrange herself. Letting out a snort of frustration, she adjusted the coverlet to conceal as much of her disarray as possible.

With no sign of effort, the Scotsman carried her into the hallway, which was marred by crumbling, mildewed plaster and cracked paneling almost black with dirt. Then he proceeded down a dusty, creaking stairway that complained so loudly she was certain their combined weights would send them straight through every step. She lifted up a silent prayer of thanks when they safely reached the bottom in a shabby, neglected parlor.

The room was saved from abysmal disgrace only by a large Persian rug of quality, the sole item that seemed to have been properly cared for. All around it, the muddy floors were stamped with porcine and human footprints, and chickens roosted in the clutter that covered what had probably once been decent wooden furnishings.

Hens and pigs in the house, like some peasant hovel! These people lived like churls, lacking even the pride to properly maintain the home that gave them shelter.

As the Scotsman carried her toward the outer doorway and the brilliant early August sunshine beyond, she thought she spied a stained-glass coat of arms inset among the ample windows' diamond shaped panes. But the glass was so grimy, she couldn't be sure.

Once outside, she had to close her eyes against the sunlight and the bright, blue, cloudless sky. A sweet-smelling summer breeze washed over them, carrying away her captor's harsh scent. The warm summer sun sent a shiver of pleasure through her.

He carried her so securely, not even breathing hard.

She kept her eyes closed until he stopped, then she opened them to see a breathtakingly beautiful valley stretching away from the ancient wall upon which he held her. Tidy stone hedges enclosed lush crops and pastures dotted with sheep and cattle. In the largest pasture, a substantial herd of sturdy border hobblers grazed alongside magnificent black, roan, and dappled stallions, ready to earn renown for the reivers who rode them into battle.

At the center of the valley, a clear, slow-moving river reflected the sky overhead and the green pastures at its banks. On the horizon, ancient trees bordered scrub forests.

Catherine was struck by the immaculate landscape's contrast to the squalor and neglect of the dwelling she had just left. But the border regions had long been a land of contrasts.

" 'Tis mine now," the Scotsman said with quiet resolution. She looked up and saw the fierce pride with which he gazed upon his land. Then his features tightened along with his voice. "Mine, despite ma bein' a bastard." He glanced at her askance. " 'Tis an irony I enjoy. But these lands, like most things of worth and beauty on the borders, come at a terrible price."

He did not need to name the cost. She—and all who lived within the marches—knew far too well the bitter heritage of greed and revenge that afflicted the region. The two of them had that curse in common, if nothing else.

Catherine was surprised to hear such a frank, philosophical insight coming from a man so clearly devoid of culture or breeding. Yet there was something about him . . .

She felt her body grow warm where his hard, muscular chest pressed against her hip and his arms circled her

waist and thighs. Suddenly all too conscious of the inti-
macy of their situation, she tried her best to wriggle from
his embrace, wishing she could demand that he put her
down.

Devil of a thing, not being able to speak!

His arms tightened around her. "Something amiss?" he
asked archly. A thin smile stretched his shapely mouth.
"Ye have but to ask, and I shall do ma best to oblige."
He ambled toward the waiting chaise.

The arrogant bonehead. Catherine mustered all her
strength to escape him, but her feeble efforts succeeded
only in tiring her and amusing him.

"Down?" he asked after a maddeningly deliberate
pause. "Wantin' down, is't?"

She nodded angrily, her lips curled inward with frustration.

"Verra well." He plunked her like a sack of oats onto
the fleece-covered chair, then turned his back and left before she could give him a proper silent scolding.

Her dignity in tatters, she shifted her thoughts away
from the ruffian Scotsman. She needed to think, come up
with some way to let her family know where she was so
her stepfather could send the wardens after her. Robert
Storey was well respected by both the queen and her men-
at-law. They would not hesitate to arrange for help from
their Scottish counterparts. She only needed to let Papa
know she was alive, and where.

Her sweet, precious Hal, the brother of her heart, if not
her blood. How she missed him already. And Papa. Did
they think she had drowned?

A sudden ache pulsed in her heart.

She must get word to them somehow. But first, she
would have to find out exactly where in God's good earth
she'd ended up.

A stab of guilt reminded her of Charles. Where was
he? Lying dead at the bottom of the sea, or held hostage
like her?

If he was dead, Willa would be crushed. And she'd

never forgive Catherine for being the reason Charles had boarded that ship.

Miserable, Catherine drew the cover tight around her and stared unseeing across the pastoral perfection before her.

She couldn't think of Charles now. She had to have a plan. And she had to grow strong.

Chapter
FOUR

Catherine started when the woman the faerie child had called Aunt Brigit pulled open her chamber door and banged into the room with a tray of food. In the week since she'd awakened at this godforsaken place, Catherine had learned not to expect any mannerly consideration from her captors. Clearly, these outlaws knew nothing of proper decorum. Yet she still hadn't gotten used to being barged in on without so much as a word or a knock.

"Food," Aunt Brigit announced grumpily. She briskly navigated the dusty baskets of wool, abandoned clutter, and broken spinning wheel between the door and the bed.

It was obvious she did not relish waiting on Catherine, but since the dour little Scotswoman had refused to starve her into submission, Catherine held out hope of winning her as an ally. Though how she could do so without speaking, she had yet to figure out.

Arriving at the bedside, Aunt Brigit shoved the tray at Catherine with her usual admonition. "Here. And ye'd better eat every scrap, for there's precious little to go around."

Catherine straightened against the pillows and accepted the coarse fare, upon which Aunt Brigit swatted at the bedclothes to smooth them, muttering her customary litany of complaints.

Catherine's stomach turned when she looked down at the tray's contents. Food, indeed . . . *swill* would be more accurate for the leaden bannocks, sour beer, and heavy, unseasoned bigg-and-bean stew she'd been forcing down in order to regain her strength. Her efforts were paying off—she was feeling a little stronger every day—but the stew left her so swollen with wind that she was wholly unfit for polite company.

Not that the outlaws who held her here were polite company. They probably passed wind in public without so much as a thought, but Catherine would rather die than humiliate herself thusly in front of them, so she hadn't even considered venturing from her chamber. Not that she could, even if she wanted to. She was still so weak and shaky, it was all she could do to get to the chamber pot and back.

She did her best to ignore Aunt Brigit, who now stood watching her to make certain she didn't waste a single morsel.

The sound of shrieks and clattering feet erupted from the house below. She often heard children running wild as dogs through the house, but only the winsome little girl and her simple brother had ventured into her room. Yet more and more often, she heard small footsteps, whispers, and giggles in the hallway outside her door. Taking a bite of bannock that seemed to get bigger with every chew, Catherine wondered idly how many children lived here.

And she wondered how much longer she'd be able to endure being cooped up in this grimy room. She scanned from the sooty ceiling past the moldy plaster to the stained paneling to the clutter that scarcely left a clear path from the bed to the door. What sort of people could bear to live in such squalor? She certainly couldn't. The stronger she grew, the more the filth and neglect around her weighed upon her spirit.

Perhaps the time had come to do something.

She cleared her throat to get Aunt Brigit's attention, then mimed writing.

Aunt Brigit tucked her chin and frowned. "Ye want to *write*?" The request clearly baffled her.

Catherine smiled and nodded, miming quill and paper again in confirmation.

"I doona ken . . ." Aunt Brigit pinched her thin lower

lip between thumb and finger, her gray brows lowered in suspicion.

Catherine pressed her palms together as if in prayer, meeting the little woman's wary, bird-bright gaze with her own look of honest supplication.

Perhaps it was that unspoken exchange, or perhaps Aunt Brigit really did have a heart beneath her crustiness, but after only a moment's consideration, the tiny Scotswoman closed her eyes and sighed, granting Catherine a glimpse of how deeply weary she really was. "Ach. I suppose there's nae harm in askin' Duncan." She opened her eyes and pinned Catherine with a withering glare. "But doona make me sorry, lass. He's cross enough with me already fer takin' your part about the food."

Catherine clasped Aunt Brigit's small, work-worn hand in gratitude. When the wardens came to rescue her and put this Duncan in irons, Catherine would repay Aunt Brigit's kindness by pleading mercy for the woman. But as for the Black Bastard, she would gladly watch the reiver hang.

Downstairs Duncan bent over his accounts in morose concentration, wishing there were some way he could stretch the supplies they had and the yields from the upcoming harvest. But the inventories and crop projections told him otherwise. The year's unseasonable weather had produced scanty crops, so his harvest of bigg and haver wouldn't hold out past December. That would mean starvation, unless he butchered his breeding stock and dairy cattle. If he did, he'd be left in even worse shape to provide for the fifty-three souls who depended upon him should they face another lean year.

Michael had ridden to Glasgow and sold the Englisher's rings, but he hadn't raised enough to carry a household as big as Annanlea through the winter. It would take three times as much as the jewelry had brought.

He slammed down his fist on the scattered inventories and accounts. Damn the devils who'd taken his salt!

Thanks to them, he now faced stealing food from the mouths of others to feed his own.

All these years, he'd prided himself on raiding only in direct retaliation for a theft or an offense. It was the one scrap of honor he'd held on to. But it seemed fairly certain now that his salt was gone without a trace. As he'd feared, the trail had led only to the firth. Unless he could find out who was behind the raid, he couldn't even petition the Crown for restitution from the thieves. So, because of someone else's treachery, he faced being dragged down to the basest dishonor himself.

Yet what was honor in the face of starvation?

The sound of Michael's familiar footsteps cut through his anger, and he looked up to see his trusted mentor carefully skirting Aunt Brigit's rug. "Any word?" Duncan asked him.

"Nae." Michael dragged a stout wooden chair onto the rug, facing Duncan, and dropped his bulk into the seat. He exhaled heavily, his wide mouth flattening within the beard surrounding it. "I saw Auld Wat maself, so's I could weigh his verity when he spoke about the salt, but he seems as flummoxed as we are." His thick brows drew together. "I've kent the man these thirty years, Duncan, and I doona think he turned on ye." He grinned. "Why he hasna, I canna guess—he's double-crossed every other friend he's ever had—but Wat respects ye as he respects nae other." He shook his head. "It's only ma instincts that tell me so, but boil me and hang me up for a haggis if I doona think the auld devil's innocent—in this, at least." He absently rubbed his ample belly. "That's a first, Auld Wat innocent of anything!"

"Wat's suffered just as we have from poor crops," Duncan argued. "There's still the chance he was behind it." The mere possibility sent a cold tingle down his spine. Walter Scott—Auld Wat to one and all—had long been his most important ally. But if the outlaw had taken their salt, retaliation would unleash a bloodbath such as even these parts hadn't seen since auld King James set his war dogs on the Armstrongs.

Duncan managed a halfhearted smile. "Your instincts are enough for me, auld man. I'd gladly trust ma children's lives to 'em." He leaned back, bleak. "We'll have to steal what we need from the Johnstones." He all but choked on the words. " 'Tis the only way."

Michael's kind face went grim. "Nay, lad. Surely there's another way. Besides the trouble that'll stir up, I canna bear to see ye—"

Whatever he was going to say next was drowned out by his aunt's strident rebuke. "Get off ma rug, ye great filthy lummox!" She grasped her skirts and stormed toward him with mayhem in her eye.

"Achen, Brigit!" Michael shot back, coloring violently to the straw-pale roots of his hair as he shot to his feet. "That voice would curdle cream!" He snatched the chair from the rug, then gestured to where he'd been sitting. "Look ye. I havna hurt the cursed thing!"

"Mayhap nae," she grudgingly allowed, straightening her tiny frame in incongruously feminine fashion as she approached. "But ye *could've* . . . Think of that!" She glided past him, sparking a carnal gleam in Michael's eyes despite his scowl. "Trample ma rug again," she snapped, "and I'll crack that empty pate of yours and prove to Duncan once and for all there's nothing between those big ears."

Duncan suppressed a smile. He'd long kent that Michael harbored a deep and abiding attachment to his aunt, and he'd suspected for just as long that Bink cared for Michael. The two certainly seemed to enjoy swapping insults, and he'd seen the way they looked at one another when they thought nae one was watching. But Duncan had nae intention of sticking his nose into the situation. Bink would assuredly bite it off.

Still, he held out hope that the two people dearest to him besides his children might somehow find happiness together.

Aunt Brigit smoothed the folds of her sturdy skirt. "I need to speak with ye, Duncan."

"In private?" he asked, doing his best to appear grave.

"Nae." She shot Michael a sour look. "I never notice he's there, anyway."

By a Johnstone's dirk, she didn't.

She turned her attention back to Duncan. "The Englisher would like a quill, some ink, and something to write upon."

"Write?" Duncan tucked his chin. "She can *write*?"

"Why does that surprise ye so? *I* can read and write," she reminded him testily. "As could your sainted mother, God rest her soul, and all your children save poor Nevin, though how those bairns've managed to learn with as little time as I've been able to teach 'em is a miracle. Ye've gone too long wifeless, Duncan."

Duncan groaned inwardly. Bink was always tearing off down that particular rabbit trail.

She shook her finger at him. "Yer children need a mother, nae a dried-up auld spinster like me. I doona ken why ye—"

He cut her off with an emphatic, "Ye were sayin' our hostage would like to write." He had enough troubles without breaking in another wife who'd only up and die on him.

At the moment, this Englisher was one of those troubles. The woman was becoming a bane. What good was she unless she revealed her identity?

The more hopeless recovering the salt became, the more important it was to get that ransom.

"Aye, she wants to write," Aunt Brigit snapped, determined as ever to have the last word in any exchange.

Duncan considered the request and decided that if he gave his hostage some rope, the haughty wench might hang herself. "Let her write." Still painfully conscious that someone from Annanlea had betrayed him, he lowered his voice so only Bink and Michael could hear the next. "There's a better than even chance she means to smuggle out a message to her kin. When she tries, we'll intercept it and learn who she is."

He rummaged up a couple of sheets of precious paper that had only been written on in one direction, and handed them to his aunt. "Here. Take her these, but keep a sharp eye out and mind if any of it goes missing."

"How could she smuggle out a message?" Michael asked in a "whisper" that carried clear to the stairs. "Nae one here would dare to help her."

"Someone might," Aunt Brigit said. Then she voiced Duncan's only reservation about the scheme. "If there is a traitor in our midst, and if she found him out, he might help her."

"Hmm." Pensive, Michael combed through his beard with three fingers. Then he brightened. "Achen. If *we* can't find 'em, how could she? The woman canna even talk. Anyway, besides your bairns, Duncan, only ye and Brigit can read."

"Doona be taken in," Duncan cautioned them. "The woman can talk. She's nae more mute than I am." He cocked his head toward the painted cabinet under the windows. "There's ink and quills in there."

He returned to his inventories. "Tell her it's all the paper she'll be getting. What little salt we have to trade must go for food, nae luxuries like paper."

Aunt Brigit glided past Michael with a definite swish of her narrow hips.

Michael responded by sucking in his belly until his face reddened, forcing him to exhale in a whoosh. He turned to Duncan. "By yer leave then, I'll be goin'."

"Aye." Duncan clasped his forearm. "I thank ye, Michael. We'll think of something to get us through the winter."

The old man nodded, but his face said he wasn't convinced.

Neither was Duncan.

While his aunt rummaged in the cabinet, he laid out a clean sheet of precious paper and began to pen yet another request for information about his salt, this time to a middleman in London who owed him a favor.

"I have it, dear boy," Aunt Brigit said as she turned to leave.

It had been a long time since she'd called him that, and it earned a smile. He looked up to see her shoulders slumped with fatigue, and her gray eyes weary. Duncan's heart caught. She'd sacrificed her youth to care for him and his mother, and now his children, making her old before her time. " 'Tis I who thank ye, Brigit Maxwell," he said with affection. "I ken how hard ye work for all of us."

It was as close as they came to saying they loved each other, but for both of them, it was enough.

Her step a little lighter, she kept on going, making no reply.

He would get another wife to ease Aunt Brigit's load—as soon as he found his salt or ransomed the hostage. Assuming anyone would marry him in light of the ridiculous rumors that he was hexed and doom awaited all his wives.

Duncan lost himself in his letter for some time before the loudness and tone of Aunt Brigit's voice from upstairs broke into his concentration.

Quill poised, he leaned back and listened.

What he heard was nae one of her usual tirades. Something had truly offended her. "The devil's codpiece," he muttered as he rose and went to see what was the matter.

In the hallway outside the Englisher's chamber, the volume and intensity of Aunt Brigit's outburst prompted him to quicken his pace.

"So this is how ye repay ma kindness! Well, ye can stick yer tongue to a hot iron, ye high-handed, useless tart!"

"How now!" Duncan strode across the room, and none too soon. "What's all this?" Bink didn't acknowledge him. Instead she raised her hand and reared back to slap the

Englisher, who glared up at her with frosty—albeit shocked—disdain.

He closed the distance to his aunt just in time to prevent her from bandycocking the Englisher. "What's this? Fisticuffs?" Grabbing his aunt about her tiny waist, he easily lifted her off the floor and drew her out of striking range. "How's a man to think with all this racket?"

Dusky with choler, Aunt Brigit went straight as a pike and waggled one of the pieces of paper in front of him. "Here! See for yourself!"

The hostage watched in silent affront as he took the rumpled sheet in his free hand and read the elegant script at precise right angles to his own unpolished scrawl.

I wish to be granted my privacy. Please leave my food outside the door and knock to let me know it is there. I shall replace the tray when I am done. You will find my chamber pot outside the door every morning. Please clean and replace it by mid-morning. Beyond that, I ask only that I am undisturbed in my chamber.

Aunt Brigit must be weary, indeed, if *this* was what had set her off. Women. Duncan had given up trying to understand them with wife number two.

But what little he did ken told him the problem here wasn't really the Englisher's high-handed request, but his beloved aunt's fatigue. To be asked for special treatment by a stranger when she enjoyed none herself . . .

"It's all right, Bink," he said, giving her arm a reassuring pat. "I'll deal with this. Go lie ye down, and don't get up till supper. That's an order."

"I willna do it," she grumbled halfheartedly even as she leaned against him. "Lucas's cookin' would kill us all if I wasna there to keep an eye on him. And if I slack off, then more's the work awaitin', and where's the good in that?"

Why did he bother? he asked himself as he put her down.

Her chin stubbornly projected, Bink crossed her arms and straightened to all four feet eleven inches of her height. "And anyway, I want to see ye put this haughty wench in her proper place."

Duncan kent better than to push her in such a mood, so he turned to the hostage. The Englisher seemed anything but repentant. She sat rigid with her own arms crossed, a cold expression on her plain face.

Blast the woman, sitting there like evil Queen Bess herself, as if they owed her the homage of waiting on her hand and foot. No wonder Bink was sorely vexed.

He fixed her with his most ferocious frown, but it had no appreciable effect. He'd told Aunt Brigit that God had sent them this hostage, but now he was beginning to wonder if she hadn't come from the other direction.

She was a *captive,* for glory's sake, not a bloody guest! "Have ye nae noticed, woman, we have nae servants in this house? At Annanlea, it's toil or perish for one and all, and Aunt Brigit works the hardest of anyone, from before dawn till long after dark." He straightened, fully expecting his hostage to cringe when he towered so close beside her, but she didn't so much as flinch. "Ye would do well to remember ye are alive, fed, and cared for at ma sufferance, and by ma aunt's good service, overburdened though she is. I willna have ye addin' to her labors. And I willna have ye wreckin' the peace of ma home." He shot his aunt a brief look of reproof. "Either one of ye."

Ignoring his rebuke, Aunt Brigit glared down on the Englisher, who responded by reaching out for the paper Duncan was holding.

When he handed it over, she dipped the quill and wrote in a quick, precise hand. Before the ink had dried, she briskly returned her response.

Duncan read:

My request in no way adds to your aunt's labors. If anything, it reduces the time required for my care.

*Though I am not yet strong enough to look after my-
self, I assure you I shall relieve your aunt of that burden as soon as I am able. I am merely asking for my
privacy, nothing more. I see no reason not to grant it.*

Aunt Brigit read the note aslant and colored up again
at its condescending tone. "Of all the bold-faced, naked-
arsed, high-handed gall!" She jabbed a work-worn finger
toward the hostage. "I've half a mind to shave that prim
hair, pearls and all, from your big-head, and see how
proud ye be then."

Duncan closed his hand over Aunt Brigit's pointing
finger and lowered it. "Ye'll do nae such thing." He
glanced archly at the hostage. "Nae *yet,* anyway."

The Englisher's eyebrows shot up in alarm. Finally,
he'd gotten a rise out of her. So she was vain about that
ridiculous, stone-hard hair . . .

Duncan guided his aunt to the door. "Please lie down
for a while, at least, Bink. I fear for your health if ye
doona get some rest."

Her expression pinched, she wrested free of him.
"Mayhap I will for a wee bit. But only because ye order
it." She glared at the hostage. "Duncan is master here. I
obey his commands. I always do."

Close to her as he was, he was glad lightning didn't
strike Bink for that particular bold-faced lie. Ironically,
she probably believed herself the most obedient of
women, though all at Annanlea knew otherwise.

Duncan gently grasped her shoulders and urged her
toward the hallway. "Off with ye, then. I'll look in on ye
after I'm done here."

With weary steps, she headed for her room. "Put her
in her place, Duncan," she said without looking back.

Duncan pivoted to study the Englisher, who recipro-
cated with disturbing intensity.

Their gazes locked, he returned to the bedside. Staring
down this woman felt like going nose to beak with an
eagle capable of striking any minute, its bright eyes

trained relentlessly on every move. Unsettling.

Despite her pallor and weakness, her large brown eyes glittered with stubborn, guarded intelligence and ... what? He would say hostility, but there was something else there.

Suddenly ill at ease in the brittle silence, he reminded himself that her muteness was a direct affront to him. So why should *he* feel awkward in the vacuum it created? It was she who should be cowering. Yet he sensed again in this Englisher the same mettle that kept Bink going.

If so, force would be ineffectual. The harder one came down on Bink, the more she resisted. Duncan smiled, certain he would find a way to bend this hostage to his will.

Perhaps it wouldn't be a bad idea to leave her to the company she seemed to enjoy the most—her own—and spare the rest of the household. He bent low, so close his breath washed back on him from her pallid skin. "Ye'll have your privacy then, wench, but only to spare Aunt Brigit the choler ye give her. And only until you're fit enough to earn your bread."

She winced slightly when he spoke, but maintained her rigid posture despite an almost imperceptible quaver.

It was a start. A quaver today, proper obedience within another fortnight.

Duncan rose and planted his fists at his waist. "And as soon as ye are fit, there's work aplenty in the scullery." He chuckled at the thought of rough, burly Lucas matching wills with this silent shrew. If that didn't squeeze an oath from her, nothing would. His chuckle bloomed to a laugh, and with that, he left her frowning in confusion.

Before he ducked through the doorway, though, a tingle on the back of his neck prompted him to turn and catch her peering at him, her gaze darting from his face to his legs to his groin.

Plainly horrified to have been caught looking at him the way women had looked at men since Adam and Eve, the Englisher averted her eyes, two harsh spots of color staining her pale cheeks.

By glory, he'd been so long without a woman that even a lecherous look from a bony Britisher like her set his cock to throbbing.

Duncan laughed in earnest now.

He hadn't thought the prim, clinch-arsed aristocrat had the juice for such a thing.

"Here," he said cheerfully. "I'll give ye a better look still." He reached for the buttons on his breeches, but before he had even one undone, she hoisted the covers over her face with a gasp.

Duncan grinned. He was making progress already.

Catherine remained beneath the musty bedclothes until she was certain the Black Bastard had left her alone. When she finally dropped the covers and saw that he was really gone, she fell back, humiliated and exhausted, onto the pillows.

Would he really have flaunted himself to her?

Probably.

It wouldn't have been the first time she'd seen a man without his clothes, but it would have been the first time she'd seen one as comely as Duncan Maxwell. She shamed herself again by wondering what his formidable body would look like proud and naked.

Her captor's breath had smelled of sour beer, but by the queen's petticoats, he was well-formed for a man of his size, made like one of the scandalous Buonarroti marbles she'd seen in the gardens of her father's Italian friend near Carlisle.

Why she'd looked at the Black Bastard as she had, she couldn't imagine. One minute she'd been recoiling from the smell of him and thinking he needed a good scrubbing; the next, she'd been caught leering like a wanton.

Perhaps she was going mad. Catherine groaned and pulled the covers back up over her head, mortally ashamed of the aching hunger inside her.

She couldn't think about it. It was too horrifying.

Determined to exorcise the incident, she willed herself to think of something else.

Her room. Yes.

She'd been granted her privacy. Now she could set her room to rights in peace. What supplies she needed, she could forage after the rest of the house had gone to sleep. Her captors rose so early and worked so late, she was confident no one would hear her. And if the rest of the house was anything like this room, they'd never miss a pail or broom or brush. If they had any!

Yes. She would show them how to clean a chamber properly.

Uncovering her face, she closed her eyes and gratefully surrendered to sleep. But when she dreamed, it was of Duncan Maxwell, clean and glistening wet and naked, laughing at her shame.

Two weeks later on August twenty-ninth, Catherine waited in smug anticipation by the door until she heard Aunt Brigit's approaching footsteps. Her hands were raw and her knees ached, but she was proud of what she'd accomplished. When she heard the footsteps reach the last turn in the hallway, Catherine pushed the door open, then stood aside to allow for the full effect.

"Achen. So her highness wants to be served after all, does she?" Aunt Brigit, head down as usual, marched right past her and took three steps before looking up. When she did, her progress halted abruptly. "By all the piss in all the waulkin' vats in Scotland, woman, what have ye done?"

Catherine surveyed her orderly chamber with satisfaction. It had taken all of her hard-won strength to bring the room to some semblance of its former distinction, but the effect was gratifying. A cool, fresh summer wind blew past glistening panes of the narrow open windows, banishing the pervasive mustiness. The wooden floors, paneling, and furniture glowed richly now that they'd been stripped of grime and rubbed with walnut oil. The toys and clutter had been collected, washed, then stored in a basket, and the neglected wool would soon be spun, now that she'd managed to repair the wheel.

Overhead, no cobwebs marred the coffered ceiling. And though the plaster was still crumbling, she'd managed to scrub away the worst of the dirt and mold, revealing sturdy brick, not daub and wattle, underneath. Catherine had also cleared the ashes from the fireplace, dumping them out the window as she had the filthy cleaning water. She'd even scrubbed the hearth and sooty mantel.

Expecting thanks, she faced Aunt Brigit with silent pride.

But Aunt Brigit's reaction was definitely not one of gratitude. In a gesture reminiscent of Duncan, she propped her bird-fists on her scrawny hips and glared at Catherine. "Ye said ye'd relieve me of the burden of your care as soon as ye were able." She shot a disdainful glance at the transformed room. "I'd say this makes a lie of *that* promise." Her gray eyes danced with anger. "If ye're well enough to do this, then it's past time ye earn your bread by helpin' Lucas in the kitchen, as Duncan has ordered."

It wasn't the grateful reaction Catherine had expected. And she wasn't prepared to be sent to the scullery!

Why, she'd had to rest every few minutes as she'd chipped away at the filth in her room, and after two weeks of relentlessly pushing herself by day and garnering water and supplies by night, she scarcely had the strength to stand.

But she'd be hung for a witch and burned before she'd let this ungrateful crone get the best of her. Catherine glared right back at Aunt Brigit with a curt nod.

"I'll bring ye some work clothes straightaway." Aunt Brigit shoved the tray into Catherine's middle. "And nae more trays for Her Majesty. Ye can eat with the rest of us in the kitchen." With that, she stomped away without bothering to close the door.

Tray in hand, Catherine drew the door closed, then

returned to her bed. Stung, she sank to the mattress.

Once again, her stubborn pride had been her undoing.

She *had* said she'd relieve Aunt Brigit of the burden of her care as soon as she was able.

Dear Lord, give me strength . . .

Ah, well. Working in the scullery should be sufficient penance for her conscience and for God. She looked at her cracked nails and red, chapped hands and consoled herself that she needn't worry about the effects of scouring. She'd ruined her hands already.

She took a bite of the chewy bannock, which she was actually beginning to get used to.

Maybe it wasn't so bad after all that she would be working with the others. The sooner she made herself a part of this barbarian household, the sooner she could find out exactly where she was and send secret word to her family.

Catherine took one look at the kitchen—and the hairy bull of a cook—and her stomach turned. She'd been eating food that came from this horrid place, prepared by that horrid man. Already light-headed from the halting journey from her room, she feared for a few awful seconds she would faint, throw up, or both. But iron will and a deep breath forestalled such a disaster.

Straightening to her most ladylike posture, she advanced on the brute at the cook fire. Lucas, Aunt Brigit and Duncan Maxwell had called him. Well, Lucas, you might as well know I'm nobody's slave from the start. And I can teach you more than a thing or two about cooking.

His back to her, the burly oaf adjusted the joint that hung from the roasting hook, setting it far too close to the glowing charcoal.

Good grief! Meat was scarce enough in this place. Overcooking it was a double sin. Catherine reached past him, keeping as much distance between them as possible, and adjusted the joint to the proper location for the heat of the charcoal.

The beast snatched up a rusted cleaver and turned on her with a roar. "Touch that meat again, and there'll be nothin' left to touch it with!" Eyes narrowing, he thrust his long jaw forward with a questioning frown. "What the hell do ye think ye're doin? Keep to the scullery, woman, as Duncan ordered!"

Confronted with the upraised cleaver, Catherine realized—as she too often did—she should have been more diplomatic. One must never give an inch with bullies like Duncan Maxwell, but the lower the rank, the more tender the ego where most men were concerned. So she dropped, eyes downcast, into an exaggerated curtsy and waited, hoping the gesture would literally and figuratively disarm the irate cook.

Long seconds passed before she sensed him ease. More long seconds of staring at the grimy hearth elapsed before he finally grumbled, "Ye do me nae good like that, woman. Up with ye, and to the pots."

She rose, but wavered from the sudden change of elevation.

Lucas actually blanched. "Here, now!" Dropping the cleaver with a metallic clank to the hearth, he caught her by the forearms, then guided her to a nearby bench. "None o' that," he blustered. "Ye'll do nobody any good cracking yer head on the floor."

Why, the old bull was a fraud, a softie! His red face and worried eyes betrayed genuine concern.

Once she was settled, Lucas stepped first in one direction, then another. "Water. Nae, spirits." He rummaged behind a nearby heap of baskets and emerged with a half-full bottle of dark liquid. Uncorking it with a pop, he thrust it under her nose. "Ma private stock. Drink! It'll stiffen yer spine."

From the smell of it, the contents would stiffen her whether she had a spine or not. Tempting though the prospect was, Catherine shook her head and pushed it away.

Though she couldn't bring herself to drink after Lucas, he'd offered her his best. Such an act of kindness from so unlikely a source touched her deeply. She smiled up at him with genuine gratitude.

The hairy old reprobate reacted as if no one had ever smiled at him in his life. Amazement, then embarrassment, flickered across his coarse features. "Fuff!" he blustered, backing toward the fire. He waggled a meaty finger at her. "Sit ye there, now, till yer feet be steady. And that's an order." He turned to stir the bubbling pot of stew that hung beside the meat. "There's sand and pumice aplenty in the scullery, and water in the barrel."

Catherine looked at the years of neglect around her and vowed to scrub more than pots as soon as she had the strength. A sudden light went on inside her. *That* would be the way to win Aunt Brigit's respect: with plain, honest toil! Surely if she made life better for those at Annanlea, she would win at least a few allies.

That would be her plan, to toil as one of them. Then when they trusted her, she'd find some way to get word to her family without the outlaws' knowledge.

It would work. It must.

FIVE

More than a week and a mountain of pots later, Catherine pumiced away the final patch of rust and grime from the last of the pots in the scullery. A household this size should properly have at least two blackguards to attend to such matters. But nothing in this nest of outlaws was as it should be.

Seven motherless children running wild and uninstructed. More than a dozen thieves and their families within the compound. And all in perpetual chaos. She marveled that anything got done at all.

Weak though she still was, at least she'd brought some proper order to the house, first in her chambers and now the kitchen and scullery. Setting things to rights created the illusion that she had some control over her circumstances. It made her feel better to see the results of her efforts.

And it had impressed Aunt Brigit. Though her complaints continued, the old woman had definitely warmed up to Catherine. Catherine had come to realize that Aunt Brigit complained about everything and everyone.

And Duncan Maxwell . . . for all the tales she'd heard of the Black Bastard, he seemed to be a reasonable man—overbearing, but neither harsh nor cruel. And he clearly adored his family. It never ceased to amaze Catherine how kind he was to his aunt and children.

Duncan Maxwell, the family man, was a striking contrast to the ruthless outlaw of fable. True, his wild, dark appearance and startling blue eyes were every bit as handsome as the stories claimed, but here in his family, he was no brigand. He showed unfailing patience with his motherless brood and was always ready with an affectionate touch, a hug, a tousle, or an encouraging word. Such a good father, despite the fact that he had had no father of his own. And the respect he showed Aunt Brigit never wavered, though she often rubbed him the wrong way.

Catherine did not know what to make of him. She could not help but like the devoted father and thoughtful leader he seemed to be, yet she hated the Black Bastard who cold-bloodedly held her hostage, determined to extort her family, and condemned her to the work of a lowly servant.

Frustrated by the warring emotions he stirred in her, Catherine focused on the mindless chore before her. When she was done, she set the iron pot down in front of Hob's-a-gibbet's simple wife, Nessa, then arched her back in weary satisfaction.

"We done it, ma lady," Nessa said with pride, her lop-sided smile exposing all three of her teeth. Patience and attention had been all it had taken to transform the fearful, reclusive woman from a burden to a productive member of this household.

Catherine smiled back, glad she'd come up with the idea of training Nessa to help—and, she hoped, replace—her in the scullery. She patted Nessa's arm. As always, even that small gesture of approval was enough to puff Nessa's chest with pride and set her wide, flat face alight.

With the slap of bare feet, Duncan Maxwell's six-year-old twin boys raced into the scullery and scrambled to hide behind the teetering pile of freshly scrubbed pots. The high-spirited lads were constantly chasing or being chased, but always with great merriment. Outlaw though they might be, children were still children.

Nessa paled. "Master Gordon! Master Kerry," she pleaded. "Have a care! The pots—"

Too late. The precarious stack shifted, teetered, then tumbled apart in a deafening cacophony of iron striking iron and stone.

"Aaagh!" Kerry cried. "Cameron'll find us fer sure now!" When the final pot struck the floor with the resonance of a great bell, both lads shrieked with laughter so infectious Catherine couldn't keep from grinning.

But Nessa was thoroughly undone to see her precious pots rolling all over the floor. "Oh, ma lady!" she wailed. "The pots . . ."

Catherine hastened to comfort her with a hug.

Sure enough, Cameron stomped into the scullery brandishing a wooden sword. "Har! I've got ye now!"

Far swifter than their methodical elder brother, the twins split up and hurtled past him on either side before Cameron had time to react. "Hey!" A heartbeat behind, he stormed off after them.

"Oh dear, oh dear." Nessa began gathering up the pots. "Oh dear."

Catherine helped Nessa gather up the wreckage. There was no harm done, really. The pots were far too stout to be affected by a mere tumble, and the insides were still clean.

Only when everything had been put to rights did Nessa relax. "May I scrub in the kitchen now?" she asked. Ever since she'd mastered the art of scrubbing, the good woman seemed to consider it not just a duty, but a joy.

Catherine nodded, leaning back against the cool wall and sinking down for a rest. She watched Nessa gather her supplies and march into Lucas's domain in search of grime. Seeing the simple woman's burning determination, Catherine couldn't help wondering if Nessa had taken sand and pumice to her husband Hob's-a-gibbet. Like everything and everyone at Annanlea, he certainly needed scrubbing.

She almost laughed aloud at the thought. Catching herself just in time, she clapped a roughened hand over her mouth. She had to be more careful.

Ironic, how protective she'd become of her self-imposed silence. She'd actually begun to enjoy not talking. It saved a lot of time and energy, and she relished the insular privacy it provided her.

"Leave that alone!" Lucas's shouts brought her

abruptly alert. "Get out, woman! Yer ruinin' it! Back to the scullery with ye!"

Oh dear. That was quick.

Catherine scrambled to her feet and hurried to protect poor Nessa from the cook's infamous temper. She found Nessa drawn back in horror from the large worktable. A gouged strip of fresh wood marked the table's darkened, workworn surface where Nessa had attacked it with sand and pumice.

Not the wood! Catherine groaned inwardly. She'd thought poor Nessa had finally gotten that straight, but clearly she had not.

"How many times must I tell ye, woman?" Lucas shouted. "Doona scrub the wood! If ye do, there'll be nae table left within the year!" He waggled the heavy ladle he was carrying. "Out of ma kitchen!" he bellowed. "With such interruptions, how's a man to cook?"

Badly, Catherine thought, just as he did without interruptions.

She fixed him with a reproachful scowl, pushing past him to rescue Nessa.

Lucas had spent the past week blustering that he could scarcely cook for Nessa's scrubbing the hearth, the mantel, and even the bricks in the fireplace. Yet Catherine knew he didn't mean it, just as she knew that despite his grumbling about her own "interference" with his cooking, he savored the way everyone gobbled down the much-improved bannocks, tansy, pear and cherry pie, and oxtail soup she'd shown him how to make. At the resulting praise, he'd preened like a reiver bringing back a herd of stolen cattle.

She stood between him and Nessa. *Back off,* her look of warning said, *or there'll be no more receipts for you!*

Lucas faltered. "I told ye all along," he said to Catherine defensively, "she's far too simple for decent work."

Nessa moved in closer behind Catherine. "I was only tryin' to clean the table, ma lady."

As always, Nessa's reverent—and inappropriate—

manner of address raised a twinge of superstitious worry in Catherine. She was nobody's lady, just a merchant's daughter. To allow herself to be called a lady surely tempted fate. But no amount of silent correction had discouraged Nessa. Even Lucas had taken to calling her Nessa's Lady.

Ah, well, she thought, *let fate take its course. How much worse could things be?* She was already a hostage, virtually a slave in this heathen, barbarous tribe.

Somehow she had to get word to her family that she was alive and held at Annanlea, so they could notify the warden and mount a rescue.

She thought of Hal and Papa, and a fresh stab of longing struck her heart.

God would make a way. He must.

But for now, in this moment of this day, all she could do was all she could do. And that meant insinuating herself into this den of outlaws.

She put her arm around Nessa's shoulders and directed her to a patch of grease on the cold stone floor that could benefit from her efforts.

NOON—SEPTEMBER 21

Golden autumn sunshine illuminated the parlor two weeks later when Duncan peered inside to see if the way was clear before entering. Since his hostage had emerged from her sickroom and managed to delegate herself out of the scullery, she'd turned the house upside down, and he couldn't say he liked it much. Without a word, she'd taken the place over.

Most baffling of all, Bink had permitted it. She grumbled about it, of course, but hadn't made a move to stop the woman.

He couldn't find a thing, thanks to the hostage's incessant cleaning and rearranging. With glares alone, she had his men scraping off their boots before they dared to cross the threshold. Most demoralizing.

By glory, a hardworking man should be able to walk into a house with the soil of honest labor on his boots without earning a look that would wither Beelzebub himself.

His hostage was as tart as a green apple and twice as hard. How she'd won Lucas over was still a mystery, but she'd done it. And the children! All except Baran seemed drawn to her by the same inexplicable attraction that had seduced his dog. Duncan couldn't imagine why. She was as silently demanding of them as she was of all the others at Annanlea, yet Amber willingly assisted in her endless labors; Erinn and her cats sought the Englisher out at every opportunity; and Nevin grinned like a beggar eating pudding every time he saw her. Cameron and the twins granted her the same good-natured acceptance they granted their own family.

"Come along, ye traitorous beast," he said to Clyde. "The way is clear."

Please, Duncan pleaded silently to no deity in particular as he carefully skirted Aunt Brigit's rug on his way to his desk. *Let me get through my accounting without the bloody Englisher's interference.* He settled into his chair and began to look through the neat stacks of paper in an effort to find his place in his accounting.

Clyde stretched out on the newly polished floor between the desk and the rug. Even he kent better than to despoil Aunt Brigit's Persian.

The barley records. He'd been working on those.

After a cursory search, he opened the household ledgers and began to enter the hay crops they'd harvested that week instead.

Yet no sooner had he begun to do some productive work than Clyde scrambled to his feet with a welcoming bark. Sure as sunrise, the Englisher glided briskly into the room. Duncan shot her a look of dismissal, but couldn't help noticing how becoming her new hairstyle looked.

She'd drawn her dark locks up softly into a shining tumble of tresses at her crown, and wisps of beguiling curl escaped at her nape and temples, making her look years younger and almost comely. But the sharp purpose in her brown eyes drove his focus abruptly back to his books.

Yet as always, even a brief look at her left a lasting impression. Her worn, handed-down attire should have looked absurd with its too-short sleeves, waist, and hem, but she wore it with such arrogant assurance and rigid posture that one came away thinking the fault belonged to the garments alone.

The floors did not even dare to creak beneath her feet, giving her the unnerving ability to sneak up on people. Clyde's affection for the woman afforded Duncan one compensation: she couldna sneak up on him as long as Clyde was around.

Ignoring her, he rummaged the desk for the blasted barley record. Her hand invaded his field of vision and plucked out the very one he'd been searching for.

How had she done that? Saints, but it rankled.

Duncan didn't have to see her to know that her plain face would be alift with smugness, but for some reason, he looked up anyway. Sure enough, she peered down at him as if she were Lady Bountiful and he a simpleton.

"This is the last time I'll be tellin' ye," he rumbled, "doona interrupt me when I'm at ma ciphers. Do it again, and ye'll find yourself countin' the cobwebs on the ceiling."

She shot a haughty glance at the ceiling, then met him eye to eye.

Blast it all. There weren't any cobwebs on the ceiling anymore.

Duncan's choler rose. His neck pulsing, he bent to his accounts. "Get out! I've work to do, and willna bear distraction."

She turned and glided out, managing to look smug even from behind.

Maddening.

Duncan had to admit, though, the food had improved drastically since the Englisher had taken Lucas in hand. The result was tasty meals, indeed. He gave her credit for that.

And for something else. Besides Aunt Brigit, his hostage was the most industrious woman he'd ever seen. Despite her weakened condition, she toiled away relentlessly under a crushing load of work. As a result, Duncan saw a gratifying change in Bink. A blessed touch of humor rang in her complaints, and she seemed far more rested now that she had someone to help her shoulder the load.

A shard of guilt reminded him of his resolve to remarry. A plump widow without too many children would suit him fine. No more virgins. He'd sworn off virgins after wife number three. Entirely too much trouble all around. And they died on you even quicker than the widows. Maybe one of his salt customers in Dumfries could scare up a widow there who hadn't heard the rumors.

When one of the twins clattered down the stairs, Duncan hailed him with a cry. "Kerry! Find yer uncle Michael and tell him I want to see him."

"Aye, Papa." Kerry spun around and tore into the foyer just in time to run head-on into the man himself.

"Whoa, lad." Michael Graham tousled the six-year-old's raven curls. "Ye found me."

Kerry grinned and sprinted back toward the kitchen.

"I swear," Michael said as he stepped inside the room. "That lad canna walk for runnin'." He took another step, then looked down at his muddy boots, retreated to the front door, and stomped the boots clean outside.

Duncan bent his forehead into his palm. The devil's codpiece! The Englisher had even gotten to Michael. "Come in," he roared. "Never mind your boots."

A troubled look on his face, Michael stepped gingerly across the polished floor, careful to avoid the rug.

"Sit ye." Duncan motioned to the chair on the other side of his desk. "We've inventories to discuss."

The auld warrior eased down with a contented groan.

"Achen, that feels good. I've been on ma feet since sunrise." It was now midday.

"Doing what?"

He sobered. "Helpin' Thurlow and Hob's-a-gibbet fix the henhouse and the sty."

Duncan stopped leafing through his papers. "They're supposed to be at the salt pans."

"And they are now," Michael said, "they are."

Duncan knew the answer before he asked the question, but he asked anyway. "Who gave them leave to work in the barnyard?"

Michael glanced toward the ceiling. "It was Brigit, actually." An obvious half-truth. Duncan smelled the Englisher in this. How she'd managed to get his aunt to go against his express orders, he couldn't guess, but this time, the woman had gone too far. She couldn't be diverting his men from their proper duties. For all their sakes, Duncan's authority had to remain absolute and unquestioned.

Temper barely in check, he asked with deceptive calmness, "Since when does Aunt Brigit have the power to override ma orders?"

Michael sighed. A direct contradiction of orders was serious business. They both knew punishment, swift and public, would have to be meted out. He gripped the arms of his chair. "Doona blame the men, Duncan. It's ma fault, nae theirs. When I didna find them at the pans, I sought 'em out. Found 'em in the barnyard toilin' away under Aunt Brigit's supervision with the Englisher lookin' on."

Just as he'd suspected!Angry, Duncan rose to pace.

Michael stood. "Ye canna fault the men fer givin' in to Brigit and the Englisher. *Ye* may be strong enough to face down those two women, but Thurlow bein' an Englisher himself, and Hob's-a-gibbet simple from stretchin' the hangman's rope, 'tis little wonder they were sucked in."

The old warrior straightened. "I should've brought the men with me then, but Brigit said 'just a little longer.' When a little longer stretched to half an hour, I rolled up ma sleeves and set to helpin' the lads to make the work go faster." He met Duncan's glare with one of grim determination. "I ken there must be a punishin', one harsh enough to show yer orders canna be ignored."

"A whipping," Duncan said without relish. "Today, in front of all." He did not enjoy disciplining his men, but harsh justice was the only way to maintain discipline in these lawless parts.

"Let me take the stripes, Duncan," Michael insisted quietly. "It'll do the most good if I'm the one. The men ken how ye love me, lad, and how hard it'll be to lash me."

The old man was right, and Duncan hated it. Yet there was no denying he could give no quarter; they both knew it. He considered a proper punishment for such a grave offense, then subtracted by a third. "Twelve?"

Michael considered. "Too few, and ye lose the effect." He cocked a wry grin. "Too many, and ye lose *me*." He nodded. "Aye, twelve."

Duncan had long loved and respected Michael as the father he'd never had, but he'd never respected him more than at this moment. "When?"

Michael curled his lips and absently combed his fingers through his beard as calmly as if he were choosing between ale and beer instead of deciding when he'd take a lashing. "Straightaway, I should think. I wouldna want to do it on a full belly." He grinned. "And if it's done anon, I should be fit to eat again by supper."

By God, there was a man. Duncan grinned. "I'll have Lucas fix ye somethin' special tonight."

Michael brightened. "That pear and cherry tart." He paused, then raised a finger. "At the lashin', put me so's I can see Brigit's face when ye do it."

Aunt Brigit!

Duncan hadn't considered the effect this would have on her. And the Englisher. He let out a low whistle. "This'll bring the lesson home with our two crowin' hens, of a certain."

Michael's smile widened. "That alone will be worth it, lad." He whacked Duncan's back harder than friendship permitted, but straightaway eased the slight by circling his shoulders for a brief, affectionate squeeze. "That alone will be worth it."

Catherine still couldn't believe what Duncan Maxwell was doing. Her eyes averted, she embraced Aunt Brigit in the courtyard among the rest of Annanlea's assembled inhabitants as Michael Graham took the last of his lashes.

A fresh wave of remorse swept through her. She'd never dreamt such a dire consequence would result from a harmless project.

It had all happened so fast. Aunt Brigit had done her best to dissuade Duncan from the whipping, but neither he nor Michael Graham would be moved. The one consolation was that the children had been sent to their rooms.

"Blast Michael Graham," Aunt Brigit said hoarsely into her shoulder, "and Duncan with him."

Duncan may have ordered her to be present, but Catherine had no intention of watching. Hob's-a-gibbet hung his head in shame next to an equally deflated Thurlow. Nessa peeked from behind her husband. When she saw Catherine look their way, she waved, then retreated. The remaining ten of Duncan's men observed in silence.

"I wouldna put it past those two to have done this simply to teach us a lesson," Aunt Brigit said in a bitter whisper. "A harsh lesson 'tis, nae just for us, but for all present." She let out a shuddering sigh. " 'Tis one I'll never be able to forget."

Catherine nodded. Judging from the grim onlookers, it would be a long time before anyone dared to do other than exactly what Duncan had bidden, no matter who ordered otherwise. Hateful though this was, she had to admit the punishment possessed a certain brutal logic. Duncan's men already liked and respected Michael. Now they had reason to love him. And to fear the Black Bastard of the Western March.

But at what cost to Michael Graham?

She forced herself to look at Duncan and was shocked to see a single tear tracking down his rigid face as he struck the final blow.

"Is it over?" Aunt Brigit whispered. "I lost count." At Catherine's nod, her gaze flew to Michael Graham's face. The old man looked back at her with stoic pride as Duncan gently laid a balm-soaked cloth over his back. "Justice has been well and truly served this day," Michael declared for all to hear. "Ma men are responsible to me, and I for them, so I have gladly borne this fair punishment."

"Idiot man," Aunt Brigit grumbled, but there was admiration in her voice.

Duncan sent a black look straight at Catherine as Michael Graham sauntered over to Aunt Brigit wearing a smile halfway between a grin and a grimace.

"Ah, Michael, ye foolish man," Aunt Brigit said as she supported him. "After all these years, ye shouldna let me talk ye into trouble so easily."

Enjoying the chance to lean against her, he took full advantage of the opportunity. "Ye always could, Bink, and I guess ye always will."

"There ye go," she muttered with what sounded like a familiar exchange, "blamin' it all on me."

"But *ye* were the one who said—"

"Hush ye, now," she chided as they approached the door. "Ye've held up well thus far. Doona be shamin' yerself at this late hour." She glanced at the blood seeping through the cloth on his back and winced. "Come along, then. I'll tend those wounds, then feed ye a special potion to ease the pain."

Catherine watched with a mixture of frustration and remorse as they disappeared into the house.

Why had Duncan Maxwell done this, really? Surely not just to teach her and Brigit a lesson.

What sort of man would publicly abuse one he purported to respect? Catherine couldn't fathom such a thing. Discipline had been firm back at River House—it had had to be—but never so brutal or monstrous as this. Yet Duncan Maxwell was unfailingly kind to his aunt and his children. Catherine could not reconcile the two sides of the man.

When he turned and headed straight for her, she resisted the urge to flee. She stood firm as he closed the space between them and brought his black-gloved hand up under her chin, forcing her face to level with his. "I doona ken how ye managed this, mute as ye are," he ground out, "but mayhap now ye'll think twice before interferin' with ma men."

He towered over her, his dark hair blowing in the wind, impossibly handsome despite the blackness of his harsh soul. Unflinching, Catherine met Duncan Maxwell's cold blue gaze, so close she could see the cobalt rims and dark flecks of his irises.

"Try a trick like that again," he fairly purred, "and I canna answer for what might happen." He looked her up and down. "I havena lashed a woman before, but they say there's a first time for everything."

The brute was probably hoping for the chance. But the next time she crossed him—and there *would* be a next time if she was ever to escape this godforsaken place— Catherine had no intention of getting caught. It would be a sad day indeed when she couldn't get the best of an outlaw like Duncan Maxwell. In future, she would simply have to be more careful.

Chapter
SIX

Perched on a stepstool at the parlor's triple window, Catherine stilled for just a moment and soaked in the rare silence of the house. Everyone had gone to Ander's cottage to await the outcome of a particularly difficult birth, so she was alone for the first time since she'd been brought here. Reveling in her solitude, she'd taken advantage of the lull to complete the last major chore in restoring the parlor to respectable condition: cleaning the soot and grime from the inside of the parlor window.

Careful not to distort the leaden framework that held the diamond-shaped panes, she scrubbed away amid the sharp tang of vinegar, taking pleasure in seeing the glass sparkle as she finished each facet. It was mindless work but not too strenuous, and it satisfied her to watch the September sunlight, pane by pane, banish the gloom and set the room aglow.

But her quiet contentment proved elusive. Thoughts of Duncan Maxwell invaded her mind like great, shadowy crows bringing with them guilt, indignation, and dark attraction on their wings. How could such a rogue so stir her blood? Yet he did. She could not deny it, any more than she could deny he had lashed his most loyal friend for her and Aunt Brigit's transgression.

A bitter shard of guilt stabbed through her indignation. If Michael Graham had not taken responsibility for what she and Aunt Brigit had done, would Duncan have publicly whipped them instead?

Catherine wasn't certain. And it was that uncertainty that made her desire so disturbing.

She banished the troubling thoughts as she always did: with work. Only when her hand began to cramp and she stopped to rest did she notice with a start that Nessa stood waiting by the stairs with two of Duncan's men.

Unnerving, how they'd crept up on her unawares. How long had they been there?

"Beggin' yer pardon, ma lady," Nessa ventured. "A word wi' ye?"

Wary, Catherine regarded the tall, lanky outlaws. They glowered at her with strikingly similar features. Brothers, obviously. One of them was standing awkwardly, his left shoulder dropped and his arm tucked into his plaid. Pain etched his haggard face. The other hovered behind him like a watching specter, radiating deep suspicion and hostility.

She looked closer at the catawise one. Beads of perspiration filmed his brow and his dark eyes were dull with pain. Shoulder separation, or break? One might be easily remedied, the other not.

She nodded her consent for them to approach.

Nessa pulled the man forward by his good arm.

"Doona tug at me, woman," he yelped, but she dragged him after her with her usual dogged insistence.

"Sorry to disturb yer work, ma lady," Nessa said brightly, "but Quinn, here, his hob tossed him yesterday, and he canna find relief."

"I'd rather have Aunt Brigit," Quinn snarled.

Nessa shook her head. "Aunt Brigit said she canna help ye now. She's busy bringin' Ander's firstborn." She nudged him closer. "Great ladies ken much of healin'. Hob's-a-gibbet told me so." She turned a trusting face to Catherine. "Quinn has nae wife to tend him, nor Rory, neither. And I doona have the wit to do it, but I ken ye can, ma lady."

Catherine wasn't a lady, but she did know how to pop a dislocated shoulder back into place. She'd seen her stepfather do it often at River House; she'd even done it herself three times. But Quinn was a large man. Even if he had a simple dislocation, correcting it wouldn't be easy owing to his size. Yet clearly he was in agony.

And if she was successful, perhaps she could redeem

herself somewhat in Duncan's eyes for her meddling with Thurlow and Ridley.

Catherine decided to take the chance. Thank goodness it wasn't his sword arm.

Drying her hands on her apron, she stepped down from her stool and motioned the injured outlaw forward. Wary as a stray cur, he sidled to within a pace of her.

Catherine drew up a chair and motioned for him to sit. He did so, but eyed her as if she might try to cut his throat at any moment.

When she tried to take hold of his arm to feel of the bones and examine the shoulder, he shot up from the chair and sidestepped right into Nessa, sending her wimple askew.

"Ach, man!" Nessa shoved him none too gently into the seat. "She canna help ye if ye pull away." Straightening her wimple, she shot his menacing brother a warning glance. "Back off, Rory. Let Ladykate see what's what." She turned to Catherine with absolute trust. "They're both corry-fisted, ye see, so Quinn's nae good this way."

Corry-fisted? Catherine frowned. Was there something wrong with his hand, too?

"Kerr-handed." Nessa mimed a sword thrust with her left hand. "Ye ken, like all them bluidy Kerrs."

Knowing nothing of "them bloody Kerrs," Catherine could only surmise from the gesture that Nessa meant they were left-handed.

This was serious, indeed. Losing the use of his sword arm was a death sentence for a reiver.

She hesitated. If she tried to help Quinn and failed, he might well hold her responsible for the loss of his sword arm. Blood feuds had been spawned for far less reason among these barbarian clans. And his brother—Rory, wasn't it?—what would he do to her if she failed?

She shuddered to think.

Yet it was not in her nature to turn anyone away when

there was a chance she could help, so she stuck with her initial resolve.

Dear God, please let it be a simple separation.

Catherine faced Quinn squarely and waited until he nodded his consent, then she felt of the upper armbone. It seemed of a piece. That meant she would have to move the limb to check the joint.

Her patient protested loudly when she did, prompting his brother to take a warning step forward, but Catherine quickly decided the shoulder was dislocated.

She pantomimed that it wasn't broken. "Ach, good," Nessa interpreted. " 'Tisna broken." She nodded to the brothers. "She can fix it. Ye'll see."

Please, Lord, let it be so. She motioned for Quinn to lie down on the rug.

"Nay." Quinn bristled. "I may be hurt, but that doesna make me a fool."

Catherine pointed emphatically to the rug.

Quinn looked left, then right. "All right, but make it quick. If Aunt Brigit should catch me—"

"If Aunt Brigit were free to find ye," Nessa scolded, "ye'd nae be here atall. Now lay yerself down."

And Nessa thought herself simple.

Quinn did as instructed, and Catherine positioned herself at right angles to his shoulder while Rory glowered down on them like an avenging angel. It took all her strength to coax the errant bone where it belonged, but just when Quinn's shriek of pain reached its peak, she felt the joint click into place. Hastily, she scrambled to her feet.

Quinn's protest died abruptly. "Flay me for an Englisher!" he squeaked. " 'Tis better." He blinked up at Catherine in surprise. "Much better." He rolled up into a sitting position, then struggled to his feet with Rory's assistance. Once Quinn was standing, he gingerly flexed his arm and worked the damaged shoulder. " 'Tis a miracle," he said to his brother. "Looka here. Still sore as a bare cuddy on a hot griddle, mind ye, but I can move it fair enough."

He grinned at Catherine. "Ye gave me back ma sword arm, Nessa's Lady." To her surprise, he managed a courtly bow. "Never let it be said that Quinn Little wasna a man to give thanks where thanks was due, so I thank ye." He nudged his brother, who bowed, as well.

"Aye, lady," Rory added, albeit grudgingly. "We be beholden to ye."

"Oh, my." Nessa's eyes widened. "Rory never speaks to anyone but Quinn."

To her amazement, Catherine felt herself blushing at the outlaws' efforts at courtly gratitude. It was certainly not what she'd expected. Flustered, she acknowledged their thanks with a curt nod.

She resolved to make up a healing poultice and send Nessa to rub it in.

To hide her embarrassment, she took up her cleaning rag and pail, then returned to the window.

Three days later, Catherine had just finished showing Amber how to spin a decent thread with some of the abandoned wool from her chamber when Erinn glided in, cats and Nevin in tow.

"We're busy," Amber said loftily to her little sister.

Catherine laid a staying hand on Amber's arm and shook her head in mild reproof. Then she turned to Erinn and opened wide her arms.

Beaming, the little girl climbed into her lap holding Twinkle, a placid calico wearing a tattered kerchief for a cloak.

All of Erinn's cats had names, but Catherine had only learned a few. Her head was too full from trying to sort out the names of Duncan's seven children, twelve men, and their families.

Tightening her arms around Erinn, she savored the welcome in the eight-year-old's smile and the simple human comfort of holding the child in her lap. Amazing, how healing it was just to know someone was glad to see her.

Hal was that glad, and she had often held him in her lap just this way when he was small. She closed her eyes to a vivid impression of those blessed moments, prompting a twist of sadness deep inside her. Would she ever see him again?

"What's the matter, Nessa's Lady?" Erinn asked, her cherubic face troubled. "Do ye wish me to get down?"

Catherine shook her head and smiled, reaching into the pocket of her secondhand skirt to retrieve the little cloak and cap she'd fashioned from a scrap of decent velvet salvaged from the ruined parlor drapes.

Erinn chirped with delight when she saw the fine new clothes for her cat. "Oh, thank you, thank you, thank you!" She circled Catherine's neck and gave her a great big kiss on the cheek.

Catherine felt an odd warmth around her heart. No one, not even her sainted mother, had ever granted her such an open display of affection. Embarrassed though she was, she felt the joy of it clear to her soul.

She covered her awkwardness by untying the "cloak" Twinkle was wearing. Relaxed and purring loudly, the little cat didn't so much as squirm when she tied on first the velvet cloak, and then the caplet.

Nevin clapped with glee at the results, and Erinn grinned. " 'Tis the most beautiful cap and cloak I've ever seen."

Even Amber forgot her pretensions of adulthood and regarded the cat's costume with wistful admiration. "I wish I had so fine a raiment." Suddenly self-conscious, she tucked a patch into the folds of her worn dress.

Catherine had prevailed in having the children bathed and sulphured from head to toe, and she'd washed and mended their clothes, but all of them needed new attire from the skin out.

The cat's cap and cloak had been an experiment. Though she was expert at embroidery, she'd never attempted to make a garment, even with a proper pattern. But her first foray into dressmaking, small though it was, had given her the confidence to attempt bigger and better projects.

She pointed to herself, mimed sewing, then plucked at Amber's dress.

"A dress?" Amber asked in awe. "You'll sew me a dress?"

Catherine nodded, smiling in spite of herself.

Amber's lovely young face grew radiant with delight, then fell. "But ye ken we have nae cloth. All we had was long since used. And since our salt was stolen, there's naught to trade, nae even for food. So Papa said there could be nae new clothes. Nae this year, anyway. I heard him telling Uncle Michael we mayn't even have food enough for the winter."

Nevin cuddled a gray tabby and chanted happily, "Nae salt, nae salt. Nae clothes. Nae food."

Erinn frowned at her sister. "Amber," she muttered, "we're not to speak of that. Papa said."

"And who's to know?" Amber retorted. "Unless *you* tell." She shot Erinn a condescending look. "Anyway, where's the harm?" She cocked her head toward Catherine. "Nessa's Lady canna speak to tell of what she hears."

Catherine felt a twinge of conscience even as she wondered about this stolen salt. She frowned, puzzled.

Duncan Maxwell, a salt merchant? She'd heard there were deposits in this area, but . . . Duncan Maxwell, a merchant? From first glance, she'd thought of him as an outlaw—a knave who stole from others and would not tolerate anyone's stealing from him.

It had never occurred to her that Annanlea might lack the stores to feed its people through the winter. And it certainly hadn't occurred to her that Duncan's household suffered want because someone else had stolen from *him*.

In a flash of insight, she realized she might turn outlaw, too, if it was the only way to feed her children.

Catherine could not bear to think of poor Nevin or

precious Erinn or Amber, or placid Cameron, or rambunctious Gordon and Kerry, or even hostile Baran going
hungry. Not to mention Nessa and Lucas and all the others. Erinn was so small and frail already.

No matter how cruel a tyrant the Black Bastard might
be, Duncan Maxwell had shown he had a gentle side when
it came to his family. Sometimes, he even made her think
of Papa. Was it a father's love that drove him to plunder
the marches?

Surely there must be some other way to spare the people of Annanlea from privation.

Your jewels.

Catherine froze. She had the means to help them: the
jewels sewn into the embroidery of her shift. But how
could she sell the jewels without betraying her treasure?

The wheels started turning in her mind. She had to find
the minister, see if he could be trusted. If he could, she
might be able to convert one or two of her jewels into
food and clothing for the children. But she would have to
be careful. If Duncan Maxwell were to learn of her treasure, she had no doubt he would seize it all and still demand a ransom from her stepfather.

Her mother's jewels were her only security.

She turned to the children and traced a cross on her
forehead with her thumb as ministers did upon christen-
ing, then gestured a query. When the girls failed to understand what she was asking, she clasped her palms flat
together as if in prayer, then spread them in question.

"Church?" Amber asked.

Catherine waggled her hand to indicate she was close,
but not correct. She repeated the prayerful gesture, then
traced a minister's stole down her chest and made a sober
face.

"The minister!" Erinn burbled in excitement.

Catherine nodded enthusiastically, then gestured
searching.

"Where is the minister?" Erinn correctly surmised.

Catherine was so pleased, she hugged the little girl

soundly and planted her own kiss on Erinn's cheek.

"I guessed it," Erinn said proudly. "She wants to know where the minister is."

"But what does the minister have to do with anything?" Amber asked.

Sharp, this one. Too sharp.

Catherine shook her head, ashamed of herself for misleading Amber. If her plan should work out, though, she could not have Amber connecting what happened to the minister.

"Where is the minister?" Amber repeated, puzzled.

Catherine nodded.

"At his house by the kirk in Annandale, I suppose," she said.

Catherine took Amber's hand and motioned again.

"Take you to him?" the girl rightly guessed. Amber drew back. "I doona ken. 'Tis a long way. And I doona think he'd be glad to see me . . . any of us."

"We havna been to kirk since Nevin's mama died, and—"

"Shhh!" Amber shot her sister a warning look. "We're nae supposed to speak of that, either, especially in front of strangers."

Erinn cupped Catherine's cheeks in her small hands. "She's nae a stranger, silly." She let go to extract Twinkle's tail from Nevin's mouth.

Amber's remark stirred Catherine's curiosity.

"Who cares what that old minister thinks, anyway," Amber huffed. "Papa says the only thing that matters is what God thinks."

Clearly, there had been a falling-out between Duncan Maxwell and the minister . . . *since Nevin's mama died* . . .

Something to do with the burial of Nevin's mother?

The only conflicts over burials Catherine had ever heard of involved questionable deaths. Had Nevin's mother taken her own life, been refused Christian burial in holy ground?

The thought sent a shiver through her. Little wonder, in a place like this. If the minister had refused the woman Christian burial . . . Perhaps that was why this household was unchurched.

As it had so often in the past few weeks, Catherine's heart went out to Duncan Maxwell's children. Shame on the man, endangering their souls by keeping them unchurched. How could he expect his children to know anything of God?

Well, she had no intention of sitting idly by and letting them be consigned to hell. No. She would take them to church herself, this very Sunday! It appealed to her sense of order that she would thus accomplish two things at once: establishing contact with the minister, and tending to the children's sadly neglected little souls.

Catherine set Erinn from her lap, straightened her skirts, smoothed the bun at the nape of her neck, then marched herself down to confront Duncan Maxwell. The children—and the cats—followed close behind.

He couldn't possibly have missed the noisy entrance of such an entourage, yet her captor kept her waiting for long minutes in front of his desk without acknowledging her presence. He didn't look up until three cats roamed the ledgers and the girls began to giggle. "I warned ye not to pester me when I'm at ma sums," he said with a mildness contradicted by his harsh expression.

Catherine curtsied with exaggerated deference. Then she rose, unafraid, and appropriated the inked quill he'd been using. She picked up a crumpled scrap of paper, smoothed it, and wrote at right angles to the words already there: *I humbly request your permission to take your children to the village church for proper religious instruction. Would you risk their souls by refusing?*

She had known he might be angry, but she was unprepared for the fury that darkened his face. Realizing too late that she had stirred a dragon in this tall, powerful man, she fully expected to wake up staring at the ceiling. If she woke up at all!

"Aunt Brigit!" Amber made a panicked flight for the kitchen, dragging Nevin and Erinn with her. "Help! Come quick! Papa's going to kill our hostage!"

A strangled sound escaped the Scotsman, and Catherine commended her soul to heaven. But she had no intention of cowering. Better to die proud than live in shame. So she met his murderous gaze without flinching, her back erect.

"What's this, then?" Aunt Brigit shouted. Her footsteps hastened across the room, quieting when she reached her beloved carpet. "Duncan!" There was real fear in her voice. "Doona kill her, Duncan. Ye canna ransom a dead woman!" She circled the desk and made to lay hold of him, but thought better of it when he turned on her like a wounded bear.

Catherine blinked in surprise at Aunt Brigit's open intervention. After the flogging, Catherine would never have expected Aunt Brigit to cross her nephew.

"Calm yourself," Aunt Brigit pleaded. "I want her alive, Duncan. She serves us well—"

"Serves?" he exploded. "The haughty wench serves nae one, just looks down her nose at us and does what suits her, turning the household upside down!"

"Well, I need her, ye great lout!" his aunt retorted. "Look around ye! She's made a home of the place, somethin' I've nae had the strength to do alone. And the children love 'er."

"Not Baran, he doesn't," Duncan countered. "She might have fooled the rest, but Baran sees through her, just as I do."

"Well, aye," his aunt allowed, dropping her tone to a more conversational level. "Baran wants nae part of her, 'tis true."

Realizing what had just transpired, Catherine looked on Aunt Brigit with a new respect. By drawing Duncan's fire, the woman had calmed the confrontation and quite possibly saved Catherine's hide.

Duncan exhaled heavily, then dropped down into his chair.

Palming the scrap of paper that had started it all, Aunt Brigit grabbed Catherine's upper arms and steered her toward the kitchens. "It's kettles to scour for you, Miss High-and-mighty, and hearths aplenty to scrub."

Once the kitchen door was safely closed behind them, she shoved Catherine up against the wall and read the note.

"Hazelnuts and whoremongers, woman!" she hissed. "Ye have nae idea what a sad poke o' trouble ye've opened up by askin' such a thing." She tucked the note into her apron.

It surprised Catherine that a drudge like Aunt Brigit could read. Was nothing as it seemed in this house?

"Ach," Aunt Brigit spat out. "He swore off religion the day the minister refused to bury poor Aselma in holy ground. And who could blame him? There was nae proof the poor, sad lass jumped instead of fell from the peel."

So she'd guessed rightly. Catherine straightened and pointed to the children, then motioned "shame" in Duncan's direction.

Brigit let out a heavy sigh. "Aye. They should be kirked, 'tis true." She glanced toward the parlor. "After he's cooled down, I'll speak to him."

Catherine pointed from herself to the children.

"Ye want to go with 'em?" When Catherine nodded, Brigit rolled her eyes. "Marry, woman. Ye are the stubbornest, most froward wench I've ere had the misfortune to come across."

Catherine smiled and pointed to Brigit.

"See here," the old woman huffed. "I'm nothing like ye." She shooed Catherine toward the back stair. "Keep ye out of his way." She glanced out the window to the fine, breezy autumn day. "The turnips are ready. Might as well pull them today." She frowned at Catherine without conviction. "We could all use some air and honest toil.

Ye can watch over Nevin while we work. I'll fetch up the others."

"Turnips?" Amber complained. "I hate pulling turnips. It ruins ma hands."

Catherine cocked her head at the girl and frowned in reproach.

"Oh, all right." Amber had the good grace to look sheepish.

"One look from you, and the lass is all meekness," Brigit grumbled. "With me, she'd drag her feet and whine all the way to the fields and back."

Catherine shrugged, then motioned Nevin to come with her, her spirits lightened by the prospect of escaping her prison, even if only for a little while.

Half an hour later, she and Brigit arrived at the turnip patch with all seven of the children, at least a dozen of Erinn's cats, and the mute lad called Mouse to help Baran stand lookout.

The only thing Mouse seemed on the lookout for, though, was Amber. He could not take his eyes from her.

When Erinn climbed the stile, Brigit stopped her and peered into her face. "Bide with Nevin, child. I doona like the look of yer eyes." She turned Erinn around and gave her an affectionate nudge toward Catherine. "I've work aplenty without havin' to nurse ye through the ague."

Erinn nodded. "I am a little tired."

Catherine marveled that anyone could know a child well enough to interpret a certain cast of the eyes as impending illness. A wistful shard of longing prompted her to wonder if ever she would know a child that well, but her practical nature squelched the thought. She had missed her chance for children and must make the best of her life as it was. Resolute, she turned to the not-unpleasant task of tending Erinn and Nevin.

The midday sun shone down so warmly that Catherine picked a shady spot beneath a larch to spread the blanket by the stone hedge.

Amber wished them well, then scaled the stile after her

great-aunt. Gordon and Kerry hurtled over the wall prac-
tically atop each other, with Cameron bringing up the rear,
as always. Baran shot her a look as murderous as one of
Duncan's, then gravely took up his post atop the hedge,
watching for trouble.

Once she had Nevin and Erinn settled, Catherine allowed herself to lean back and relax amid the comforting
sound of crickets and the gentle breeze redolent with the
sweet smell of grass.

"Do Evil Jack," she heard Nevin say to his sister in
his slow, thickened tones. "S'ma favorite."

"Aye. 'Tis my favorite, too," Erinn agreed. After a dramatic pause, her voice shifted to a stage falsetto. "Oh, no!
It's the evil pootenanny Jack, come to rob our kine!"

Pootenanny? Catherine watched in amusement as Erinn
lifted up a thin, black kitten, then herded several others—
the cattle, no doubt—into her lap. She set down the evil
pootenanny Jack and picked up a calico by its middle,
then pretended to gallop it across the blanket to Jack.
"Har!" she snarled in as deep a voice as she could manage, much to Nevin's delight. "We rode to trot and got
'im straightaway!"

She released the calico, then raised "Evil Jack" up at
arm's length. "Hang the varlet!" she said roughly. "But
flay the skin from his hindside first, and cut off his balls!"

Nevin clapped, enthralled, but Catherine sat straight up
with a gasp to hear such atrocities roll so easily from the
mouth of an eight-year-old.

Lost in her brutal game, Erinn took no note. She held
the bored kitten tenderly under its forearms as she pretended to lash it with a blade of dried grass. "Let his blood
run red, and that'll be a lesson to any man who steals
from Duncan Maxwell," the little girl growled in imitation
of her father.

Bile rose in Catherine's throat. The brutality of this
place was so pervasive it had already poisoned Erinn. And
now she was unwittingly passing it on to poor, simple,
innocent Nevin.

"Fetch the gelding scythe," Erinn went on, appropriating a twig to serve as one.

Catherine could bear no more. She reached over and rescued the bored kitten from "torture," peering at Erinn in dismay.

"What's the matter?" Erinn seemed genuinely puzzled. "Ye look so sad. And angry." She rose up on her knees and bracketed Catherine's cheeks with her small hands. "Are ye ill? Does your head ache? Papa frowns like that when his head aches."

The child had not the slightest inkling that the brutal game had caused Catherine's distress.

A pox on Duncan Maxwell, for polluting his children with such barbarism while keeping them from the Word of God!

Too angry to remain seated, Catherine stood and strode to the stile to glare toward the rolling hills. She wasn't certain how long she'd been standing there when she realized something on one of those hills was moving. She tensed, her eyes narrowing.

Riders. Many riders. Moving fast, straight for them.

A shout of alarm almost escaped her. Frantic, she plucked up a small stone and flung it straight for Mouse, who was so busy watching Amber he hadn't seen the danger.

When he whirled on Catherine, she pointed frantically toward the oncoming throng.

Erinn chose just that moment to climb up beside her. "Raiders!" she shrieked, pointing.

All eyes turned to the horizon.

"Stay with the women," Baran commanded Mouse. "I'll run for help!" He launched himself toward Annanlea, which now seemed hopeless miles away, its gate on the opposite side of the barnekin.

None of the others cried out. Instead, they abandoned the turnips and, bending low, hurried for the shelter of the wall.

"Quickly," Brigit ordered as she hastened the others

toward the stile. "Keep ye down, then over the hedge. We'll hide there till Duncan comes."

Her heart pounding with fear, Catherine snatched up Erinn and Nevin and took shelter under the drooping boughs of the larch.

Reivers. The hateful images of Erinn's game still fresh in her mind, Catherine conjured up unspeakable possibilities of what might happen should the raiders find them. She heard the others come running, then saw them leap the wall—even Brigit!—and scramble toward her to hide.

Not daring to show their heads above the hedge, they all leaned, panting, against the stones and peered through the larch boughs toward the walls of Annanlea. There were no signs of life atop the corner peels, and they heard nothing.

Then the alarm bell sounded, faint and distant, but blessed to Catherine's ears.

"Doona fear, ma bairns," Aunt Brigit said, breathless. "None shall harm ye. Duncan willna let 'em. Ye heard the alarm. He'll come ridin' round that corner in no time, with all his men. Just ye watch."

Dear God, please send Duncan Maxwell and his men to rescue us.

What was she saying? Asking God to allow Duncan Maxwell to rescue her? What if the riders weren't raiders, but rescuers?

Catherine went rigid at the thought.

Was it possible? Could Papa have discovered her whereabouts and mounted a trod?

But if he had, would the children be harmed? There might be shooting.

She should have been hopeful, but fear piled upon fear instead, making it hard to breathe. Raid or rescue party, the children were in danger.

A raid, though . . . From childhood, Catherine had seen the aftermath of the Steel Bonnets' pillage and destruction. How could she forget the blank faces and torn, brutalized bodies of rape victims, some of them younger than Erinn?

She strained to hear the approaching hoofbeats over her own hammering heart and the ragged panting of the others.

Louder and louder the thunder came. Many horses, thudding heavily across the field, headed straight for them!

The hoofbeats bore down on them, then more than thirty riders leapt the wall on either side of the larch.

Catherine held on tight to the children and closed her eyes until all the horses had cleared the hedge. Then she opened them to see the foulest, most disreputable-looking company of bandits she'd ever laid eyes upon. At the fore, a big-bellied bear of a brute leered down at her.

"And who's this wench I'm seein', Mistress Brigit?" the leader bellowed, prompting a guttural clamor from his men. "Looks like Duncan's been holdin' out on his old friend."

"Hazelnuts and whoremongers!" Brigit shot to her feet, vibrating with fury, and shoved clear of the branches to confront him. "Ye scared the life from us, Wat!"

Wat! *Auld* Wat? The most notorious reiver of the marches? Catherine's blood went cold, but to her amazement, the children all relaxed.

But Aunt Brigit didn't relax. She was angry as a vixen in a snare. "What in all the parishes of all King James's realm were ye thinkin', comin' up aforce on an ally with nae word given?" she demanded. "God only kens what might've happened!"

"Calm yerself, woman," Wat retorted. "We never expected to get this far wi'out challenge." He pinned Catherine with a lecherous look that made her feel as if he could see through her clothes. "Duncan's slippin'," he ground out.

Brigit faltered, but only momentarily. She pointed to the corner of the castle walls. "Tell him yerself, then, for here he comes."

Catherine had never thought she would be glad to see Duncan Maxwell and his band of ruffians, but she was glad now, and even gladder to see them fully armed.

Auld Wat shot her another leering glance, then turned his attention to the approaching horsemen.

Riding as one with his massive steed, Duncan Maxwell made straight for them, reining in only at the last possible moment. "Wat, ye unwashed son of a weasel!" He grinned, but his eyes were cold. "To what do we owe the honor of this visit?"

Wat ogled Catherine again. "A little bird told me ye had plucked a hostage from the sea." He leveled a stony look at Duncan. "I doona like relyin' on little birds, though, Duncan. I expect ma friends to keep me informed."

"She washed ashore on ma land," Duncan said smoothly, "which makes her mine by right. But she doesna speak and willna write her name, so I doona ken who she is or if she's worth a ransom. To my way of thinkin', that's hardly much to tell."

"Ah, Duncan." Wat angled his mount in close beside him. Tension crackled between them, yet both were smiling. "If I didna love ye so, I'd be tempted to kill ye." His coarse face cleared. "But I do love ye, so there's an end to it." He cocked his head toward Catherine. "I might like a taste of that, though."

Horrified, Catherine clutched Nevin closer.

"Ye wouldna like it," Duncan said archly. "Pure English vinegar, that one, I can tell ye, and stiff as a stick."

Catherine was so outraged by Duncan's implication that he'd "tasted" her himself that she almost missed the reference to her being English. Almost.

"English!" she exploded. "How long have you known I was English?"

Everyone turned to her in surprise as she emerged from the protection of the larch. "Answer me," she demanded of her captor, "you unwashed, unchurched, *uncivilized* heathen varlet."

"I see she's got ye pegged well enough," Wat said dryly, "but I thought ye said she couldna speak."

"I didna say she *couldna* speak, Wat," Duncan corrected mildly. "I said she *didna* speak."

Catherine would have liked nothing better than to slap both of them, outlaws or not. "How long have you known I was English?" she repeated, her voice resonant with anger.

A slow smile of grim amusement slid across Duncan Maxwell's handsome features. "Since I fetched ye."

All her efforts to remain silent, for naught. That galled her most of all.

Catherine felt two small arms circle her hips. "Ye can speak," Erinn said, quiet tears streaming from her blue eyes. " 'Tis a miracle."

" 'Tis nae miracle, so dry yer eyes," Duncan Maxwell corrected. "She could speak all along. Her muteness was but a deception." Erinn recoiled in confusion. "She tried to fool ye, darlin'," he said to his daughter, "just as she tried to fool us all."

The little girl's look of disillusioned reproof cut straight to Catherine's heart.

That was the final straw. Catherine advanced on Duncan Maxwell's Percheron with mayhem in mind. It had been a long time since she'd lost her temper, but she lost it now. "You varlet!" she ground out. "You knew I could talk, yet you allowed me to go on in silence—"

"I liked it that way," he shouted over her, much to the amusement of the men. Catherine's mouth snapped shut. "Ye were irritatin' enough, as it was," he went on. "I guessed that tongue was sharp, and why ye kept quiet. But it suited me so. I kent what a thorn ye'd be if anyone loosed it, and I was right, eh?" He looked to the gathered throng, who roared with laughter.

All the anger and frustration of the past weeks rose up in Catherine and propelled her toward the man who now taunted her. "You low-minded, yellow-livered, unshriven, uncouth excuse for man!" She flailed away at his booted leg. "Jackanapes! Kidnapper!" She was hurting herself more than him, but Catherine didn't care. It all came pouring out. "Whoremonger! Outlaw! Devil's spawn!"

Through it all, Duncan ignored her, a smug expression on his face amid the hilarity of the other men.

All but spent, Catherine exploded with a final parting shot. "Wife-killer!"

The accusation echoed in a sudden, chilling silence. All eyes focused on Duncan, including Catherine's. Never, in all her life, had she seen a more daunting reaction.

His expression froze and all the color left his face, putting his blue-black brows and stubble in sharp relief. But it was his eyes that frightened her most. Stark in their blueness, they radiated pure menace.

"Escort our honored guests to our home, Aunt Brigit," he clipped out, "and see them well fed." With one mighty swoop, he bent low, captured Catherine's waist and drew her up across his lap, then kicked his horse to a gallop toward open country.

As she had so many times in her life, Catherine realized too late that she had gone too far. Watching the grassy road flash past beneath her, she wondered in a panic where was he taking her. And what he meant to do to her when they got there.

Every time Duncan felt his temper fading, the impossible shrew across his lap opened her big mouth again and fanned his anger even hotter. Both he and Rogue were winded by the time she'd been joggled into silence and he'd gotten a grip on himself, and none too soon. He'd run out of moor. Breathless from holding her across his lap, he reined in on a wide patch of turf overlooking the firth.

When he felt his passenger's stomach muscles spasm, he hastily dropped her to the soft turf, whereupon she raised herself up on all fours and scrambled several yards before collapsing onto her side, exposing the fancy shift that hung below her skirts.

She glared up at him with a decidedly greenish cast on her plain face, her dark eyes burning in accusation. "If you mean to kill me," she half groaned, half snarled, "then do it and be done."

Her adder's tongue squelched whatever admiration he might have felt for her courage. Ever the shrew, giving orders even after the thorough jouncing she'd just endured.

"Well," she challenged. "Get on with it."

"I rode ye here to *keep* from killin' ye, ungrateful wretch of a woman," he panted out. "And to prevent Auld Wat from takin' that 'taste' of ye he wanted."

"He wouldn't dare!" She sat up, attempting, in a ridiculously futile feminine gesture, to smooth her ruined coiffure. For once, her dark hair was all askew, a condition he found richly satisfying.

"Aye, he'd dare." Duncan allowed himself a smile at her discomfiture. "I've seen Wat do worse. And with thirty of his men to ma twelve, I'd nae have been able to stop it."

Those hard brown eyes of hers narrowed. "But Brigit said he was your ally. Surely he wouldn't—"

"He is ma ally!" Clearly, the woman had no concept of when to shut up. "And ma friend, as well." Duncan dismounted to pace. "So I ken well enough that Wat takes what he wants when he wants it. And for some odd reason, he seems to want ye." He couldna resist the opportunity to nettle his hostage by way of retaliation for the endless annoyance she'd brought him. "Of course, with the notable exception of his lady wife, Wat never has been too particular when it came to women. As long as there's a scabbard for that nasty great sword of his . . ." Stilling on the turf, he looked her up and down. "But why he should want to sheathe it into such a dried-up old skank of a prim virgin is beyond me—"

Blushing crimson, his hostage shot to her feet in outrage. "Hold your tongue, knave! No decent man would speak thus of a woman's maidenhood!" She faced him rigid and full of fire.

So he'd guessed right. She was an old maid.

Blast. They rarely ransomed well.

"How dare you speak such coarseness in the presence of your betters!" she railed at him.

"Ma betters?" Duncan laughed, placing his fists on his hips, feet firmly planted. "And who would that be?"

"*I* am your better, you unwashed, unchurched, sorry excuse for a man."

" 'Tis true I'm a man," he said equably. She hadn't taken the bait and told him who she was, but Duncan was confident she would. No sour, overbaked spinster was going to get the best of him. He circled her at a safe distance. "A man who has it in his power to grant ye something ye want in exchange for something I want."

Her hand darted again to her ruined coif. "Aside from my freedom, which I know you will not grant," she countered, "what could I possibly want from the likes of you?"

Duncan smiled. "To kirk ma children."

The choler ebbed abruptly from her face. In its place, a flash of awareness, then something else . . . What? "But that would be for their sakes, not for mine," she said, clearly flustered. "Surely you would not keep them from the word of God."

What was she up to with this church business?

"We have a Bible," Duncan said mildly. He strolled apace to peer out over the firth. The wind that buffeted his cloak was brisk and clean and held a hint of winter yet to come. "They can learn their Scriptures well enough from that."

"But denied the sacraments . . ." Her arrogance faded. "How could you withhold those from them? Amber and Baran are past time for their catechism, and the younger ones . . . what have they learned of the Psalter, or the *Book of Common Order*?"

"More than ye, ye Englisher," Duncan shot back, surprised to find an Englisher who knew so much of Scottish Reformed ways.

She had a point, though, blast her. He'd meant to take over his children's religious instruction after the disaster with the local parish, but there never seemed to be the time. Again and again, more urgent matters had commanded his attention until his resolve had been forgotten.

"Please." His hostage approached him, a welcome sign of submission. "If you would but allow me to take them to church, it would cause no burden to you or Aunt Brigit."

She seemed so determined to take them herself that Duncan decided to use her insistence to his advantage. He'd find out why she was so insistent later. "Ye may take them," he said offhand, then turned to face her. "If ye meet ma terms."

Despite her efforts to conceal the conflict in her dark eyes, he saw it clearly before wariness erased it. "And what would you want of me in exchange?"

He moved in close, so close they were almost touching.

Duncan knew she wouldn't give ground, and he was right. She stiffened as he bent near to her face. Just when his lips were about to touch hers, he brushed past her cheek to her ear. "Only your name," he whispered seductively. "As simple as that. Tell me your name, and I'll let ye take ma children to worship."

"You are an evil man." Her low voice shook. "To trade on your own children's souls."

"Ah," he said lightly. "The pot calls the kettle black." When she went even more rigid, Duncan drew back with a grin. "Ma children's souls are secure as any mortal's. But if ye want to kirk them, ye must tell me your name."

She was torn; he could sense it. "And how do I know you'll keep your word?" she asked.

So. The deal was done. Now all that remained was to tidy up the terms. Duncan met her suspicious gaze straight-on. "Ma word is ma bond," he said. "If I say I'll do a thing, I do it." He grinned. "Ask Wat, if ye doona believe me."

At the mention of Wat, he saw a flicker of fear in her expression, but she quickly reclaimed her stiff composure. The wheels were turning behind those dark eyes, though. He could almost hear them.

After a long, thoughtful pause, she nodded. "Very well. But first you must swear to keep your end of the bargain."

The woman was as stubborn as an otter with a clam. "If I swear first, how do *I* ken that *ye*'ll keep your end of the bargain?"

"If I say I'll do a thing, I do it," she said in a startlingly accurate imitation of his Scottish accents.

Duncan laughed in spite of himself to discover that this green persimmon of a hostage was a talented mimic. But he'd known from the moment she'd feigned muteness that there was more to this one than met the eye. He extended his hand to seal the bargain. "Aye, then. Give me your name, and ye may kirk ma bairns."

"Very well." Her own hand was surprisingly warm

when she took it. Meeting his gaze, she shook with a firm grip. "My name is Catherine."

He waited for the rest. When it didn't come, he felt his temper rising. "Your whole name, or we have nae pact."

Her haughty features hardened in condescension. "You said nothing of both names when we made our pact. A man of his word does not change the terms of an agreement after the fact."

Why, the nit-picking, backhanded little vixen! "Ye kent full well I meant both names!"

"You said I must give my name, not my *names*. If you are a man of your word, the pact stands."

Curse her arrogant hide! A tide of blood rose to his face, betraying his anger. Duncan didn't know which galled him more, the fact that she hadn't given him what he wanted, or the fact that she was right in saying he hadn't specified first and last names.

No one got the best of the Black Bastard. Especially not a woman!

Damn it, though, she had him.

Bested by a willful old maid. If word got out . . . With that mouth of hers, he had no doubt it would.

Vexed beyond speech, he circled her waist and snatched her from her feet, holding her like a sack of haver under his arm.

"Unhand me!" She flailed ineffectually as he marched toward his stallion. "Where are you taking me?" The question held more than a hint of panic. "I demand to know!"

"I'm takin' ye home," he said with grim satisfaction. "And thanks to your all-fired cleverness, Kate, ye'll ride the way ye came." That ought to jounce the smugness from her.

"My name isn't Kate," she protested as he slung her across Rogue's withers. "Oof! It's Catherine, and I'll thank you to address me properly."

Duncan mounted, then pulled her none too gently

across his lap. "It's Kate from now on," he announced, then spurred the Percheron to a gallop.

Kate, for good and all. In that, at least, he would have his way.

Duncan had deliberately avoided Wat until the feast to allow time to cool whatever bruised feelings might have resulted from the afternoon's incident. Now that everyone had gathered at the makeshift tables in the parlor, though, the time for truth had come. He stood and lifted his goblet to Wat, bringing everyone else to their feet. "To friendship!" He leveled a probing stare at his guest of honor.

If their understanding had been breached, he would see it in the outlaw's eyes, for though the aging reiver was as fierce a raider as ever had ridden the marches, Wat lacked Duncan's ability to conceal his true thoughts.

"To friendship," the old reprobate replied without hesitation, his answering look one of mild reproof but no real malice.

Relief eased Duncan's tight grin and loosed the knot inside his chest. Thanks be to God, the matter of the Englisher—including today's unfortunate incident—hadn't seriously damaged the crucial alliance.

But Duncan's relief was short-lived. From the corner of his eye, he spotted Kate hovering near the kitchen door, directing the servers.

He felt his face congeal and the knot inside his chest cinch tight. Fool woman! Was she *trying* to bring about her own destruction—and his with it? He'd ordered her to keep to her room for her own protection, yet here she was, flirting with disaster. If Wat should spy her, Duncan couldn't answer for the consequences.

Fortunately, Aunt Brigit chose just that moment to refill his goblet.

"What the hell is Kate doing here?" he murmured through a forced smile. "I ordered her to her room."

Aunt Brigit motioned to Nessa as if he'd asked for more food. "More beef for the master and our guests!"

She dropped her voice back to a discreet whisper. "I locked her in maself, but she managed to get out. She seems determined to stick her nose in all our business."

Duncan closed his eyes briefly in frustration. As if his life weren't complicated enough already. Wat had most likely come to appropriate Kate in the first place. If he followed through, the rift would be fatal.

"Should I have one of the men drag her away?" Aunt Brigit murmured.

"Nae. If she puts up a fight . . ." Duncan struggled to hide his anger beneath a cheerful countenance. "We dare nae draw attention to her," he said through a fixed smile. If he left the table to take care of her himself, all eyes would be on him. "Tell Lucas to entice her into the kitchen somehow, then lay hold to her. Gag her and bind her if ye have to, but make sure she isna seen again until Wat and his men have left."

"I'll do ma best," his aunt replied with more than a hint of reservation.

Curse the Englisher. So far, she'd brought him nothing but trouble. Much more of this, and he'd willingly hand her over to Wat or anyone else who would take her.

Turning his attention back to the gathering of Scotts who flanked the long table, Duncan directed the conversation to a topic sure to please his guest of honor. "Have ye news from Edinburgh?"

Auld Wat preened like a son of Annan sitting on an English warden. "Aye. Justice was done." His barrel chest inflated despite the glowers of the relatives he'd so recently locked up to keep them from loosing a bloodbath in retaliation for the slaying of one of his many sons. "And justice was all I asked. When a man's own kinsmen kill one of his sons, the traitors should pay, and pay they have," he said smugly. "King James granted me their lands in recompense."

"Their lands. Fah!" one of his nephews protested. "They should have paid with their lives!"

Wat shot the man a baleful glare. "Traitors or nae,

they're Scotts," he asserted. "And they've paid with all their lands and goods. 'Twas well worth a son, by my way of thinkin', and there's an end to it."

A wave of resentment rippled through Wat's surviving sons, but none was foolish enough to challenge his father's statement. Wat ruled his men—and his family—with an iron hand.

How any father could barter his own flesh and blood so shamelessly, though, was completely beyond Duncan. He couldn't forgive the loss of any of his children for all of England and Scotland.

How do ye ken what ye'd do under the circumstances? an inner voice chided. *Unless ye can ransom Kate, who could guess what depths ye might be forced to?*

Shoving the thought aside, Duncan stood. "More wine," he ordered. "We'll drink to the one who was slain." He nodded toward Wat's sons.

They rose as one in gratitude for the gesture, bringing the rest of the house to their feet in solemn tribute.

When all had drunk, Duncan bowed briefly toward his guest of honor. "And here's to royal justice and new lands for all true Scots, as are those gathered here."

A hearty cheer rose from the assembly, and the table shook neath pounded fists.

Satisfied, Duncan settled to his seat. Only when Wat was engaged in a deep conversation with his eldest son did Duncan risk a glance at the spot where Kate had been standing. Good. She was gone.

He resolved to order her kept to her room until Sunday. Without visitors. That would teach her to disobey.

The woman would be the death of him yet.

The very next Sunday, Catherine ushered an uneasy brood from the carriage to the door of the kirk in Annandale. Duncan Maxwell's men did not come in with her. The silent, brooding Norseman Ander Mord stayed in the driver's seat, and Quinn and Rory Little remained mounted beside the coach, but Catherine refused to let their lack of participation dampen her spirits. Despite the cool wind that blew in dark clouds overhead, it felt glorious to be outside after the better part of a week confined to her room.

Erinn and Nevin in hand, she lifted up a silent prayer as she approached the church. *Please, Lord, let this be to all our benefit.*

Rambunctious as usual, Gordon and Kerry bounced past her and rushed to the doorstep. Placid Cameron ambled behind, but Baran stopped short beside the graven cornerstone that read 1554. "I'll nae go in," he declared. "Ye canna make me."

Amber held back, as well, her lovely young face troubled. The other boys, true to pecking order despite their obvious disappointment, retreated to Baran's flank.

Catherine had been afraid of this. When she'd announced their father's decision, the two eldest had bluntly refused to go, Amber with tears and Baran with sullen rebellion that only Duncan Maxwell's harsh command had overridden.

Amber had given in to gentle pressure, but Baran was as stubborn as his father.

Catherine knew better than to pull rank on the twelve-year-old now. Years of dealing with Charles had taught her that confrontation, particularly in front of witnesses, only made things worse. Baran already disliked her; he'd hate her forever if she embarrassed him in front of his siblings.

"Young sir," she said softly and with respect, "as eldest male, you bear the grave responsibility of setting an example for the others."

"We Scots doona single out our firstborn for special treatment like ye corrupted Englishers," he shot back at her. "Every son of this land has equal inheritance and worth to his family."

Gremlins and grindstones! Catherine had meant to calm him, not step on his blasted oversensitive Scottish toes. "Pray forgive me." She had to convince him. Everything depended upon it. "Your sire has directed you to worship with your brothers and sisters. I know you do not intend to disobey his express wishes."

Consternation replaced the harsh set of Baran's handsome young face.

An inspiration hit her. "It's only natural that all of you feel strange about coming back after what happened," she went on, praying this tack would work. "But you and your family have as much right to be here as anyone. Do not let what happened with the minister keep you out."

"Keep us out?" The boy tucked his chin, indignant. "Naught could keep us out if we wanted to go, but we doona."

Catherine shrugged. "As long as you stay away, the minister will think he's won." She transferred Nevin's and Erinn's hands to Baran. "This is your chance to show him you've nothing to be ashamed of. Hold your heads up high and take your place in the congregation, now and every Lord's Day hence."

Baran regarded the open doors with narrowed eyes, then straightened. "We've every right to be there." After only a moment's hesitation, he snapped a nod to his elder sister. "Wipe that worried look off your face, Amber, and stand proud. We're goin' to worship."

Catherine went almost limp with relief. When she entered at a respectful distance behind the children, she could not help enjoying the looks of shock and curiosity their presence caused. A buzz of speculation slithered through the gathered worshipers until the presiding elder put a stop to it with a harsh rap of his staff on the stone floor.

Proud and resolute, Baran marched his brothers and sisters to the very front and led them into the pew that bore the graven name of Kinnon Maxwell above the date 1554.

An ancestor?

If he was, he must be pleased to look down from heaven and see the courage of his descendants. Catherine's own heart swelled. *God forgive me, but it does me good to see these children take their rightful place in Your house after everything that's happened.*

So you say, an inner voice chided, but would they be here if it did not serve your own selfish designs?

Catherine guiltily banished the disturbing thought.

The white-haired minister entered and mounted the pulpit. She'd expected a harsh, unforgiving man—God knew, there were said to be many such souls presiding over the spartan kirks of this barbaric land—but when this pastor saw the children, his kindly, aging face fairly radiated joy.

"This is the day that the Lord hath made. Let us rejoice and be glad in it," he said with happy conviction. He looked straight at the children. "May we begin our service with a special prayer of thanks for every precious soul here today. Ye are all well come."

Bowing their heads, Baran and Amber exchanged surprised glances, then shrugged.

Suddenly it did not matter quite as deeply that Catherine establish a contact she could exploit with this minister. For this moment, at least, it mattered more that these children were once again where they belonged, in the house of God.

Under the drone of the minister's long-winded prayer, she made her own petitions. *I would still appreciate it, Lord, if You'd allow me to get word to my family, though. And safely redeem a jewel or two to help the children.* It was a lot to ask, but considering what He'd put her through lately, she asked it boldly.

Catherine shook the minister's hand in the open doorway after the service. "Thank you so much, good sir, for your heartfelt, moving sermon. I look forward to next week's message."

"I am gratified ma words touched ye," he said with convincing humility, "but I canna take the credit. I share only what the Lord has laid upon ma heart." He beamed at the children. "I must tell ye, though, how blessed we are to see these fine young ones again. Blessed, indeed."

A moist gust of wind funneled through the opening, tugging at their clothes. The minister looked up to the dark clouds rapidly piling in on the last remnants of blue sky. "There's quite a storm blowin' up. Will ye not consider bidin' with us till it passes? Ye've such a long way to go."

Catherine had intended to wait a few Sundays before trying to arrange a meeting with the minister, but this opportunity was heaven-sent. "It does look rather threatening."

He nodded to the small, timid woman standing beside him. "Ma wife, Sarah, and I would be honored if ye would join us for a meal at the parsonage."

His wife blanched, yet managed a dismayed smile. "But of course," she murmured, "please join us. What little we have, we are blessed to share."

From the couple's thin, threadbare condition, Catherine judged that what little they had to share would be precious little, indeed. "You are so kind. We accept. But I had already packed a meal for all of us," she hastened to reassure. "Perhaps you would allow us to share ours with you."

Before the minister could protest, his relieved wife jumped in with, "That would be lovely. Our home is just by. Pray, come with me."

"One moment." Catherine turned to the children. "Baran, would you please supervise the others in getting the food from the wagon. We're going to eat at the parsonage and wait until the storm has passed to leave."

Amber and Baran regarded her with a mixture of surprise and resentment. As Catherine turned back to the pastor's wife, she heard Amber mutter, "Papa's not going to believe this."

"He's not going to *like* it," Baran retorted, but he did as Catherine had asked. Nevin and Erinn in tow, he shooed the others toward the coach.

Catherine was so grateful Baran hadn't embarrassed everyone by refusing, her smile was genuine. "My name is Catherine," she said to the thin older woman.

"I'm Sarah," her hostess said. "Sarah Maxwell."

"Is everyone in this parish a Maxwell?" she couldn't resist asking.

"Oh, we have our Bells and Armstrongs and Irvings and Carruthers," Sarah answered easily. Her voice dropped to a stage whisper. "And a few Johnstones, of course." She reverted to her cheery tone. "But we Maxwells outnumber them all in these parts. As a matter of fact, ma husband was first cousin to Duncan's grandsire." Once she got past her initial shyness, Sarah Maxwell enjoyed her conversation, even with a stranger—and an English one, at that.

Catherine hoped she'd be as garrulous at dinner.

Catherine lingered at the table with Sarah and Angus Maxwell after the children had been excused to gather in the parlor for rest and quiet conversation. Outside, the late-summer storm sent sheets of rain across the town.

Her hosts had entertained the children with fond stories of their mothers, with the notable exception of Nevin's. The tales were touching, but not informative. Yet Catherine knew better than to ask probing questions. And despite their obvious curiosity about her, the Maxwells hadn't pried.

Catherine had learned something from the conversation, though. If these people were as they seemed, God had smiled on her, for she sensed a deep honesty and a good heart in both of them. "Thank you so much for offering us shelter," she said to the elderly couple. "You were quite right about the storm, Reverend. What a blessing that we were not caught out in it."

"The blessing is ours, good lady," Angus Maxwell replied with conviction. "I'm that glad for a chance to help Duncan Maxwell and any of his own." There was a prolonged silence. "So," he continued, "what brings ye to our humble parish?"

"Angus." His wife's eyebrows shot up in reproof. "Have ye abandoned yer manners entirely? If our guest had wished to tell us, she would've done so."

"It's all right, really," Catherine reassured them. The truth was always safest, and giving it extended a bridge of trust. "I am not offended by your question." She faced Angus Maxwell squarely. "I was shipwrecked in the firth and washed ashore on Duncan Maxwell's land. He now holds me for ransom."

"Oh, my," Sarah said in dismay, her gentle soul clearly wounded by such a revelation. "Ye poor, dear lass. Oh, my."

Her husband reddened. "A foul and evil practice, hostage-taking, one I have preached against since the day I took this pulpit." He sighed heavily. "But in such a hard and hostile region, even men as fine as Duncan Maxwell often fall into such a sin. One despairs. One despairs indeed to see his flock so far astray."

As fine a man as Duncan Maxwell? Catherine retracted some of the hopes she'd pinned on this first meeting.

Yet if the minister disapproved of her being held for ransom, perhaps she had found the ally she needed to gain her freedom.

"Reverend and Mrs. Maxwell," she began.

"Angus and Sarah, please," the gentle pastor's wife insisted.

Catherine nodded. "Sarah . . . I am deeply troubled by some pressing concerns . . . rather personal ones. Would it be an imposition for me to ask for a few moments to speak with the pastor in confidence?" There. She'd done it.

Sarah Maxwell looked on her with sympathy. "Of course ye shall, ma dear." She rose. "And while ye chat with Angus, why don't I entertain the children with a few ripping good morality stories?"

Angus smiled. "All the wee ones love her stories. She makes 'em quite excitin'."

Sarah rose. "Take all the time ye need."

Catherine wanted to squeeze the little woman in a bear hug, but she confined herself to a heartfelt, "Thank you, and God bless you."

"This way." Angus Maxwell guided her into a small book-lined room barely large enough for its well-worn desk and the chairs on either side. "Sit, please." As she did, he drew the door only partway closed, then worked his way around to sit facing her. "Now, how may I help ye?"

Catherine hesitated. Dared she risk it? Her instincts told her she could trust this man. And he had spoken out so plainly against ransoming hostages. There was no question that he felt sympathy for her plight.

But could she count on him to help her? Especially when it meant acting against Duncan Maxwell, his own kinsman—and a dangerous and powerful one at that.

Still, Angus Maxwell was the man he was. Either he would help her, or he wouldn't. Better to find out sooner than later.

Through the crack in the door, she heard the children laughing and clapping as Sarah Maxwell entertained them with her "ripping good" stories.

"Pastor, I beg you to help me," she ventured, her voice so low he had to lean forward to hear her. "I have not told Duncan Maxwell who I am, where I came from, because he means to demand a ransom from my stepfather." She peered into his kindly eyes, praying he was truly a man of principle. "My stepfather has no money for ransom. What with the poor crops these past few years, our lands cannot produce enough to provide for our family— my stepfamily," she corrected. "We survive by working as simple merchants. There are no coffers of gold or silver. Only debts, hard work, and hope."

And the jewels sewn into your shift!

"Ach." Angus Maxwell exhaled heavily, nodding his head in sympathy.

"My family doesn't even know that I'm alive." She leaned closer, tears escaping unbidden. "Please let me send them word that I did not perish."

Angus Maxwell frowned, his brow furrowing beneath his white mane of hair. "What ye ask—"

"I know. I know. I'm asking you to do something without telling Duncan." She had to convince him. "But what harm could come from it? As God is my witness, I speak the truth when I tell you that my stepfather has no money for ransom." Never mind the treasure she carried with her. "So you would not be hurting Duncan by helping me."

She could see he was wavering.

"I must let my family know I'm alive," she went on. "I could send the message in a letter addressed to my own dear pastor back home. He'll see that they get it. I only want them to know that I'm safe and where I am."

The minister curled his lips, clearly torn between mercy and the worldly ties of blood. "But Duncan . . ."

"The only way he could find out would be if you tell him. Are not the confidences of your office sacred?"

"Aye, but . . ." Angus Maxwell stared into space. "Child, ye doona ken what yer askin'. There are wounds yet unhealed twixt me and Duncan. To go against him yet again . . ."

"I judge you to be a man of conscience, sir. You say you have gone against him before. It must have been a matter of deepest spiritual principle." She gripped her hands before her. "Is this too not such a matter? You say you've preached against hostage-taking since you came here. Would you then deny me, a hostage, what little help I ask for? Help that it is well within your power to extend?"

Angus Maxwell braced his elbows on the desk and scrubbed his lips back and forth across his linked fingers. "I must think on this and pray."

"Of course. Of course." But what if something kept

her from coming back? What if this was her one chance? She fought down a spike of panic. "May I write the letter now and leave it with you?" she pleaded. "That way if you decide to help me, as I pray you will, you can simply send it."

He frowned. "Well, I doona suppose there's any harm in that."

Catherine's heart throbbed with hope. "You may read it, of course." She struggled to remain calm. "I want you to see I have nothing to hide."

Only your jewels!

"Verra well. But I canna promise that I'll send it," he said with a gentle shake of his finger.

"I trust your conscience, good sir. If God is truly merciful," she said in earnest, "you will send it."

Angus Maxwell drew out a clean sheet of paper, a quill, and ink. "Write, then."

Catherine creased the paper, tore it in two, then addressed the first note to her pastor, William Braithwaite, at the Church of the Assumption in Corby. She guessed at the date, then wrote a guarded plea for him to deliver the enclosed note to her stepfather. Her words were chosen carefully, lest the missive fall into the wrong hands. The only full name she used was Duncan Maxwell's.

The second letter was more difficult, because as she wrote, her eyes filled with tears. Beginning with simply "Beloved Papa," she took great care to betray as little as possible of her family while letting them know where she was.

Papa would know what to do. He always had.

After sanding and blotting the message, she handed the two notes to Angus Maxwell and watched with bated breath as he read them. But his studious frown and the occasional lift of his brow told her very little.

He returned the letters without comment, then lit a candle and gave her a stick of sealing wax. "As I said," he cautioned gently, "I canna promise ye anything."

Catherine nodded, a lump the size of a plum in her

throat. She folded the letter to her father, then tucked it, unsealed, inside the one to her pastor. With a silent prayer, she sealed the outer missive, then handed it over to Angus Maxwell, the man who now held her fate in his hands.

Papa, Papa, how I pray you get this. I can bear anything, as long as you know I am alive.

It was several seconds before she found her voice. With that out of the way, she decided she might as well forge ahead. "There is one other matter . . ."

The beleaguered minister drew back in dismay.

"Baran and Amber are overdue for their catechism," she hastened to say, fearing he might bolt from the room. "Would it be possible for you to supervise their instruction after worship on Sundays?"

Relieved, Angus nodded. "Of course. As long as Duncan gives his permission."

"I'm certain he will," she said calmly. "As you said, he is a fine man." She surprised herself at how sincerely she was able to say the words, for she did not believe them.

"Then I'd be delighted," he rolled out in his thick Scottish accent.

Catherine rose. "Thank you so much, sirrah." She watched in silence as Angus Maxwell tucked her letter into the desk drawer and closed it.

Please God. Please.

She wanted to see Papa and Hal again.

And River House. She wanted to go home. Her troubles with Charles now seemed so inconsequential.

She'd even be glad to see her stepmother, Willa. And Charles, if by some miracle he'd survived. A wave of homesickness swept through her. Then she remembered. She'd given up River House, and her family.

Would they take her back?

Could she face going back?

Though her stepmother had been unfailingly courteous to Catherine, no warmth had passed between them, especially after Catherine had championed Hal when Willa's obvious preference for Charles had surfaced. And if Charles had perished, there was little hope that Willa would tolerate Catherine's presence, much less forgive, despite the fact that Charles had accompanied her only at his mother's insistence.

Catherine would cross that bridge when she got to it. First, she had to besiege heaven with prayers that Angus Maxwell would send her letter—and that the letter would find its way home.

Chapter

EIGHT

Duncan did his best to concentrate on his correspondence, but it wasn't easy. Worry stabbed at him like a busy little demon with a needle. Not to mention the fact that Michael Graham had been nervously prowling from the desk to the parlor window for almost half an hour.

He closed his eyes and inhaled deeply in an effort to calm himself. The crisp evening air was sweet with the aroma of autumn. If he hadn't been so anxious about his children, he would have gone to the peel and savored the pastoral peace of his holding. But as it was, he tried his best to distract himself with his ever-demanding inventories and correspondence.

Michael peered through Kate's handiwork into the darkening twilight, rocking on his feet at the window with his arms locked behind him. "Shouldna we go after them?" he asked for the third time. "They're perilous tardy, Duncan."

Duncan glanced at the clock. Again. Over an hour had passed since he'd sent two men to look for the coach.

"If we have nae word from Logan and Carlin within the hour," he told Michael, "I'll take Thurlow and ride." Leaving Annanlea and its families far too thinly defended. "More than likely, the coach has mired down somewhere," he said to reassure himself as much as Michael. "Ye ken the roads after a storm." He prayed it was true, but for the past few hours, a dozen chilling possibilities had swooped into his thoughts like nasty, giant bats.

He'd never been a worrier until Kate washed up; nor had he second-guessed himself. Now here he was, fretting like a broody hen who'd lost her chicks.

But if any harm had come to his children . . .

He loved them as he loved nothing else in this world.

They were more than his future; they were his life, each one a precious jewel, unique and irreplaceable. Duncan had long ago steeled himself to the harshness of the world beyond these walls, but when it came to his family, he was wholly vulnerable. He'd buried six wee ones already. And four wives. Each death had wrenched great holes in his soul. Was that not grief enough for one man?

He'd paid his penance in this life, branded a bastard, despised not only by the world, but also by his own grandsire. He'd witnessed the scorn heaped on his gentle mother and known that he was the cause. He, and his cowardly English father. The blood of a coward ran through his veins, and Duncan had sworn from childhood to purge himself of any trace of cravenness. Every indignity he'd suffered had only fueled his hatred for his father and hardened his determination to protect and love his own children.

His children. Where *were* they?

While Michael paced, Duncan forced his mind back to answering yet another unproductive response about his missing salt.

Blast. He miswrote—again. He slashed through the word and continued. But the mounting tension put him so ill at ease, he could not concentrate.

Michael's constant motion set his teeth on edge.

Ye should have gone with Logan and Carlin, at least.

Still pacing, Michael smacked his hands together behind his back.

Torn between protecting his own family and those of his men, Duncan finally exploded. "Pick a place and settle, man. I canna think with ye flitterin' about that way."

"Forgive me, lad." Michael stilled, his expression one of sympathy instead of recrimination. "Go back to yer letters. I think I'll head for the kitchen and bedevil Lucas fer a bit. We both enjoy it."

"I'm sorry, Michael." Duncan abandoned his quill and stood. "I had nae call to speak so sharp with ye. I didna mean to run ye off."

Michael raised a staying hand. " 'Tis nothing, truly," he said with a wistful smile. "Enough, the burdens ye bear for all of us. Now this worry. 'Tis a testament that ye've stayed as calm as ye are. I'll leave ye to yerself." He turned and made for the kitchen. "Do sing out if there's word, though."

"Aye. Ye'll be the first to know." Duncan went to the fire and poked at the glowing peat. More agitated by the minute, he felt as if the sparks were swarming through his veins instead of rising up the chimney.

Blast Kate and her conniving. He should never have let her take his children from the safety of Annanlea, no matter what he'd promised.

Your word is the only honor ye have left, his conscience reminded him. *Ye had to let them go. But ye should have gone along yourself, instead of sending Quinn and Rory.*

It was true, he had to admit. Only pride had kept him from going. Pride, and smoldering anger. The last thing he'd wanted to do was endure sitting under Angus Maxwell's preaching, putting himself on display to the congregation after they'd denied poor Aselma Christian burial.

But what was pride compared to his children?

Lord God, bring them home safe, and I'll take them to kirk maself every Sunday, he vowed in earnest. Then he felt obligated to add, *Unless there's trouble afoot, of course, and it isna prudent to stir abroad.* Surely God wouldn't be offended by that one condition. The Lord ought to understand trouble well enough; He'd allowed enough of it in these parts.

Duncan's vow brought him little peace. He paced to the window. Outside, the older lads set torches at the gate and the front door in anticipation of the coach's return. A brazier glowed to life atop the northern peel, then the western.

The lookouts were in place. Yet still no word of his family.

"The coach!" Thurlow's shout resounded from the northern peel. "The coach! Open the gate!"

Thanks be to God!

Relief flooded through him. "Michael! Aunt Brigit!" he called. "They're back."

His aunt was halfway down the stairs already amid a tide of Erinn's mewing cats. "Worked ma fingers to the bone this day without Kate or Amber here to help me," she said with a note of edgy relief that told Duncan she'd been worried, too. "Shoo." She nudged a cat out of her way. "How in purple perdition do the beasties ken when Erinn's comin' home?" his aunt asked rhetorically. "They started fer the stairs the moment the shout went up."

"Doona ask me. I'm just glad she's home." Duncan halted in the middle of Bink's precious Persian rug, whereupon a dozen noisy felines surrounded him. He plucked up Twinkle. "Goodness, such complaints." He rubbed his finger just below her ears as she liked, but the forlorn creature wouldn't be consoled. "There, there, kitty. She'll be home anon."

"Get those beasties off ma rug," Aunt Brigit commanded, "and take yerself with 'em."

"Doona worry, Bink. Nae harm'll come to your precious carpet."

Through the window, Duncan saw Logan and Carlin ride in first, muddy to the chest. Then, with great clatter and clop, the muddy coach rumbled through the gate. By the light of the torches, Duncan saw that Ander seemed relaxed at the reins, with Quinn and Rory—as mud-caked as the others—riding close behind.

So the coach had mired down.

"Come along." Aunt Brigit sailed toward the door, her precious rug forgotten. "They'll be here any second. Ye should be there to greet them."

"I'll wait right here," he said, relishing the reception he had planned. "Just send them in."

* * *

Catherine's arms had long since gone numb from holding Nevin as he slept, but she did not mind, for he made a precious burden. Owing to the mired roads, their trip home had taken twice as long as the one out, but even that hadn't dimmed the hope that now burned bright within her heart.

Surely God would direct Angus Maxwell to send her letter. Surely.

The children had long since lapsed into weary silence, but Baran roused to stick his head out of the window and wave. "Haloo!" He drew back inside and shook his brothers. "Wake up. We're home." The boys yawned, grumbled, poked each other, and scratched themselves in a most ungentlemanly fashion.

Catherine looked ahead through the window and saw Brigit Maxwell and Michael Graham waiting on the front steps.

Not Duncan? An unexpected sliver of disappointment surprised her.

Erinn roused from her lap, waking the fluffy gray kitten she'd wheedled out of the Maxwells. Amber stretched beside her with a long, satisfied moan. At last the coach swayed to a halt.

The door swung open to reveal a grinning Michael Graham, with Aunt Brigit hovering anxiously on the step above him, surrounded by Erinn's mewling cats. "How was kirk, then?" Michael asked, beaming. "I do believe ye all look a bit holier than when ye left."

"Uncle Michael!" Erinn took one look at him and without a second's warning or hesitation, hurled herself—and the kitten—straight into his arms. Catherine's heart lurched and Aunt Brigit gasped in fright, but Michael managed to catch the child.

"Give an old man warning before ye jump him, darlin'," Michael scolded gently, setting Erinn to her feet.

"See what Cousin Sarah gave me?" Erinn asked blithely, holding up the kitten. "Isna he beautiful?"

Aunt Brigit recovered sufficiently to comment, "Ah. Just what we need. Another tomcat."

"Go hug yer dear old auntie," Michael told her. "I'm off to aid Quinn and Rory with their horses. Baran can help the rest of ye down."

Baran's chest swelled. "Aye." He clambered out, then turned to extend his hand. "Ye next, Amber."

Once she was back on solid ground, Amber reached back for Nevin. "Here, Ladykate; let me take him."

"Thank you, dear." Afraid she couldn't trust her leaden arms, Catherine handed the still-sleeping child over with great caution. She would have followed, but it felt so good just to be still from the ride that she permitted herself a moment more to watch and rest.

Amber carried Nevin to Aunt Brigit, who gathered him gently to her chest. "Worried me half to death, ye all did," Aunt Brigit grumbled without conviction. "I feared some heinous fate had overtaken ye."

"Cousin Angus invited us to wait out the storm at his house," Amber explained.

Brigit's wiry little frame snapped taut. "Oh, he did, did he?"

"Aye," Baran piped up. Oblivious to his aunt's obvious resentment of Angus Maxwell, he helped the sleepy twins and Cameron from the coach. "And good thing we did."

"The roads were beastly mired after all that rain," Amber said dramatically. "We got stuck four times."

"It was only three," Baran corrected.

"Nae." This, from Cameron. "If ye count that wallow at Cousin Angus's yard, 'twas four."

"Well, if ye count *that* one," Baran conceded. "But it wasna on the road."

Catherine had learned much from such exchanges on the long journey, but now all she could think about was being home. Back, she corrected.

All she wanted now was her bed. To get there, she'd have to move. She rose stiffly and gladly accepted Baran's assistance debarking. "Thank you, Baran." As it always did after a coach trip, the ground felt as if it were moving, and her legs were reluctant to function.

Next Sunday would come too soon, her weary body told her.

Ander cracked the whip and urged the horses toward the stable.

"Come along then, all." Aunt Brigit shooed the older children up the wide brick stairs. "Yer Papa's waitin' fer ye in the parlor." She motioned to Catherine. "Step lively, Kate."

Catherine forced her legs to follow.

"So Angus Maxwell invited ye to his house," Aunt Brigit said defensively when she caught up with her. "So's he could fill your ears with slanders, nae doubt."

"On the contrary," Catherine was quick to say. "He showed nothing but kindness and concern for this family."

"Hmph." Brigit looked past her into the parlor, and her scowl eased into a delighted smile. "Well, would ye look at that."

Catherine did, and was completely unprepared for what she saw: the Black Bastard of the Western March waited crouched in the middle of the rug, a huge grin on his handsome face and his arms opened wide to his children in joyous invitation.

"There they are!" Duncan cheered. "Come to Papa. I've missed ma children, one and all." The twins and Erinn raced toward him in delight.

"He was fair distraught when ye went so tardy," Aunt Brigit confided to Catherine in a whisper, cradling Nevin in her arms.

"They're on your rug," Catherine couldn't resist saying.

Smiling, Aunt Brigit shook her head in dismissal. "And welcome to it for such as this. They're long overdue for a tussle, all of 'em."

The children launched themselves onto Duncan with such enthusiasm that he tumbled to his back on the floor.

He not only didn't seem to mind, he reveled in it. "Aaagh! Massive forces!" he cried in mock alarm.

Catherine watched in delight as Duncan played with his children. Baran watched with adolescent disdain, while Amber held back wistfully, but the others had a grand tussle with their father. Laughing and writhing, Duncan looked ten years younger, his cheeks ruddy below bright blue eyes and his wavy hair mussed.

If only he didn't wear black all the time . . .

Lucas had told her that there had been strife between Duncan and his grandsire, and for that reason, Duncan had refused to wear the Maxwell plaid. Curious, she ventured, "I've heard there was no love lost between Duncan and his grandsire." She leveled a frank look at Aunt Brigit. "But was your sire good to you, at least?"

A shadow crossed the little woman's face. "I willna speak ill of the dead."

So that's how it was. A wonder indeed that Duncan could be so affectionate with his own children. His mother must have been a woman of exceptional warmth. "Please forgive me for prying."

"I will, but doona test me again," Aunt Brigit snapped.

"Down." Nevin wriggled in Aunt Brigit's arms. When she set him to the floor, he toddled to his father and flopped like a plank against him. "Huh, huh, huh," he said in what, for Nevin, was an outburst of hilarity. Duncan drew him close and gave his head a kiss.

The children attacked en masse, so Duncan countered with a tactical tickling.

Such play. The joy was contagious.

Catherine had never seen the like. She and her stepfather loved each other dearly, but Robert Storey was not the sort of man to make public displays of affection, much less tumble on the floor with anyone. He'd been a different sort of father, but a good one. Her vision lost focus as she remembered his kind face and patient, gentle ways.

And darling Hal. How she missed him. He was the same age as Baran—twelve—but still had the look and innocence of a boy. She missed the chance to talk with Hal and hug him and tousle his wavy chestnut hair. Such a gentle soul. Catherine had sensed it from the first moment Willa had allowed her to hold him. Hal's quiet spirit was better suited to peaceful games than rough play.

But her memories triggered unasked-for images of strife: Charles's relentless, hostile resentment and Willa's failure to discipline him for it. Catherine shuddered, abandoning her reverie for the buoying sound of children's laughter that refreshed her smile—and her soul. She came to herself to find Duncan Maxwell lying on his back covered by a tangle of children, his neck craned to peer at her with the strangest quizzical expression.

Her easy grin froze. Why would he regard her thus? What had she given away in those few vacant moments? There was open curiosity in his face and . . . something else, something she couldn't identify.

Feeling as if she'd been caught naked, she glanced away, nervously smoothing down the stray tendrils the journey had worked loose around her face.

She did not want to look his way again, but found herself doing so just in time to see a flicker of regret in his eyes. His expression shifted abruptly to consternation, though, when Cameron launched another sneak attack: a direct hit to the midsection.

"Oof!" Duncan recovered from the assault to his dignity with another lion's roar. Then he rolled carefully back onto all fours and began to prowl the rug, dragging all five children with him.

"Easy, now," Brigit scolded her nephew. "Doona be too rough wi' them, Duncan."

"Rough with *them*?" Duncan blew a stray lock of black hair from his sparkling azure eyes. "Can ye nae see, woman? *I'm* bein' mauled, by ma own flesh and blood," he said theatrically, resuming his assault on their ribs with a mighty roar like a lion.

This time, though, Catherine detected the tiniest note of hysteria in Erinn's laughter. Duncan must have, too, for he promptly put an end to the game. "I surrender!" he conceded. "I yield to superior numbers." He stood and extracted the hangers-on one by one, giving each a hug before setting the child onto his or her feet.

Mottled and panting, the boys scampered to the chairs and settee to rest.

Aunt Brigit scooped up Nevin. "There's ma little buttercup," she cooed, tenderly cuddling the little boy to her.

Erinn made straight for Catherine's skirts and leaned against her waist. "Too bad ye didna join us, Ladykate. We had such fun."

The idea of tussling with Duncan Maxwell appealed to Catherine far more than she cared to admit.

"Really, Papa," Amber chided, above it all. "Must ye be so undignified?"

Baran said nothing, but his expression seconded his sister's criticism.

Ah, the young, Catherine thought. So harsh in judgment, yet wise in their own eyes.

Duncan shook where he stood like a great, shaggy beast, then smoothed his tousled hair with exaggerated gentility. "Some of us are not too old to make merry, Amber," he said with a sly smile as he crossed to where she was sitting. Catching her at the waist, he snatched her into the air for a twirl full-circle. " 'Twas nae so long ago, Miss Prissyface, that ye liked to tussle as well as the others."

When he set her down, Amber was smiling despite a flush of embarrassment and guilty pleasure. "Papa, I'm too old for such nonsense—old enough to marry."

"Nae, ma darlin', too young to marry yet." Duncan's wistful smile bloomed into a dazzling grin. "But grown enough to lift a foot with your *undignified* old Papa." Taking her hands, he began a lilting song in a strong baritone, leading her in a stately dance. Amber blushed happily and followed her father's steps with equal grace and poise.

The children clapped and began to sing along. Even

Aunt Brigit joined in. As with many Scottish songs, the words were dire and morbid, but the tune was sweet.

Profane songs and dancing? On the Sabbath!

Why should that surprise her, though? Duncan was a lawbreaker. Little wonder that he broke God's laws as well. But the children . . .

Cast not the splinter from thy neighbor's eye before thou removest the beam from thine own, she chided herself. She had no right to judge. She had danced and sung often enough on the Sabbath, herself. Was she any better simply because no one else knew?

No. She was worse, because she'd enjoyed it and never truly repented. Even now, her toe tapped the lively rhythm of the song, and her body longed to join the dance. So by intent, she was just as guilty of breaking the law as Duncan.

And she could not help marveling at the grace with which he led his daughter through the intricate steps. Catherine never would have imagined a man his size could be so fluid yet precise, but he was. Not to mention devastatingly handsome.

Still singing along, Cameron left his chair and swaggered up to Erinn. He bowed, then drew her into the dance. With lofty expressions, the two of them managed a reasonable approximation of the complex motions.

The patterns seemed familiar, like a dance Catherine had mastered in her youth.

She watched in astonishment when the twins straightened up in their chairs and sat like little gentlemen. As if someone had waved a magic wand, the entire family suddenly comported themselves as if they had been manorborn.

Baran approached his great-aunt. He bowed, his hand extended. "Pray, honor me with this dance, fair lady."

Aunt Brigit actually blushed! Smiling, she handed Nevin to Catherine, then curtsied gravely to Baran. "Aye, young sir." She took his hand and moved into the music with the elegance of a queen. Still, she couldn't resist firing off a smug "Uncivilized, eh?" at Catherine.

A powerful tug pulled at Catherine to join them. She'd already sinned by intent, and sin was sin. In for a penny, in for a pound. So she extended Nevin's stubby little hand in her own and joined the couples on the rug.

How long had it been since she'd danced? Longer than she'd realized. It had been years since she'd retreated to widow's corner at festivities back home. Long, lonely years since suitor after suitor had sought her hand only to forsake her after seeing how plain she was.

Even now after she had put her girlhood dreams to rest, the pain of those rejections throbbed dull inside her, but she steadfastly ignored it for the pleasure of the moment.

She rubbed noses with her little partner. "May God forgive us all, we're dancing now."

Nevin rewarded her with a welcome "Huh, huh, huh," prompting even Baran to grant them a smile.

Amber drew her attention with a melodious laugh. Catherine turned, smiling, to find Duncan Maxwell peering at her in the same odd way he had before. A self-conscious flush betrayed her, but she refused to allow him the satisfaction of knowing how he'd rattled her.

Never mind, she told herself. Angus Maxwell would send her letter, and she would be shed of Duncan Maxwell soon enough—and the inappropriate feelings he stirred within her. She would make it back to River House and never leave again.

Buoyed by that hope and the magic of the music, she forced herself to relax and enjoy the movement and the feel of precious Nevin in her arms. It was the happiest she could remember being in a long, long time.

Dancing closer, Amber whispered something to her father, whereupon Duncan glanced at Catherine, but made no reply.

Amber . . . what are you up to?

When Amber whispered again, Duncan sighed in resignation, then steered her straight for Catherine.

"Change-about," Amber called as they reached her,

pulling free of Duncan to whisk Nevin from Catherine's arms.

Before Catherine could protest, Baran and Cameron had swapped partners, too, and Duncan Maxwell drew her to his side with practiced assurance, his large, capable hands warm on her skin. Still singing, he leveled a beckoning gaze to hers, sending a jolt of physical awareness through her. They'd been far closer when he'd carried her, yet she suddenly felt as ill at ease as a callow girl.

Aunt Brigit and the others kept up the song, but Duncan stopped singing and looked into her eyes. "Relax, Kate," he murmured. "I doona plan to bite ye."

"Lions bite," she said crisply. He was easy to dance with, she had to give him that. For some odd reason, they seemed to fit, and the touch of his hand on hers sent tingles through her whole body.

Which signified nothing. She was going back to River House as soon as her stepfather could muster the warden.

"I'm nae a lion." A smile crinkled the corners of Duncan's deep blue eyes. "Just a man."

Which man? she wondered. The devoted father or the ruthless outlaw?

Both, an inner wisdom guided. *They're two sides to the same coin, and both sides spend.*

He twirled her into the next move and stepped in close behind her. The heat from his long, hard torso warmed her back, and his hands tightened on hers.

What would it feel like to have those hands caress her body? she wondered perversely. Would it be like her dreams?

The images that notion spawned set loose an exquisite flood of yearning within her, so strong she faltered in her steps.

She pulled away from Duncan. "The children must be starving. I should go help Lucas ready supper."

There was that flicker of regret again, just like before. "As ye wish." Duncan nodded. "Go hide behind yer pots then, Ladykate." She felt stripped naked when his hungry gaze met hers. "But I'll still be here when your chores are done. And I'll still be just a man."

That was the trouble, Catherine thought as she hastened to the safety of the kitchen. Duncan Maxwell was a man, all right—too much of one.

Chapter
NINE

Catherine did her best to avoid Duncan in the week that followed. The sinful desires of her dreams had bled into her waking hours. Now all it took was the sight of him to feed her growing attraction to her captor. Yet she fought to remain aloof. It wasn't easy; he kept turning up, and he'd been more than charming all week. But Catherine knew he was only trying to coax her identity from her. Still, it was only her hope of deliverance that gave her the ability to resist.

So far.

Every day, she prayed fervently for strength to win this battle with her flesh. And just as fervently, she prayed that Angus Maxwell would send her letter.

She awakened long before sunrise on Sunday, too anxious to go back to sleep. She would see the minister today. Would he tell her his decision?

Catherine pushed back the covers and sat up. Brrrr. Though the days were still warm, the late September nights had grown chill. Rubbing her arms through the coarse nightgown they'd given her, she relieved herself in the chamber pot, then hastened to dress. Still shivering when she was clothed, she drew one of her woolen blankets around her shoulders for a shawl, then loosed her long braid and brushed her hair free, thankful for the curtain of warmth it provided her back. She yawned with a satisfying stretch.

Might as well get breakfast started for Lucas. Careful of her steps, she crept into the hallway to find the rest of the house still silent.

Good. She would have a few peaceful moments to say her prayers by the warmth of the cook fire. She tiptoed past the other bedrooms and descended the stairs with a minimum of squeaks and creaks.

Seated at the worktable in the kitchen, Duncan heard someone approaching and wondered who he'd wakened. Last night he'd slept only fitfully, deviled by the prospect of facing his cousin and the congregation. He'd finally given up and dressed, then rummaged the darkened kitchen for a quaich of beer and the stale bannock he now nibbled.

Memories of the last time he'd been to kirk dimmed his appetite. He'd lost his temper completely that dark day, but Angus Maxwell had bowed to the will of his congregation and refused to allow poor Aselma Christian burial. That had grieved Duncan almost as much as losing his emotionally fragile wife.

And now, thanks to his rash vow a week ago, Duncan was obliged to do what he'd never intended to do again: go back to church with Angus Maxwell still in the pulpit.

Vows. Why did he make them? They always caused him trouble, especially where Kate was concerned.

Quiet footsteps preceded the creak of the opening door.

Speak of the devil. It was Kate.

Her hair unbound in a dark curtain down her back, she clutched a blanket around her shoulders and made straight for the fireplace. A few weeks of good, plain food had eased the sharpness from her sturdy frame. Her figure had softened to that of a woman instead of a rawboned lad.

Duncan decided to wait and see how long it would take her to discover she wasn't alone. He watched as she knelt at the hearth and stirred the ashes. In the darkness, the resurrected embers bathed her strong profile with a ruby glow and highlighted the thick waves of her hair.

Beautiful hair. Thick, shiny, and lustrous, it cascaded to the floor as she knelt. He wondered if it felt as soft and silky as it looked.

She added a few small faggots of straw to the embers, then fed twigs into the growing flame until the fire sprang to life. Her movements slow and graceful, she carefully arranged peat and charcoal to complete the fire. Then she sat back on her haunches, hands extended toward the coals to warm herself, a faraway look on her face.

No longer was she the bossy spinster. In this most private moment of vulnerability, she looked like a wistful young girl. A single tear caught the light as it coursed down her cheek.

Suddenly Duncan felt like the basest spy. But just when he opened his mouth to tell her he was there, she folded her hands and closed her eyes.

"Dear Lord," she said aloud, "I confess the sinful urges Duncan Maxwell has aroused in me—"

Sinful urges!

So his efforts had been successful after all. Yet Duncan felt no sense of triumph, only embarrassment to be eavesdropping on her prayer.

"—and I humbly beg You to cleanse those urges from my body, soul, and spirit." Kate's troubled frown eased. "Please send legions of angels to keep everyone at Annanlea safe and protect us as we travel to and from Your house." She smiled. "And I pray again Your blessings on darling Nevin. He is Yours and always will be. Please keep him safe and well, so that we who love him may continue to enjoy the gift of his innocence."

Duncan squirmed. A cynical inner voice told him that she knew he was there and was saying these things aloud for his benefit, but the better part of him suspected she wasn't. He knew he shouldn't be hearing this, yet he was touched by her concern for his child. And fascinated by this glimpse into Kate's hidden heart.

He listened to her pray with insight and compassion for Erinn—and her cats—and Cameron, and the twins, then Amber and Aunt Brigit.

By that time, Duncan was so chastened he'd resolved to spare Kate's dignity by slipping away before she finished. He eased himself from the stool and tiptoed toward the service hall.

"And Lord," Kate prayed with heightened urgency.

"Baran especially needs Your spiritual guidance and protection. He's trying so hard to come into his manhood. It's only natural that he wants to be like his father, but Duncan Maxwell is hardly a fit example." Duncan stopped in his tracks. "I pray that the power of Your Holy Spirit would break the curse of the generations and reveal a better way to live, before Baran is corrupted—"

He pivoted, appalled. "Corrupted?" The single word resounded off the brick and stone.

Kate shot to her feet and whirled to face him in horror. "Gremlins and grindstones! Where did *you* come from?"

"I was here when ye came, Miss High and Holy!" Outrage hammered just below his ears with every step as he closed the distance between them.

She stiffened. "How much did you hear?"

"From the beginnin'."

The color ebbed from her face.

"I heard ye curse Baran for things he didna do," Duncan went on. "Curse of the generations, indeed . . . And I heard ye call me a bad example."

As seemed her wont when she was cornered, Kate went on the offensive. "Ye *are* a bad example, man!" she rolled out in her unwitting brogue. "I've heard the tales of yer raidin' and yer murderous ways. Ye canna deny it!"

Her accent was so ridiculously authentic, and she so unaware, he almost laughed. Almost. "Most of those tales ye heard are just that," he shot back, "mere tales. If ye want the truth, then here it is: I'm a man of ma word. How many can ye say that of?" Why was he defending himself? He wanted to stop, but the words flooded out unbidden. "Before God, I have never killed a soul without good cause. Nor have I taken food from another's mouth to feed any of ma own, but that may have to change, for I willna stand by and watch ma people starve because someone stole from me."

Kate remained skeptical.

"I have nae shame for what I've done," he went on, "and what I must do yet to protect ma kin and those who depend upon me." Frustrated by her lack of response, he deliberately crowded her back toward the fireplace.

Instead of being intimidated, Kate shoved hard against him in an ineffectual bid to gain ground. "Oh, you're shameless, all right," she spat out. "And heartless, for holding me hostage."

Far too conscious of the feel of her body against his, he struggled to maintain his righteous anger. "I doona ken where ye come from, Kate, for ye havena deigned to tell me. But clearly, it canna be near here."

"What does that have to do with anything?" Kate's eyes reflected consternation at their proximity, yet she refused to give an inch.

Duncan's body responded all too eagerly. "Ye doona ken what it takes to survive here, woman," he snapped. "Ma sons will learn from me how to stay alive! And how to care for those who depend on them. If ye think that's a bad example, ye self-righteous codfish, then so be it. 'Tis nae a curse. 'Tis the only way to survive amid the chaos that surrounds us here—a chaos I didna cause and canna cure."

Why did she have to smell and feel so . . . so like a woman?

He could see she'd taken his point, but her nature forbade her from admitting it. "What sort of man would eavesdrop on a person's *prayers*?" she parried.

" 'Tis ma house, woman!" he said, indignant. "I've a right to be where I choose in it. If ye wanted privacy, why didna ye say your prayers in your room?"

She wavered, but her brown eyes still blazed up at him with fire. "You should have made your presence known, sirrah."

"Verra well." Giving in to his own "sinful urges," he grasped her upper arms and drew her even tighter against him. "I'll make it known right now." He kissed those stubborn lips and pressed his aching member hard against the resistance of her belly.

Kate fought back only briefly. Then her hands splayed

on his upper arms and her mouth went supple. She tasted like a woman ripe and full when his tongue met with hers in hungry exploration. His hands slid through the silken thickness of her hair to caress her body.

Duncan had the oddest sensation, as if he were falling inward on himself. He ran his hands down the long, pleasing curve of her back, then cupped her buttocks. So soft, yet resilient beneath her skirt. And all the while, the pressure of her pelvis sent waves of exquisite agony radiating from his swollen manhood. Growing hunger drove him to deepen their kiss and embrace.

With a shudder of surrender, Kate's body melted to his, almost sending him beyond the brink.

What was happening? Duncan had bedded four wives and his share of willing wenches in between, but nothing like this, ever. He wanted to devour Kate, possess her wholly. Consumed by passion, he hiked her skirted legs around his hips. Now only a few layers of fabric and leather separated her sex from his aching member.

God, it had been so long. Nae, it had never been like this.

Her "sinful urges" getting the best of her at last, Kate moaned beneath his lips and writhed against his erection, her fingers threading into his hair to draw him closer.

An overpowering urge assailed him to snatch aside her skirts and find release inside her, but a whisper of reason pulled him back. *Stop! Think!*

What was he doing? Contrary to Kate's assessment of him, he had his scruples. He would never take advantage of a maiden, even one as old as Kate. But the taste and feel of her drove him almost beyond reason. He wanted her.

Bewitched, by Plain Kate.

But the moment he slid his hands up her legs, the door squeaked loudly open. "Hazelnuts and whoremongers!" Aunt Brigit roared from somewhere beyond the haze of lust that surrounded them. "What in purple perdition is goin' on here?"

Her voice hit Duncan like a pail of icy water. He wrenched his lips from Kate's, hastily lowering her to her feet. But when he felt her sag, he caught her up against his side, inadvertently revealing the formidable proportions of the bulge at his crotch to Aunt Brigit's disgusted perusal.

For the first time since she'd abandoned her silence, Kate seemed at a loss for words. She flushed crimson, tugging to straighten her clothes, but said nothing.

"I asked ye a question, lad," Aunt Brigit demanded. "What mischief is this?"

Mischief? His manhood throbbing, Duncan rounded on his aunt. "I canna see how it's any of your business, Bink."

"Aye, and 'tis, when it's smack in the middle of the kitchen!" she shot back. "Duncan Maxwell, have ye nae sense of shame?"

"I don't think he does," Kate volunteered, reverting to her usual ramrod posture. "We settled that earlier."

Aunt Brigit laid two firm fingers across her lips to stop the smile that threatened to escape.

Kate had been as drunk as an otter in a barrel of beer from acting on her "sinful urges," but now she recovered her customary primness. "Goose feathers," she moaned into her hands. "What have I done?"

"There, there," Aunt Brigit soothed. "We caught it just in time. Nae harm done, lass." She glared at Duncan in reproof. "Kate is nae some wanton to be dallied with. She's a virgin, an innocent."

"It was just a kiss," he shot back. "As ye said, nae harm done." *Nae thanks to ye,* his conscience chided him.

A shard of lingering passion sang through him. "She didna seem to mind, Aunt Brigit. 'Twas just a kiss." He grinned at his aunt. "Have ye never shared a kiss with a man?"

"Nae like *that,* I havena," she retorted. "I may be auld, but I'm nae naïve. That was more than a kiss. Admit it.

Ye ken as well as I what would've happened if I hadna interrupted when I did. The poor lass—"

"I am not a poor lass," Kate snapped. "I'm a grown woman, fully capable of taking responsibility for my actions." Back to her old, abrasive self. "Pray excuse me. I must go and dress my hair." She shot Duncan a frosty look. "Rest assured, my lapse will not be repeated."

She nodded briskly to Aunt Brigit. "I'll be down to help with breakfast anon. I implore you to forget what you saw. I shall." Head high, she sailed from the room.

Aunt Brigit turned to Duncan after she was gone. "She's quite a woman, Duncan. I warn ye, doona toy with her." A shadow of long-past hurt dimmed her gray eyes. "Kate's too fine to be used by any man. Underneath her crusty ways, the lass has a heart as big as a house. I remember when I was . . ." Her vision glazed, but she quickly came back to herself. "Doona steal her innocence, lad. 'Tis all she has left. Trust me, I ken too well."

Chastened, Duncan nodded. "Aye." He'd only been seven or eight when Aunt Brigit had staged her last, desperate campaign for the right to marry, yet he could still remember her hoarse pleas and bitter tears, and his mother's. And the hateful coldness with which his grandsire had refused to part with her dowry.

Little wonder Aunt Brigit felt compassion for Kate.

The truth was, Duncan felt compassion for her, too. And admiration for her courage.

And undeniable, unexplainable desire for her body. A desire that could lead them both only to disaster.

He sighed heavily. "If Kate would only tell me who she is, I could send her back to her family."

His aunt unhooked the porrich pot and set it on the table. "She says her family has nae funds to ransom her."

"And ye believe her?" Duncan picked up the heavy milk pitcher, removed its cloth cover, then poured the pot three-quarters full.

"Aye." Aunt Brigit bent almost double in the oat bin to fill a bowl full. Almost empty, Duncan noted with a sick sense in the pit of his gut. Bink continued when she came back up. "I see truth in her eyes when she speaks it. But there's somethin' she hasna told us. I can sense it in her."

She dumped the oats into the pot, added salt, then gave them a stir. "I've come to wonder if Kate doesna want to be sent home."

"Well, she surely doesna want to stay here." He picked up the filled kettle and carried it to its hook at the fire. "She's made nae bones about her disdain for Annanlea, and us."

"Not us, Duncan," his aunt corrected. "*Ye.* But judgin' from her state when I walked in, she may have changed her mind."

"May have?" Of course she had, his pride told him.

"So certain, are ye?" Too perceptive, Aunt Brigit pinned him with a pointed stare. "Have ye changed yer mind about her, then?"

"Nae," he said a few heartbeats too late to be convincing. "She's still a crowin' hen and a bluidy nuisance." Aunt Brigit scowled as she stirred the porrich, prompting him to add, "She's earned her keep, I'll give her that. It's done me good to see the help she's given ye."

"Hardest worker I've ever kent," his aunt declared. "And precious good with the little ones. Even with Amber."

Duncan remembered the look on Kate's face as she'd prayed for his children one by one. "Aye, she loves them. And they love her." Even Baran, he suspected.

His aunt softened. "For both yer sakes, Duncan, keep yer distance. What if she should get a child? Remember yer blessed mother's humiliation, and yours. Would ye sentence Kate to that, or the child?"

Aunt Brigit had raised the one objection he could not dismiss. It resurrected a stab of bitterness and his hatred for his English father. "Nae." Nary a woman deserved to be punished forever for a single mistake. And no innocent child deserved to carry the shame he'd borne for a life-time.

Suddenly weary, he looked up to see the first rays of dawn illuminate the rafters. "I'll go rouse the children." Duncan headed for the stairs, but paused in the doorway. "Will ye be goin' with us to kirk then, Aunt Brigit?"

His aunt bristled like a hedgehog. "Ma shift will sprout diamonds and rubies before I sit under the preachin' of that heartless hypocrite."

Duncan chuckled. "Down, woman; I only asked." It was good to see her back to normal.

Whether he would ever be back to normal, Duncan couldn't say. Not until Kate was long gone, and maybe not even then.

Blast her. How had she managed to bewitch him?

Chapter

TEN

Two hours later, Catherine shepherded the children toward the front door where the coach was waiting. Bright sunshine had burned away the morning's chill and fog, presenting them with a fine, golden day for their trip to church. "Come along. We don't want to be late for worship. That would just give everyone good reason to stare at us."

Baran glanced back from the threshold. "It doesna matter, Ladykate," he said without rancor. "They always stare anyway."

So much for her theories about reasoning with children to get them to behave properly. It did no good if they reasoned back better than she, as Duncan's children often did.

Erinn, Nevin, and Cameron lagged behind as usual, but today even they were ahead of Amber.

Concerned, Catherine waited for her. "What's the matter, child?" she asked gently. "You seem even more reluctant to go than you were last week."

Smoothing self-consciously at her patched skirts, Amber turned troubled eyes to her. "Did ye mean it when you promised to make me a new dress?"

"Yes." Catherine circled the teenager's sagging shoulders with a consoling arm. So that was it. Amber was ashamed of her clothes.

How many lovely gowns Catherine had taken for granted at Amber's age. Papa had seen to it that she never lacked for anything, even after her mother's death. But Papa had had only the business and their family to worry about. Duncan and Aunt Brigit had far more pressing concerns than new clothes to preoccupy them. "I'll make you a new dress as soon as God provides some fabric." She leaned close to Amber's ear. "But until then, wear your clothes as if they were the finest raiments in God's good earth. Then no one will notice your patches. They will see only your pride.

"Look at me." With a rueful smile, she drew back the shawl she was wearing to expose her own too-short sleeves and hem. "How easy do you think it's been to walk around with my wrists and ankles hanging out? And my shift."

Gratitude erased the shame from Amber's face. "Thank ye, Ladykate." She stood straight and proud as she climbed into the coach behind the others.

Thurlow offered his hand to help Catherine board. "Ah. Saved the best for last," the Englishman said with a shy smile.

"Thank you, Thurlow." Catherine took great comfort from the familiar accent of his speech, but a shock was waiting for her inside the compartment. "Duncan." She almost fell back out the door. The Scotsman's dominating presence filled the large coach, his long legs aslant across the floorboards. Wedged into the far corner of the floor, Clyde wagged his tail as best he could and let out a happy bark.

"Oh, no. Not the beast, as well."

Duncan caught her hand and drew her in. "Glad to see ye, too, Kate."

The warm strength of his flesh against hers sparked a humiliating jolt of unbidden desire. And on the *Sabbath*.

Dear heaven. After this morning, how could she possibly endure being shut up so close to him all day? She could almost hear the pulsing attraction that thrummed through his touch.

She snatched back her hand.

Lord, I'm trying to resist, but my body betrays me.

Pitchforks and panderers! That one fatal kiss had done this. She never should have given in. Now that she'd sampled real passion, her body wanted nothing else.

Oh, *why* did her fool cheeks insist on going hot?

"Papa," the twins asked as one. "May we ride with Rory?"

"Me, too," Cameron added.

"Aye. But only if ye behave."

The boys scrambled up to sit with the driver.

Catherine barely heard the coach door close and latch behind her. Squeezing onto the seat as far away from Duncan as possible, she was grateful for the distraction provided by the remaining children.

Duncan relaxed in his corner, watching her like a hawk.

She tried her best to seem unconcerned. "What made you decide to come along? You said nothing about it at breakfast." Despite her efforts to the contrary, her words came out sounding like an accusation.

"I'm simply going to kirk," he said with an enigmatic smile. "And ye were right. We shall be late unless Rory can make up the time." He pounded the ceiling with his fist, and the coach jostled into motion.

Eager for the outing, Erinn peered out the windows and chattered in excitement, but Amber and Baran—old enough to sense the tension between the adults—surreptitiously watched every move Catherine and their father made.

"Ye asked me why I came." Duncan granted her a lazy, rakish smile. "I decided it would be best to go along. To keep an eye on things." He put a subtle emphasis on the last.

An eye on things? Kate went still.

Could he possibly suspect her of plotting with the minister?

But how? Why?

Had Angus Maxwell betrayed her?

Surely not. Catherine's instincts said no, but was that merely wishful thinking? Blood was thicker than water in these parts. And she was, after all, an "Englisher."

Even if the minister hadn't betrayed her, how could she possibly steal even a few moments alone with him without arousing Duncan's suspicions? With her captor "keeping an eye on things," she feared last Sunday's private conversation with Angus Maxwell might end up being her only one.

And her plans . . . The two rubies she'd carefully freed from her shift and hidden in her bodice now grew hot against her skin. She had planned—if Angus Maxwell had sent her letter—to enlist his help in trading the jewels for ransom silver, and supplies for Annanlea and the needy of the parish. But Duncan's presence made that far too dangerous.

Or did it?

Surely God did not want the children to go hungry, or her to remain a prisoner.

Since she'd surrendered River House and all its lands to her stepfamily, her mother's jewels were all Catherine had left in the world. She had no intention of allowing an outlaw like Duncan Maxwell to rob her of that legacy. He would do it, too, without compunction, for even by his self-professed code of conduct, he wouldn't be taking food from her mouth. Just her future and her independence.

Well, she wouldn't let him.

Catherine drew Erinn into her lap. "Have I told you the story of Sleeping Beauty? It's a beautiful tale brought from France by my Norman ancestors."

Erinn frowned. "Who's Norman?"

"Dear me, I can see we need a history lesson." Catherine gave her a hug. "But no history lessons today. Instead, I have a magical tale to tell of Sleeping Beauty."

Duncan Maxwell pinned her with a piercing stare as she began the ancient story. "Once upon a time . . ."

This was going to be a long day. A very long day.

A single consolation occurred to her.

Catherine paused in her story and granted Duncan her own smug smile.

At least she would be there to witness the reaction when Duncan Maxwell returned to church. For all she knew, the congregation would take it as a sign of the End Times and repent en masse.

Duncan exited the coach and was gratified to see that the kirk doors were still open. Not, as Baran had said, that it made any difference. He would still have to run the gauntlet.

Being a bastard was good for one thing, at least. It had taught Duncan to hold on to both his dignity and his temper when he faced the scorn of others. So when he marched his brood up to the kirk, it was not as a prodigal, but as David, triumphant, returning to Jerusalem.

When they reached the open doors, Kate leaned over and murmured dryly, "You know, Duncan, your presence here today might spawn a great revival."

He almost chuckled, but he refused to give her the satisfaction of knowing how much he enjoyed her acerbic wit. Instead, he took her arm and escorted her into the kirk.

Sure enough, jaws dropped, and three people sank to their knees in amazement as he led his family to their pew at the front. A startled hum prompted the presiding elder to stamp his staff three times for silence, but even that could not quell the whispered speculation.

At least Angus Maxwell had the good grace not to make a fuss. As he stood to begin the service, the minister nodded with pleased acknowledgment, but to Duncan's relief did not single him out for comment or condemnation.

That was one less hedge to jump. Duncan allowed himself to relax a bit.

Ye can do this, and with dignity, he told himself. *Just get through the service and afterward, then the catechism lesson, then the leaving.*

He managed fine until Nevin passed wind so loud it could be heard in the last row, and the boys—even Baran—wriggled in mock suffocation from the fumes.

Duncan could have stilled them with a word or a touch,

but pride prevented him from correcting his own in front
of these sanctimonious hypocrites.

At the subtle disturbance, the elder wavered, staff in
hand. Duty bade him to reprimand the offending children
with a public prod, but Duncan's presence—and his un-
resolved conflict with the church—kept him planted
firmly where he stood. With a nervous cough, he directed
his attention sharply to Angus Maxwell, who continued
with his opening remarks as if nothing had transpired.

"Phew." Erinn waved a hand in front of her face, yet
maintained her bewildered decorum while Amber wilted
in shame.

Kate was the exception. Though her face contorted to
keep from smiling, she glanced to Duncan in question,
clearly expecting him to discipline his children.

Suddenly defensive, he stilled each lad with a touch.
Then he did his best to concentrate on the service. It had
been a long time since he had sought God's presence. He
decided this was as good a time as any to make a new
start with his Creator.

But when Duncan opened his eyes after the general
confession, Gordon and Kerry were missing. Alarmed and
annoyed in equal measure, he craned about for sign of
them. They popped up like woodchucks in an empty sec-
tion of the pew three rows back.

The little devils! Still up to the same tricks they'd per-
petrated as four-year-olds. Only now did Duncan remember that he and Aselma had been forced to separate and
lay hold to the twins to prevent just this from happening.

When he got his hands on them . . .

Visibly alarmed to have been discovered, the two boys
dropped from sight as if they'd fallen into a hole. Then,
after surprisingly little scuffling, they reappeared even farther back, closer to the doors and escape.

Duncan had no intention of humiliating himself by rising from his seat to deal with this. Teeth clenched in fury,
he aimed a commanding stare at the elder and willed him

to look his way. The man was actually trembling, his gaze fixed on the minister in silent desperation.

Ordinarily Duncan would have been pleased to know his mere presence could provoke such fear, but now, he just wanted the blasted elder to look at him. Frustrated, he scowled up at Angus, then cut his eyes toward the elder. Angus took his meaning and relayed the gesture.

As if he'd been commanded to face the devil himself, the poor elder dared to look Duncan's way.

At last. Duncan nodded, then cocked his head toward his errant sons.

Permission granted, the man hastened to the back of the kirk and captured the two escapees by their worn collars, then delivered them to their father. It was the twins' turn to tremble now.

Though the entire congregation watched every move in breathless anticipation, Angus Maxwell continued the service without missing a beat.

Duncan simply pointed to the pew on either side of him, and the boys sat, humbled and quaking. Catching a glimpse of Kate, Duncan was appalled to discover her watching him through welling tears of amusement, her lips curled into a tortured line to preserve propriety.

Fry his liver for bacon if she wasn't enjoying this! Why, he couldn't imagine. Yet there she sat, making merry at his expense.

That, more than anything, threatened his self-control. Duncan jerked his chin to ease the growing tightness of his collar and did his best to focus on the sermon Angus Maxwell had just begun.

In a heated message about the persecutions of the early church, the minister's deep voice rose by degrees until it boomed across the little church. The meek cowered, and the dourest of the elders nodded in agreement, adding their somber *ayes* and *amens* with every rising indictment.

Nevin, however, did not approve.

Disturbed by the tone and timbre, he squirmed in Kate's arms and pressed his palms against his ears. She struggled to calm him, but in a rare display of pique, he buried his head under her arm and continued to wriggle and grunt in displeasure.

Nevin reached the end of his limited endurance just as the sermon came to a crescendo. Hair askew, he emerged from neath Kate's arm and turned toward the pulpit. "Ouch!" he shouted louder than he'd ever said anything in his entire young life. "Doona say dat words! Dey hurts ma ears, auld man!"

Angus Maxwell halted, dumbstruck, in mid-gesture.

Kate and the rest of his children froze, then looked aslant to Duncan in wide-eyed dread.

In the deafening silence that followed, Duncan wished the floor would open up and swallow him, but he calmly took his son from Kate's arms and held him close. Only then did he glance through the appalled assembly. "Ach, he only said what half o' ye were thinkin." Dandling his son, he turned back to the minister. "I never thought I'd see the day when a mere bairn could silence the likes of Angus Maxwell."

The minister let out a bark of surprised laughter that loosed a cleansing tide of good humor throughout the congregation—excepting, of course, the inevitable handful of raisin-faces who considered it sacrilege even to smile in the Lord's house.

For some reason, the laughter narrowed the gap between Duncan and the others, perhaps because they were laughing with him, instead of at him.

"Ah, Duncan," his cousin Angus said with a grin. "What a gift your honesty is to our assembly."

"Carry on, man," Duncan urged, fondly patting Nevin. Only then did he note that Kate was staring at him as if he had just materialized out of thin air.

What had she seen in him that had caused the wonder in her face?

And why did he care so much that the wonder was there?

Before he could address the question, his forearm

bloomed with warmth and wetness under Nevin's bottom.

Perfect.

Duncan extended the toddler out over the stone floor where Nevin finished with a beatific smile of satisfaction on his little face.

Now he remembered why he hadn't been to church in two years. It wasna just his feud with Angus Maxwell and the elders.

Catherine yawned contentedly in the shade of the giant oak beside the parsonage. The minister and his wife had returned to the house, ostensibly to prepare for the catechism lesson, but Catherine suspected they'd wanted to allow the family a private interlude.

Even Quinn and Rory and Thurlow had retreated to stand sentry at a discreet distance.

Seated on a springy pillow of moss, Duncan lazed against the tree trunk, his black hair in stark contrast to the gray bark. Looking at him, she was overtaken yet again by that same nagging sense of familiarity, as if she had seen him somewhere in the past, but banished the notion in favor of enjoying the domestic tableau he now presented.

Erinn and Nevin slept curled against their father, heads in his lap, with Clyde sound asleep beside his master's long, muscular legs. Cameron snored stretched out on the moss, while Baran and Amber returned the last of the lunch things to the basket.

Duncan yawned. "I havena felt so peaceful since . . ." He closed his eyes. "Since . . . I canna remember."

Catherine could have said the same. It was peaceful here. And it felt safe, removed from the dangers that surrounded them. She glanced across the yard, checking on the twins, and found them moping at opposite sides of the clearing, forbidden each other's company or conversation for the rest of the day for their antics in church.

Catherine had feared Duncan would beat the little boys. Most fathers would have, long and hard. But Duncan's choice of discipline had impressed her deeply as not only wise and merciful, but also effective. Judging from the twins' exaggerated misery, they'd have preferred a beating to prolonged separation.

Remembering the chain of calamities, she allowed herself the chuckle she'd had to suppress in church. Duncan Maxwell had conducted himself in church with forbearance, dignity, admirable fatherly devotion, and best of all, redeeming humor.

The Black Bastard and Duncan Maxwell might share that magnificent body, but Catherine's healthy instincts for self-preservation warned her never to forget the dangerous side of the man who now seemed so appealing.

The Maxwells emerged from the house and strolled over arm in arm. When they reached the shade, Sarah proposed softly, " 'Tis such a lovely day, Duncan. Would ye have any objections if I took over Amber and Baran's catechism lesson?" She patted her husband's arm. "Angus has been cooped up all week working on his sermon. I was hoping he might take a stroll in the orchards with ye and Catherine. He's off for Glasgow this week, so I think he could benefit from stretching his legs."

"Mmm." Duncan's lids bobbed like apples in a stream. "Fine with me, Cousin Sarah, but if it's all the same, I'd rather sleep than walk. Kate can go with him if she wishes."

Catherine couldn't believe her ears. She'd given up completely on being able to speak in confidence with Angus, and now Duncan himself had provided her the perfect opportunity. Heart pounding, she rose. "I'd be delighted." She took the pastor's arm, then forced a measured pace and prayed no one would notice her agitation.

Step by endless step, they strolled across the meadow, the sun warm on her hair and the comforting sound of crickets all around them. She dared not look back. Only a little farther, she told herself again and again, just to be certain they were well out of visual range before she dared to speak. Finally, she judged it safe. "Reverend Maxwell,

I do not wish to pressure you, but I must ask—"

"Think nothing of it, child," The minister's blue eyes twinkled—eyes similar to Duncan's, but not as arresting. "Why do ye think Sarah and I arranged this stroll?"

"Arranged this?" Catherine didn't understand. "But how could you possibly have—"

"Today is not the first time Duncan Maxwell has settled down for a nice, long Sabbath nap under that oak tree. And God willing, it willna be the last. I've invited him for many a stroll, ma dear, but he's yet to prefer a walk to his nap. Predictable as clockwork."

She regarded her host with a new appreciation. "Why, Reverend Maxwell," she rolled out in roughened Scottish tones, "ye sly auld fox."

He cocked his head in surprise. "Doona be tellin' me now, lass, that ye're really Scottish."

"Nay." Embarrassment tingled through her. "Just a foolish mimic."

"That's a relief. I doona think I could handle any further complications."

Catherine couldn't hold back her question a second longer. "My letter? Have you reached a decision?"

"Aye." He stopped to face her. "I rode it to Dumfries maself on Wednesday and sent it along to England with a trusted friend in the clergy. He'll see it well delivered."

Overwhelmed by relief and gratitude, Catherine sank to her knees and allowed her tears to come at last.

"Here, here. Get up, child." Angus drew her to her feet. "What if someone should see ye thus?"

"Forgive me." Brushing away her tears, she forced herself to rise and keep on walking. "I just . . . you cannot know how deeply I—"

"I simply did as God instructed," he demurred. "Both Sarah and I were strongly led to help ye."

Sarah, too. God bless them both. She'd been right about them after all.

Catherine was so happy she hugged herself. But when

she did, her arm detected the resistance of the two jewels tucked against the side of her breast.

The rubies. Did she dare to ask . . . ?

Did she dare not to? He was going to Glasgow next week. How perfect was that?

"Reverend Maxwell, there's something else . . ."

He halted, his kind face wary. "And what precisely would that be?"

"I need silver for my ransom. And Annanlea needs food and cloth and supplies for the winter." Catherine plunged her hand into her bodice to retrieve the rubies hidden there. "These are all I have," she lied, "but—"

Angus Maxwell drew back in horror as if he might expire on the spot.

"Oh! Forgive me. It's not what you think" She turned her back and located the jewels, then pivoted. "Please forgive me. I've kept them hidden . . ."

Ruddy as a milkmaid, the minister raised a staying hand. "Ye needna say where. I saw where plain enough." He mopped his forehead with a rumpled linen square. When he'd recovered a bit, he ventured, "Kept what hidden?"

Catherine opened her palm to reveal the two large, rectangular rubies. Reflecting the strong autumn sunlight, they glistened like the very blood of Christ.

Angus Maxwell gaped. "Where did *those* come from?"

Glancing nervously to the surrounding rows of trees, she closed her fingers. "They were my mother's, now mine. All I have in the world."

Lying to a man of God. On the Sabbath! And after he helped you, and the Good Lord allowed your letter to be sent!

She would roast in hell, no doubt about it. But she might, just might, get to go home before she did. Catherine was more than willing to take the risk.

"You said this afternoon that you'll be attending the regional assembly in Glasgow next week." She pressed the stones into his hand, then closed hers over it. "Please take these with you. Surely there is someone there who will buy them for silver." She searched his eyes for some sign he might agree. "Keep half of whatever they bring for food and supplies—not just for Annanlea, but for the poor of the parish." She withdrew her hands. "I ask only half for my ransom. If Duncan demands less than that, I'll gladly donate the rest." She leveled her gaze to his. "As God is my witness, my family has no silver to redeem me. This is my only hope."

That much, at least, was true.

"Surely Duncan would accept just one of these as ample ransom," the minister argued. "Why give them both to me? Do ye ken how perilous such a thing would be, not just for me, but for Sarah. Duncan—"

"Duncan Maxwell must not know about these jewels." Catherine had to make him understand. "He's desperate since his salt was stolen, and desperate men do hateful things. Can you be so sure he wouldn't simply take my jewels and still demand a ransom from my family?"

"Nae." Angus's shaggy white brows drew together. "But I doona think he would. Duncan's nae like the others. Even when we stood at odds, he conducted himself with honor. Maybe it's the hardship of his past, but he's never sunk to the level of most men in these parts."

"But can you be sure he would not take these from me and still keep me prisoner? I cannot." Worn out, she sank to the golden grass. "I want to go home. Is that so much to ask? I only want to go home."

And keep your mother's jewels.

Angus Maxwell sat beside her. When he tried to return the rubies, she refused to accept them. "Look at them," she challenged, her voice hard.

He opened his palm.

She pointed to the stones. "You're holding God's provision for all of us." It could be true. "For Annanlea. For your poor. And for me. Can you not accept it as that?"

"God's provision?" He shifted the rubies in the light.

"Or the devil's." His fingers closed and he sighed heavily. "Again, I must pray for an answer."

"And again, I shall trust your conscience and God's compassion."

If God was just, the answer would be no.

But Catherine continued to hope that He was more merciful than just. And that by some miracle, He would move Angus Maxwell to help her again.

This had been a day of miracles and unexpected joys.

What was one more miracle to God?

Three miles out from home, Duncan shifted in his seat, careful not to disturb the sleeping children in the coach. Only Amber remained awake, her head on Kate's shoulder, their fingers intertwined.

"Tell me about London again, Ladykate," she murmured wistfully.

Kate smiled. "Again? I should think you'd be tired of hearing."

After two times already today, Duncan couldn't help thinking Kate must be weary of *telling*.

"Nae." Amber stared out the window at the evening sky. "I'll never tire of hearing. Or of dreaming that one day I might see such places." Amber pulled back to regard her. "And please, doona leave anything out."

Deep affection softened Kate's features. "All right, then." She truly seemed to care for Amber, just as she did for the others.

She began the story for the third time, sparing no detail. "I was just your age. Thirteen." Word for word. Duncan smiled. How many times had Amber made her tell it before this? he wondered.

"Never in my wildest dreams had I ever imagined I might go to London, but one fine June afternoon when I was mending in the arbor, my dear, sweet Papa came to me with a big smile on his face. 'How would you like to go with me to London?' he asked."

Amber listened with rapt adoration on her young face as the story unfolded.

Seeing his daughter thus, Duncan thought back. Even as a tiny girl Amber had begged the adults, any and all, to share the tiniest details of their own small travels and excitements. She'd always been a dreamer, never content with the limited horizons of their lives. Still, he feared he was doing the lass no favors by allowing Kate to fill her head with stories far beyond the ken of ordinary people.

But the truth was, he liked to hear those stories almost as much as Amber did. Not for the exotic and colorful descriptions, but because of the way Kate told them, her voice relaxed and animated. He found it soothing. And she gave away far more about herself than she would have imagined. From the sound of it, she too had once been as dramatic, joyous, and starry-eyed as Amber.

What had happened, he wondered, to drain the life from her? It occurred to him that he probably wouldn't find out, for she would be on her way home as soon as he coaxed her identity from her.

In a flash of insight, he realized that the children might well suffer Kate's leaving as if they were losing another mother—especially Amber. And Erinn. A deep, small ache awoke inside him.

Much as her froward English ways galled him, the thought of life without Kate seemed wrong somehow.

Had it really only been weeks ago when God had literally tossed her, half-dead, into their lives?

Aye. Eight weeks.

Duncan couldn't pinpoint how it had happened, but in those short weeks, Kate had somehow gone from being a stranger, peripheral to the circle of their lives, to a steadfast anchor at the hub.

Even Baran had begun to soften to her.

And despite the inconveniences her obsessive cleaning had visited upon him, he had to admit it did him good to see the house returned to a semblance of its former grandeur. Kate had made Annanlea a home in a way none of his other wives ever had.

If it weren't for the ransom, he might even consider . . . A pungent thrust of remembered desire reminded him that such a match might have its compensations.

Duncan caught himself in mid-speculation, appalled. Kate? What in Beelzebub's hoofprints was he thinking? Must be his own blasted English blood that drew him so. She was a stranger, he reminded himself—and his body. She did not fit into his world and never could.

Flustered, he redirected his attention to her story.

When Kate described the people in the prosperous merchant districts of London, Amber interrupted at precisely the same spot she had with every telling. "Describe their clothes again. Especially the lasses ma age." Unaware she was doing it, his daughter spread her hand across a conspicuous patch on her worn skirt, and for the first time, Duncan noted how shabby her simple clothing was.

All his children's clothes were shabby, he suddenly realized. Twice turned, patched, and faded.

It did no good to question fate, but Duncan couldn't suppress the anger that rose inside him. He worked so hard to provide for those who depended on him, and for what? So he could watch them suffer hunger and humiliation?

If ye would eat, work, the Bible said. Well, he worked from dawn to dark, and so had everyone else at Annanlea, only to have the fruits of their labors stolen. Where was God's provision in that?

All God had sent him was a feisty spinster who'd been nothing but trouble!

Not all the unpleasant kind of trouble, his body reminded him.

"Ladykate," Amber said with longing in her voice after Kate had described a sumptuous meal. "Please teach me proper table manners. Our food is simple, but may we set a proper table so I can learn how decent folk eat?"

Decent folk! Duncan stiffened. "We are decent folk," he clipped out. "Doona ever doubt it." His bastardry had long since inured him to the scorn of outsiders, but his own daughter's subtle disdain stung him deeply. "What have I taught ye, lass?"

Amber rolled her eyes. "That honor isna born into us, but created one decision at a time," she recited, "and it only matters what God thinks, nae other people." Her lovely young face softened. "But Ladykate says that good manners are really about consideration. Like the Golden Rule. I want so much to learn, Papa."

Manners, indeed. Duncan's grandsire had been a man of impeccable manners, but they hadn't signified. Laird Kinnon Maxwell had never been rude or impolite, but he'd never been kind, either. And Duncan's mother, God rest her soul, had been a lady in every sense of the word, yet little good it had done her or her bastard son.

Amber turned to Kate. "Please, will ye teach me?"

Kate looked to Duncan with a compassion that nettled worse than her customary sarcasm. "I would be pleased to teach you what little I know of such things," she said to Amber. "But only with your father's permission."

"Amber, Amber." Duncan shook his head. "Your life is here with us, nae in London or Edinburgh or even Dumfries. What good will airs and affectations do ye?"

A young life's worth of secret dreams shone from her eyes. "If God is willing, I shall see Edinburgh before I die. And maybe even London. But even if I doona make it, I want at least to ken how to make things special, Papa. The way our Mimi did, your own blessed mother. Nae just for me, but for you and all the others."

"Ye do make things special, child, just by bein' who ye are." His mother had clung to the vestiges of respectability long after they had lost their meaning.

Yet how could he deny his daughter's harmless dreams? Duncan's hope had long since deserted him, but he saw it burning now in Amber's pleading face. "Verra well," he conceded. "Manners it shall be."

Kate granted him a respectful nod. There was that open, assessing look again. "Tomorrow night, then?" she asked.

"Suit yourself."

"Thank ye, Papa. Thank ye." Amber reached for his hand and gave it a squeeze. "I canna wait."

Duncan could. But then again, this just might provide an opportunity for him to show Kate he hadn't been born in a barn. As a matter of fact, he might just stand the spinster on her ear. It had been a long time, but he still kent how.

The next evening Catherine was in the kitchen ironing dry the last of the freshly washed linen napkins when Lucas approached her.

"Soup's done," the cook announced. "Will ye sample it?"

She gladly set aside the iron and crossed to the hearth. At the worktable Amber polished away on the pewter flatware they'd found with the napkins in a long-forgotten trunk.

With Lucas hovering nearby, Catherine dipped up a spoonful of the kettle's aromatic contents and blew it cool. Closing her eyes, she tasted his first attempt at her receipt. "I don't know," she said to herself as much as to the expectant cook. "Something's missing. What did I leave out?"

"And how could I be tellin' ye what's left out if *ye* didna tell *me* in the first place?" Lucas grumbled, wounded. "I browned the bones for the stock and made it as ye said. Then I cooked the onions slow in drawn butter as ye instructed, and added the roasted garlic at the last minute, along with salt and pepper."

"Mustard seed," Catherine realized aloud. "I forgot to tell you to put in the ground mustard seed." She fetched the bottle of precious seeds, crushed a judicious measure in the mortar, then added it to the soup. A taste was inconclusive. She offered Lucas a spoonful. "See if that's better."

He closed his eyes in unconscious imitation of her as he swallowed it down. Opening them again, he shrugged. "I couldna say, Nessa's Lady. It tasted fine enough the way it was."

Nessa's Lady . . . He, alone, still called her that. Catherine found it endearing.

"Amber," she called as she dipped up another spoonful of soup. "Come taste this for me, please."

Amber set aside the pewter implements and hurried over. When Catherine tipped the spoon to her mouth, the teenager sampled the broth and rolled her eyes. "It tastes divine," she gushed. "What is it?"

"Nothing fancy." Catherine stirred the rich brown broth. "Just onion soup, with a touch of roasted garlic." She smiled up at the cook. "You've done fine, Lucas. Fine indeed."

"Hmph." Flushed with pride, he returned to basting the capons on the spit.

Amber leaned close to whisper, "Lucas's onion soup never tasted like that before."

"It will from now on," Catherine whispered back. "Once he learns how to make a dish, he never forgets."

"Ye needna bother ta whisper," Lucas said equably. "I can hear every word ye say." He pointed a meaty finger at Amber, then aimed it to the floor. "I'm off to the cellar fer some wine, so ye can talk about me all ye want."

Amber had the good grace to blush as she hurried back to her task.

Catherine gathered the carrots she'd pulled and began to wash them.

"I'm almost done with the knives and forks." Amber held up a fork with pride—an implement that hadn't graced the table since Catherine had come here. "I'm so glad we found them. But I doona think Papa will want one. He does well enough with just his knife and spoon. Truth be told, I canna remember seeing Papa use a fork, even when Aselma was alive." She paused, thinking. "Or Leslie. Or Beth, for that matter."

Catherine had heard those names, but couldn't remember where. "Who are they?"

"*Were* they," Amber corrected wistfully. "Leslie was Erinn and Cameron's mother. She died tryin' to bring another sister to us. Beth was the twins' mother, used most foully and killed by Robin Johnstone. Papa took care of him," she said ominously, then reverted to her matter-of-fact account. "Peggy was my mother and Baran's. She was the first, of the Bonshaw Carruthers. Died of measles when I was six, along with two of our little brothers."

Catherine sighed at the sad account. As with most families, life and death lived hand in hand.

"Aselma was the last wife; she gave us precious Nevin." Amber shook her head. "Poor Aselma. Papa was so unhappy when she . . ." She stopped short, catching herself, making Catherine more suspicious than ever that Aselma's death hadn't been an accident. Amber met Catherine's curious gaze with one of resignation. "We loved our mothers well, all of them." The pain of loss aged her lovely young face. "But they died. 'Tis the curse of Annanlea: our mothers die. Even Papa's."

"Do you remember your papa's mother?" Catherine was bold to ask, wondering what kind of woman had spawned a handsome rogue the likes of Duncan Maxwell.

"Aye, I remember Mimi well." Amber smiled. "She was so kind, and always such a lady." She shot an appraising glance at Catherine. "Ye remind me of her in that way, Ladykate."

Embarrassed, though she had no idea why, Catherine concentrated on the carrots. Duncan Maxwell's mother, a lady? One certainly couldn't tell it by her uncouth son.

"Poor Papa," Amber lamented, taking off down a conversational rabbit trail as she was wont to do. "He swore he'd never marry again after Aselma died."

Duncan must have loved his wife deeply to swear off marriage after losing her.

Amber held up a fork and digressed again. "Did ye use forks where you came from in England?"

"Aye." Catherine started slicing the carrots. "We used them every meal. And linen napkins." Her heart warmed with the memory of River House in peaceful days, before Charles's selfish temperament had spoiled things. She'd left her home behind so Papa and Hal could have some peace. Now she wanted nothing more than to return to it—spoiled stepbrother, cool stepmother, and all. She would suffer them gladly.

"Ye were rich then, aye?" Amber's face glowed with happy jealousy.

Compared to the Maxwells, Catherine supposed she had been rich—still was, thanks to the jewels hidden in her shift. But she shook her head in denial, hating the necessity for lying to trusting Amber. "Not rich, but we had enough." Her conscience prodded her to add, "My mother used to say that anyone who had enough was rich, so aye, perhaps I was rich."

"Your mother, is she—?"

"She died when I was twelve," Catherine offered. "My father died when I was just a babe."

"Had ye nae brothers nor sisters?"

"Not until later, when my stepfather remarried." And Willa had subtly made Catherine feel like an interloper in her own home. "And my two stepbrothers were born." One a bane, the other a blessing.

Amber's face went slack with sympathy. "Ma poor Ladykate. When ye were ma age, ye had nae parents nor brothers nor sisters. However did ye manage?"

Realizing she'd said too much, Catherine tensed. "Papa—my stepfather—took care of me. He always has, and I love him very much. I was provided for." She carried the board of sliced carrots to a kettle of boiling water and dropped them in. "As I told you, my family are merchants. Nothing grand."

"What do they sell?"

Catherine knew Amber wasn't trying to pump her for information, but her guard heightened just the same. "A little of this, a little of that." She shifted the subject. "If you're done with the flatware, I'll show you how to set the table. Then you may tell the others to wash up for dinner."

"I can *tell* them," Amber said archly, "but it'll take some muscle to get the lads to do it. I vow, ye'd think they'd melt, the way they avoid water."

Boys. Catherine smiled. Even her darling Hal hated washing, but when it came to cleanliness, her stepmother Willa ruled her two sons with a velvet glove. "They won't mind it so much once they're used to it. I've been encouraging them to practice." She picked up the stack of pewter chargers Nessa had scoured, then headed for the dining hall.

"Will ye give me a few pointers before the others come?" Amber pleaded as she followed with her apron full of flatware. "I want to show Papa."

Catherine doubted Duncan Maxwell would notice, much less care. Then she remembered the wounded sadness in his eyes when Amber had contrasted the family—including Duncan—to "decent people." Perhaps he had sensibilities, after all.

As if summoned by her very thoughts, Duncan Maxwell chose just that moment to enter the room. Fresh from a ride, he was ruddied by the wind that had pulled free shining black wisps of his queue, and his startling blue eyes flashed with life. He looked so handsome, Catherine's heart lurched and her body ached with forbidden longing, but as usual, he seemed oblivious of the effect his appearance had on her.

"Hello." He crossed to Amber and dispensed a fatherly kiss on her forehead. "What have ye there?"

Amber extended the apron to show off her handiwork. "Knives, forks, and spoons, Papa, for the table," she bubbled. "So we can eat with gentle manners."

Duncan recognized the flatware. It had been his grandsire's, banished to the attic along with all the other useless niceties after Duncan's mother died. He and Aunt Brigit had been united in that as well as their grief. They both despised the "civilized" tyranny of Laird Kinnon Maxwell and all that represented it. Almost as much as Duncan despised the shame of his own bastard English blood and the scorn it had earned him from his own grandsire.

The light faded from Amber's face. "Is something wrong, Papa?"

"Nae." Duncan forced a reassuring smile, refusing to let the ghosts of the past control him. He had given his children the loving acceptance his grandsire had never given him, and he didn't mean to let the memory of Kinnon Maxwell's coldness poison Amber's happiness. "Your great-grandsire's pewter looks fine, lass. Fine."

He turned to Kate and caught her studying him again. When their gazes met, he saw a flicker of remembered passion that was swiftly overridden by embarrassment.

An answering stab of lust struck him. For a brief instant, Kate was not the sturdy, repressed ruler of the hearth. Instead, he saw her with her hair tumbling loose, her woman's body melting in his arms, and a look of hungry, astonished curiosity on her face.

Duncan shifted uncomfortably. The flirtation had barely begun, yet it was getting out of hand already. He had to woo the truth from the woman, not ravish her.

The thing was, he'd never before lusted for a woman he couldn't have. It was most discomfiting.

He reminded himself that she was English, through and through. That alone was enough to stand between them.

"Will ye, Papa?" Amber seemed to expect an answer.

Duncan directed his attention to his daughter. "Will I what, lass?"

"Will ye dress for dinner?" She tucked her chin shyly. "Ye ken, the fancy clothes stored away in the chest upstairs."

He'd completely forgotten them. "Aye." As a matter of fact, they could be of great assistance in the wooing of Ladykate. He gave Amber a quick hug. "I'll even join in Kate's manners lesson. I could do with some polishin' maself."

Aunt Brigit caught only the last as she entered from the parlor. "Polishin', Duncan? Ye?" She planted her fists on her narrow, bony hips. "We have Nessa for that. What nonsense is this?"

" 'Tis nae nonsense, Aunt Brigit," Amber said brightly. Flatware and all, she fairly danced across the floor. "Ladykate has promised to teach us to eat like civilized people. Even Papa."

Duncan flattened his lips to keep from smiling at the look of outrage on his aunt's face.

"Civilized people!" She turned on Kate. "Ye brazen upstart, we *are* civilized people! Ma father was a great laird and chieftain. He often sat at Queen Mary's table, though she feared him greatly. Our great-great-grandsire on our mother's side was king! And Duncan's mother was as highborn and gracious a lady as Scotland ever saw."

But my father was an English rogue who made a bastard of his son, Duncan finished silently. *And 'tis true, I have nae manners left.*

Kate refused to take Aunt Brigit's bait. Instead she beamed. "That means you're the great-great-granddaughter of a king, Aunt Brigit. A princess." She nodded to Amber. "And you, my lovely little lady, are a princess unawares." Kate's impish smile faded to one of regret. "I never intended to imply that any of you were uncivilized, Aunt Brigit. Truly."

Duncan couldn't resist the opportunity to get the best of his prim spinster. "But ye did speak it, Kate. At least about me." Predictably, she bristled. "I seem to remember your calling me a barbarian on a number of occasions. And there was more. Uncouth. Unwashed. Unchurched. Un*civilized*."

Kate's brown eyes sparked and her plain face rosied. Saints, but she was lively with her feathers up.

"I fear my circumstances have made me forget my upbringing." She dropped him a curtsy so low it was insulting. "I humbly beg your pardon, sirrah."

"Just like an Englisher," Aunt Brigit snapped. "Slander ye till the cows come home, then expect ye to forget it for a simple 'Pardon, sir.' "

Kate rose, turned to his aunt, and dropped an even deeper curtsy. "A simple 'Pardon, *ma'am*.' "

Amber giggled, but Aunt Brigit snorted and strode from the room. "Don't include me in yer bluidy manners lesson," she said as she left. "I'll sup in the kitchen with Lucas, thank ye."

Duncan savored Kate's obvious consternation.

"Oh, Ladykate, I'm so sorry." Amber rushed to her side. "I spoke without thinking, and now Aunt Brigit is angry with ye."

" 'Tis not your fault, dear one," Kate responded with convincing contrition. She circled his daughter's shoulders with a consoling arm. "You did nothing wrong. I'm the one who must beg your pardon for speaking such foolish, rash words in the first place."

Amber leaned into the embrace, and it occurred to Duncan how starved the lass—and all his children—must be for a mother's caring touch. Aunt Brigit loved them deeply, but she was as cuddly as a basket made of brambles. It wasn't her nature to hug and console.

"Come." Kate gave Amber another squeeze before releasing her. "I'll show you how to set a lovely table."

"If I'm to dine at such a lovely table," Duncan offered, "then I suppose I'd better clean up a bit. I've been ahorse all day."

He started for the stairs, then paused, unable to resist a parting shot. "I'm brutal saddle-sore, Ladykate," he teased. "Perhaps ye could find some salve to rub away the—"

Coloring, she cut him off abruptly. "The sea will spit nightingales before I'd rub any part of you, sirrah," she snapped. "Now off with you. Dinner in half an hour."

She was such an easy mark. Grinning, he executed a perfect courtly bow, then left her with, "Listen well then, Kate, for soon enough, the waves shall sing at moonrise."

Half an hour later, he entered the dining hall to find his family—minus Aunt Brigit—gathered around the immaculately set dinner table. His stomach growled at the sight and smell of the food. A heavenly scent rose from the steaming tureen in front of Kate at the far end of the table. Fresh oatbread, butter, two roast fowls, and bowls of parsnips, carrots, and tansy completed the repast.

But it was the shocked looks on everyone's faces that pleased him most. "Close your mouths," he said to his sons as he took his seat. " 'Tisna polite to show your tonsils at table."

Gordon and Kerry erupted into giggles behind their hands, but Baran reddened and snapped his jaw shut. Cameron just grinned, staring at Duncan as if he were made of pixie dust.

Kate stared as if an elephant had just strolled in. Clearly he had, in fact, set her on her ear.

"Papa," Amber breathed. "Ye look like a prince in a fairy tale."

"Nay," Erinn's tiny voice said in awe. "Not a make-believe prince. A *real* one."

Duncan had to admit that the transformation was startling. He'd hardly recognized himself in the mirror. A good scrubbing head to toe, a shave, and a fine suit of clothes could make a gentleman of any man, even the Black Bastard of the Western March.

His hair was still damp in its tidy queue.

"Your clothes, Papa," Baran said with pride. "Tell Ladykate where they came from."

Duncan grinned. "After I was done with him, Robin Johnstone had nae more use for them." He raised his elbow and pointed to the doublet's lush black silk and velvet chevrons. "See? Ye can scarce see the stain where I ran him through."

The children guffawed, but Kate blanched.

Seeing the depth of her reaction, Duncan sobered slightly. "There is nae stain, Kate. 'Twas but a jest."

She remained wary. "So you didn't slay him, then."

He met her gaze straight-on. "Oh, I killed him, but I stripped him naked first. I doona often have the opportunity to kill a man whose clothes'll fit me."

Kate paled in earnest. For a moment, he feared she might faint.

" 'Twas justice, Ladykate," Cameron calmly explained.

"The varlet shamed and killed Gordon and Kerry's mother when they were but bairns."

Kerry nodded in solemn confirmation. "Eye for eye. Life for life."

A tide of red abruptly replaced Kate's pallor. "Children," she snipped out, "our first lesson will be about proper subjects for dinner conversation." She glared at Duncan. "Out of consideration for those present, unpleasant matters should never be discussed at table. Such things as illness, injury, crime"—she arched a haughty brow at Duncan—"or murder must be avoided at all costs."

"Hist. Our Ladykate has spoken," Duncan said, his mettle raised by her high-handed disapproval. Typical Englisher, condemning them for the harsh realities that were forced upon them daily. "Let's eat, before everything gets cold," he said coolly. "I'll have some of that soup, Kate."

A stab of uncertainty gave him pause. Soup did come first, didn't it?

Aye. Soup first, then meat and vegetables, then tansy. Carve the meat and hand around the vegetables to the right. It was all coming back.

He met Kate's disapproval head-on as she gracefully filled the bowls and passed them down. "Ye can never go wrong if ye watch your host or hostess," Duncan instructed his children. "Doona start to eat until everyone at your table has been served and your host takes a bite."

Kate glanced sharply at him but kept on serving. Her surprise went a long way to lightening his mood.

"What's a host, Papa?" Erinn asked.

"At home, your papa is the host," he answered. "Away from home, it's the master of the house." He shot Kate a half-smile. "Or the mistress."

Before Duncan could swallow his first mouthful of soup, the children attacked their bowls with a clatter of spoons. "I fear for the pewter," he quipped. The smooth linen napkin felt good against his lips and shaven skin, bringing back memories of his mother and happier days.

And the soup! "Delicious." He lifted his goblet to Kate. "Ye've done wonders in the kitchen, Kate. I have to give ye that. We're in your debt."

"I . . ." She faltered, caught off-guard by his compliment. "Lucas . . . is an apt pupil. I merely taught him a few receipts."

He looked around the room. "More than that, ye've made this place a home. For that too I am grateful."

"I'm nae grateful," Baran muttered. "I liked it better before. Nae one makin' ye wash all the time or clean yer shoes before ye come inside."

"I think it's wonderful." Amber clasped her hands dramatically before her heart. "Everything's so clean and lovely and . . ." She groped for words. "And *civilized*."

"Civilized," Nevin echoed flatly from atop his pile of pillows.

"Even Papa," Erinn chimed in, beaming up at him.

Kate expressed her skepticism of that statement with a most unladylike snort.

"I fear our Ladykate doesna think your papa is civilized, poppet." Duncan turned his most winsome smile on the Englisher. Then he had an inspiration. "But perhaps we can convince her." All his wives had loved his music. "After dinner, I've a mind to play a bit."

"Yay!" The children clapped and bounced in eager anticipation. "Huzzah! Papa's going to play."

"And what instrument do you play?" Kate asked with obvious disdain. "The Scottish pipes?"

"Nae the pipes." Duncan signaled his eager children to silence before they revealed the instrument. "Ye shall see soon enough. I'll wager ye'd never guess."

Kate studied him with guarded curiosity. "You are a complicated man, sir."

"Nae half as complicated as ye, ma Ladykate." Small steps. He would win her over and find out who she was with small steps.

They just had to be *quick* ones, for he must succeed in

sending her back to the father and brother she claimed to love so deeply, yet had forsaken.

The sooner Kate was gone, the better for everyone—but most of all, for him.

Chapter
TWELVE

Catherine sat by the fire in the parlor with Nevin in her lap. What instrument would Duncan Maxwell play? she wondered. The recorder, perhaps? Or a lute?

Nay. Neither of those was a man's instrument, and Duncan was a man's man.

He drew up an armchair for Amber and Erinn, then pulled the heavy settle close to the hearth for the boys. Only when everyone was seated did he unlock the chest in the corner and draw out the instrument he meant to play.

Not a recorder or a lute! A violin, superbly crafted and clearly well used.

Catherine did her best not to show her disappointment. She'd heard quite a few fiddlers among the traveling performers who had come to River House, but their raucous efforts had set her nerves on edge even more than the pipes.

Ah, well. The children seemed excited. They, at least, would enjoy their father's playing.

Duncan adjusted the bow, then began to tune the instrument, stroking a few rich, soulful notes to check the pitch. They should have prepared her for what came next, but they didn't.

"Ready?" he asked with a contagious twinkle in his eye.

"Yes!" "Play, Papa!" "Don't keep us waiting," the children urged.

And play he did, such as Catherine had never heard, a melody as bright and clear and true as larksong on a sunny summer's day. Listening, Catherine felt as if time and care had suddenly suspended, leaving only the magic of Duncan's music. The sounds he coaxed from his violin were as far from the ragged squawks of other fiddlers as a brilliant sunset from the musty depths of the deepest cave.

He played on, and the tune mellowed, softened.

It was spellbinding, even for the children. All seven of them sat at peace, lost in the music. Amber cuddled Erinn close, and the boys had wiggled down to a frieze of knees, elbows, and feet on the settle.

She feasted her eyes and ears on Duncan Maxwell, letting the artful melody resonate within her. The song was eloquent of love and loss and hope. Unlike the intricate, structured pieces of the day, Duncan's music was fluid and free, ripe with deep emotion.

Whose music was it? she wondered. Catherine had never heard the like, not even in London.

Such magic this rough Scotsman wove with his bow, his eyes closed and his expression of one transported. The man before her was no boorish outlaw; he was a person of sensitivity and consummate artistry. But how could that be? Catherine could not reconcile this side of him with the uncouth father who'd just made sport with his children at table about killing an enemy and wearing his clothes.

Yet his music . . .

It lulled her, drew her. Wooed her.

Excited her desire.

What a paradox Duncan Maxwell was. For every wild and fearsome thing about him, he hid a secret, cultured counterpart. First he'd surprised her with his dancing. Then he'd set her blood afire with his kiss. Then he'd shocked her with his transformation into a gentleman— the handsomest she had ever seen. Now this.

Watching him now, Catherine had to admit there was far more to him than she had ever imagined.

One by one, the children relaxed and nodded off, even Baran, leaving the two adults alone in the moment with only the music between them.

She'd been staring at Duncan for some time before she realized he was staring back, his blue eyes hungry.

She recognized the raw desire in his gaze, and an answering twist of passion sprang up deep inside her. She shifted in her chair, ruing yet again her weakness in allowing Duncan to open with a kiss what she feared could never be shut again. Fortified by the reality of their one encounter, her dreams were almost all of Duncan now, passionate or otherwise.

His song became impassioned, romantic, and he peered at her in open invitation.

A swell of defiance rose inside her. Duncan felt free enough to strip her bare with his gaze whenever it suited. What was wrong with her retaliating in kind? She was no coy young girl. She was a mature woman, and he the handsomest man she had ever seen. With his clean, shining black hair pulled softly back into a queue, the strong bones and classic planes of his face showed stark and elegant in the firelight.

Erinn was right. He did look like a true prince with his broad shoulders encased in lush black silk and velvet, his narrow waist accented by the elegant doublet, his powerful thighs rippling beneath the tooled leather of his breeches, and his muscular calves strongly outlined by his supple leather boots.

Nay, not a prince. A king.

And the shocking truth was, Catherine wished with all the pent-up longing in her solitary heart that she could be his queen, even if only for a night.

Silent alarms went off inside her brain. Dangerous, such rash conjecture. Rocking the sleeping child in her arms, she struggled to pull herself together. Duncan Maxwell was a bastard, a rogue, a man of violence, she reminded herself. Yet his burning gaze held her riveted even as his music drew her soul and body like a golden cord.

Could he sense what she was thinking? She shivered at the provocative notion.

Ridiculous, such an idea in a sensible, plain woman far grown beyond such fancies.

Perhaps he had bewitched her. If so, she did not want the glorious spell to end.

Too soon, the last plaintive note of the music echoed in the silent room, and Duncan stared unseeing into the glowing fire.

"Please," she asked softly, "would you play that piece again?"

He shook his head. "I canna do it, Kate."

"But why? It was magnificent."

Duncan rose quietly to replace the violin into the chest and lock it. "I play what is in ma heart." He shrugged, then shot her a glance that was almost shy. "It changes every time."

That glorious music, his and his alone?

Catherine stared at him in awe. To have heard his music . . . she recognized the privilege for what it was, a rare and precious moment in time, never to be repeated.

She was humbled to have been granted such a glimpse into the heart of this complex man who now held more than her body captive. "Thank you for allowing me to listen."

Gordon stirred, setting off a chain reaction of shoves and mumbles on the bench, but the sleeping boys subsided quickly.

Slowly, deliberately, Duncan approached her, blatant hunger in his eyes.

What did he mean to do? Catherine's arms tightened around Nevin, her heart beating faster. Part of her wanted to flee, but the greater part of her wanted Duncan Maxwell to kiss her again.

Closer. Closer. He was moving so slowly she wondered briefly if he was prolonging his approach on purpose, drawing it out.

At last, he reached his arms toward her and bent down, bringing with him the scent of soap and spice and wood smoke. Catherine held her breath. His lips were so close.

"It never fails," he said in a whisper as soft as black velvet, his breath warm against her ear. "They beg me to play, then always fall asleep." He scooped Nevin from her arms and straightened, a triumphant gleam in his eye.

"I'll take care of the bairns, Kate. Why doona ye run along to bed?"

Run along to bed! As if she were one of the children.

Anger and shame brought Catherine abruptly to her feet. She opened her mouth to speak, but words deserted her, so she snapped it shut.

Judging from the twinkle in Duncan Maxwell's eyes, he was enjoying her discomfiture immensely.

Cursed man! Bloody Mary would come back from hell and walk the streets before Catherine would allow Duncan Maxwell to play her like a foolish girl again! Pulse pounding now in fury, she marched straight to her room, slammed the door, and took to her bed.

With her last conscious thought as she drifted off to sleep, she wished he would drop into the deepest hole in the deepest ocean.

But far into the night, he came to her in dreams, all clean and hard and handsome, just as he had been at supper. He put his arms around her and drew her close, his body firm against hers. Then he kissed her. His hands caressed her ribs, her back, her breasts, and she melted from the inside out.

And then his hand slid between her legs and—

Catherine woke up throbbing with need.

Faith, what was happening to her? Her wanton dreams had birthed a wanton mind within her, one that grew stronger every time she got close to Duncan Maxwell.

She must be rescued, and soon. She had to escape Annanlea and Duncan Maxwell's spell. She could not answer for her sanity if she didn't.

Or her honor.

"I'm glad you decided to eat with us," Catherine ventured as she and Aunt Brigit cleared the table that Thursday night. It was good, having time and privacy to talk alone. "Your family is not complete without you, Aunt Brigit. And our conversations were far less interesting."

Aunt Brigit let out a benign grunt. "English airs and

fancy ways. Useless." Her gray brows lifted. "Mayhap even treasonous."

"Nay, none of that, now," Catherine cautioned with a smile. "I have it on good authority that Duncan's own mother insisted upon eating here every night, with pewterware and proper table manners."

Her arms loaded with bowls and chargers, Aunt Brigit halted. "And what blabbermouth tattletale went and told ye that?"

"I really couldn't say." Catherine transferred the last of the goblets and utensils to the tray she carried.

" 'Twas Michael, aye?" Aunt Brigit accused.

"I could not say," she repeated. Actually, it had been Amber.

"The auld fool has developed an uncommon fondness fer ye, Kate," Aunt Brigit said with more than a hint of jealousy. "Take care he doesna corner ye."

"Ach," Catherine replied in brogue, "the man has eyes for no one else but ye, and doona doubt it."

"Hmph." Aunt Brigit's grudging smile warmed Catherine's heart.

"Why haven't you married him?" Catherine was bold to ask.

"Married? Michael?" Aunt Brigit colored. "Nae that it's any of your business, Miss Poke-a-nose, but he hasna asked me."

"Nonsense." Catherine pushed open the door to the kitchen so Aunt Brigit could enter ahead of her, then followed. The kitchen was redolent from supper, and warm from the fire still glowing under the kettle of washwater. Catherine sprinkled a handful of soap chips into the pot, then laid in the chargers, goblets, and utensils. "I have it on good authority that Michael Graham has proposed marriage to ye a dozen times if he's asked ye once."

"Doona mock ma speakin', lass," Aunt Brigit deflected. "I warn ye."

"I'm as stubborn as ye are, woman," Catherine shot back in her best brogue, "and I'll nae be put off so easily.

Admit it. He's asked. But ye always said nae."

Aunt Brigit deflated. "Well, he stopped askin'," she said with obvious regret.

Catherine was gentle. "A man has his pride. Perhaps he gave up."

"Aye, perhaps he did." Aunt Brigit busied herself with the dishes. "So it's too late."

How many years had Duncan's aunt denied the love everyone else could see so clearly? "If he asked you again," Catherine challenged, "would you accept?"

Aunt Brigit shook her head in denial, but her words contradicted the gesture. "Who kens? Mayhap I would."

"Then I shall pray he does," she said with genuine affection.

"He willna do it," Aunt Brigit huffed, requiring the last word on the subject as usual. They finished the washing, rinsing, drying, and putting away in companionable silence. When that was done, Aunt Brigit headed up the back stair. "Are ye comin' to bed, Kate?"

"Not just yet." Catherine removed the apron she wore. "It's such a beautiful evening. I think I'll walk about outside for a while before I turn in."

Aunt Brigit paused. "I'm grateful to ye, Kate, fer all ye've done here. And fer bein' so good wi' the children."

"I've come to love them," Catherine surprised herself by saying. Moved almost beyond speech by the emotions her simple statement stirred within her, she covered with, "Anyway, staying busy keeps my mind off my predicament."

"Aye." Aunt Brigit regarded her with compassion. "Nae one kens better than I how lonely 'tis to be a woman wi'out a family of her own. And I doona grudge ye sharin' ours. But ye must ask yerself how hard it will be for them when ye leave us, Kate."

"I have." And she hadn't liked to think of what a wrenching parting that would be for her, as well. But she *had* to escape this place.

Didn't she?

Papa was probably already on his way, she told herself. Yet the affirmation seemed to have lost its power to encourage her.

Aunt Brigit nodded. "Good night to ye then, lass. Sweet dreams."

No dreams, if Catherine had any say about it. "Good night."

She retrieved her shawl from its peg by the back door, then exited into the twilit courtyard. As she strolled across the brick paving, she spotted Duncan Maxwell standing in stark silhouette atop the northern peel, his foot propped on a crenel. Motionless as the stone beneath him, he stared across the lands he'd fought so hard to keep.

From that high up, he must have a fine prospect. On impulse, Catherine walked to the door of the peel, then went inside to mount the stairs. She fully expected to pass Duncan on the way, but she arrived at the top to find him transfixed on the parapet. Sleek and still as some great ebon cat, he stretched forward with one arm braced across his thigh, the muscles of his legs accented by his position.

She coughed, just to let him know she was there, but Duncan did not stir, so she approached him with caution from behind.

Drawing abreast of him, Catherine forced her eyes from the man to the view spread out below her. It was even lovelier than she'd imagined it would be. From so high up, Duncan's fields and pastures formed a fertile counterpane on either side of the Annan, accented by the trees that were reaching the peak of their color. Such a tranquil, idyllic picture it made, so deceptively peaceful. " 'Tis a lovely illusion, is it not?"

"Aye." He exhaled heavily. "All ma life, I've had to content maself with only the illusion of peace." A cool breeze stirred his dark hair as he turned a guarded look on her. "But I suppose 'tis better to cling to an illusion than to have nae hope at all."

An outlaw who hoped for peace.

Like it or not, she felt compassion for him. And for

his children. What choice did any of them have? The curse of violence ran deep in these hills and vales, yet their family remained an island of love amid the chaos.

And her family had become an island of chaos amid the relative security of their own river valley across the border.

Catherine tightened her shawl.

"Are ye cold, then?" Duncan put his arm about her shoulders and rubbed her through the woolen fabric.

"I'm fine. Truly." She wanted to lean back against him and soak in the heat from his body, but she drew away instead.

He allowed her to retreat, yet she could sense the tug their nearness had on him, too. "The wind is rising," he said. "We might best go inside."

Catherine shook her head. "If you don't mind, I'd like to stay up here for a while."

"I doona blame ye." He scanned the darkening scene below. " 'Tis ma favorite place to come when cares weigh heavy."

"What cares have brought you here tonight?" she asked impulsively. He might not answer, but at least she'd asked.

"That's ma Kate," he said dryly. "Straight to the heart of the matter."

"Or the heart of the man," she parried.

"I'd be less than prudent revealin' ma weaknesses to a hostage."

"Is that all I am to you?" She faced him squarely without anger. "A hostage?"

He reached up and brushed a stray tendril from her temple. " 'Tis what ye are, ma Ladykate," he said as softly as any endearment.

"I am not your Ladykate." A pulse of aching desperation thickened her voice. "I am a human being, Duncan, a woman with a family who thinks I am dead. Let me go home to them. Please."

He closed his eyes briefly. "Beelzebub's hoofprints,

woman," he said wearily. "Doona ye ken I would if I could? I'm nae claimin' ma ransom for spite, but from necessity. God didna send ye to someone else. He spit ye out on ma lands, and I mean to have ma ransom."

"I have told you and told you," she snapped, "my family *has* no money for ransom."

"Then why would God send ye to me?" he shouted.

Catherine shouted even louder, "Perhaps as a penance to us both!"

After a heartbeat of silence, Duncan surprised her by laughing. "Aye God, woman, ye may have hit upon it." He threw back his head and laughed full and free, breaking the tension. "We probably do deserve each other!"

The absurd truth of it kicked over Catherine's tickle-box, too. The more she thought about it, the harder she laughed, until both of them were sagging helplessly on adjacent crenels.

When at last her hilarity began to fade, the evening stars were blurred by mindless tears. Her cheeks aching, Catherine wiped her eyes. "Hoo. That felt good." She straightened, completely relaxed.

"I doona ken what it is about ye, Kate," Duncan managed, "but every now and then, somethin' does me good." He looked at her with open fondness. "The rest of the time, ye vex me fearsome. But I think I shall miss ye when you're gone." Night was hard upon them, making it difficult to see his expression, but he cut a magnificent silhouette against the cobalt October night sky.

Catherine stepped in treacherously close. She could feel his body tense with need, and her own answered. A dangerous game, they were playing. "Before I do go, there's something I'd like you to do." So close, she could scarcely think.

"And what would that be?" His voice was low and husky.

"Play for me up here," she said brightly, shattering the mood. "Just the two of us." Now they were even for his "run along to bed."

It was still light enough to see the flash of his grin. Catherine had to give him credit; he was a good sport, at least.

"I'd be glad to play for ye here alone," he said seductively, "as long as I can play *with* ye after I've finished with ma fiddle." He drew her close and brushed his hand up the side of her breast, causing her to resonate like the strings of his violin.

"Very well, it's agreed," she said breathlessly. "I shall ask you to play for me when I'm ready." Heaven help her, she was planning her own downfall.

Duncan enfolded her for a passionate kiss, just as she'd secretly hoped he would. Hunger, frightening in its depth and power, consumed her. She kissed him back with abandon, reveling in the taste of him, the firm resistance of his body, and the heady scent of him.

Abruptly, he pulled away and strode to the stairs, leaving her alone to sway in the empty air.

She should have been angry that he'd left her so, but oddly, she wasn't. Instead, she let out a hearty, cleansing chuckle. Catherine had no idea what would come next, but she suspected Ladykate was about to get herself into some serious trouble—trouble named Duncan Maxwell.

Chapter

THIRTEEN

"Lone rider comin' in! Fast!"

The alarm echoed from the peel, reaching Catherine and the girls in the sunny parlor. She halted in mid-stitch. A messenger.

Word from Papa? The notion lodged with the force of an arrow.

A charge of anticipation shot to her fingertips. Aye, this could be the day, she let herself hope.

Erinn and Amber abandoned their sewing and rushed to the window with Nevin toddling after. Amber peered toward the gate. "Who could it be?" Fear edged the eager curiosity in her voice.

Frowning, Erinn turned from the window. "Messengers never bring good news. Ye ken 'tis true, Amber." She took Nevin's hand and started back to her chair.

"Perhaps it will be happy news for someone, poppet," Catherine said. Feeling as if she were moving at half-speed, she laid aside her mending and rose. "Continue with your stitching, girls. I'll see what it's about." Her fingers fumbled with the ties of her apron.

Aunt Brigit entered from the kitchen, the furrows between her brows deeper than usual. "What now?"

"A messenger," Catherine explained. "I was just going to investigate."

"Ye'd best stay here and let Duncan handle it," Aunt Brigit called after her. "Ye nosey thing." Her voice subsided to its usual rumble of ineffectual complaint. "I doona ken why I bother. Blasted Englisher never listens, just does as she pleases."

Catherine exited the front door just in time to see Duncan striding to the gate with Michael Graham and the boys close behind. His expression grim, he looked every inch the Black Bastard.

"Baran, ye may stay wi' Michael," he shouted to his sons. "The rest of ye lads, back to Aunt Brigit. Now."

The twins and Cameron obeyed without hesitation, making a race of it as they streaked past her.

Hands clutched at her waist, she fixed her gaze on the rising portcullis. Moving in an envelope of silence amid the chaos of the alert, Catherine was drawn to the gate and the incoming messenger like one of Nevin's pull-toys compelled to motion by its string.

"Rider at the gate!" came Darby Carlisle's shout from the peel.

She didn't know how or why she was suddenly so certain the messenger was from Papa, but she was.

The portcullis creaked to a halt at the top of the gate. Catherine stepped behind Duncan in the cool shade beside the guardhouse and waited, almost afraid to hope.

Duncan's long, elegant fingers played at the hilt of his sword, the only betrayal of his concern. Otherwise, he stood as formidable and composed as Hades himself. He and Michael exchanged meaningful glances.

"The salt?" Michael murmured so low she could barely hear him.

"By courier?" Duncan shook his head in contradiction to his next words. "We could hope."

Catherine realized that Duncan was probably praying even now for a very different message than the one she wanted.

"Open the gate," he commanded. Quinn and Rory put their backs to it. As soon as the massive bars cleared their seats, Ander, Thurlow, Lucas, and Mouse shoved open the iron-clad gates.

A muddy rider, heaving from exertion, slumped in his saddle as he prodded his lathered mount toward Duncan. As soon as he was through, the gates were closed behind him. He halted at a respectful distance, slid to ground, then bowed low, presenting Duncan a sealed roll of parchment.

Catherine felt as if a dozen ravens were flapping inside her chest and shrieking, *"Open it. Open it Open it."*

But Duncan did not open the missive. "Who sent ye?" he demanded of the messenger.

"I doona ken," the man responded. "A stranger come to ma stable in Dumfries just after dark last night. English, I'd have to say. Saw ma hob and asked what I'd want for deliverin' this message. I told him 'twould have to wait till day. Then I named a price three times fair, and he met it."

"English?" For the first time since she'd arrived, Duncan acknowledged Catherine's presence—with a sharp glance of suspicion. "Was he mounted?"

The stableman shook his head. "Shank's mare." Afoot. "What did he look like?"

"Nae tall, nae short." The messenger shrugged. "I couldna see his face. He kept to the shadow of his brim, and he was cloaked."

"Cloaked?"

"Aye. Wi' a garment well above ma station, but nae so fancy as a laird's."

Never mind who gave it to him, Catherine railed inside. *Read the letter.*

"His name?"

The exhausted rider lifted his chin, defensive. "His coin was name enough."

Duncan scowled his dismissal, then pivoted. "See to him, Michael. Baran, go with them. I'll be in ma study." He glanced up to the armed men and women on the battlements. "Stand ready."

He strode toward the house, where seven faces—including Aunt Brigit's—hovered at the window.

"Duncan." Catherine had to hitch up her skirts and sprint to keep up. "Wait."

He neither slowed nor looked back. "Return to your work, Kate. This is none of your affair."

"We shall just see about that." She followed him through the foyer. By the time they reached the parlor, it was deserted, but she saw several telltale toes and hems protruding just beyond the open doorway to the corridor.

He turned and faced her. "You're settin' a bad example for the children, Ladykate, by ignorin' ma orders," he warned. "This is none of your business, woman. So go!"

"And what if that message *is* my business?" she blurted out.

Duncan halted, his eyes narrowing. "Why would ye think such a thing?"

"Read it and see," she challenged.

Duncan took his time settling into his chair—just to vex her, she was certain. She moved in close enough to see the imprint in the wax. Papa's three diamonds!

Thanks be to God! I knew it. I knew it.

She held her breath as Duncan lazily broke the seal, then unrolled the parchment and read.

His pretense of ennui didn't last long. He couldn't have gotten much farther than the first sentence when his color rose and the muscles rippled over his clenched jaw.

Stand firm, she told herself. Anger was to be expected. But she knew enough of Duncan Maxwell to trust that he would not harm her.

At least, she hoped she did.

When he looked up at her at last, his expression was grim, but instead of anger, she saw frustration and . . . what? If she hadn't known better, she would have thought it pity. "I doona ken how ye managed this, Kate," he said. "But since this does in fact concern ye, I suggest ye hear it sittin' down."

Bad news? Nay. "I am no frail maiden, sirrah," she shot back. "Read away."

"Verra well." He spread the letter between them, revealing Robert Storey's familiar hand. Just the sight of it was enough to hearten Catherine. " 'To whom it may concern,' " he read aloud. " 'It has come to my attention that my stepdaughter, Catherine, is being held for ransom on

Scottish soil by one Duncan Maxwell, a common outlaw and criminal who styles himself the Black Bastard of the Western March.' "

That hardly sounded like Papa. Catherine had scribed many a letter for him, but never—even in the most serious of matters—had he been so cold and stilted in his wording.

Duncan read on. " 'As my stepdaughter has doubtless revealed, she has recently severed all ties with our family—' "

Severed all ties?

" '—and was on her way to Cornwall to serve as a companion for a distant relation who, word has just reached us, died August fifteenth.' "

Cousin Thelma, dead?

A rising thread of warning crept into Catherine's hope.

" 'Irrespective of that,' " Duncan read on, " 'I am certain my stepdaughter must have informed you that neither I nor any of my family has the means to procure even a modest ransom. According to the terms of Catherine's parents' wills and her own, the home in which we live and the surrounding lands may not for any reason be sold or encumbered.' "

Had the world gone suddenly atilt? Catherine's will had no such stipulation. Why would Papa say it did? Wrong. Something was very wrong here.

"Let me see that," she demanded.

"After I've finished." Duncan regarded her with dark compassion. "I'm only readin' what it says, Kate, and I doona like it any better than ye."

Catherine's stomach plunged. Maybe she should have taken that chair. "Go on, then."

" 'As for Catherine herself,' " he read, " 'we bear her no ill will and wish her Godspeed, but as we are deep in mourning for the loss of our eldest son in the wreck of the *Dere,* we are neither able nor willing to pursue this matter any further.' "

Charles, dead—gone, just as some secret, selfish part of her had hoped.

A low moan escaped Catherine. Out of nowhere, the feel of strangling brought her hand to her throat as her mind flashed a blurred image of a dark silhouette against the storm, followed by the sensation of falling, then smothering cold, wet silence.

Abruptly, Catherine remembered. Someone had tried to choke her, then thrown her overboard! Before the wreck.

Duncan paused, his brows drawn together in concern. "Are ye all right, Kate?"

"Fine," she managed to get out. He'd just told her Charles was dead, yet here she was, thinking of herself. Guilt washed over her.

God forgive me, she prayed. *I didn't really want him dead. Truly.* But she had.

No wonder Papa's message was so cold and distant. Charles was dead, and he blamed her. Blood and love had been tested, and blood won out, even with Papa.

In life, Charles had done his best to poison Catherine's relationship with her stepfather. Now in death, he'd succeeded. And Willa . . . An involuntary shudder wracked Catherine at the thought of how Willa must hate her for living when Willa's darling Charles had died.

Duncan cleared his throat and resumed reading. " 'Therefore, address no further demands or communications to me or my family concerning Catherine. Whoever holds her may keep her. Perhaps she will prove as useful to them as she once was to us.' "

"Useful?" She gasped out the word. Her stepfather's hateful rejection tore like teeth into her soul. "Keep me?"

"There is nae closing," Duncan concluded. "Nae signature." He turned the letter facing her. "Very clever. Nae last names. Nae clues about his location. I canna even send an answer."

Reeling, she bent forward to brace herself on the desk. Papa did not want her back!

"Papa . . . blames me for Charles's death." She heard her own words as if someone else were speaking. "But it was Willa who insisted Charles accompany me." She met Duncan's somber gaze. "I did not want him to come. Truly, I didn't."

But she'd wanted to be rid of Charles, and now she was. They all were.

"Papa blames me." Whose harsh voice was that? Surely not hers. Those were her hands, though, blurred by tears as the fingers splayed on the desk to keep her from falling into the huge, black chasm of her stepfather's rejection. "He said he loved me as if I were his own. But Charles was his child by blood."

Only when she felt Duncan draw her to him did she realize he had left his chair and circled to hold her. He picked her up as if she weighed no more than a basket of bread. "Shhhh, Kate. Shhh." He swung her gently side to side, his great head bending to hers in comfort.

But Catherine could not be comforted. She'd lost everything that mattered. Everything. Her home. The love of the only father she had ever known. Every constant upon which her life had been structured. How could she go back to River House now? She'd surrendered it to the very people who now hated her.

She'd lost everything.

Not everything. You still have your mother's jewels, an errant thought injected. At least she would not starve. And neither would the children.

Angry tears displaced the wayward thoughts. "They've thrown me away," she rasped out, curling into a wretched ball in Duncan's sustaining arms. "For all they know, you could be the most depraved and abusive of men, yet they left me to you, at the mercy of your will!"

She thought of Hal, and her heart broke even further. Did he know what they'd done to her? Or did he hate her, too? "How could they do this to me?" She clutched at Duncan's jacket. "How could they?"

"I doona ken," he said quietly. "Perhaps abiding love is but a myth."

Erinn burst into tears and ran forward from her listening post in the hallway. "We love ye, Ladykate," she bawled, setting Nevin off. "I'm glad they didna want ye back. I prayed ye wouldna leave us. Now ye can stay." Followed by her big sister and Nevin, Erinn latched onto Duncan, hugging Catherine's skirts. "We want ye, Ladykate. Doona cry."

"Aye. We want ye here with us." Amber joined the awkward embrace as best she could. "Our papa will take care o' ye, won't ye, Papa?"

Duncan Maxwell let out a deep sigh. "Do I have a choice?"

Even Aunt Brigit had to speak up at that. "Duncan!" She appeared in the doorway, stiff with indignation. "Of course she can stay."

"Papa," the girls wailed.

"Aye, ma darlin' lasses," he assured his daughters. "Kate can stay with us, if that's what she wants."

Catherine didn't want to stay at Annanlea. She *wanted* to go home. She *wanted* her stepfather to love her enough to accept Charles's death as God's will, not her fault.

And as much as she loved the children, she did *not* want to become one of Duncan Maxwell's band of ragtag outcasts.

"Stand aside now, ma lasses," he gently urged his daughters. "Ladykate has had a nasty shock; let me take her to her room to recover."

Through her haze of pain and guilt, Catherine felt young hands pat her in reassurance. "Aye, rest, Ladykate," Amber said after a most unladylike sniff.

"I'll bring ye some autumn leaves to cheer ye," Erinn offered.

Bless their precious, unsullied hearts. Catherine realized with a dull ache that theirs was the only love she had left in this world.

She closed her eyes and willed the world to go away,

only dimly aware when Aunt Brigit joined Duncan at the bottom of the stair. "The putrid, heartless buzzards," she snarled. "But Duncan, an Englisher? What will all the others think? Auld Wat will—"

"And since when do I give an ant's arse what anybody thinks, including Wat?" Duncan clipped out as he carried Catherine up the steps. She wanted to shut them out, but their words penetrated the fog of denial into which she was trying to vanish.

"But wi'out the ransom," Aunt Brigit whispered, "how will we manage? Another mouth—"

"Has your tongue run away wi' ye, woman," Duncan snapped, "or do ye mean to twist the dagger deeper into Kate and me both?"

Catherine should have been glad to hear him defend her, but she felt little. A blessed numbness was slowly overtaking her.

"Forgive me, lad." Aunt Brigit followed them into the upstairs hallway. "I was just so worried."

Again, he cut her short, but this time with less choler. "We will manage. We always have." He ducked into Catherine's room and carried her to the bed. "Draw down the covers, Bink. She's shiverin' like a rabbit in a snare."

Cold. She was so cold.

When Duncan laid her down, she missed the warmth and reassuring strength of his body. She curled onto her side and was glad when they covered her.

Papa didn't want her back.

Odd, how quickly it had gone from a shattering, rending thing to a flat finality with the smell of death about it.

Papa didn't want her back.

The rest of her life, forever changed, began this day, here and now. Held in this godforsaken place by a handsome rogue who played her body to his tune the way he played his fiddle, and the children who had somehow won their way into her heart.

"Sleep, Ladykate." Duncan stroked his thumb across

her temple. "And when ye wake, we'll sort things out. Everything will come round right."

How could he believe that? She didn't. Not anymore.

Catherine's limbs felt like long loaves of sodden dough when she woke at last. She opened puffy eyes to see that it was morning. She stretched beneath the covers. Stiffness and sore muscles told her she'd been abed for far too long, but she wanted nothing more than to pull the covers over her head again and hide. Yet as she forced herself to awareness, she discovered that the pain which had driven her to seek oblivion had faded to a distant ache. Just a moment more, then she would face the day. She closed her eyes to the sound of someone at the door.

"Scat," Aunt Brigit chided. "Ye can see her later. Now run along wi' ye."

Catherine recognized Amber and Erinn's disappointed moans before the closing door shut them out.

Aunt Brigit's familiar brisk cadence approached. "Aha. Yer awake, then." She loomed into Catherine's narrow field of vision with tray in hand, bringing the mouthwatering aromas of golden onions, spiced wine, and fresh bread. Catherine's stomach answered with a formidable roar. "Get up, Kate," Aunt Brigit ordered. "Lucas made yer favorites, onion soup and sage bread."

When Catherine didn't move, she smacked the tray onto the dresser, threw open the tattered draperies, then returned to jerk back the covers. "I said sit up, woman. This has gone on long enough. If yer to be one of us, ye must carry yer weight." She drew the empty chamber pot from beneath the bed and thwacked it down beside Catherine. "Anyway, Duncan wants to see ye. Get up and tend to yerself. He'll here anon."

The mere sight of the chamber pot was enough to make Catherine realize she was about to pop. "All right." She swung her legs over the side and rubbed her face. Her clothes were mashed and twisted, her stockings gone, and she felt deep creases in her cheek.

Where were her shoes?

She lifted the covers and found them at the foot of the bed, along with her stockings.

"That's more like it." Aunt Brigit turned to leave. "Ye have fifteen minutes, then I'm sendin' Duncan up." She exited and closed the door behind her.

Fifteen minutes!

Catherine relieved herself, undid her ruined coiffure, brushed her hair and hastily twisted it into a chignon, then washed her face and hands. Despite her best efforts to smooth her clothes, they looked as if she'd slept in them for two days, which she probably had.

She had just settled down to eat when Duncan entered. He appeared to have been up the entire time she'd been sleeping. Yet though his blue eyes were sunken and bloodshot, his cheeks haggard, he looked even handsomer than he had at the gates.

"Kate." He drew up her side chair, turned it backward, then sat straddling it. Clearly, he had something on his mind, but Catherine wasn't ready to face whatever it was. Not quite yet.

"How long have I been sleeping?" she deferred.

"Three days." He seemed glad to avoid the matter at hand, as well. "Aunt Brigit wanted to roust ye out yesterday," he said, "but I wouldna let her. Four wives were enough to teach me that it's best to let a woman sleep it out when she's had a shock."

"Thank you," she said. Suddenly, she wasn't hungry anymore. The emptiness loomed deep and dark within her. She rose and went to the window to stare across the courtyard to the autumn countryside beyond the wall.

What should she do? Should she offer Duncan jewels for her freedom?

But if he knew she had them, would he find the rest and take them—not for himself, but for his people?

Nay. She dared not tell him about her jewels. They were all she had left in the world now, her only connection to her past, her parents. With Angus Maxwell's help, she could still ease the privation at Annanlea while keeping her secret.

What good would it do to win her freedom, anyway? Even if she had somewhere to go in England, Duncan could not spare his men to escort her, and she dared not trust anyone else to do it, not even the warden. A woman alone . . .

It seemed she had little choice but to stay.

At least here the children needed her, and there was honest work aplenty to keep her mind off her family's rejection.

Duncan moved in close behind her, but he stopped short, setting the hairs on her neck alert in anticipation of his slightest touch. Heaven help her, she wanted him close. Wanted his arms around her, his mouth on hers, his hands on her body. "Kate . . ."

"Yes?" She knew what he was going to say. Duncan Maxwell needed a mother for his children. Aunt Brigit needed help running Annanlea. And Catherine had nowhere else to go. She would have to marry him, she supposed.

Odd, how things worked out. She had long since reconciled herself to spinsterhood, yet here she was, trapped in the wilds of the Scottish borderlands, preparing to accept a union that would make her a mother seven times over and join her to a bastard and an outlaw. A very handsome and compelling bastard and outlaw, but a bastard and outlaw, nonetheless.

All too aware of Duncan's presence behind her, Catherine was reminded by a paroxysm of desire that such a match would not be all bad. If he was as accomplished in the marriage bed as he was at kissing, she would have that, at least, to look forward to.

"Kate." His hands closed gingerly on her upper arms, sending chills to her fingertips. "I've been thinkin.' The children love ye. Well, most of 'em."

"I have come to love them, too." An unexpected surge

of emotion made it difficult to speak. "Even Baran. He's trying so hard to come into his manhood."

"Yes, well . . ." Duncan gently chafed her arms. "And ye've been a great help to Aunt Brigit. She's grown quite attached to ye, in spite of your bein' a 'blasted Englisher.' " He paused.

"Spit it out, Duncan." The sooner she got through this, the sooner she could get on with her life. Such as it was.

"I was thinkin' ye could stay on as housekeeper," he blurted out at last.

"Housekeeper!" He might as well have shot her through. Catherine pivoted on him and took a step backward. "What do you mean, housekeeper?"

Puzzled by her reaction, Duncan tucked his chin. "What I said. Housekeeper."

Aunt Brigit picked just that moment to join them unannounced. "Ah. I see ye've told her." She crossed her arms at her waist. "Well, Kate. What say ye?"

Catherine glared up at Duncan. "I had thought, sir, that you would at least offer me an *honorable* position in this household. Especially after the liberties you have taken."

"An honorable position?" Duncan shot back. "And what's nae honorable about bein' a housekeeper, might I ask ye?"

"Liberties?" Aunt Brigit scowled at Duncan. "What liberties? Are there more, besides the one ye took in the kitchen?"

"A kiss or two," he said defensively. "I told ye I wouldna take her maidenhood, and I havena."

"Of all the arrogant, ill-bred, *uncivilized* nerve!" Catherine exploded. "As if I would ever let the likes of *ye* come close to takin' ma maidenhood, Duncan Maxwell!"

Duncan grinned. "Listen to her, Bink. Nae matter where she came from, that temper's so Scottish it bleeds a brogue into her speech."

"I am not Scottish, sirrah," Catherine clipped out, "but English to the bone, and proud of it. God save the queen!"

"How did he kiss ye, lass?" Aunt Brigit demanded.

Catherine crossed her arms at her breasts. "With his hands all over me and his tongue half down my throat, and his codpiece grinding into me, that's how!"

"Did ye like it, then?" Aunt Brigit prodded.

"What difference does that make?" Catherine railed. "Aye. I liked it. No one's ever kissed me that way before."

"I told ye, Bink," Duncan protested. Why was she taking Kate's side against him? " 'Twas just a kiss or two. Nae more."

"And how would ye, a man, ken what a kiss means to a maiden," his aunt shot back, "especially one who has reconciled herself to celibacy?" She looked from Catherine to Duncan and back again. " 'Tis clear enough, Duncan. Ye must marry her. For honor's sake. And for the children's."

Duncan looked at his aunt in shock. "Marry her!" Had Bink lost her mind? She might as well have suggested he lay his cock on the chopping block! "Who said anythin' about marriage?"

Kate's mouth flattened into a thin line, her brown eyes blazing. "I would not marry him if he was the last man in the last parish in the last shire in all of Queen Elizabeth's realm."

Duncan refused to lose his temper. "Might I remind ye, Kate," he said, "that Scotland is a free and independent realm under our own King James, nae your doughty, bald old queen."

"A king who is king only by Her Majesty's sufferance." She drew back her hand to strike him. "And how dare you insult our sovereign's person?"

Duncan easily captured her wrist. "She's nae ma sovereign." He had to give it to Kate, she was stirrin' with her mettle up. None of his other wives had ever dared to cross him.

His other wives . . . The devil's codpiece! Aunt Brigit had him thinkin' it now, too.

"Let go of me, you varlet," Kate fairly growled.

Aunt Brigit headed for the door. "I'll send for Angus

right away and start Lucas on the weddin' feast."

"Nae!" "No!" they shouted in unison.

"I willna marry her!"

"I shall *not* marry him!"

Aunt Brigit whirled and marched back to confront Duncan with grim composure. "Ye shall marry her, Duncan, for if ye doona, I shall pack ma bags and leave ye. And if any ill befalls me, it'll be on your head."

He'd made a sacred vow to his mother on her deathbed that he'd care for Aunt Brigit as long as she lived, and Bink knew it. "That's extortion!"

"Aye," his aunt said calmly. "And I mean every word of it." For all her idle complaints, she had never been one for idle threats. If she said she'd leave, she would do it. Blast her.

She pointed a finger at Catherine. "Ye, Miss Ladykate, should marry him fer your soul's sake, lass. He's already seduced ye with the flesh." Her tone softened. "Do it for the children, Kate. They need ye almost as much as I do."

Duncan couldn't believe his ears: Aunt Brigit, admitting she needed anyone, much less Kate? "Ma children were fine wi'out ye," he countered, "and they will be again!"

"Fine, were they?" Kate turned on him. "No decent food. The girls in rags and ignorant of all but the basest women's ways. The lads as wild as rats. No lessons. No religious instruction. No one to teach them that there's more to life than a hand-to-mouth existence. Oh, they were fine, all right."

Now she'd gone too far, questioning his fitness as a father. "Ladykate the expert, after all of three months? What gall. I've loved 'em and reared 'em for the past thirteen years. Ye havna even a bairn of your own. Keep your hands off mine."

Kate's mouth dropped open in an exaggerated gasp. "That was low, you peat-eating, kitten-kicking, swell-headed . . . *troll*. But you have no cause to question my affection for those children, or what I have done for them." Her voice broke. "I need them. And they need me."

"Duncan needs ye, too," Aunt Brigit declared, "though he's a man, so he canna see it."

Kate looked at his aunt with the oddest expression on her face. Were those tears in her eyes? Surely not. And Aunt Brigit, smiling at her that way. It wasn't natural.

Duncan didn't like the turn this had taken. "I need Kate like I need a boil on ma cuddy," he protested. "Hell, I'll take her back to England maself, this very day."

"Nae, lad." Bink took Kate's hands in her own. "Ye'll marry her this very day, and nae regret it."

Nae regret it? Kate had been nothing but trouble. And that tongue of hers—the idea of a lifetime of her chiding made him shiver.

Of course, she had seemed more than eager for his kisses. With a little encouragement . . .

The devil's codpiece! He was thinking with the wrong head.

Catherine gave Aunt Brigit's hands a grateful squeeze. Only another spinster could begin to understand what she was going through at this moment, and Aunt Brigit did. Catherine needed a home, a new life, and Aunt Brigit had become her ally in procuring one.

Most comforting of all, she knew how much Aunt Brigit loved Duncan. For all the little woman's bluster, she would never insist on a match she felt would be harmful to him. That confidence went a long way toward shoring up the shattered remnants of Catherine's confidence. If Aunt Brigit thought this was best for everyone, Catherine could believe it just might be. It wasn't as if she had any other options, after all.

Thanks to the children, she could love and be loved. Have a family. It was what she had longed for. She just hadn't ever imagined she would get it by ending up in the perilous, untamed Scottish borders, married to a proud, untamed Scottish bastard. That part would take some getting used to, but life as Duncan Maxwell's wife . . . a jolt of pure lust erupted beneath the sodden blanket of grief, guilt, and regret that weighted her.

She leveled a decisive gaze to the handsome, flustered man before her. "Very well, Duncan Maxwell. I will marry you."

A tumult of giggles and thumps erupted from the children beyond the door.

"Ah." Aunt Brigit beamed. " 'Tis settled, then."

Duncan couldn't believe his ears. "What d'ye mean, settled?" This was like a bad dream. "She canna accept anything. I never asked her!"

"Ye didna have to say the words, man," Bink informed him. "Yer actions made the promise. By the laws of God and king, ye must marry her." She looked ridiculous, circling Kate's waist protectively as if the Englishwoman were some foolish virgin he'd led astray instead of a mature female taller by a head than his aunt.

"I told ye I would get another wife," he parried. Duncan shot a caustic look at Kate. "One with a goodly dowry."

"Fah!" Bink swatted off the suggestion as if it were a gnat. "Ye've already married every decent woman within fifteen parishes who would have ye, dowered or otherwise. Nae, Duncan." She smiled at Kate. "It must be Kate, and now."

This was preposterous. "I only kissed her!"

Why was he defending himself?

"If ye have a whit of honor in ye, man, or care fer yer children, ye'll marry her," Bink roared. Reclaiming her composure, she actually bestowed a dainty peck on each of Kate's cheeks. "Amber and Erinn will be beside themselves wi' joy. I'm sure they'll want to help ye prepare fer the nuptials."

"Nae the children, Bink!" He'd never hear the end of it. And Baran would sulk for months—years, maybe.

"I doona have to tell them, lad," his aunt informed him. "They've been listenin' at the door."

Duncan groaned. This had gotten completely out of hand.

Aunt Brigit glanced out at the bright fall morning, then directed her attention back to Kate, who seemed strangely serene. "Michael won't be back with Angus until mid-afternoon, so ye'll have plenty of time to prepare."

"Michael?" Duncan bristled. "Doona drag him into this, Bink, I warn ye."

"Doona dare to warn me, lad," she said with a twinkle in her eye. "Ye're still not quite as tall as I am when ye bend over and catch yer ankles."

She hadn't threatened him with that since he'd been a callow, insolent brash of a lad. His cuddy warmed at the mere thought of the swift but just punishment she'd administered with her wooden cutting board back then.

But Duncan wouldna be put off so easily. "I am nae a lad to be spanked, Bink," he cautioned her, "and I have nae intention of marryin' Kate."

Was that injury he saw in Kate's eyes?

Blast the woman. Why did she have to turn that same wounded look on him that he'd seen when he'd read of her family's rejection?

He had nae reason to feel guilty. He'd only kissed her. Why should her anguish cut him so?

"Come along, Duncan." Bink drew him toward the doorway. "I'm sure ye've much to do before the weddin'." Before Duncan could set her straight, four of his children mobbed him.

"Thank ye, Papa! Thank ye." Erinn leapt into his arms and hugged his neck till he could scarcely breathe. "I've prayed for this so long."

The twins pounded him on the back. "Ladykate's a good one, Papa," Gordon asserted, "even if she is an Englisher."

"Aye," Kerry seconded. "Thurlow's English, too, and he's all right."

"We need a mother, Pa," Cameron added. "And she's a good cook and a fair hard worker, even if she is plain."

"And makes us wash," Gordon added with a frown.

Only Amber and Baran held back. To Duncan's surprise, Amber seemed subdued, and Baran wasn't sulking.

Nevin pulled loose from Amber's hand. "Mama." He toddled straight past Duncan to Kate's waiting arms.

Baran shot him a wry look. "Ye were right, Papa. 'Twas extortion." He shook his head, surveying the tumult. "Are marriages always made this way?"

"They're nae supposed to be." Duncan set Erinn to her feet, then turned to his elder daughter. The way she doted on Kate, he'd have thought Amber would be happiest of all with the idea, but instead she seemed on the verge of tears.

"What is it, Amber?"

"How could you do this to her?" she accused, her eyes welling. "Kate deserves better than we can offer her, Papa. And she deserves a husband who wants her, nae one who's forced to take her."

Why in blazes was she blaming him? "Ye heard the same as the others, lass," he explained. "This wasna my idea. I never asked the woman to marry me."

"Well, ye should've," she said, contradicting herself in the baffling way of her gender. "Shame on ye for nae askin', Papa," she whispered dramatically through her tears. "Shame on us all fer keepin' her here." She bolted for her room. "Now I'll never see England!"

Women! Duncan rolled his eyes heavenward.

Maybe Angus Maxwell could talk some sense into them. *He* certainly couldn't.

And he had no intention of marrying Kate!

Chapter
FOURTEEN

Duncan sat in the parlor at the head table with Kate to his right, Angus Maxwell to his left, and Annanlea's noisy, celebrating inhabitants crowded about him. The sound of lute, timbrel, and wood pipes mixed with a festive roar of conversation. Underneath the table, Clyde lay across Kate's feet, panting happily.

Duncan still couldn't believe it.

He'd married Ladykate.

And she had married *him*—a bastard, a man with no name to give her save his mother's.

The pain of that still smarted, though why it did, he couldn't fathom. It had never bothered him before. But none of his other marriages had been even remotely like this one, and none of his other wives remotely like Kate.

Duncan looked around him. Aside from Baran and Amber, no one else seemed loath to accept it, though. After so many months of strain and worry, his people had grasped with gusto this opportunity to forget their troubles and revel, even if only for a few hours. And in spite of the fact that he'd married an Englisher.

An Englisher. Too ironic to be borne. All her British ways were constant reminders of his tainted blood and abandonment. Duncan still couldn't believe he'd married her.

He turned to find Kate watching him. "I know," she said. "I can't quite believe it, either."

How did she *do* that? He cocked a half-smile. "This will never work if ye read ma thoughts, Kate."

"Then don't look so transparent, husband." Her gentle tone took the sting from her retort.

Pitcher in hand, Amber approached them wearing a face more fit for a funeral than a wedding. "Mead?"

"Aye." Kate held out her goblet, clearly aware of Amber's dark mood but prudently silent about it. After a heavy sigh, Amber poured the wine, then left them.

"Such a difficult age," Kate observed when his daughter was out of earshot. "Everything is either a tragedy or a miracle. Nothing in between."

Duncan wondered what Kate had been like when she was a girl. Now that they were married, she was free to tell him. If she would. "Were ye like that at Amber's age?"

A faraway look tinged with both sadness and nostalgia stole across her face. "Aye. Very much so."

"So which did ye have more of then, Ladykate?" he prodded. "Miracles or tragedies?"

"Miracles, when I was small," she said without hesitation. Then her brown eyes dimmed. "Later, tragedies." She shook her head. "At Amber's age . . . Ah, such dramas. Far too much wear and tear on the emotions."

Duncan wondered what Kate's dreams had been and what had stolen them from her. Her stepfamily, no doubt. "And after that?"

"I grew up and made the best of my lot as a spinster," she said without a trace of self-pity.

"Spinster nae more," he reminded her.

A subtle wonder crept into her expression. "Aye. I'm Dame Maxwell now, aren't I?" She said it as if she didn't mind a bit.

Duncan followed Kate's gaze to Baran, who sulked in his seat. "Give them time," he told her. "They'll get used to things."

The question was, would he?

Duncan still wasn't certain how matters had gone so far so fast. True, Angus Maxwell—the traitor—had insisted he was obligated to wed Kate, but why in blazes had it had to be so quick? The minister had acted as if she were nine months gone!

Bink was behind the whole thing, really.

Hell, he chided himself. Blame was for small children

and horse races. Duncan couldn't even muster up enough outrage to convince himself. The truth was, he could easily have stopped the marriage at any point along the way. It would not have happened if he hadn't let it. That was the most baffling thing: he'd let it happen.

He had married an Englisher whose surname he hadn't heard until the middle of the ceremony: Armstrong. Even that had told him little. There were Armstrongs, and then there were Armstrongs. He didn't know yet exactly where she'd come from, or the name of the stepfamily who had turned their backs on her.

Sitting there, looking at the plain, proud, stubborn woman who was now his wife, he realized that for some perverse, unimaginable reason he had *wanted* to marry Kate, God help him.

Bink had only provided the momentum.

Speak of the devil, his aunt arrived with pieces of Lucas's infamous wedding cake. "Eat up, for luck," she admonished. "And doona leave a crumb." She handed Duncan his piece, then wagged a finger. "When it comes to wives, ye need all the luck ye can get."

"I ate every scrap of ma cake four times before," Duncan shot back, "and all I got for it was bad luck and a bellyache." Realizing too late that he'd probably been impolitic in mentioning his previous fated weddings, he shifted his attention to the dry, heavy slab of cake. "It appears Lucas has got nae better with practice."

Yoicks. He'd done it again. Fortunately, Kate seemed unperturbed.

"Never mind what it tastes like, Duncan," Aunt Brigit dismissed as she slapped Kate's down before her. "Tradition demands it. Ye'll eat it for Ladykate's sake." She pinned Kate with a warning look. "And she'll eat hers for ye." She left them to supervise serving the others.

Kate inspected hers. "Lucas and I never got around to cake-baking lessons. It appears he could use a few."

"Weddings are the only time he makes them," Duncan

explained. "To everyone's relief. Eating it is a rite of passage, a shared ordeal."

Duncan broke off a bite of the heavy, dark slice. "Looks awful dry." Wary, he raised the morsel to his nose and sniffed. It had an odd, but not unpleasant, odor. "Spicy."

Kate broke off a bite of hers and sniffed it, too. "Aye. Mayhap it won't be as bad as his others." She held hers poised, eyeing him askance. Duncan noted that they were not alone in their hesitation. Everyone else seemed to be waiting for them to eat theirs first.

When it became obvious that both bride and groom were each hoping the other would go first, Kate spoke up. "What's the matter, Duncan. Afraid?"

" 'Tis prudence, nae fear, that holds me back," he said, sanguine.

A small frown tugged her ample mouth. "We have to eat this, you know. We'll invite disaster if we don't. 'Tis the custom on my side of the border, too."

He exhaled slowly. "Tradition demands it."

"A wager, then," she challenged, lifting the cube of cake between her fingers. "Whoever finishes last must obey the other without question until sunrise."

"Done," Duncan said, then promptly shoved the small cube of cake into his mouth, followed immediately by the rest of his slice.

Letting out a muffled cry of protest, Kate popped hers in, but she had to break the rest of her slice into pieces to fit it into her mouth.

Only when both of them, cheeks stuffed like squirrels, began to chew in earnest did the wretched taste and dryness hit them. Eyes watering, both grabbed for their goblets and did their best to wash the noxious mess down with mead.

A roar of laughter went up among the celebrants, followed by a pregnant silence as they devoured theirs, as well.

Adults' eyes watered and children gagged and uttered

protests, but everyone joined in the ceremonial sacrifice.

In the end, Duncan's superior size enabled him to win the wager. Kate was still chewing frantically when he swallowed the last of his and opened his mouth wide to claim victory. "Aaah. Gone. I win."

"Mmph!" She struck the tablecloth with her fist in frustration. As soon as she choked down the last of hers, she stretched out her goblet toward Amber's pitcher. "Quickly. More mead," she pleaded with a mixture of humor and desperation. "Leave the pitcher."

Only when she'd washed away some of the taste did she turn back to him. "Very well, you rogue, I concede. I shall obey you," she said without the slightest trace of submission. "Until sunrise, at any rate."

"That should be long enough. For a start," Duncan answered. How he savored the idea of having Kate at his whim on this of all nights. A number of delicious possibilities sent a shot of desire straight through him.

As if she had read his thoughts, she colored, then looked away.

Duncan studied her classic profile and her straight, strong torso as she watched the crowd. He certainly could have done worse. She was no great beauty, true, but her ill-fitting clothes hinted she was woman aplenty, and her big brown eyes, ample mouth, and willful chin had grown on him.

Yet there was far more to Kate than her woman's body. She was a survivor, a force to be reckoned with. They had that much in common, at least. And her intelligent wit often made him smile despite the barbs that came with it.

Irritating though the woman could be, she possessed a rare spark that brought light to the dark corners of his life. Maybe that was why he'd married her—for her spark.

Better the devil he knew than the devil he didn't, and he knew this one well enough. Kate would soon be back to her bossy, irritating ways, but with luck, her spark would warm his life. And his bed.

She caught him looking at her and actually blushed. "Look as you will, husband, but I am still the woman I was when you married me," she said with a tiny edge of defensiveness. "Too late to change your mind now."

He didn't want to. Not yet, anyway. Looking forward to doing more than kissing her, he took her hand in his. "Nor can ye. We're stuck with each other, Kate."

Kate blushed, then retracted her hand in a decidedly virginal gesture.

Fool that he was, he actually hoped they might make merry in bed this night. If his previous wedding nights were any portent of this one, though, the odds of a happy consummation were not good.

Not that Duncan had any reservations about his skills as a lover. He'd bedded a few willing wenches before and between wives, and they had made it clear they reveled in his attentions. 'Twas a matter of pride to bring pleasure to his partners, not to rut with them like an animal. But his brides . . . they had been nothing like the wenches.

Like Kate, two of his late wives had been virgins. The first, poor Peggy, had burst into torrents of tears upon seeing his erect member, setting the disastrous tone for their fated union. No amount of patience and consideration had eased her revulsion for what she called her "wifely sacrifice." It had been a miracle indeed that Amber and Baran had issued from her martyred couplings.

His last wife, fragile Aselma, had been no better when it came to conjugal matters. Mating with her had been like making love to a creature made of glass. Despite his best efforts to woo her gently, she'd wept in silence almost every time he'd taken her, convinced that sexual pleasure was the devil's snare.

Ach, Aselma. She'd endured his attentions only in hopes of the children she so desperately wanted.

His second and third wives, Beth and Leslie, had been widows, simplifying things immensely, but only Beth had enjoyed their lovemaking. At least, he'd thought she had. She'd never come right out and said so, but she'd responded readily enough whenever he'd reached for her under the covers. Leslie, though . . . Her lack of response had left him feeling as if he were making love to a woman in a trance.

If only tonight could be different.

Kate certainly was. There was nothing fragile about her, nothing passive. And definitely nothing timid. He'd caught her looking at him more than once this day with a hungry curiosity that had pricked his male instincts.

"Here, Kate." He refilled her goblet with sweet spiced wine. "A maiden only marries once. Drink up."

She drank as if it were a physic, then set the goblet down with another of those half-shy, half-brazen looks that set his loins atingle.

Aye. They might make merry, indeed.

As the lower tables were taken down to make way for the dancing, Duncan's men approached to pay their respects. Lucas came first, as drunk on pride as he was from wine. His daughters hovered behind him. "Hullo, the newlyweds," he bleared.

"Excellent feast, Lucas," Kate complimented him with a dazzling smile. Wisely, she said nothing about the cake. "The touch of sage on the roast pork was inspired." Duncan noted her speech was just the tiniest bit slurred from the mead she'd drunk.

"Thank ye, Nessa's Lady," Lucas boomed, then turned to Duncan. "Good choice, man," he said with characteristic frankness. "I hope she lasts."

Duncan recoiled at the crass reference to his fatal bad fortune with wives, but Kate laughed aloud. "I might not want to, Lucas." She grinned at the three young women hiding in their father's wake. "I see you have your girls with you."

"Aye, and promised all, thanks to ye." Lucas beamed as the three sturdy lasses crept into the open to offer Kate a curtsy.

"I wish you great happiness and many healthy children," Kate said graciously.

"An' great happiness and many healthy children to ye and Duncan, too," Lucas chimed in over his daughters' murmured good wishes.

"What was that about?" Duncan asked as Lucas's daughters steered the drunken cook back to his seat.

"Happiness, or healthy children?" Kate said in mock innocence.

"Nae. The promised part."

She kept her eyes on the crowd, continued smiling, but her body tensed. "Nothing, really. I simply noticed three of Auld Wat's lads eyeing Lucas's daughters when they ate here, so I arranged for each girl to serve the one who'd taken a fancy to her. Then I merely suggested to Lucas that he might wish to mention to Wat's captain that the girls were all good cooks and hard workers who would bring with them his best receipts as dower."

So *that* was what she'd been up to that night.

"A letter or two went back and forth." Kate shrugged, still not looking at him.

Duncan straightened in alarm. This was serious. "Ye've been correspondin' with Wat?" How had she gotten past him?

"Not I," she said evenly. "Lucas was corresponding with Wat's captain. I simply wrote the letters and read Lucas the replies."

The trouble she might have gotten them into . . . By Saint Matthew's wallet, she could have written anything! And Lucas! "I'll deal with Lucas later about this," he snapped.

Kate faced him. "Lucas did nothing wrong, Duncan. He has as much right as any man to see his daughters wed."

"Nae without ma approval." It sounded petty even to him, but Duncan could not allow such a breach to pass unaddressed. If anyone but his bride had done such a thing, he'd have been forced to execute speedy and public justice. But in deference to the occasion, he choked down his temper. "Never do that again, Kate," he said gruffly.

"I won't need to." A smug smile curled her lips. " 'Tis done, and as the bard said, 'All's well that ends well.' "

Blast her insolence. Had the woman no grasp of the risks she'd caused? The smallest slight could have transformed his most important alliance into a deadly enmity.

Ended well, indeed.

Duncan wondered. "So Lucas marries off three daughters," he said with an evenness he did not feel, "and Annanlea loses three good cooks and hard workers."

"Nay." Kate forked up a delicate morsel of pork and ate it. "You lose two barely adequate cooks to Wat. The best lass stays here, and brings her husband with her."

What? "And Wat agreed to that?" Nobody got the best of Wat, not even Duncan himself.

She cocked her head with a benign smile. "Wat dearly loved my tansy. That particular receipt cost him a man."

"Well, I'll be skinned." He assessed his bride with a new respect—and wariness. The woman wasn't a wife, she was a secret weapon. But he had to break her of this meddling. It was far too dangerous. "In the future, Kate, doona communicate with anyone beyond these walls wi'out ma express permission. There's too much at stake, especially with Wat."

She nodded, but her eyes did not relent. "As you wish, my lord."

Quinn and Rory Little approached with a posy of yellow mums apiece. Flowers were the one thing she'd neglected in the hurried preparations. Rory handed his to Kate first, granting her an unprecedented smile. "Long life and happiness, Ladykate. And thank ye for the salve."

Hearing Rory speak, Duncan couldn't believe his eyes, or his ears. "Rory?" In the seven years since the brothers had thrown in with him, this was the first time the man had made polite conversation, much less smiled.

Rory met Duncan's surprise with calm appraisal. "Well done, Duncan."

Quinn parried his flowers like a sword toward Kate in jest. "Good as new, Ladykate. Good as new." He grinned

to Duncan. "She saved ma sword arm, just like I told ye."
He added his posy to his brother's. "Long life and happiness, Ladykate. Even if ye are an Englisher."

Her laugh was as clear as meadow song in spring.
"Thank you for the flowers. They will make a perfect bridal crown." She spread the blossoms on the table, then deftly began to weave the stems together into a golden halo.

Quinn bowed as if she were a duchess. "May our new mistress be as good for Duncan as she's been fer all of Annanlea."

Kate nodded, her smile one of genuine affection as the two men left them. An unexpected twinge of jealousy made Duncan wonder if she would ever regard him so.

He told himself it didn't matter. None of his marriages had been love matches. Why should this one be any different? Kate needed a home, a protector. He needed a mother for his children and help for Bink. 'Twas reason enough to marry.

Aye. 'Twas reason enough.

So why did his innerds tug at him when he saw her smile on others as she had never smiled at him?

Kate finished her crown of golden mums, then donned it to welcome the people who were now her own. One by one, Duncan watched and listened as his men, some of them with their families, came forward to offer their good wishes. But more than that, his people offered something else: their thanks to Ladykate for touching their lives in the few short weeks she'd been there. A poultice here, a wound stitched there. A pot of stew when a wife was ill. Shoes sewn from old grain sacks. Clean water. A few extra turnips for those with growing boys. As the list of unsung kindnesses came to light, Kate accepted their thanks with simple grace and genuine humility.

Duncan was astounded. When had she had the time, especially with the ruckus she'd stirred up cleaning his house to within an inch of its life?

"Are you all right, Duncan?" Her dark brows drew

together beneath her golden halo of flowers. "You look worried."

"Nae worried. Amazed," he murmured. In a jarring flash of insight, he realized he'd never really *seen* the woman he'd just married. Who she was beneath her crusty ways and outspoken opinions.

For every strident word, a quiet kindness had passed unnoticed as she'd embraced his people in a way he never had. For every criticism she'd directed at him, she'd liberally dispensed encouragement, hugs, and loving discipline to his children. Even Aunt Brigit loved her, and now he realized why.

Kate was as big a fraud as Bink, the auld softy! Why hadn't he seen it?

Knowing it lifted some of the weight from his careworn shoulders.

Perhaps this could work out. But if the marriage were to have a chance, Kate must stop writing letters without his knowledge. That could be their downfall.

"Yeek!" His bride let out a most undignified shriek, then snatched up the edge of the tablecloth to glare down on Clyde. "Kindly discipline your dog, sir," she ordered Duncan in her old high-handed tone. "He's trying to swallow my foot."

Sure enough, Clyde appeared to be sucking on her toes, shoe and all.

"Ach. He's only adorin' ye," Duncan explained, "kissin' your foot as if ye were a saint. Ye should be flattered." He scratched the hound's head affectionately, but he made no move to stop him. "There's nae a bit of pressure in his jaws."

Kate grimaced with distaste as she gingerly took hold of Clyde's well-lubricated dog lips in an effort to open his mouth. "Nay, Clyde. Nay," she scolded in irritation. "Let go."

Clyde just wagged his great tail harder, delighted that she'd made eye contact and touched him. The fool animal truly adored her, but he had not one whit of respect for her.

Duncan took pity on Kate and snapped his finger, then pointed to heel, whereupon Clyde released her toes and stood up—shaking the table and everything on it—before he settled obediently where Duncan indicated.

"Ick." Kate scowled at her soggy shoe. "My foot is soaked." She washed her hands in the laver, then dried them.

The music grew louder, inviting everyone to dance.

"Your foot may be wet, but I'll wager it works as well as ever." Duncan stood to draw her up beside him. "Dance wi' me, Kate, and show the world you're mine."

"My name is Catherine, not Kate," she answered.

Duncan searched the rich brown depths of her eyes and found hope and humor there, along with a tempering measure of dreams surrendered. " 'Twas nae the wedding a young lass imagines, was it?"

"I'm nae a lass," she answered with a straight face in that annoyingly accurate brogue of hers, "and I'd long since given up on ever having a wedding of any kind." She pressed close to conceal the hand that cupped his member. "Or one of these."

"Whoa." Duncan's manhood jolted alive at the unexpected caress. "What shall it be, Catherine?" he whispered in her ear, the flowers soft against his temple. "Dance or play? It's up to ye."

She stepped back and drew him toward the open floor. "First we dance. Then we play."

And dance they did, with Kate sipping down at least two more glasses of mead between the lively tunes. She picked up their local dances with formidable ease and grace. And with every dance, she grew freer with her manner, her body, and her wine. Though Duncan enjoyed seeing his prim bride make merry, after an hour he signaled Aunt Brigit to stop the wine for fear Kate would lose consciousness before she retired to their bridal bed.

When the music ceased after a particularly merry jig,

Kate staggered, breathless, against him. "Whew, that was lively. Ask them to play a slower one while I catch my breath." Her color was high, her eyes bright but slightly glazed, her mouth ripe, full, and ready for the taking. Seeing her this way, he realized she wasn't plain, but quite a striking woman, indeed.

"Nae." Duncan swept her up into his arms. " 'Tis time we were abed, ma Kate."

Their guests caught hold of his words and raised a rowdy chant, "To bed! To bed! To bed!" followed by a flood of ribald comments that turned Kate's cheeks even ruddier.

Mayhap it was the spirits, but instead of hiding from the good-natured coarseness, Kate looked him in the eye with unabashed conjecture. "Aye, then, husband." She dragged her fingertip seductively along the juncture of his lips, then whispered for his ears only, "Take me to our bed and show me what it's like to feel my body like a woman full, at last."

Duncan's manhood leapt. Impatient to do just that, he kissed her right there in front of everyone. Yet what began as a stamp of possession quickly became something else entirely when she yielded to his lips with a hungry eagerness that propelled him far beyond mere lust. Suddenly the presence of the others became unbearable. He wanted to get Kate alone, strip the clothes from her body, and savor her awakening.

Trailed by clapping women and hooting men, he carried her to the room they now would share. Aunt Brigit followed hard by, swatting at anyone who got too close or too unruly.

At last, he ducked through the open door into his chamber, which had been flowered and scoured beyond all decency.

Clyde trotted in behind them, grinning his slack dog grin.

"Out." Kate pointed to the door.

Clyde sat.

"Duncan." She appealed to him. "I married you, not your hound. May we not be alone in our bedchamber, at least?"

"Aye." Duncan wanted no distractions. He lowered Kate to her feet then pointed to the door. "Out, Clyde."

The hound turned soulful eyes at them, then slunk halfway to the hall and stopped. Another soulful look.

"Out," Duncan commanded.

The picture of dejection, Clyde pushed past Aunt Brigit and disappeared into the crowd.

Bink's voice rose above those of the revelers: "Oyez! Oyez! Oyez!" She laid her insubstantial weight to the door, shooting Duncan a parting wink as she sealed their privacy. "Back downstairs!" came her muffled instructions through the closed door. "We've saved the sweet rolls for last. Back downstairs, now." Within seconds, the hallway fell silent.

After the heat and noise, the cool silence of the room made Duncan self-conscious. "Well, then. Here we are."

Kate's earlier abandon seemed to have evaporated along with the noise, but he was pleased to see a keen spark of anticipation in her big brown eyes. "Aye," she said shyly. "Here we are." She looked lovely standing there, almost like a girl, her dark hair framed with golden flowers and softly caught up into a bun at the nape of her neck, her simple clothing accenting her narrow waistline and womanly curves.

He shifted from one foot to the other, still eager to have her, but all too aware of her inexperience.

Why was he nervous? He had more experience with wedding nights than most men.

Suddenly feeling as if his collar had shrunk a size, he tugged loose the neck of his doublet. "If ye like," he offered, "I could turn ma back while ye make ready for bed."

"Thank you." A touch of the old, prim Kate crept into her voice. "I would."

Duncan did, conscious of her every footstep and each

soft scrape of fabric as she removed her clothing. Absently, he unbuttoned his jacket the rest of the way, then shrugged it off onto the chair facing him beside the bed. "Just tell me when you're ready for me to turn around."

"I shall." Her voice had tightened; he could hear it. The mead must be wearing off.

By the devil's codpiece, what in blazes had possessed him to marry a middle-aged virgin? And why was he standing here hoping their wedding night could be anything but difficult?

But his lower lip tingled with the memory of Kate's finger tracing along it, and his member leapt at the memory of her hand upon it.

He heard the sound of a brush sweeping long, careful strokes through her hair, and it made him wonder what that hair would feel like dragging gently across his naked body.

Fry his liver for bacon, but he'd been too long without a woman. His manhood swelled so full it ached. Yet she was a maiden, he reminded himself, so he must take her gently.

Duncan did not understand it, but he wanted Kate in a way he hadn't craved the others. He wanted to waken her to the binding consolation he'd heard the marriage bed could be. Wanted to find that consolation himself, with her. Was it too much to hope that they succor each other now?

"You may look," she said.

He turned to find her sitting up against the pillows, the covers drawn to her chest and a high-necked nightgown tied up tight below her chin. Her dark hair tumbled loose around her shoulders, and her great brown eyes peered up at him with open candor.

She looked like the girl she might have been before life had hardened her spirit and sharpened her tongue. Softer. Younger. Beautiful, in her own distinctive way.

"Would you like for me to close my eyes while you

make ready for bed?" she quipped. Leave it to Kate to shatter the spell by speaking.

"Nae." He cocked a wry half-smile. "I'm made the same as any man. Ye might as well see what ye're getting."

"In my duties with the sick and injured back home I've seen many a man, Duncan Maxwell," she said, "in many a state of dress and undress. But never have I seen one like you, nor ever shall, methinks."

Uncertain just how to take that, he paused with his hand on the buttons to his breeches. "Then ye have seen a man as God made him?" He didn't want a repeat of the disaster that had transpired with poor Peggy.

"Did I not say as much?" she shot back, blunt as ever. "But only seen. Never touched or been touched. Never even kissed, except by you."

"I'm glad." And he was—more than glad, surprising himself with the possessiveness he felt. It made no sense, but there it was.

He unbuckled his scabbard, then his belt, and hung them on the arm of the chair. Then he sat down to remove his boots.

"Here, let me help you with those." She slipped from beneath the covers and circled the foot of the bed to kneel before him, her wavy hair catching the shine of the candles and the fire. She gripped the burnished leather boots with expert competence and easily slid them from his feet.

"Thank ye." Part of him was moved by her simple gesture, but the other part wondered if she was up to something. Yet she looked so lovely there, her simple white gown pooled on the floor, her dark hair cloaked against it.

She stood his boots neatly beside the chair. "There. I used to help my younger brother, Hal, with his," she said. "He was always getting stuck with them half off, calling for Catherine—" She faltered, eyes averted, and Duncan wondered again what sort of family would have thrown her away. When she stood, her gaze was bruised, but steady. "Taking off boots is so much easier with someone to help."

Duncan grasped her hands in his and rose, achingly conscious of her woman's body beneath the fabric of her borrowed gown. "We can help each other now, ma Kate." He drew her close, savoring the feel of her softness against him as she willingly curled into his arms.

"Why did you do it, Duncan?" she whispered. "Why did you marry me, really?"

"It was ye and Bink who cooked this up. And ma blasted cousin Angus, who said I had nae other honorable choice," he said lightly over the top of her head, knowing that wasn't the reason. All he knew was, he wasn't sorry.

It felt so good to hold her. They seemed to fit. And he wanted her as he'd wanted no other woman. Yet he knew that gentle talk and listening were love to a woman, so he stayed the urges of his body.

"Nonsense," she murmured. "Nobody forces you into anything, Duncan." She burrowed deeper into the shelter of his chin. "You've never bowed to anyone else's will and likely never shall, especially Angus Maxwell."

Why did she have to be so right all the time? "Well, what about ye?" he countered. "Why did ye marry me? And doona try to tell me ye were led astray. The devil himself couldna lead the likes of ye astray, ma Ladykate, unless ye willed it so."

She stilled. "The truth?"

"Aye, truth." For some unknown reason, he believed she would tell him.

She let out a pensive sigh. "I love your children." She paused. "Even Baran." Another pause. "And I needed a place to belong. A home." Another pause. "I can be useful here. My life will have meaning."

He sensed she had given all her reasons but the real one. "Is that all I offer ye, Ladykate?" he asked her softly. "Ma children and a useful existence?" Duncan smoothed his hands down her buttocks to cup them hungrily, eliciting a sharp intake of breath from her. "Ye wound ma manly pride."

"Nay. That wasn't all." Her words were breathy as she leaned against him, the pressure of her body exquisite torture against his erection. "I wanted more." She pulled back and searched his eyes, her own shadowed with fear and longing. "I wanted this." She ground her hips against him even harder, releasing shards of pain and pleasure. "I wanted you. Us." Her voice was thick with desire. "Together like this. I want you inside me. I want to feel what I've only dreamed. You haunt my dreams, Duncan Maxwell."

Duncan almost spilled his seed. No woman had ever spoken to him so frankly, or so erotically. Yet he could not deny the innocence behind her boldness.

"Do ye ken what passes between husband and wife, Kate?" he asked.

"I've heard the serving wenches talk," she answered. "Staff and shaft, they said. I know what goes where."

"There's more to it than staff and shaft, ma Ladykate. So much more."

"Aye." Her color heightened. "They spoke of that, as well."

He caught her up into his arms, then laid her on the bed. She made no effort to cover up or hide herself, just stretched there without artifice or shame. The way she looked at him . . . Duncan recognized and appreciated passion in a woman, but this was different. He saw a hunger far deeper than lust and more provocative than mere desire in Kate. She looked on him with dreams, and in her dreams he saw his own, long since lost yet resurrected. They resonated from her bones to his, invading on her gaze, her touch, her very breath.

Beneath the threadbare linen of her gown as she lay before him, he could see the shadow of her breasts and the dark vee at the apex of her legs. His manhood throbbed harder and tighter with every heartbeat.

He wanted to make her sing like his violin, to stroke

her dreamsong from her soul the way he stroked his music from its strings. To pluck the notes of her long-denied desires.

The way she looked at him . . .

Suddenly he was smothering inside his clothes, couldn't get them off fast enough. He dropped his breeches, taking his stockings with them, then stepped free and stripped off his shirt. Naked at last, he stood beside the bed to see her eyes widen.

She scanned his body without fear, without coyness, without cunning. Seeing the overt approval in her expression, it was all he could do to keep his headlong passion in check.

Catherine took her time looking over the magnificent man who was now her husband. For once in her life, her vivid imagination had failed her. He was more than she had conjured—harder, more muscular, more glorious. Real. Lethal. The battle scars that crossed his torso only enhanced the masculine perfection of his body.

She followed the scattering of ebon curls that tapered from his chest to his groin. His proud erection nestled there in a state of arousal worthy of fable. As if he had felt her gaze, his member leapt, setting loose an answering paroxysm deep inside her.

The way he looked at her . . . as if he wanted to feast on her, ravage her, gobble her up. Never had she thought a man would look at her that way, especially one as powerful and handsome as Duncan Maxwell.

Could she dare believe it? Did he want her?

Her mind knew better, but her body . . .

Her body overrode everything, sweeping her on a tide of emotion and desire past logic and reality, beyond safety. This night, she would be a queen. Wanted. Desired. Beautiful. This night, her hunger would be enough to make her believe that his desire was real.

What came later did not matter. She would have this much, at least.

In a haze of passion, she rose to her knees at the edge

of the bed and drew him closer, reveling in the sharp tang of man-smell that filled her nostrils when she circled his waist. She laid her cheek to his chest, his erection firm and hot against her waist.

Duncan threw his head back with a groan. His hands roamed her like those of a blind man, stroking, caressing, setting every nerve on edge as he claimed her with his touch.

Driven by a wisdom as ancient as man and woman, Catherine responded in kind. Her fingers savored the smooth ripples of his ribs, then glided over the sharply defined muscles of his back, across the taut hardness of his buttocks, down the corded power of his thighs. The more she explored, the more ragged his breathing and urgent his own hands became. They followed each other in a glorious fugue of desire and sensation.

Abruptly, he pushed her from him. "I want to see you," he said, his voice hoarse.

She untied the ribbons of her gown as quickly as her shaking fingers could, but Duncan was too impatient to wait. After only two ties were free, he brushed her hands away and pulled loose the ribbons himself, then smoothed the fabric from her shoulders. As it fell to the bed around her, his blue eyes darkened with raw desire. "Saints," he breathed out, "that's some body you've been hiding."

The conviction in his words sent Catherine's heart soaring. For so long, she'd believed no man would ever want her. Yet Duncan did. This beautiful, terrible, unsettling man did. He looked on her as God had made her, and lusted.

It drove her beyond the brink of boldness. Her naked skin burned despite the cool night air that stood every hair on her body aright.

Duncan drew her up to plunder her mouth, bringing her breasts into contact with the hard muscle and crisp curls of his chest.

Catherine felt herself spinning. What was it, this power he had over her, this magic he worked with touch and tongue to make her melt inside? Her body wept in exquisite agony. He had only to kiss her, caress her, and suddenly there was no world beyond these walls.

No past. No future. Only Duncan.

Suddenly fierce, he grasped her buttocks and drew her astride his hips, nestling the length of his shaft against the hot, wet slash of her desire.

Catherine heard her own cry as if it had come from someone else. Explosions of lightninglike sensation erupted from the point of contact. He shifted her upwards bringing the tip of his member into maddening contact with the mouth of her femininity.

She fought the overwhelming compulsion to impale herself. Instead, she closed her eyes and focused on the delicate torture. She shuddered, afraid the emptiness welling inside her would swallow her whole, yet held herself on the brink. "Take me," she gasped out.

To her dismay, he swung her into his arms and laid her on the bed again, then lay beside her, his hungry gaze glowing like the heart of a forge. "First, let me give ye pleasure, Kate." His tongue flicked her earlobe, then he playfully closed his teeth on the tender flesh, sending a thrill clear to her toes. "Ye told me the wenches said there was more than staff and shaft. What did they say?"

"They spoke of their lovers caressing their breasts," she answered, "teasing the nipple between their fingers, suckling like babes."

She felt his body quake at her shameless words.

"Like this?" He bent his head to her breasts, and she arched in ecstasy as his fingers did as she'd described. Then his lips brushed across the sensitive flesh. When he stroked her tight nipples with his tongue, Catherine thought surely she would die.

She cried out, grasping his thick, wavy hair close to the scalp and drawing him closer. "Don't stop. Aaagh. Nay, the other now. Yes. Oh, yes."

Maddeningly, he pulled away. "What else did the wenches say," he goaded.

"They said..." She couldn't. It was too coarse. "They...I—"

"Did they speak of this?" His fingers probed the hidden flesh between her legs. Catherine's body contacted hungrily in response. When he probed deeper, sliding his finger inside of her, she could not help herself, but thrust to meet him. "Duncan," she gasped out, "end this torture. Take me."

He nibbled at her breast. "Nae until you've felt your body like a woman full, Kate."

She gripped the sheets in exquisite frustration, her legs stiffened and toes pointed. "I have. I am."

"Nae yet." His gaze locked to hers, Duncan knelt between her legs and pushed them apart, stroking the inside of her thighs, preparing the way with his fingers, kissing her low on the belly, driving her mad.

But when his fingers closed on the pearl of her desire, gently but insistently rolling it between them, she came straight up off the bed with a cry and wrapped herself around his torso. "Now!" she demanded. "I cannot bear it. Now."

"It's your first time." Genuine concern clouded his face. "There will be pain. We must take it slowly."

Heart pounding, she met his worried look with one of deadly determination. "Let me be the judge of that." She kissed him with fierce abandon, her nails digging into his shoulders, her body demanding what was rightfully hers.

Even Duncan Maxwell had his limits. With a primal growl, he lifted her into position, but halted when he met resistance.

Catherine didn't. She thrust herself downward with all her might, and an explosion of pain erupted into a scream.

"My God, Catherine," he choked out, "are ye all right?"

Catherine wasn't sure at first, but then a warmth began to spread where the pain had been. Tentative, she shifted with him inside her, and a wondrous filling diffused her being.

He eased her back onto the bed, but she held on tight, forbidding him to part from her. "Duncan," she whispered. "Do not leave me. Stay inside me. Move inside me."

Propping himself with his arms, he rose to look at her in wonder. Then slowly, he began to draw, then thrust.

Catherine leaned up and peered at the point of joining, which caused his member to twitch inside her. "Oooh, that felt good. Make it jump again."

"Ye did it, Kate, not I, with your brazen eyes."

Smiling, she reached down and slid her fingers on either side of his member so she could feel him moving in and out of her body.

The unexpected pressure almost sent him out of his skin with excitement. "Ach, I've married Venus!" he gasped out, the thrusts growing deeper, faster.

And then they were both lost in joining. She met him thrust for thrust, building frantically toward what she knew not, until at last, something huge and glorious exploded inside her, setting loose a wave of flutters.

Duncan let out a guttural bellow of satisfaction, then collapsed panting atop her, their bodies fused with the sweet sweat of passion.

After only a moment, he tried to roll free of her, but Catherine held on to him. "Nay."

"But I'm so heavy," he said groggily.

"I can breathe," she murmured, more content than she had ever been. "I like the feel of your weight atop me. The scent of you against me." His body relaxed. Catherine said a heartfelt prayer of thanks. She did not want the dream to end. Reality would catch them soon enough. But for this golden moment, she was content.

Chapter

FIFTEEN

Far into the night, Catherine drifted up from a dreamless sleep to a new sense of warmth and safety. And satisfaction. Gradually she realized she was curled into the shelter of Duncan's body, caged securely by his arms and legs.

One by one, her senses woke to his presence. The wild, distinctive scent of him filled her nostrils. The soft curls of his forearm brushed against her cheek. The heat of him warmed her back, her buttocks, her legs. The sound of his deep, even breathing marked a slow and easy cadence like the measured heartbeat of some great enfolding guardian.

Afraid a single movement would break the spell, she lay there savoring every sensation, remembering the three times they had made love. Until tonight, she had rushed to escape into the sweet illusions of her dreams. Now she did not want to sleep away a moment of the even sweeter reality of Duncan's arms around her. Yet just as surely as the sunrise would steal him from her, she lost the battle and was drawn back to the faded realm of her imagination.

ANNANLEA—NOVEMBER 23, 1590

On a crisp morning nine days later, Michael Graham galloped up to Duncan on the windswept height where they were hunting. "I told ye that ugly great musket of yours was precious little use! Give me a good longbow, any day. What happened? Did it seize up on ye?"

Duncan started. Blast. Caught daydreaming like a callow lad whose prong ruled over his pate. "Seize up?"

"Aye." Michael pointed the arrow nocked in his longbow toward a thick swath of trees a hundred yards away.

"I'd have taken a shot at that stag maself, but I was out of range." He halted, peering at Duncan. "Duncan? Did ye even see the beast?"

The sides of Duncan's neck grew warm with embarrassment. "Nae. Ma mind was . . . elsewhere." In bed, with Kate.

Just the thought of her dark-eyed passion sent yet another twist of desire through him. The woman was insatiable. He couldn't stop thinking about her. Them. Together in bed.

Michael guffawed. "Split ma gizzard! You're smitten!"

"Smitten?" The heat in Duncan's neck deepened. "Ach, you've lost your mind, auld man." Distracted, aye, but that was all. "Nae smitten. Preoccupied." A half-smile escaped. "I must admit, though, that the longer it's aged in the keg, the stronger the spirit. And the sweeter."

"Hah!" Michael gave his arm an affectionate whack with his bow. "So all Kate's fire isna in her tongue."

"Very little of Kate's fire is in her tongue," Duncan said with wry appreciation. He couldna allow her to affect his work, though. "Now. Let's run us down a stag."

The next morning at his desk, Duncan did his best to focus on his inventories, but those same intrusive thoughts of Kate kept unseating his concentration.

How much longer would this go on? he wondered. He'd expected the physical attraction between them to fade, but it hadn't. With every coupling, it had intensified, until now he couldn't look upon his wife without wanting her, couldn't imagine sleeping without her soft within his arms.

So quickly, she'd gotten under his skin. Pleasurable for them both, but most disruptive to his duties.

More than that, he had become aware of her—her stamp upon his life, his home, his soul.

Distracted, he scanned the parlor, soaking in the orderly structure Kate had worked in his house. For all his complaints about her stubborn routines and compulsive cleanliness, he had come to appreciate the quiet patina her efforts had brought to Annanlea and his family. Bink laughed now more than she had in memory. He often caught the two women with their heads together. And the children . . . Baran and Amber excepted, they seemed happier than he could ever remember their being. Even the twins had settled into the routine of study, cleanliness, and decorum Kate had imposed, for she was just as quick to comfort and encourage as she was to correct.

Froward she might be, but she was an impressive woman, one he was coming to respect. And sharp though her wit might be, he often caught himself chuckling over one of her clever retorts. If she could just learn to keep that razor of a tongue of hers inside her head . . .

Thoughts of Kate evaporated when Clyde sat up, ears pricked, and growled.

"Lone rider comin' in," Thurlow shouted from the peel.

The mastiff rose to his feet, hackles raised.

What now? Duncan headed immediately for the gate, wary of what new disaster the messenger might bring. He caught up his dark cloak from its peg in the entry hall, then left behind the warmth of the house for the cold, brisk wind that scoured the bailey.

Clyde raced ahead, then planted himself on rigid legs square in front of the gate, barking as if the devil himself was about to come through.

As the rest of his men assumed their defensive posts, Cameron loped over from the smithy, and the twins erupted from the barn at a dead run. Michael emerged from his cottage with Baran in his wake.

"I recognize him," Darby called down from the parapet of the guardhouse. " 'Tis Bruno Jenkins from Annandale."

Duncan's wariness eased, but only a bit. Bruno often picked up extra coin by delivering messages, but he wasn't particular about who employed him. The message could be anything. From anyone.

Duncan reached the sealed gate just as Bruno tossed

the folded message up to Darby, who relayed it immediately.

The paper was thrice-used, but of good quality. He turned the letter over and saw that it was addressed to his wife. No imprint marked the sealing wax.

Kate! What mischief was she up to now?

Who would be writing her? Certainly not her family. They'd made it clear enough they wanted no part of her.

Blast the woman. He'd hoped marriage would bring an end to her meddling.

He opened the message and read:

> *My dear Cousin Catherine,*
> *On our sojourn to Dumfries, Angus and I were able to obtain the goods and provisions ye requested, which amount to six wagonloads. Would ye wish to collect them when ye come this Sabbath, or shall I send them to ye sooner? Please advise, as the tariff for the wagons and drivers is accounted by the day. I await your response with joyous anticipation, and have more happy news to share that prudence forbids my committing to paper. May God be praised for His bounteous provision in time of trouble.*
> *Your most Humble Servant and Sister in Christ,*
> *Sarah Maxwell*

Goods! Provisions!

Cold fury tightened the cords of his neck and sent his heartbeat pounding.

What in blazes was Kate doing ordering goods and provisions? And how in blazes did she expect him to pay for them?

"Kate!" Duncan bellowed across the compound, prompting his men—and everyone else in earshot—to duck for cover. Clyde slunk to a safe distance and regarded him askance as Duncan jabbed a finger toward Darby. "Bring Bruno in and hold him for a reply."

Kate would answer for this, as would Angus Maxwell!

Betrayal. Intrigue. Corruption. From his own bed. With his own kinsman!

And after he'd forgiven Angus for the blight he'd put on his family!

Duncan strode toward the house and confrontation. Losing his salt was one thing. Bad enough, that one of his own people might have betrayed him. But his *wife!*

Was this how Englishwomen reverenced their husbands? With schemes and plots?

Or was it simply Kate? Had he married a spy, a conniver?

Either way, she had some tall explaining to do.

And he knew just where to find her. He burst into the house. "Kate!"

Nothing.

Blast her hide, leave it to Kate to make him come to her. He stormed into the morning room and found her pretending to be engrossed in her mending. Cats scrambled for cover, but Amber and Erinn sat in wide-eyed fear beside Kate while Nevin, oblivious, played with a wooden darning knob at their feet.

"Leave us," he ordered his daughters. "Take Nevin with ye."

The two girls shot Kate a questioning look before they obeyed, scalding his masculine pride. "I said leave us!"

Kate nodded her confirmation to the girls, then met his glare with cool aloofness as they hurried away. "If you have a grievance with me, sirrah, pray do not take it out on the children."

How dare she lecture him on how he treated his own children! He opened his mouth to set her straight, then realized the trap he'd almost fallen into.

No, no. He would not be deflected.

Reining in his anger, he approached to stand towering over where she sat, deliberately crowding her. He thrust the opened letter forward. "Explain this. Now."

He might as well have been across the room for her lack of reaction to his presence, which galled him even further. Kate accepted the message and read the graceful script running at right angles to the supply list and the household inventory that had been the paper's two previous uses.

Her calm features congealed. She glanced down and to the right, a sure sign of dissimulation.

Aye, Kate. Your sins have found ye out.

She hesitated for long seconds before meeting his accusing glare with one of calculated composure. "Am I to expect that you will open *all* my mail now that we are married?"

Duncan was in no mood for her verbal parrying. This was not some game or idle spat between them, and he would not be put off. "We'll discuss that later. I want an explanation, Kate."

Her expression closed up tighter than a tortoise harried by a hound. "Annanlea needs food. The children are in desperate need of new clothing, as am I. I simply asked your cousin Angus to purchase some yardage for us when next he went to Dumfries. And a few other household items we are lacking. And food for our people." She met his gaze in challenge. "*Our* people."

Stifled whispers and rustles erupted in the hallway.

His girls. Confound Kate and her schemes. Already, she had his daughters eavesdropping. Who knew what other bad habits they had picked up from her? "I told ye to leave us," he shouted toward the hallway. "Now begone, or feel ma strap!"

As always, the mere threat of punishment was enough to bring his daughters into line. He waited until the clatter of their footsteps retreated to the kitchen before he turned back to glare down on Kate.

She eyed him with guarded condescension, as if he were an unruly toddler and she his nursemaid. It made him want to heave her headfirst into the river. An excellent idea, but one he'd save for later.

"These goods and provisions," he said with strained control. "Did ye once ask yourself how I'm to pay for them? Ye ken we have nae money and precious little salt to trade."

"I had the means." She calmly directed her attention back to her sewing. "Consider it my dowry. I paid for everything myself when I asked for Angus's help."

"Paid?" Duncan was so taken aback he could not hide his surprise. "With what?" He made the sign against evil. "Ye came here all but naked, empty-handed."

"Aye, but not destitute." Kate lifted her stubborn chin. "I had secreted two jewels on my person."

He heard a gasp from the hallway, but was so shocked at Kate's disclosure that he ignored the eavesdroppers.

Jewels!

How? *Where?*

And why hadn't she used them to ransom herself in the first place? That would have neatly solved both their problems. As it was, the two of them were yoked for life, God help him.

Anger, suspicion, and more than a snatch of relief wrestled his emotions. At least she hadna indebted him, and the food would be sorely needed. "What jewels?" he challenged. "I checked ye over top to toe maself when we brought ye here, and I found nae jewels."

"You did what?" She glared at him, her brown eyes sparking fire. "You searched me when I was all but naked and unconscious and could not defend myself?" She drew her mending protectively to her chest. "How dare you. What other liberties did you take, sir?"

He recognized the question as a spurious one. At least she did not employ the usual feminine weapons of martyred silence, swoons, or tears. Kate was no faint-hearted opponent in an argument; he had to give her that. She attacked or deflected, but never retreated.

A soft swish from the hallway reminded him they were not alone. Knowing that only Bink would dare to risk listening at the door after he'd banished the children, he raised his voice so she could hear him clearly. "If ye worry what I might have done to ye, Kate, ask Aunt Brigit. She helped me search ye."

"I did nae such thing!" Bink appeared in the doorway, irate. "Aye, he checked ye over, Kate, but ye were clad in yer shift, and cold as a cod. There was nothin' improper. I wouldna stand for such."

Women. They stuck together even over blood.

Duncan leveled a trenchant stare at his aunt. "Now that you've made your peace with Kate, Aunt Brigit, please leave us alone. This is a private matter between husband and wife."

Bink hesitated, clearly worried what he might do to Kate, but for once, the discipline of his household won out. "Aye. But doona make me ashamed of ye, Duncan." She turned and aimed a stage whisper at Kate before leaving. "Never fear. I'll have ma liniments at the ready, in case he beats ye."

Duncan could kill without compunction when he had to, man or woman, but he'd never laid so much as a hand to any of his wives, as Bink knew full well.

Kate's eyes widened in dismay.

With a final glare at him, Bink retreated.

Duncan gripped the arms of Kate's chair, penning her in, and dropped to one knee before her to bring his eyes level with hers. "Now, Kate," he said smoothly. "Ye were telling me about the jewels." He ran one hand up her leg beneath her skirt until he reached the top of her thigh.

Kate sucked in a shocked breath and went rigid, thoroughly undone by the unexpected turn of events. "Duncan, stop this. It's broad daylight. We're in a common room—"

"And willna be interrupted," he said ominously. "So the jewels were secreted on your person." He stroked his thumb across the mouth of her sex. "Surely ye didna hide them here. 'Tis every maiden's treasure chest, true, but—"

"Stop it," she demanded. "Unhand me this minute."

"Ah, Kate," he said, wondering how angry she would

have to be before she betrayed her secrets. "Ye ken I canna keep ma hands off ye."

"Then face the consequences," she snapped, placing her foot on his chest and shoving with all her might in a futile effort to topple him. He clamped an iron grip around her ankle.

Duncan had never been more tempted to beat a woman, but he had no intention of allowing her to bring him so low. He did, however, intend to nip her violent tendencies in the bud. "Now, Kate. Is that any way for a lady to act?"

She struggled to free her leg, but he held her fast. "I told you, I'm nobody's lady." She glared up at him. "Let me go, Duncan."

"Doona dare to kick at me again, Kate. I canna tolerate such *uncivilized* behavior in a wife. 'Twas a useless effort, anyway. It takes more strength than ye can muster to topple me." He dropped her foot with disdain.

Kate sat rigid and unbowed.

The muscles in his jaw fluttered. He'd had his fill of her reckless plots.

He fixed her with his most intimidating stare. "We are married now, Kate. There must be nae lies between us. I'm waitin' to hear the rest about these jewels." He noted her slight hesitation to meet his gaze, another telltale clue that she was keeping something from him.

"Those rubies were all I had left of my heritage," she said softly. "I gave them to Angus and asked him to redeem them for food, yard goods, and wares for Annanlea." She met his gaze. "A harmless request, Duncan."

"Harmless?" Grateful though he was for the food she'd provided his people, Duncan's temper flared. He bent close. "Are ye simple, woman, or merely ignorant? Have ye nae concept what peril this placed Angus in? Nae to mention how dangerous such intrigue and betrayal are?"

"Intrigue and betrayal? Nonsense. You make too much of little." Her protests lacked their earlier conviction. "I merely wanted to help."

"Spare me, Kate. If ye'd merely wanted to help, why didna ye come to me?"

The fire returned to her eyes. "You were my captor. You held me against my will."

"Of course I held ye!" How many times would they have to go over this before she got it through that thick skull of hers? " 'Twas by God's good pleasure ye ended up with us, to be a ransom for many."

Finally losing her composure, Kate exploded with a completely unintelligible expletive. "Did it never occur to you that God might have brought me here so you could save me and send me back to my family?"

"Of course not! What good would that have done us?" Women. Why couldn't they simply see things for what they were?

Kate threw up her hands and rolled her eyes heavenward. "I give up."

Duncan wondered for a heartbeat how they'd gotten so far off the subject, then realized she'd lured him down another rabbit trail. He took a deep breath to restore his self-control. "I am master here," he ground out. "Ye shall nae go behind ma back again, Kate."

Damn, but it galled. She'd been among them less than four months, yet already she'd corrupted his cousins. "Ye should have trusted me with the jewels, Kate."

"Nay, Duncan," she said, defiant. "For then I'd have had no say in how the money was spent." She let out an exasperated sigh. "They were my jewels, Duncan, to do with as I saw fit. I see no reason for your choler. All I have done is see that our people will be fed and provided for. Can you not let it go at that?"

By Hades, the woman could provoke a saint to slap his dying mother.

It was up to him to make her see her folly and repent it, or none of them would be safe.

Ever the optimist, he tried reason one more time. "It remains to be seen what trouble ye might have stirred up with such a reckless scheme. At the least, this puts bad blood between me and ma meddling cousin for life."

"Duncan." Kate looked up to him in alarm. "Surely you don't mean that. Angus was only trying to help us and the poor of his flock. How could you possibly blame him for—"

"Easily. Ye were ma hostage! He went behind ma back, and on the word of a stranger, an Englisher. If I were a less forgiving man, I'd call him out this day and send him to the God he claims to serve."

Her knuckles whitened on the arms of her chair. "But you are a forgiving man, aye?"

Now that he had the advantage, he moved in. "I could be, if . . ."

Taut silence stretched between them, but ultimately it was Kate who capitulated. "If what?"

"If ye swear to me on the souls of ma children that ye will never communicate with anyone beyond the barnekin without ma express permission." Any other oath would have no meaning, but Kate loved his children. This vow alone might seal her obedience in this all-important matter.

Might.

"And if I do not?"

Duncan was no man for idle threats, but he decided to risk just one. "I would demand satisfaction from Angus Maxwell," he said with deadly conviction, "nae just for this, but for the undeserved shame he brought down on ma clan when he refused to let us bury Aselma in holy ground. With nae a shred of evidence that she jumped instead of fell. That puts bad blood between us."

No need to let on that he'd since decided to move past the unfortunate incident. A man of God was, after all, still just a man, as fallible as any.

Kate blanched.

He could see she believed him. Good. If she relented, he might still hold out some hope of taming her.

Her tongue darted again across her lip, and she took up her mending with shaking hands.

Aye, Kate. There are consequences to your blasted schemes. Best to ken it now.

"Very well, then," she clipped out. "I swear it. I shall never communicate with anyone beyond Annanlea without your express permission."

"And?" Without the rest, her words would hold no weight.

"I swear it on the souls of our children," she added, resentment burning in her face.

Duncan let out a sigh of satisfaction. The tension broken, he stepped back and assayed his proud, angry wife.

Faith, but her feisty spirit made him randy. Or was it victory? Either way, he had to fight to quell the urge to snatch her close and turn her anger into flame.

Instead he bent to her ear and murmured, "It's up to ye, ma Ladykate. We can be at war, or we can be at peace. If ye choose war, ken one thing: I willna be the loser."

She waited until he drew back to slap him with all her substantial strength. "We shall see, Duncan Maxwell. We shall see."

The next day Duncan was conspicuous by his absence—as was Aunt Brigit—after word came that the six wagonloads of supplies were approaching, but Catherine breathed easier for their absence. Things would definitely be smoother, and less dangerous, without Duncan around. And she did not wish to get Aunt Brigit into deeper trouble by association.

But when she announced to the children that her dowry had arrived, they were beside themselves with excitement. Word spread faster than a summer storm crossed the moors, and in a trice most of Annanlea's inhabitants were waiting in the bailey, huddled against the wind as the end of November held its last beneath a wintry, overcast sky.

The girls twittering with excitement in her shadow, Catherine scanned the gathering for the other children. Cameron held Nevin on his shoulders beside the guardhouse, watching and waiting as always. Baran scowled down on the proceedings from a superior position—and attitude—on the parapet. Only the twins were unaccounted for, but she knew they'd turn up soon. Sure enough, they raced through the crowd wielding clay pistols to shouts of, "Stop. Ye're dead! I got ye!"

"Nae, ye didna! I got ye first."

"Nae, that shot didna count. Ye didna have time to reload." Chaser became chased, and the hot pursuit continued.

Michael Graham bellowed, "Open the gates!" He approached to stand beside her, watching Carlin, Ander, Thurlow, and Logan do as he had ordered. "Duncan told me," he said quietly.

The sad reproof in Michael's expression stung her. "Do you think I am a traitor, too?"

He exhaled heavily, clasping his hands behind his back. "I think ye doona understand the danger ye caused, Kate. This was nae small matter. More than goods and provisions might have been lost. What ye did could have cost lives. Might cost them still." He faced her, sober. "Duncan is yer husband now. Ye canna imagine the things he has endured to keep us safe. Ye must trust him without reservation. I do. So does everyone else here. That trust is all we have. Our lives depend upon it."

Catherine wasn't certain she could trust anyone as he'd asked her to trust Duncan, not after what her family had done to her. Still, she appreciated Michael Graham's candor. "Thank you for your honesty, Michael." Perhaps if she knew more of Duncan's past, it would be easier to trust him. "I'd like to learn more of Duncan's life. Could you tell me some time soon?"

"Aye." He nodded with approval. "I'll be glad to." He bowed briefly, then left to help the men.

Angus Maxwell rode in on the first wagon, wedged between the driver and his burly helper. Catherine was disappointed to see no sign of Sarah, but excitement about the arrival overrode both her disappointment and the lingering disquiet from her conversation with Michael.

The twins raced around the lead wagon. "What's inside? What's inside?"

"Can we climb on?"

"There's a crack in the spoke on this wheel."

"Look at the marking on that gelding's belly. It's shaped like a fish."

"Boys! Boys!" she scolded. "Give way to the wagons. Not so close."

Only when they obeyed did she wave to the beaming minister and walk alongside the slow-moving wagon. "God bless you, Angus Maxwell." Her pleasure at seeing him was tainted by Duncan's threat. What trouble would Angus suffer for helping her?

"God has blessed *ye*," Angus corrected, "for your stones were worthy of a king. The jewelers of Dumfries bid up the price on yer jewels. We ended up wi' twice what I'd expected. And had nae a stitch of trouble getting yer goods bought and delivered safe. In these parts, that amounts to a miracle, indeed."

"So it does." Aware now of the perilous risk he had undertaken on her behalf, she sent up a brief, heartfelt prayer of thanks for God's protection.

The wagon halted so Angus could clamber down to join her on the ground. "I never would have managed wi'out Sarah." He slapped the dust and straw from his clothes. "She decided how to spend some of the overage. Even bought some ribbons for the girls."

"Ribbons," Amber squealed to Erinn, abandoning her moroseness to bounce on tiptoe, taking Erinn with her.

Angus pressed a small, heavy leathern pouch into Catherine's hands and murmured confidentially, "Eighteen silver pieces left over."

"Silver," Amber repeated in an awed whisper.

"Ooo, silver," Erinn echoed.

Catherine was every bit as impressed as the girls. Guilt and gratitude prompted her to open the pouch and extract half the coins. "Please keep half of these, at least." When Angus held up a staying hand, she dropped the coins back into the pouch and tried to return it all. "Take it all. We would have nothing without your help."

Amber became suddenly earthbound until Angus shook his head and pushed the pouch back into her hand. "Ye would have nothing wi'out *His* help, lass." He let out a contented sigh. "Keep the silver. Ye can use it toward God's glory as well as I. Thanks to your generous heart, the poor of our parish needna starve this winter. I trust ye and Duncan to use what's left of the money well."

The driver cracked his whip and urged the weary dray horses toward the house. Catherine and Angus walked alongside, the girls following with whispers and giggles.

Angus granted her a beatific smile. " 'Twas a blessed day indeed when the Good Lord brought ye to us, Catherine. A blessed day, indeed."

"I fear my husband does not share in your opinion," she confided. "He accused us of betrayal, intrigue, and of conspiring behind his back."

"Oh, aye. We did all that," Angus said with a boyish twinkle in his bright blue eyes. "We stand convicted without excuse. But God forgives. And He can use even our sins to work His greater good." Not a shred of remorse.

"Why, Angus Maxwell, is that any way for a minister to talk?"

"It's the only way for a minister to talk," he answered brightly. "Without guile or hypocrisy." He scanned the bailey. "That's what I love best about Duncan, among his many other fine qualities. He has nae guile, and there's nae a speck of hypocrisy in the man." He looked about again. "I doona see him."

"He left early, claiming he had better things to do than wait around for my dowry to arrive, and lucky for us. Aunt Brigit made herself scarce, as well, though frankly, I'm astounded that she could resist the opportunity to supervise the unloading." She sighed. "They both disapprove most vehemently of what I've done. Duncan and I had quite a row when Sarah's letter came."

Again, Angus's blue eyes sparkled with mischief. "Aye. I thought as much."

Catherine halted in her tracks. "You knew he would read the letter?"

"Of course, child." As before, Angus showed not the slightest contrition. He took her arm and eased her back toward the house. "Duncan has his pride, after all. If we had simply shown up with these wagons, I tremble to think what might have happened. He verra well might have slain me on the spot, and that would have caused all sorts of trouble for everyone here, nae to mention the parish and poor Sarah. I couldna have that on ma conscience, so I made certain he was forewarned." He raised his bushy eyebrows, looking for all the world like a little boy despite his snow-white hair. "Do ye forgive me?"

"Of course I forgive you," she blustered, "I just cannot understand why you would deliberately do such a thing. The risk—"

"Ach, but 'twas nae risk, ma lass," he reassured her. "Duncan has a fearsome temper, true, but given time to think, he's a most judicious man. I trust that wi' ma life." He grinned. "And I kent full well ye could handle the situation. Duncan's met his match in ye, he has." He shook his head. "And some poor souls think God Almighty hasna a sense of humor."

Catherine straightened in mock offense. "Are you implying that I am God's joke on Duncan Maxwell?"

"As the Christ spoke in Scripture, 'Ye have said it,' " he quoted irreverently. "But if ye are, the converse is also true, for all the Lord's workings are perfect."

Catherine chuckled. "So Duncan would be God's joke on me."

"Ye must admit, it reeks of divine irony."

They laughed together, to the children's confusion.

Angus sobered. "But there is also blessing, him to ye and ye to him. For all the Lord's workings *are* perfect."

"I fear this will end badly," she confessed. "Duncan

still harbors great resentment about the church's position
when Aselma died."

Angus's humor faded. "I was wrong in that, Catherine.
I shouldna have let the elders sway me from mercy to
judgment. That was ma failing, and mine alone. Duncan
has every right to be angry."

Catherine's already healthy respect for the minister
swelled. "You're quite a man, Angus Maxwell."

He met her eyes frankly. "Nae half the man as yer
husband, Catherine, for my calling allows me the liberty
of peace. Duncan has nae such luxury."

Gordon and Kerry interrupted their conversation by
dragging branches around them.

"Here come the other wagons!" Kerry shouted. "Look
at the size of those horses!"

"Yoicks!" Gordon exclaimed. "So many barrels!"

"Listen to those pigs! There must be a dozen!"

"May we climb up to ride with the drivers?"

"Nay, let's ride the cows!"

"Stay away from the cows," Catherine called after
them, "and the wagons."

One by one, the other wagons rolled into the bailey,
each of them trailed by livestock. Catherine counted six
fat dairy cows, one bull, four beef, and half a dozen nanny
goats. Only the first wagon was loaded with household
goods. The rest held food: fat sacks of turnips and parsnips, cured meats, plump swine, beer, dried beans, and
grain. "Empty the foodstuffs first," she directed from the
front step, then stood back to bask in the hope she saw
in the faces of their people as they unloaded the unexpected bounty. For the first time since Catherine had come
here, she sensed a vaulting optimism within the ancient
walls.

Erinn started bouncing again, warming Catherine's
heart to see the joy in her glowing face. "What's in the
first wagon, Ladykate? Please let us see."

"Aye." Amber nodded, her hands clasped before her in
anticipation, completely forgetting to be tragic. "Please,

will ye ask one of the men to unload it now? I doona
think I can stand to wait."

Catherine grinned, eager to see their faces when the
fabric was brought out. "All right." She motioned to one
of the burly hired workmen. "Here! Could we have a man
here, please?"

He lumbered down from the next wagon, then climbed
up into the first one and started handing down boxes and
baskets. The first few held cooking utensils, bedding, and
crockery. Then came a coffer that sent the girls into peals
of delight when they opened it to find polished shears,
pins and needles, silken thread, cunning thimbles, tortoise-
shell combs and hairpins, a looking glass, three hair-
brushes, several serviceable caps and wimples, and a bolt
of bright red velvet ribbon. Every new discovery
prompted fresh squeals of delight.

"Oh, Angus," Catherine breathed, "Sarah did well, indeed."

At last, the workman emerged with bolt after bolt of
rich red woolen plaid shot through with wide bands and
narrow stripes of dark green. Each bolt was slightly different, but all were variations on the same basic color
scheme, a pattern of vibrant green on a brilliant red background, lively and becoming. "Look, girls! The best surprise of all. Lovely fabric for new clothes." Catherine
clasped her hands in excitement. "New clothes for all of
us. Warm and sturdy and fine as any in the parish." She
approached the wagon. "May I have one, please?"

The workman handed one of the smaller bolts over the
side. Catherine's breath caught when she saw the fine,
dense weave up close and felt the smooth texture. This
was wool worthy of a laird, thick yet elegantly soft and
supple. She could not wait to see Amber in it. All of them.

She had assumed the girls were speechless with
delight, but suddenly their silence seemed ominous. Bolt
in arms, Catherine turned around to find them staring at
the material as if it were soaked in blood. "Girls, what's
wrong?"

Angus shifted uneasily beside her. "I'm sorry, lasses, truly I am, but this was all the merchants had. They were even out of black. Everything but Maxwell plaids had long since sold to the gentles at the fall markets. There willna be anything·else until spring." He glanced at their threadbare clothing. "With winter comin' on, I reckoned even Maxwell plaid would be better than nothing."

"But that's perfect," Catherine argued, wondering why it clearly wasn't. "Maxwell plaid for Maxwells."

The picture of misery, Amber stroked the fabric with longing. "Papa will never let us keep it." A tear rolled down her cheek. She leaned close and whispered, "Maxwell was Papa's mother's name, and he hated her cruel sire. So he has never worn the Maxwell plaid, and neither have we. It goes against his pride."

"Faith, how Byzantine." Catherine looked to Angus in consternation.

" 'Twas all they had, so I must believe Divine Providence figures in this somewhere. But even my faith has its limits. I wouldna like to be around when Duncan sees it."

Neither would she. Catherine motioned to Thurlow as he carried a sack of grain toward the larder. "Thurlow, please put down the grain and take these fabrics to the girls' room posthaste. And make certain they are stored well out of sight. I do not wish to offend my lord husband." Not, at least, until she'd figured out some way to get around his blasted pride.

Thurlow eased the grain reluctantly to the ground, his eyes darting nervously the length and breadth of the bailey.

"It will be all right," Catherine told him, wishing she believed it. "Duncan need not know you ever touched the stuff."

"Aye, Ladykate," he said with trepidation. Then he hurried to make away with the contraband.

Why couldn't anything be simple and straightforward with this family? she wondered yet again. Catherine circled the girls' shoulders for a reassuring hug. "Don't worry, darlings. You shall have your dresses. And warm shawls, and thick cloaks. Ladykate will think of something."

Now all she had to do was think of something.

Duncan sulked through the rest of that day and slept with his back to her that night, but at least he did not forsake her bed entirely. For though his manner was cold as the northeast wind, his body was warm, and she had already grown dependent on his presence beside her in the night.

The next morning he rose and left her without a word.

Catherine understood it would take him time to get used to what she'd done, but she also realized confrontation would only make it harder to bridge the gap once he'd come to his senses. So for the time being, she declared a tacit truce.

The following week things remained strained between them, except in bed. Duncan's coolness there had lasted only one more night. After that, neither of them could keep their hands off each other. But their lovemaking took on a decidedly aggressive flavor, one she found as exciting as it was disturbing.

By the following Monday Catherine had wearied of Duncan's cool politeness, so she enlisted Lucas's help in making a meal that would serve as a peace offering: Duncan's favorite, pigeon pie.

She had just shown Lucas how to sweeten the flesh by rubbing the birds with lard and honey before roasting, when Duncan stormed into the kitchen, white around the eyes and nostrils flared. Without so much as a hail-fellow-well-met, he crossed the stone floor, took firm hold of her arm, and propelled her into the parlor.

When he reached his desk, he left her standing by a chair and sat facing her. "Sit down, Kate," he ordered, prompting her to remain standing. "Wat has sent for us."

Wat?

Good glory, what now?

Oh, dear. Not something to do with Lucas's girls, she hoped.

Catherine decided sitting down might be a fine idea. She eased onto the edge of the seat. "Why?"

Duncan propped his elbows on the arms of his chair, steepling his fingers. "I thought perhaps you could tell me."

"He did not say?"

Duncan flicked a thick sheet of folded vellum toward her. Saints, but he looked handsome—and dangerous— when he was in these darkish moods.

She picked it up and read in an elegant feminine hand:

To our esteemed friend, neighbor, and ally,

Walter and I would so enjoy your presence and that of your bride at race this Saturday afternoon hence and a feast afterward in honor of your nuptials. Pray, do accept our hospitality for three days' time at least. I am eager to meet your Catherine and share with her the particulars of her new homeland, and Wat wishes to try his new Arabian against your Rogue.

Your most obedient servant,
Mary Scott

Horse races—and the illicit trading that always accompanied them—were the favorite entertainments of border life, erasing the lines between Scot and Englishman. More than that, though, they provided an excuse to strike deals, gather information, further plots, and turn a profit. Catherine supposed their marriage was as good an excuse as any for Wat to stage a race. But the feast in their honor . . . such a thing would serve as public confirmation of Wat's continuing alliance with Duncan. For that, she was truly grateful.

And she was grateful that her intervention on Lucas's behalf hadn't stirred up any trouble with Wat. "It seems straightforward enough," she told Duncan. "Your friend and ally would like to race his new horse against Rogue, and his lady wife wishes to meet me." She dropped the letter back on the desk. "How kind of them to honor us with a feast. I should think you'd be pleased, Duncan."

"Ye've been here long enough to ken that nothing in these parts is what it seems, Kate." Duncan fixed her with those piercing blue eyes. "Mary Scott has never summoned me with any of ma other wives. I have to ask maself why she does so now." His face was cold as stone. "Is this one of your schemes? Have ye written Mary Scott?"

"Of course not," Catherine shot back, wounded by his quickness to judge her. "Your accusation insults me, sir. I gave my solemn vow to do no such thing, and I keep my vows."

He continued to study her closely, making her uneasy despite her innocence. "If I've misjudged ye, I beg your pardon." His posture relaxed, but only slightly. "I havena kent ye long enough to be certain how ye keep your vows."

"Nor I, you. Time will tell, sir." She rose and turned to leave.

Today was Monday. They would have to depart early on Friday to reach Harden by the race. That gave her only four full days to get her clothes in order. Catherine paused. She could not face another woman in these threadbare tatters. "Duncan," she ventured, "there were several bolts of fabric among the goods I asked Angus purchase." She met his suspicion without flinching. "To go in these clothes . . ." Her hands spread the patched, ill-fitting skirt. "I fear it would bring shame on you for me to meet your most important ally wearing these tatters. May I make some dresses from the woolens? And some clothes for the children? Theirs are almost worn through."

Judging from his guarded expression, she might have suggested asking a Johnstone to ride along with them, but after a long pause, he assented. "Verra well. Gaud yourself as ye wish, as long as the clothes are decent proper. And sturdy."

They would be all of that. The only catch was, they would be Maxwell plaid. Yet if she played her cards right, Duncan wouldn't know until it was too late.

"Would you ask Aunt Brigit to help me, please? There's little time left—"

"Ask her yourself," Duncan grumbled. "Tell her I said she should help ye, but only if she has the time."

Perfect. Perfect. Thank you, Mary Scott.

Catherine was glad they'd be there for three days at least. By the time they got home, Duncan would have gotten over the worst of the shock. She hoped.

Chapter

SIXTEEN

Duncan peered across the coach at Kate in the early morning light, enjoying her discomfiture. She sat wedged into the farthest corner of the seat, nervously glancing out the windows, at the ceiling, at her feet, even at Clyde . . . anywhere but at him. Every time she looked at the dog, though, the mastiff took it as an invitation and tried to nudge closer. This time, he actually levered the front half of his body across her lap.

"Oof! Clyde, *nay!*" Her cloak askew, she shoved at the adoringly oblivious canine without result. "Get *off* me. Down!"

She might as well have been murmuring endearments for all the effect it had on the animal. He just panted happily, then swiped a big, wet kiss up the side of her horrified face.

Ach, but it warmed Duncan's heart to see her infernal primness crumble under Clyde's moist affection. He did his best not to gloat—openly, anyway.

The dog had provided the only break in the tension since they'd left Annanlea—and safety—behind the day before. "I should be jealous, Kate," Duncan said in mock seriousness. "Clyde doesna love me even half so well."

"Well, I wish he did not love me at all." Retracting her chin in thinly disguised abhorrence, she tried again to free herself of Clyde's adoring bulk. The mastiff responded by dropping his broad head flat into her lap, begging for a pat. Kate tried to salvage her dignity by straightening her clothes, but that proved impossible with half of Clyde pinning her down. "Aren't you going to do anything?"

she scolded Duncan. "He's your dog. Did you allow him to maul your other wives this way?"

"I've only had him these past four years," Duncan qualified. "He usually doesna let anyone but the children or me near him." He shrugged. "Aselma tried to befriend the beast—even brought him meat—but he growled at her as if she were a Johnstone. Shunned the meat like poison."

Judging from the way Kate looked at Clyde, she probably thought poison would be a fine idea. "I certainly wish I knew why he liked me so well," she despaired. "I'd move heaven and earth to undo it."

Duncan decided to be merciful. He snapped his fingers and pointed to the scant floor space beside his hip. Clyde whipped around and settled there so abruptly he flung up Kate's skirts, but only a little. Duncan thought he caught a flash of red before she smoothed them down in panic.

"Ye need nae get so riled about showin' your ankles, Kate. I've seen ye naked, so what's a little ankle between husband and wife?" The mere mention of naked was enough to conjure the notion that it had been a long time since he'd made love in a coach.

But Kate looked anything but approachable. As a matter of fact, she retreated from him even farther.

He'd suspected all day that something more than the trip was bothering her. Probably nervous about meeting Wat's wife. Women worried about that sort of thing.

He decided to ask Kate straight-out what was troubling her. Give her the opportunity to tell him. "What's the matter with ye, Ladykate? I'm your husband. If something is amiss, I could help."

"Nothing, Nothing." She shook her head just a little too briskly. Her tongue swiped across her full lower lip, another betrayal that she wasn't being truthful. "I simply . . . well, I'd like to remind you," she said defensively, "that you were the one who asked Aunt Brigit to help me with my new clothes. It wasn't her idea."

"Aye." Why had she brought *that* up? "I did. But only because ye asked me to."

Duncan knew better than to run that rabbit. Trying to follow a woman's logic was like leaping into the great-grandsire of all rabbit holes. You lost your bearings straightaway and always came up empty-handed.

A shadowy little niggle directed his thoughts back to a single phrase: new clothes. Then it dawned on him.

New clothes. Could *that* be behind her nervousness?

He'd wondered why she'd turned up for the trip yesterday wearing the same old ill-fitting hand-me-downs, especially after she'd spent the week holed up in Aunt Brigit's room sewing with the girls.

At least, he thought she was wearing the same old clothes. He looked her over critically. Same worn cloak. Same bodice. Same blouse. And that same shift of hers hanging below the same too-short skirt.

Yet something about the way she looked in them seemed different, but he couldn't put his finger on what. A bit bulkier, perhaps? "It has something to do with your clothes, doesna it?"

Kate blanched as if he'd pointed a loaded pistol at her. Nostrils flared, she smoothed at her skirt. "Nay. I was just worried about the race. And the feast afterward. And what Wat's lady wife will think of me."

Ah. He'd been right, then.

But that wouldn't account for the signs of deception in her manner. "Then why didna ye wear your fine new clothes?" he asked evenly.

Her face congealed. "I did not want them soiled by the journey. Once we are near Wat's, I plan to change."

Duncan's eyes narrowed. She was up to something. He could smell it. "Ah, really? And where would ye plan to do that?"

"I don't know." She waved a hand, attracting Clyde's unwelcome attention. "Behind a bush, if necessary. When next we water the horses."

Duncan stayed his dog with a look. "We just did that.

We canna stop for anything else until we're safe at Wat's."

He could see the wheels turning behind those eyes as she bit the side of her lower lip. "Well," she said, trying unsuccessfully to seem offhand, "I suppose I could change in the coach." She straightened. "But only if you swear not to look until we get there."

What sort of nonsense was this? "Kate, doona be silly. Why shouldna I look?"

"Promise," she challenged, "or I shall not change until after we've arrived, and whatever happens then, just remember that it was because of you I waited."

If that wasn't an "I told ye so" in the making, he'd never heard one. But before he could probe the matter further, Clyde sat up rigid and growled just as Duncan heard a cry from one of his men. He looked out the window to see a bolt lodged in Darby's left arm.

Attacked!

Quinn and Rory drew their pistols and bent low on the necks of their hobs. Darby managed to stay ahorse, bolt and all.

Deadly battle-chill shot through Duncan's veins, bringing everything into crystalline focus and charging him with bitter strength and clarity. With one powerful swipe he threw Kate to the floor just in time to avoid the bolt that whizzed through the window. It lodged with a thunk into the upholstery where her face had been.

Mouse cracked the whip, and the coach leapt forward as fast as the team could take it. Behind them, the stallions whinnied in alarm.

Duncan motioned Clyde to lie atop Kate, shielding her from further attack. "Stay! Both of ye!"

A muffled oath escaped. "Duncan! I cannot breathe with this animal atop me! Get him off!"

"Stay," Duncan repeated to the animal, knowing that Clyde, at least, would obey. He rose up just in time to see another bolt emerge from a copse of trees and underbrush ahead. Only the angle of its flight prevented it from going straight through the door and striking one of them.

He threw open the opposite door of the hurtling coach, climbed outside to untie his stallion, then whistled the animal alongside. "Those trees yonder!" he shouted to his men. "Darby and Rory, stay with the coach! Quinn, circle wide! I'll follow!" With one well-aimed leap, he hooked his foot into the stirrup and swung into the saddle, then galloped behind Quinn toward the source of the attack. But by the time they reached the evergreens, they found only a smooth indentation beneath the trees, four spent long-range crossbows, and fresh tracks of a single hob leading into the nearby woods.

Alarms went off inside Duncan when he looked at the crossbows. This was no random brigand's attack. The weapons were powerful and crafted for deadly accuracy. No lone highwayman in his right mind would attack a well-guarded coach. And he hadn't spent his bolts on the guards, as one might have expected. After striking Darby, their attacker had definitely aimed for the passengers.

Quinn picked up a crossbow. "Expensive." The accomplished tracker scanned the markings in the evergreen needles on the ground. "Alone." He fixed a worried look on Duncan. "Someone who kent we were comin'?"

They both knew what that would mean: an assassin.

The coach rumbled closer and slowed. "We're all right," Duncan shouted. In response, the brake screeched loudly, bringing the vehicle to a halt on the road.

Quinn picked up the second crossbow. "Think ye 'twas one of Wat's men?"

"I doona ken what to think," Duncan said, grim. The crossbows were unlike any he'd seen in Walter Scott's arsenal. "But I'm nae inclined to suspect Wat. He's never been one for subterfuge. If he wanted me dead, he could easily have overwhelmed us. Why bother sending for us, only to have a lone attacker waylay our coach? Nay, it doesna fit." Yet it had to be someone who knew Duncan would pass this way.

A renegade in Wat's camp, perhaps? If so, why? And who?

"We'll hide these in the coach and sort this out later." With Darby wounded, he could not spare a man to track the assassin. He started back toward the road. "Come. Let's see to Darby."

When they emerged into the open on foot leading their horses, Darby declared with his usual swagger, "It'll take more than a bolt through the meat to unhorse me." Still mounted beside a grim Rory, he clutched the bloody bolt in one hand and clasped his other over the wound in his upper left arm. " 'Twasna barbed."

Clyde barked loudly from the coach. "Clyde, come!" Duncan called to him, whereupon the mastiff squeezed himself through the window and leapt to the ground, sending the stallions into nervous rearing at their tethers. Single-minded, Clyde anxiously sniffed away down the trail Duncan had just made from the evergreens.

Kate opened the door and got out, wrinkled, cloak awry, and hair askew, but all business. She took one look at Darby and altered her course in his direction. "Darby, you're hurt!" She hurried over. "Have I leave to tend your wound?" she asked him with an inordinate deference that pricked Duncan's curiosity.

Darby looked to Duncan.

"I think we're safe here for a moment," Duncan told them. Clyde would have let him know if any danger lingered. "Our attacker is gone. We have his arsenal. And my guess is, he's nae long for these parts, since he failed to kill me."

Mouse didn't look convinced. The reins still firmly in hand, he glanced nervously around them for signs of further attack. Quinn remounted and patrolled the area around the coach while Darby slid to the ground, where Kate busied herself getting his doublet off his injured arm.

"Goodness, such a lot of blood," she commented, solicitous as a mother hen. "Perhaps you should lie down."

Why was she making so much of a flesh wound? There was blood, true, but hardly enough to generate such grave concern. Yet Kate certainly wasn't the type to exaggerate the severity of anything—except perhaps Duncan's faults.

"Ach. 'Tis nothin'." Darby's thin chest swelled with pride under her ministrations.

"Pray forgive me if I hurt you."

"Do what ye must."

"You're a tough man, Darby Carlisle," she said without a hint of sarcasm as she inspected the seeping wound.

Duncan finally realized what she was up to. Kate must have noticed how the other men sometimes made sport of Darby's lameness, small stature, and swaggering manner. By the time she had bandaged the wound with her kerchief, the little man all but glowed from the respect she lavished on him.

Her work done, she turned to Duncan. "What happened? Who would waylay us thus?"

"I doona ken."

"Could Wat be behind this? He was the one who invited us."

Duncan scowled. Typical. She'd asked a question, he'd answered it, yet she'd kept right on asking because his answer wasn't to her liking. He'd had that problem with all his wives to some degree, but Kate was by far the worst.

Quinn rode up, providing a welcome interruption. "I doona like stoppin' here, Duncan," he said. "We're easy prey. What if he comes back with friends?"

"He won't." This was the work of an assassin.

Duncan would have preferred a straightforward raid. That, he would have understood; even expected. His known enemies lacked the means and the inclination to hire a paid killer. Such methods raised alarming possibilities.

Perhaps Quinn was right to be cautious. The sooner they were safely at Wat's, the better.

Unless Wat really had been behind this. If so, Duncan's days were numbered anyway. And so were those of his men.

He nodded to Darby. "Are ye fit to ride, then?"

"Aye." Buoyed by Kate's attentions, the bandy little man swung into his saddle with scarcely a wince, her blood-soaked kerchief a badge of honor on his sleeve. "Fit as any man here," he said with a forced grin.

"Then we ride." He turned to Kate. "Back in the coach wi' ye, Kate."

She glanced up sharply. "You're not riding in the coach? Duncan, someone just tried to kill you. Surely—"

"I'm nae ridin' in the coach," he snapped. He looked over the nervous, lathered team and called to Mouse. "Are the horses good for the rest of the way wi'out a rest?"

Mouse nodded, clearly anxious to be off.

"Aye, then." Duncan mounted Rogue. "Into the coach wi' ye." Then he let out a piercing whistle through his teeth, and Clyde scrambled from the trees, his hackles down and his huge pink tongue flapping as he ran. Duncan pointed to the coach, and Clyde streaked past Kate, then leapt inside without breaking stride.

"Oh, Duncan." Kate scowled up at him. "Please don't inflict Clyde on me all by myself. He'll squash me dead before we get to Wat's."

Duncan concealed his amusement behind a concerned frown. "He's just a simple beast," he told her. "Ye mustna let him disobey. Just show him you're in charge."

She shot him a look that would curdle milk. "*Who's* in charge? The dog weighs more than I do, and he knows it," she grumbled as she stomped back to the coach and boarded. "How in blazes am I supposed to convince him I'm in charge?" Still muttering hostilities, she slammed the door, and Mouse cracked the reins to set the coach in motion.

"Awk!" came Kate's voice from inside the compartment. "Get off me! Sit! Stay." The next was muffled. "Off! Off!"

If he hadna been so troubled, Duncan would have smiled as he rode beside them. But as it was, he kept remembering the sight of those crossbows and what they signified.

All this time he'd been worried that someone might move against them or Annanlea on the trip, but never had he considered an attack like this.

Duncan kept his eyes wary for trouble up ahead, but his mind whirled.

Treachery. First his salt, now this.

His instincts told him Wat was not behind today's attack, but if not Wat, who? he asked himself in the same words that had annoyed him so when Kate had uttered them.

Johnstones?

That would be the easy answer. There had been blood feud between their clans for as long as Duncan could remember. But an assassin from the Johnstones?

They might have been behind the salt raid. That had been a highly organized, efficient foray with no bloodshed, just the kind of attack he'd expect from his rivals. Business as usual on the borders. But the Johnstones had never used assassins.

Things just didn't fit here.

He checked the brace of pistols he carried and wished Wat's wasn't so far away.

Inside, Catherine finally managed to keep Clyde off her by scratching the back of his neck with her foot as he lay across the floorboards. At least that way, he was not drooling into her lap, wetting through her old skirt to the new one underneath.

Catherine had calmed quickly after the attack. Since random danger was a fact of border life, she—like everyone else she knew—had a sanguine attitude about close escapes. They had survived; it was that simple. But it did bother her that someone had tried to make her a widow while she was still a bride. And the thought of losing Duncan troubled her far more than she would ever have imagined.

She craved the man, not only for the pleasure he gave her, but for the sense of protection. And for the way he loved his children. And for his fierceness in defending what was his. The list grew with every passing week.

A reiver of principle? A just outlaw? Those had been contradictions in terms until she'd gotten to know Duncan. Now she realized those terms did apply to Duncan Maxwell.

But that didn't keep her from being afraid of what he'd do when he saw her in her Maxwell plaid. At the moment, she feared that far more than she feared another attack.

Would he do away with her when he saw her draped out in Maxwell plaid? Surely not with the Scotts looking on. She hoped.

But she dared not change into her new clothes too soon. Just to be safe, she stuck her head out of the window and called to him. "Duncan! Will you let me know when we're nigh to Wat's?"

He frowned, puzzled, and rode in closer so he could hear her repeat the request over the clatter of the coach. When she had, he nodded.

Catherine retreated into the compartment for another hour of holding Clyde at bay before Duncan rode up and shouted, "Wat's is but a mile ahead."

"Thank you!" She dropped the curtains on the windows and tied them down. Only then did she pull her new skirt out from under her old one, leaving the old one underneath to supplement the petticoats she'd scavenged from the wives' chest.

That done, she retrieved the valise she had stowed beneath the seat and took out the rest of her new clothes. She felt exposed and vulnerable removing her old blouse in front of Clyde's watchful eye. He was simply a beast, but his rapt stare was most unnerving. It wasn't easy doing up the buttons on her new blouse in the moving coach with Clyde bumping against her, but at last she tucked it into her skirts and fastened up the high, ruffed collar.

Donning her new plaid jacket was far simpler. Just putting it on gave her a confidence she hadn't felt since leaving River House. The coat was tailored in simple lines, with no slashed sleeves or fancy embroidery, but it hugged her body comfortably from the pointed tabs below her waist to the plain stand-up collar that supported her blouse's small ruff at her throat.

Once that was all fastened up, she drew on the fine leather gloves Aunt Brigit had given her for a wedding present, along with the simple shoes Quinn had hastily fashioned from an old leathern pouch.

Back at River House, Catherine would have scorned such attire as far too crude and rustic, but this was such an improvement over her castoffs from the wives' chest, she almost wept for joy. For the finishing touch, she unfolded her elegant new hooded cape and arranged it on her shoulders. Then she stood as best she could in the cramped, swaying compartment and allowed the graceful sweep of fabric to fall into place. Only when she sat back down did she realize that Clyde sat poised and alert, studying her with the same intensity he granted Duncan.

"Clyde?"

Gone was his witless dog-grin. His big tongue swiped across his jowls, then promptly disappeared.

Catherine didn't know what to make of it. On impulse, she pointed to the far corner of the floorboard. "Lie down."

Clyde backed away and lay down where she'd pointed, eagerly watching her in anticipation of another command.

"Sit up."

He sat up.

Catherine couldn't believe it. What had come over the beast? Whatever it was, she was grateful.

But why? Only minutes before, he'd considered her his personal plaything.

Then it dawned on her. The clothes! It had to be. Something about her new clothes had tamed the unruly beast.

If only her Maxwell plaid would have the same effect on Duncan Maxwell!

An effervescent chuckle rose from deep inside her. Catherine let it come, and the ones that rose up after, until she was bent over, laughing to the point of tears from an overwhelming sense of the absurdity of her situation. Her life!

It fortified her for the confrontation to come.

So when the cry of "Wat's ho!" came through the curtains into the dim compartment, she was better able to face what was waiting for her at the end of their journey. She peeked out to see a large, forbidding fortified house atop a hill, surrounded by a huge encampment of wagons, tents, horses, and border men of every station and description.

Excitement was palpable in the shouts, the smell of cook fires, the whinny of horses, and the cries of vendors.

Good. The more witnesses, the safer she'd be when Duncan saw her.

And then there was the matter of Wat and his lady wife. Catherine had been so worried about her clothes, she hadn't even addressed the challenge of meeting Mary Scott. For the family's sake, it was important that she make a good impression on the wife of so powerful an ally.

Suddenly nervous, Catherine dropped the curtain back into place.

What would Mary Scott be like? Married to a lout like Wat . . . And Duncan had mentioned a daunting number of sons.

Catherine envisioned a coarse, worn-out old drudge.

The coach slowed to a crawl, then halted. "Brace yourself," she said aloud. She stole another peek at her husband as he dismounted at the foot of the stairway leading up to Wat's. "And brace yourself, Duncan Maxwell."

"Duncan!" Catherine heard Wat bellow from the top of the stairs. "Come let us congratulate ye, lad!"

Duncan's response was lost in the welcoming shouts, the crunch of hooves as the men arrived, and brisk footsteps in the gravel around the coach. One particular set of footsteps grew louder and louder.

She should have been prepared, but the opening of the coach door sent her heart to her throat.

Fortunately, the face that peered inside was not her husband's. A sturdy servant boy extended his hand to help her out. "Ma'am." For once, she was glad for Duncan's lack of manners.

Clyde tensed and let out a low growl.

"Nay, Clyde. Easy," she said, her attention drawn to the stairway where Duncan strode up to greet Wat and the beautiful woman standing beside him.

Surely not Mary Scott!

Duncan had said she had children almost as old as he, yet only a few gray hairs streaked her hair, and her lovely face was that of a young woman. Catherine watched the lady take both Duncan's hands and kiss him fondly on each cheek while Wat beamed.

Mary Scott. It had to be.

Never in all of Christendom could Catherine have imagined a more unlikely pair than Auld Wat Scott and his beautiful wife.

After a brief exchange, Duncan and the Scotts turned expectantly toward the coach, jarring Catherine into action. The last thing she needed was for Duncan to come down to collect her. She wanted him as far away as possible when she got out in her Maxwell plaid.

She stood in the cramped compartment, gave her cloak

a quick shake to straighten it, then accepted the serving boy's hand and exited with all the regal grace she could muster. A vigilant Clyde followed obediently behind.

Duncan took one look at her and his face set in stone, eyes blazing. She'd known he would be angry, but even from this distance the force of his cold fury made her mouth go dry.

'Tis done, she told herself. *You cannot show weakness now.* She lifted her chin proudly and glided up the stairs as if nothing were amiss.

"Dame Scott." She extended her hands to her hostess. "Duncan did not tell me you were so beautiful."

Wat preened, but Mary Scott responded with genteel candor as she took Catherine's hands. "Once, perhaps, but those days are long gone. I'm a grandmother sixteen times over, and a great-grandmother thrice." She touched her cheek to each of Catherine's. "Please call me Mary."

"If you'll call me Catherine." So far, so good. Duncan hadn't reacted violently. Yet.

Mary drew back to look her over. "What a lovely bride ye are. And how well ye wear the Maxwell plaid."

In the awkward silence that followed, Wat rolled his eyes and peered skyward. Catherine dared not look at Duncan for fear of what she might see.

Mary Scott came to the rescue. "Tell me, Catherine, did ye drive straight through or stop for the night?"

"We stopped at the home of one of Duncan's friends in Hermitage, a William Croser," Catherine answered. The house had been humble and the mattress sour, but Duncan's ally had treated them like visiting royalty and regaled Catherine with stories of Duncan's fearless protection.

Catherine stole a look at her husband and found him grim as death, so she directed her attention to the encampment below. "I've heard of these races, but never attended one. Are they all so big and lively?"

"Nae." Mary smiled, a knowing sparkle in her eyes. "I

think most of the folk here came to honor ye and Duncan
at tonight's feast."

"Don't let yer head swell, Duncan," Wat chimed in
with a clout from his meaty hand. "Free food and drink
brings 'em out of the bushes every time. But we'll have
a hefty purse for the contest."

Mary shot him a quelling look, but Wat was oblivious.
She circled Catherine's waist and waved her small hand
across the gathering. There must have been at least two
hundred people there—dandies, rustics, vendors, cutthroats, and even a few gentles. And prime horseflesh of
a dozen breeds and colorations. "These events are the
black heart of the Scottish Marches, Catherine. Horse-
racing is the least of what goes on. There's secrets bein'
made and sold down there. Alliances forged and broken.
Trusts betrayed. Wagers made." She shook her head.
"And all of it well lubricated with spirits."

Mary Scott's frank intelligence impressed Catherine
greatly. She had not expected a stranger to treat her as an
intimate so quickly.

Wat pointed to the two stallions Quinn and Rory were
leading toward the stable. "I see ye brought your two-
year-olds along with the Percheron." His bloodshot eyes
narrowed. "I thought ye said ye wouldna sell them."

"I changed ma mind," Duncan said with deceptive
calmness.

"We've more than a few from across the border who'll
want to see them run." Wat pointed to three well-dressed
gentles who were already eyeing the stallions from a discreet distance. "Look yonder, next to our warden. That's
his English counterpart. Word is, he's in the market for a
stallion." Wat barked a laugh. "God save us from lawmen.
Arrestin' people for sellin' horseflesh across the border
one day, buyin' it themselves the next."

Catherine was well aware of Her Majesty's edicts
against horse-trading between the two nations, but she
also knew that the laws were almost never enforced. Why,
Papa's finest gelding had come from—

The fond memory stopped short with a wrench of loss that swelled heavy as a stone where her heart had been. Maybe someday she'd be able to think of Hal and Papa without pain, but not now. Catherine forced her attention back to Wat.

"There's even a few Johnstones lurkin' about who just might overlook their differences for the right piece of horseflesh," Wat told Duncan. "That makes at least a dozen who'll want to see yer stallions run today."

"Rory will ride the dapple." Duncan's tone was offhand despite the anger in his eyes. "If Darby's well enough, he'll ride the roan."

Wat's manner sharpened. "Well enough?" He peered at the unloading of the coach and spotted Catherine's bloody kerchief on Darby's arm. "Looks like one of yer men's been hurt. Trouble along the way?"

"Nay." Duncan was quick to contradict. "Just an accident. His hob threw him into a tree, and a branch pierced his arm."

When Catherine glanced at him in surprise, his blue eyes dared her to contradict him. She knew well enough when to keep her mouth shut, so she said nothing. She did, though, note how keenly Duncan measured Wat's response.

So he did suspect Wat, after all.

"Hah!" The outlaw whacked him on the back, clearly enjoying the irony of Duncan's fiction. "With all the brigands in the marches, to be run through by a tree! Hah!"

"I'll send one of my women to tend your man straightaway," Mary offered, solicitous.

Duncan opened his mouth to thank her, but Catherine cut him off without thinking. "Thank you so much. My handkerchief was all I had to bandage it, and the wound could use a good cleaning."

"Consider it done." Mary shepherded her toward the house. "Ye must be weary from yer sojourn. 'Tis a fearful long way from Annanlea. Come. Let us go inside where it's warm."

Inside. Closer to facing Duncan about the plaid. Catherine steeled herself for the inevitable confrontation. "I am a bit stiff and chilled."

Her hostess led the way out of the cold. "Here we are, then."

To Catherine's amazement, the inside of Auld Wat's house was as much a contrast to the outside as he to his lovely wife. Mary Scott's warmth and elegance permeated the place. Colorful hangings, rugs, and fabrics warmed the stone walls and floors, and artful arrangements of fall foliage and dried flowers brought life to the rooms. Best of all, a welcome blaze crackled in the fireplace of the main hall.

Mary introduced the three women who were putting the finishing touches on the rooms as her daughters-in-law, then the women and servants departed, leaving the two couples alone in the cheerful space.

"How charming." Catherine crossed to the hearth where she gladly warmed her hands. When Mary followed, she turned to her hostess. "You and . . ."—she could not bring herself to call her host "Auld Wat"—"Walter are so kind to invite us. And most generous to stage a feast in our honor."

Mary's laugh was as cultured and unaffected as the rest of her. "Nae one calls him Walter, child. He'll think ye mean his sire, God rest his soul." She shook her head. "He's Wat to his friends and Auld Wat to his enemies. And as ye are now counted a friend, it's Wat to ye."

"Wat, then," Catherine amended. She put her back to the fire, careful to keep her cape well clear. The movement attracted Duncan's unwelcome attention from across the room, where Clyde now stuck close by his master, tense in the company of Wat's dogs.

Duncan turned back to his host, who held forth loudly about cattle, recent affronts, and other border small talk. Despite the outlaw's good-natured bluster, she sensed a growing tension between the two men.

Little wonder. Duncan was probably as worried as she that Wat had been behind the attack.

Catherine resumed her conversation with Mary Scott. "After I've rested, I look forward to talking with you. I have so many questions about my new homeland."

"I am at your disposal." Mary paused, glancing back to the men as if she too sensed the tension in the air. "Pray continue with your conversation, gentlemen. I'm taking Catherine to her room for a nice rest before the race." She took Catherine's elbow. "After ye've had a chance to refresh yerself, I'll send up food to fortify ye for the contest." She grinned. "It gets quite exciting." After another glance at the men, she led Catherine from the room.

Chatting amiably, Mary led her down several narrow halls and up a flight of stairs, then down another corridor to a chamber with a brightly painted coffered ceiling, a large bed with elegant hangings, and a soft hooked rug on the floor. The room was large enough for a whole family, but Catherine feared it would seem small indeed when she was shut up in it with her angry husband.

Mary paused before leaving her. "Pray forgive me for being so inquisitive, but I couldna help noticin' that Duncan seemed a bit . . . surprised when ye got out of the coach."

Sensing a kindred spirit, Catherine decided to risk the truth. "You are a most perceptive woman, Mary Scott." A wry half-smile cocked her mouth. "I lost everything but my shift in the wreck of the *Dere,* so I ordered fabric to make new clothes for me and the children from Dumfries. This plaid was all that could be found." She met Mary's eyes. "I didn't know that Duncan had forbidden his family to wear the Maxwell plaid until the children saw it and told me." Catherine removed her cape. "I couldn't bear to disappoint the children. They were running about in rags. Nor could I bear to come here looking like a beggar. So Aunt Brigit and I made the clothes in secret. The first time Duncan saw them was when I got out of the coach."

"Ye got Brigit Maxwell to help ye?" Mary asked, astonished. "I am in awe, Catherine."

"She was reluctant at first, but when she saw the truth of the matter, she agreed." Catherine smiled with affection for Duncan's aunt. "Aunt Brigit may seem cross, but she loves Duncan's children as much as he does, and she wanted them warmly clothed."

She shrugged. "I decided that the safest way to break it to Duncan would be to appear in company without warning. It seems to have worked." She raised her eyebrows. "So far. He made no move to beat me."

Mary waved off her comment. "Ach, he's never laid a hand on a woman. Much to his credit, in my book. With most men, violence is their first resort. For Duncan Maxwell, it's the last, but one he's nae afraid to use."

She shifted the subject abruptly. "But let's talk about ye." Her lovely face went merry. "What fun we'll have, ye and I. At last, a woman after ma own heart in these parts." She chuckled strong and easy. "So ye just popped out of the coach in Maxwell plaid like a chick pippin' from its shell. Brilliant. Just brilliant. And I was there to see it." Mary shook her head. "By glory, I do believe Duncan Maxwell has met his match at last! And an Englishwoman, to boot. Droll, droll, droll. Ye've brightened ma dull old life considerable, Catherine Maxwell."

Dull life, married to Auld Wat?

Mary headed for the door. "And I had feared this would be a dour three days when Wat proposed it. Fie. I canna wait to see what ye do next." She paused in the opening, her smile fading to a concerned frown. "Shall I prepare another room for Duncan, then? Just to be on the safe side."

"Nay," Catherine said just a little too quickly. To her consternation, she felt her cheeks warm. She'd rather face Duncan's censure than sleep without him, even when he turned a cold shoulder to her. "We'll be fine here. But I would like some time to myself before he comes up."

"T'll see ye have it. We border wives must stick together, after all." Mary was chuckling when she closed the door.

We border wives.

She was a wife now. No longer was she relegated to the outer fringes of feminine society. And despite the rustic nature of that society on this side of the border, she allowed herself to hope that she had found a true friend in Mary Scott. In a flash of insight, she realized Mary would be her first real woman friend besides Aunt Brigit.

All those years back home, she'd insulated herself from the pain of her single status with work. Now she was no longer single. She had children. A husband. And friends.

She should have been happy, but the specter of suppressed loneliness rose up inside her, opening the door on the void her family's rejection had created.

Papa. Hal.

Catherine lay on the bed and curled upon her side. *Oh, Mama,* she cried out inwardly as she hadn't in years. *I miss them so. And I miss home. This place is so wild, so dangerous.*

She could almost hear her mother's voice saying, "What's done is done, child. You have another family to love now."

Her life had many blessings. God had not left her bereft. Catherine had the children to love. She even loved Aunt Brigit. And gruff Lucas. And simple Nessa. And sweet, silent Mouse. So many at Annanlea had found their way into her heart.

Love was her blessing. But it was also her curse. Lying there in the quiet, she finally admitted the secret she'd kept from herself for many weeks: God help her, she loved Duncan Maxwell, too—beyond reason, beyond safety, beyond hope. She was besotted with her husband.

It was the most disastrous mistake a wife could make.

Downstairs, Duncan sat opposite Wat in his study and wished the auld man would stop beating about the bush and say what was on his mind. But Wat had no penchant for indirectness. His clumsy attempts invariably involved a flood of inanity, followed by a blunt attack. True to form, he finally made an end to his tale of an inconsequential skirmish and leveled Duncan with a scowl. "So, Duncan. What's this I hear about these rubies? Have ye been holdin' out on yer auld friend Wat, now?"

Duncan had known Kate's scheme would come to trouble. Now Wat thought he'd struck treasure without telling his ally.

He kept his face impassive, his tone light. "There was naught to tell. Kate was ma hostage. She had two rings and two rubies. I sold the rings first, but since ma salt was gone, we needed more supplies for Annanlea. The rubies bought more. Where's the mystery in that?" He smiled. " 'Twas all she had, and a miracle she didna lose them in the wreck. To my way of thinking, the Almighty sent those jewels along with Kate by way of recompense. She's a mighty froward creature, that one. What a mouth!"

Wat guffawed. "I heard for maself when last we came to call." He shook his head. "Ach, women. They all have sharp tongues."

"Nae your Mary, ye auld reprobate," Duncan deflected. "The woman's a saint, to put up wi' the likes of ye all these years."

"Aye, well." Wat's ruddy face softened. Despite his wenching, everyone in the Western March knew he adored his beautiful wife and always had. The auld man relaxed back into his chair. "Doona let her smooth ways fool ye," he said with pride. "Ma rose is made of iron underneath."

Now that Duncan knew what had been troubling Wat, he allowed himself to relax a bit, as well. He sensed no more unasked questions in his ally.

As for the attack on the road . . . Duncan would get to the bottom of that. He'd instructed his men to nose about for anything suspicious. Perhaps they would come up with something.

"Odd, what we end up gettin' with our wives, and how, eh?" he mused aloud.

The reference was not an arbitrary one. Wat had won his wife and lodged with his father-in-law for a year solely on the strength of his promise not to attack Mary's family in future. It was a vow he'd kept.

"I've lived a rogue's life," Wat said, "but I must've done somethin' right to end up wi' a bonnie lass like Mary."

"Aye." Mary Scott was as clever as she was beautiful. She'd kept Wat happy, provided him with an impressive crop of sons, then gladly left him to his wenching, content to be his friend as she quietly provided a refuge of calm and comfort amidst the tumult of the borderlands.

Duncan noted the cleanliness and order of this house and thought of Annanlea. He realized with a shock that aside from Kate's tongue and Mary's beauty, his bride and Mary Scott had much in common. Both women were well bred, clever, and industrious. And both, compelled by expediency, had married far beneath them.

He wondered with an unexpected tug if he and Kate would ever settle to the comfortable relationship Wat and Mary shared.

He doubted it. The woman drove him to distraction.

Right now, he'd like nothing better than to take Kate across his knee and whale the stripes clean off the Maxwell plaid that covered her backside. But afterward, he'd like to do something else to that backside . . .

Catherine woke with a start in the dusky bedchamber. She hadn't meant to fall asleep.

Across the room, Duncan sat in a chair by the fire with his boots off, eating a chicken leg and drinking what smelled like spiced cider.

"Duncan."

"Aye," he said, his expression impassive.

He was there. And he wasn't angry. "How long have you been here?"

"Nae long," he said in guarded tones. He picked up the steaming pitcher from the well-laden tray on the table beside him, then poured more cider.

His controlled reserve worried her more than overt anger would have. What was he up to?

He lifted his mug. "My congratulations, Kate. Your little plot with the plaid seems to have captured Mary Scott's admiration. She kept me tied up with small talk downstairs for almost an hour, nae doubt to give ma temper time to cool."

"It seems to have worked." Catherine got up, wary. "You appear to be composed."

" 'Twas nae the small talk that cooled ma blood," Duncan informed her.

"No?" Blast the man, he was going to make her pull this out of him. "What did?"

"The fact that she was so eager to protect ye."

He peered at her head and frowned. "I think ye might want to do somethin' about your hair, Kate. 'Tis standin' rather odd."

She went to the dressing table and picked up the ornate silver looking glass. Sure enough, her bun had come loose, and her hair jutted up comically on one side while hanging in straggles from the other. "Goose feathers."

"Nae," he commented, deadpan. "More like a wild hob's tail, I would say."

"When is the race?" Would she have time to repair it? "What time is it now?"

Duncan waved the chicken bone toward an hour-candle. "Nae yet two. The race willna be run until four. Then afterward, the feast."

The smell of food reminded her that she hadn't eaten since dawn. Hair still defiantly awry, she joined Duncan at the table and poured herself a goblet of the sweet-smelling cider. "So Mary was eager to protect me, was she?"

"Aye."

"I liked her, too." She took a draught of the spicy liquid and almost choked. The apple juice was liberally laced with hard cider. It burned all the way down. "I hope she and I can become fast friends," she managed in a choked whisper.

"I would like nothing better," Duncan said. "For an alliance with Wat is nae half so reliable as one with Mary. She's the voice of reason in this house. Always has been." He lifted his tankard. "Here's to ye, Kate. Well done, so far."

Taking another swallow for courage, Catherine decided she might as well address the matter of the plaid and get it over with. She'd certainly prepared her argument thoroughly in all those hours in the coach. "I had thought you would be angry about my clothes."

His blue eyes darkened. Clearly, this was no idle matter to him. "Oh, I was. When ye came out of the coach, I'd have loved nothing better than to turn those plaid skirts up and spank your bare cuddy on the spot in front of everyone for darin' such an affront." His features tightened. "Ye were wise to wait until we were in company." He shook his head. "And Bink helped ye," he accused.

"Only because you asked her to," Catherine reminded him. "And only when she realized we hadn't planned to buy the Maxwell plaid. I bear sole responsibility for this, Duncan. Do not blame Aunt Brigit, or the girls."

She took another sip and decided it wasn't nearly so strong as she first thought. "I did not choose this plaid to insult you, and neither did Angus. The children needed clothes. I needed clothes. I simply asked Angus to get us yard goods in Dumfries."

Duncan remained impassive.

"The markets were out of everything but Johnstone and Maxwell plaids. Angus knew how badly the children needed new clothes, so he decided Maxwell plaid would be better than Johnstone or nothing, and he bought the Maxwell." Catherine leaned forward, hoping he would believe her. "I didn't know how you felt about it until the girls saw the bolts and told me."

She could not read her husband's expression, but he listened to her intently. "Duncan, Amber wanted a decent dress so badly that she wept when she told me you would never allow us to use the cloth. How could I deny her and the others warm clothes for the winter? I couldn't. I didn't."

He remained silent, his face and eyes as impenetrable as basalt.

She raised her chin. "Beyond that, I freely confess I did not wish to come here looking like a beggar." She noticed that her tongue had thickened from the cider, so she took great care with her words. "I understand why this plaid offends your pride, but what sort of pride would I have as your wife if I came here looking like a peasant?"

"Ye could be wearin' nothing but rags and goose shite, Kate," Duncan observed dryly, "and nobody would ever mistake ye for a peasant. You're far too uppity and head-strong."

"Nevertheless," she asserted, "I bear full responsibility for this matter." She probably should have eaten a bannock before drinking so much cider. She couldn't feel her chin. When she reached over to get one, she almost lost her balance.

"That cider seems to have gone straight to your head," Duncan said with a familiar carnal gleam in his eye. "Perhaps ye should lie back down for a while." He rose to his substantial height, which made the generous room suddenly seem more close and intimate. He unbuckled his belt and scabbard. "We're nae expected downstairs for at least another hour." After laying aside his weapons, he moved behind her chair and began to pull the pins from her bun. "As I said, ye might want to attend to your hair."

Warmth suffused her nether regions, awakening Catherine's own ardor with a spasm. "I'd rather attend to something else."

He loosed her hair, then ran his fingers through it to shake it free, releasing chills of pleasure from the gentle tug at her scalp. She closed her eyes and leaned back, giving him easy access to her lips.

Duncan stroked her neck and bent to kiss her lids, then stepped back, drawing her to her feet. "I'll be takin' off that Maxwell plaid, then, Kate," he murmured thickly. "We've cheated death this day. Let us make a sacrifice of life."

Here, there were no children to intrude, no emergencies to be dealt with, no chores to preoccupy either of them. She and Duncan had not been this alone and unfettered since they'd married. And fate had given them a golden hour.

She stood, as hungry for him as she had been on their wedding night—and every time since. Eager to be shed of the clothes she and Aunt Brigit had worked so hard to make, she gladly turned her face to his and allowed him to kiss her thoroughly. The room was warm, almost as warm as Duncan's hands upon her skin.

There was no coyness between them. There never had been, and she prayed there never would be. What they had discovered in each other's arms was a force of nature: real, unvarnished, and without artifice. Urgent.

Deftly, he undid the buttons of her blouse, then the cuffs while she loosed the closures on her skirts and petticoats. Once her skirts were free, she let them fall, and the red plaid settled to the floor around her like a great scarlet blossom. She discarded her blouse atop it.

Duncan shucked her shift from her and tossed it aside, reveling in her nakedness before him. Then he drew her close to claim her body with his hands. His rapt gaze darkened. His breathing deepened. It still amazed and excited her to see the effect she could work on him.

Catherine closed her eyes and rode the welling tide of longing and sensation. He feathered kisses down her neck, then kissed her eyes, her breasts, her ears. His teeth teased shudders of delight from her lobes and her nipples. And all the while, his fingers gripped her, smoothed her, cupped her, and probed her until the longing overwhelmed even the glory of his touch, and she had to have him.

No words passed between them. Need was the only language they required, and it told no lies.

She tugged loose the laces of his shirt, then pulled it from him. Eyes locked to his, she unfastened his breeches and shoved them low enough for him to step clear. Then she thrust him backward onto the bed and crawled up his powerful legs to nestle astride his pulsing manhood. It felt hot and thick and ready between her nether lips, but she decided to prolong the gentle torture just a little longer. Balancing her weight carefully against the pressure, she shifted slightly from side to side, setting off wave after wave of pleasure from the pressure of flesh on flesh.

"Aach." Duncan arched his back with a grimace. "Ye drive me mad, Kate." He bucked beneath her, pushing her over the edge.

No longer able to endure the emptiness inside her, she sheathed him brutally in her body, then slid back and forth in a driven rhythm he joined by grasping her waist and drawing her harder and harder, faster and faster.

Then, just as she thought she could go no higher, he rolled over and flipped her to all fours, entering her womanhood from behind, filling her as she had never been filled before.

Hoarse cries of satisfaction escaped her with every thrust. She stretched her hands to the headboard and pushed to meet him. It was a savage taking, one that sent her to new heights of ecstasy and release. Catherine surrendered to the purging, primal rhythm and lost herself completely. When at last the sweet explosion came, she cried out in glorious abandon, her voice joined by Duncan's own coarse shout of release. Buried to the hilt, he arched his back behind her with a bone-deep shudder, then dropped to his side still holding her, still joined.

Catherine wasn't certain how long they had lain there when Duncan rolled onto his back beside her with a satisfied huff. Sated, she turned to nestle her head on his chest, threading her fingers through the hair of his loins that was still damp from her desire. Then she hefted the weight of his now-flaccid member.

"Ma pike's havin' his nap, Kate," Duncan rumbled. "Nae manner of handlin' will wake him before he's ready."

She chuckled. "I don't want to wake him, just to hold him. Get to know him."

"I doona mind, either way." He stretched, his feet hanging off the end of the bed. "Ach. I don't suppose we could just stay abed and skip the feast."

Catherine knew better than to let him suck her into *that* game. "Yes, let's. I'm sure Mary and Wat would understand."

A dry chuckle escaped Duncan. He rolled her atop him. "Ah, Kate." The smile lines around his eyes made him look years younger. "You're too clever by half, ma lass." He gave her behind a playful swat, then heaved her back to the bed and got up. "Ach. I'm fair sore from that pell-mell ride."

"The one we just took, or the one after the attack?" she retorted. She stretched long and hard with a most unladylike yawn, then reluctantly got out of bed. "I don't suppose I could go like this." Two could play that game.

Duncan laughed. "Oh, aye. That would give 'em something to celebrate." He looked her over with an approving eye. "I do believe ye lost your modesty entirely with your maidenhead, Kate." He picked up his shirt and breeches. "Suits me fine if ye go naked. At least ye'd nae be wearin' Maxwell plaid."

Catherine took it as a good sign that he could joke about it, but the matter hadn't been resolved. She collected her own clothes and began to dress, glad her new, longer skirt now hid the embroidery that concealed her jewels. "You did not tell me what my punishment will be, Duncan."

"Punishment?" Pulling up his breeches, he regarded her in mild surprise.

"Aye. For insulting your pride with the plaid." She

faced him without fear or anger. "What shall my punishment be?"

Duncan gathered his hose and boots, then sat back down to don them. "Nae punishment, Kate," he said as he drew them over his muscular calves. "I think, instead, a reward."

Catherine paused with her skirt midway up her thighs. Duncan seemed entirely too smug. "I see. And what would that be, then?"

"Ye shall wear your Maxwell plaid, Kate." He stood, the embodiment of male beauty with his bare chest, snug leathern breeches, and high black boots. "Wear it and nothing else, forever. That shall be your reward."

"Forever?" If Duncan Maxwell expected her to show one atom of disappointment, he had another think coming. Kate would wear his blasted Maxwell plaid with alacrity until the day she died! "Oh, thank you, Duncan," she responded with what she hoped was convincing sincerity. "Such kindness, and after I upset you so. Bless you."

His smug look promptly went sour.

Kate smiled. Papa had always said red was her best color, anyway.

EIGHTEEN

Catherine girded her courage to face Mary Scott's female guests who were now chattering in the parlor. She had no illusions about how they would respond to an English stranger in their midst.

She'd never been good at women's gatherings anyway, even under the best of circumstances. She had no patience with small talk and detested gossip.

If only Duncan could be here with her. But he had already left to prepare for the race. She would have to face Scottish society alone.

Scottish society. 'Twas a contradiction in terms.

She took a deep breath, then glided into the crowded room.

"Ah, Catherine, there ye are." Mary Scott motioned to her from across the parlor.

As Catherine had expected, her entrance met with mixed reactions, from thinly veiled curiosity to not-so-thinly veiled hostility, but Mary promptly went on record with her own personal endorsement. "Our guest of honor, ladies, and a precious new friend to me. We are so blessed to have her among us. Pray, welcome her as ye would me. I ken ye'll want to make her feel at home." Catherine detected an instant, though perhaps only superficial, thawing.

She'd never attended such a varied social gathering. The gathered women were dressed in everything from fine silks to coarse, drab plaids and spanned the gamut of age, appearance, and sophistication. One thing they all had in common, though; they looked on Catherine with curiosity—and varying degrees of reservation.

When Catherine had married Duncan, she hadn't even considered life beyond the walls of Annanlea. Suddenly, she felt very much like an unwelcome invader.

"Come." Mary took her arm and led her toward a whispering cluster of well-dressed women about Catherine's own age. "Let me introduce ye to my daughters and our friends." She started with her daughters, then progressed through her daughters-in-law to the wives of Wat's allies and fellow reivers.

Catherine's warm new cloak would keep her from the winter wind outside, but among these women, she had only her pride to protect her from the chill. So she moved with dignity and assurance to Mary's side, making eye contact with each woman along the way and nodding. They could think what they might of her, but they would know one thing: she was not afraid of them. Now that she was under Mary's sponsorship, though, not a single woman present would dare to cut Catherine directly, and some even showed the glimmerings of welcome.

The last introduction had scarcely been completed when a horn sounded outside.

"The race," Mary announced as everyone started toward the door. She motioned the servants toward the dogs. "See that the dogs are kept tied here."

"Stay, Clyde," Catherine instructed. He halted obediently at her word.

Mary ushered her toward the door. "Come, Catherine. My lord husband awaits in the watchtower. Pray, join me there. We'll be able to see most of the race."

More than a few pairs of feminine eyes cut their way in surprise or envy.

"Thank you, Mary." Catherine wound her woolen Maxwell plaid scarf around her throat, then raised the hood of her cloak.

Outside, a strong wind tore at the gray clouds, exposing patches of brilliant blue above the noisy, smoky encampment. Mary looked up. "How fortunate. Perhaps we'll have some sun for the race."

But Catherine wasn't looking up. She was looking down, at the ragtag encampment and daunting collection of armed outlaws waiting at the bottom of the steep stone stairs. She was hardly reassured by such "guards." This looked like a case of the wolves being given charge over the sheep.

Where was Duncan? she worried. Would the assassin strike again? Among such tumult, he would have a perfect opportunity. Duncan's powerful height and huge mount made him an easy target.

Shivering at the thought, she followed Mary down the long stairway toward a thick path of fresh hay that led to the watchtower. Surrounded by Wat's vigilant cutthroats, they passed uneventfully through the smoky, boisterous camp.

"I'm afraid we'll have to climb the ladder," Mary said when they reached the wooden tower. "There's only room for the two of us up there besides Wat and his chief race wardens."

Wat's bearded face loomed over the edge of the platform. "Come on up, lasses." He winked at Catherine. "We can squeeze ye in."

Squeezed in with Wat and his race wardens? Catherine resolved to keep Mary Scott between her and the old reprobate at all costs.

Nagged by concern for Duncan, she searched the crowd, but saw no sign of him. Where was he?

Once they reached the crowded platform, she pulled her cloak close against the wind and looked down. Just below the tower, the riders gathered for the start. She searched again for Duncan, but he wasn't there. Neither were Rory and Darby on the other stallions. She saw several horses that might put Rogue to a test, but one in particular caught her eye—a big red ridden by a foul-looking bear of a man.

As if he had sensed her looking at him, the rider turned to leer at her, exposing his scarred, pocked face distorted into an evil grin. His brittle gaze sent a chill down her spine.

Catherine pressed in closer to Mary and redirected her

view to the panoramic countryside. Bright swaths of sunshine illuminated the burgundy hills, green pastures, and
spent fields outside Harden.

"Our race is a single run on a circular course," Mary
explained. "Nae weapons allowed. The riders begin and
end here." She pointed to the hills and dales before them.
"If ye look close, ye'll see the flags that mark the way."

Catherine picked out the small white banners. They
traced an irregular pattern down the moss, across the narrow valley, up another hill, back down into a crooked,
sandy ravine, over more moss and field and streams, then
back up to the finish line. It was a treacherous course with
many jumps and hazards. "We can see almost everything
from here," she commented.

"Aye." Mary took her arm. "But sometimes I doona
want to. Three of our lads are runnin' today. Even without
weapons, things get brutal."

Catherine had heard of men dying in these wild Scottish races. A shiver of foreboding prompted her silently
to admonish God, *You left me no choice but to marry the
man. Kindly do not kill or maim him now.* The words *I
love him* tacked themselves unbidden onto her prayer.

She turned back to Mary, certain that the time set for
the race was well past. "I thought the start was to be at
four," Catherine said, anxious.

Mary laughed. "Ach! That's Scottish time, ma dear.
Approximate, at best. They'll go when everybody's here."

Horses and riders now crowded the starting line. The
stallions reared, snorted, and sidled. The level of noise
and excitement heightened as furious wagers changed
hands among the spectators.

"Hear ye! See the prize." Wat drew all eyes to him
when he raised a fat purse. "Ten gold pieces to the winner!"

A great tumult went up. Then Catherine saw the crowd
part, and Duncan rode forward on his Percheron ahead of
Rory and Darby on the stallions. A murmur of speculation
swished through the spectators. The women looked on the

Black Bastard with candid appreciation, but the men regarded him with envy, respect, or resentment.

Catherine scarcely noticed the crowd's reaction for Duncan, himself. Faith, but he looked glorious on his magnificent black stallion, his ebon hair whipped back by the wind, his fair skin burnished to a ruddy glow, and his perfect body molded in black leather. She waved to him without thinking, then hastily retracted her hand.

Foolish, acting like a moonstruck girl over her own husband.

Duncan granted her a nod, then eased his mount into the line of racers. Darby and Rory wedged in on either side of him. Two of the race-wardens' assistants subjected them to a cursory search to make certain they were unarmed, then nodded up to the tower.

"All set." Mary tugged gently at the red plaid wrapped loosely about Catherine's neck. "Hand me your scarf, lass. I'll use it to start the race."

Catherine removed it and gave it to Mary, wondering if she would get it back.

Mary shared a conspiratorial wink. " 'Tis our custom for the winner to tie the openin' scarf about his arm."

"Duncan, in Maxwell plaid?" Catherine shook her head. "Queen Elizabeth will have twins before that would come to pass. And anyway, he might not win."

"Oh, he'll win," Mary assured her. "And fairly, too."

Catherine wondered how she could be so certain.

Wat motioned his wife to the railing. "Come start this thing, woman, before the horses maim each other."

Mary extended the bright red plaid above the racers while the warden silenced the crowd by bellowing, "Oyez! Oyez! Oyez! At the droppin' of the scarf, let the race begin."

As if in collusion with her, the wind died along with the hubbub. Mary waited until the only sounds were the chuffing and writhing of the horses and their tack. Duncan peered up at the scarf along with everyone else. Then Mary's fingers released the cloth, and the pack of racers launched into a shouting press of man and horseflesh amid an explosive cheer from the crowd.

Catherine leaned against the rail, her pulse pounding now with a mixture of fear and excitement. The head race warden shouted out a rapid-fire chronicle of riders and positions to the crowd.

From the beginning, Duncan was closely matched with the ogre on the roan. The lead swapped back and forth between the two, often violently, with the rest of the pack well back. Catherine's heart went to her throat and stayed there.

Beside her, Mary rooted for her sons, but most of the crowd was shouting for the two front-runners. After the third near-disastrous change of lead, Catherine closed her eyes and prayed that Duncan would simply survive.

She couldn't bear to look until she heard them thundering toward the finish line. Unable to help herself, she looked down to find the rider of the roan half a nose behind Duncan and viciously whipping him across the small of his back.

Duncan stood in his stirrups, bent low over Rogue's neck, moving as one with his horse. He did not whip or spur the animal, but relied instead on the same devotion that all he mastered gave him willingly. Catherine knew Rogue would run till his great heart burst if Duncan asked it of him.

They were only fifty yards away when something shiny in the other rider's hand caught the race warden's attention. "Foul!" he shouted, pointing. "McGinty's got a knife!"

Catherine saw it, too, clumsily concealed by the man's whip. He was lunging toward Duncan's thigh with all his might. "Duncan!" Catherine's mouth went dry as the dust of a crypt, her chest tightening.

"A knife?" Mary glanced frantically about the platform. "Where's a musket! Give me a musket, I say! I'll put a stop to Gareth McGinty's treachery!"

Duncan reined his horse sharply, then, as McGinty

started past him, loosed his foot from its stirrup to strike a precise kick at the hand bearing the knife. The weapon went sailing, in clear view of everyone.

A collective gasp went up from the crowd, followed by a tumult. "McGinty is disqualified," the race warden roared, "for drawin' a dirk."

Exposed and furious, the brigand hurled himself at Duncan in an effort to rob him of his win. But Duncan, his foot already free of the stirrup, swung his leg to the opposite side of the horse, leaving his attacker with only his upper body to grab on to.

Spectators raced for a look at the fight. Rogue slowed from the extra weight, allowing Darby and Rory and Will to gain on him.

Approaching the finish line, the two men struggled back and forth until Duncan managed to wriggle free of one of McGinty's hands. The crowd shrieked as the outlaw began to slip away, but just when Catherine thought it was over, McGinty caught his foot into the empty stirrup and managed to regain his balance.

Then, in a maneuver too quick for Catherine to follow, Duncan swung over Rogue's withers, facing backward, and kicked McGinty loose. The brigand landed on his back and was hastily dragged from the path of the advancing racers while Duncan crossed the finish line alone—riding backward on Rogue's withers.

The crowd went wild. Catherine shoved her way to the ladder and clambered down. She reached him as he gingerly put himself to rights in the saddle. Dozens of potential buyers crowded around to inspect the front-runners, but none approached Rogue, for all knew he was not for sale.

Catherine gazed up at Duncan with pride. "Well done, husband. Well done."

Laughing, he took hold of her arm and hoisted her into the saddle in front of him. Where he found the strength after his ordeal, she couldn't imagine, but it felt wonderful sitting there with him above the crowd.

A horn sounded three long blasts, and everyone quieted.

"By Jupiter!" Wat bellowed down on them. "Ye'll nae more be the Black Bastard of the marches, Duncan! After today, ye'll be the Ass-Backward of the marches forever and anon!"

A roar of laughter rose among delighted cheers.

Duncan's hands rubbed her upper arms, and she felt distinct evidence against her hip that his "pike" had not suffered too badly from straddling Rogue's withers.

Wat raised the purse. "To the winner, and well earned!" He tossed it down to Duncan, who caught it in his left hand, then deftly tucked it into his jacket.

Another cheer went up.

Catherine couldn't keep herself from grinning. Then she saw the race warden approach bearing her scarf, and her smile faded.

A tense hush fell on the crowd. Duncan's feelings about the plaid must have been common knowledge. "Will ye wear the lady's token, Duncan?" Wat challenged.

Duncan shot a sardonic glance at the scarf. "Give it to ma lady wife," he ordered gruffly.

Catherine accepted it with tingling fingers, afraid the plaid would ruin this triumphant moment for both of them.

Then Duncan brushed a kiss to the back of her neck and extended his arm. "Tie it on me, Kate," he declared for all to hear. "I'll wear it proudly for ma lady wife, Catherine Armstrong Maxwell."

Never in her life had anyone honored her so profoundly, or so publicly. Her eyes blurred with happy tears, Catherine tied the fabric around his upper arm.

Then Duncan kissed her soundly, right in front of everyone, to the uproarious delight of the crowd.

But no sooner had they parted, than Rogue reared with a whinny, sending them both tumbling onto the moss. Catherine heard cries of alarm, but only when she righted herself and stood did she see why. Rogue fought his reins, unhurt, but two bolts were buried in the thick crest of his saddle.

Some of the crowd were pointing toward a wagon at the edge of the gathering, but there was no sign of anyone near it now.

Stone-faced, Duncan glared toward Wat. As host, he was responsible for the safety of his guests.

"Duncan Maxwell is more than ma ally!" the outlaw thundered from the platform, his face livid. "He's son to me, deep as blood. Whoever harms him or one of his will answer to me and mine!"

Mary looked on in shock and sympathy.

"Come." Duncan took Catherine's arm and drew her toward the house. "We're going home."

Chapter

NINETEEN

By the time he'd reached the house, Duncan realized it would be foolish to set out for home so late in the day—particularly with someone determined to kill him—but he sent Kate to their room and let Wat plead with him for another fifteen minutes before he agreed to stay the night. "Verra well. On the strength of our friendship, we'll wait until the morning to leave."

"And ye'll nae return home wi'out a proper guard," Wat admonished. "I'll send a dozen of ma best men wi' ye."

Duncan nodded, more convinced than ever that Wat himself was not behind the plot to take his life. Yet he couldn't eliminate the very real possibility that one of Wat's men—perhaps even one of his sons—had decided to eliminate the Black Bastard.

But he couldn't think of that now. The trials of the last twenty-four hours slammed home with a vengeance, leaving him drained, unable to reason. He bowed to his distraught ally. "Until the morning, then."

Duncan left the parlor, his senses strained for any sight or sound that might bode of another attack. On the one hand, he had a sanguine attitude about the two near misses. Clearly, it wasn't his time to die, or Kate's. But he had no intention of tempting fate.

He reached the door of their room without event and gladly closed it behind him, sliding the bolt securely into its fitting. The moment they were safely locked in, the last of his energy ebbed away. He'd have lain on the floor, but Kate was waiting for him at a table laden with succulent food.

"Mary knew you would be hungry and tired," she said quietly as she rose to approach him, "so she sent the choicest morsels from the feast." She unbuckled his belt. "Here. Let me help you undress."

No questions, no theories, no histrionics. No sharp-tongued comments or accusations. She simply ministered to him, unbuttoning his jacket. When she reached inside it for the purse of gold, though, he caught her wrist on reflex.

" 'Tis your prize, Duncan," she said with a blessed note of humor. "I'm not trying to steal it from you. But you must put it down sometime."

"Sorry." He released her wrist. "Pure instinct."

"And a good one, but not necessary in my case." She carried the purse to the bed. "Here. I'm putting it under your pillow."

Duncan shook his head. "Put it under yours, Kate. I'm too tired to look after it." He yawned hugely. "Just doona spend it on Maxwell plaid before I wake."

Half-asleep on his feet, he could not keep his eyes open, but sensed her smile.

Kate returned from the bed to remove his jacket. The room was warm. Peaceful. By Saint Columba's kneecaps, it felt good to be taken care of.

She loosened the cuffs and ties to his shirt, then pulled it off. Before, when she'd undressed him, it had been a prelude to their passion. Now the act was one of gentle reassurance, and it soothed his troubled soul. Unable to fight off the stupor that had been trying to overtake him, he surrendered to her attentions, thanking God for Kate's sensible kindness.

The air cooled as she left him, then he heard her pour something, followed by a clank of metal at the fire. The sizzle of a hot iron in liquid released the spicy aroma of mulled wine. Kate returned to press the handle of a tank-ard into his right hand and a chicken leg into his left. "Here. Eat this, before you fall down." She drew him toward the chairs. "Now sit, so I can take off your boots."

Dragging his eyes open, he took a grateful sip of the rich, spicy liquid, then sank into the chair. After only a bite of chicken, he must have dozed off, because the next thing he knew, he was barefooted. Kate had stoked the fire to a blaze and drawn a shallow tub to the hearth beside a steaming kettle.

"Come." She urged him back onto his feet, unbuttoned his breeches, and drew them down. "Let me wash you off, then you may sleep in peace." Weary though he was, his manhood tightened from the pressure of her touch.

Kate chuckled. "By my faith, Duncan. You can hardly keep your eyes open, but your pike leaps to attention if I even get near it. Are all men so single-minded?"

"Aye. We canna help it," he confessed, too exhausted to follow through on what his body had started.

She stooped to tug at the breeches that lay around his ankles. "Step out." He did. "Now come over here, into the tub." Duncan took another bite of chicken, then stepped into the tub and closed his eyes.

The first ladle of warm water spilled down his shoulders, sending delicious chills over his entire body. "Aaah. God love ye, woman." He shuddered.

Another ladle and another released waves of pure pleasure. Then she began to wash him with a warm, soapy cloth. Face, neck, shoulders, arms. One by one, her hands swiped smooth, soapy arcs across his flesh, followed by warm water and a toasty towel to dry his skin. At first, he closed his eyes and reveled in the sensations without response. But by the time she got to his manhood, he was full to bursting and miraculously energized.

Kate used her hand, not the cloth, to soap his throbbing member, her touch possessive. When she rinsed him with warm water, his whole body wracked, and he opened his eyes to find her gaze boldly fixed on his manhood. Her wet, warm hand circled it and slid to the base, tightening the sensitive tip.

Undone by her brazenness, Duncan crushed her lips to his with ferocious hunger and snatched her hard against him. She met him with equal fervor, pressing her body to his. Duncan half carried, half dragged her to the high bed,

breaking their kiss only when he thrust her onto her back
and lifted her skirts.

Kate raised her knees, opening herself to him. "You're
wet," she chided playfully.

Standing at the edge of the bed, he probed the dark,
erotic flower of her desire with his fingers. "And so are
ye." She was past ready to receive him. Her eyes, the
hungry intensity of her expression, her body itself betrayed her. Unable to hold back for another instant, he
buried himself inside her.

Kate wrapped her legs around his naked hips. "Aye!"
She drew him flesh to flesh with eager force, her fists
gripping the bedclothes. Duncan lost all sense of time and
place. He thrust into her faster and faster, unable to hold
back a primal groan with every stab. Kate reached her
pinnacle quickly, letting out a feral crow of triumph that
summoned forth his seed, as it always did.

Head thrown back, he executed two more mighty,
quaking thrusts, then went still, remaining inside her until
nature took its course and separated them. Only then did
he fall like a massive oak to the mattress and allow oblivion to overtake him. But as he sank into the inviting vor-
tex of darkness, a troubling realization bloomed:
Catherine Armstrong had bewitched him, body, mind, and
soul.

The following Thursday back at Annanlea, Catherine was
listening to Amber's catechism when the familiar call
came from the peel. "Lone rider comin' in. Slow."

Slow.

The fear that had sprung up in Catherine abated just a
bit. There had been trouble at the salt pans, so Duncan
had been out there for two days. She'd had to muster all
her willpower to keep from worrying herself sick about
his safety.

Erinn shook her head over the slate of subtractions
Catherine had given her to solve. "Ach. More bad news,"
she announced to the cats that surrounded her in various

states of repose, sounding entirely too much like her great-aunt.

Plodding away at his mathematics, Cameron didn't even look up from his fractions.

"A message!" The twins erupted from writing their alphabets.

"Who do ye think 'tis?" Kerry asked.

"Trouble, maybe." This from Gordon. "Ye ken what we heard about Papa and Ladykate."

"Oh, aye. That."

"Trouble," Gordon gravely confirmed.

What had they heard? Trouble? Catherine lowered the shirt she was sewing for Cameron. "What have you boys heard about your father and me?"

"Someone's out to murder Papa," Erinn answered for them.

"Erinn!" Amber glared at her.

Erinn ignored her sister, informing Catherine, "People have talked of nothing else since ye came back from Harden."

"Thank you, Erinn, but I directed my question to the twins." The twins who were now harassing each other on the library bench. "Is this true?"

"Oh, aye," Gordon stated cheerfully. "Someone's always tryin' to kill Papa. He's used to it, and so are we, but Amber said ye didna understand how things were here, so we shouldna speak of it around ye."

"Can ye nae keep anything to yourselves?" Amber chided.

Kerry crossed his arms and pouted. "I didna mean to tell her. It just came out."

Drawn by her unerring nose for trouble, Aunt Brigit appeared from the kitchen just in time to catch the last of Kerry's protest. "What just came out?"

Amber fixed her brothers with a baleful eye. "Sit ye down and shut your teeth, ye blabber-traps. Now ye've got Aunt Brigit in on it."

Catherine stood and approached the boys. "Are you

suggesting that people have tried to kill your father before?"

"Oh, that." Aunt Brigit dismissed the matter with a wave. "Old news."

"Aye, people try to kill Papa," Erinn answered, uninvited. "Every so often. But we doona hear of it till after and he's done them in, instead."

Catherine turned to Aunt Brigit. "Is this true?"

"Of course." The old woman regarded her as if she were simple. "We live in the borders, Kate, nae fairyland. Scotland is a bluidy country. Surely ye thought of that before ye agreed to marry Duncan."

Catherine hadn't thought of anything but refuge then. And desire. Only later had she seriously considered the desperate perils of the world beyond Annanlea's island of safety.

She jumped when someone pounded on the front door.

"I'll get it." Catherine laid aside her sewing. "Aunt Brigit, would you please supervise the children until I get back?"

"Aye." Clearly, Aunt Brigit would have preferred to go to the door herself, but as lady of the house, Catherine had the prerogative, and she was every bit as curious as Duncan's aunt about who had come to call.

She opened the door to find Angus Maxwell waiting in the raw winter wind, his cheeks rosy from the cold and his white hair blowing loose beneath his broad-brimmed cleric's hat.

"Angus! What a pleasant surprise." She drew him inside. "What brings you to Annanlea?"

"A pastoral call." Angus glanced nervously about the foyer and parlor. "I heard of your trouble and kent Duncan wouldna risk sendin' ye or the children to Annan for a while. So I decided to bring the catechism lessons to them."

Something was bothering him. His smile was too brittle, his speech too quick, and his gaze too wary.

"How kind of you. Please let me take your cloak and bring you some mulled cider."

Angus removed his hat, then unhooked his cloak. After smoothing down his white mane and the tabs of his clerical collar, he asked, "I doona see Duncan aboot."

"No." Catherine hung his cape and hat on a hook, then escorted him into the parlor. "He's been out on business for two days." She wasn't certain why she hadn't told Angus where. Perhaps some of Duncan's wariness had rubbed off on her.

Angus turned her toward the front window and dropped his voice to a barely audible whisper. "This is important, Catherine." He slipped a folded note from his pocket and pressed it into her hand. "It's from someone who loves ye. Wait until ye're alone to read it. May God have mercy on me if Duncan should find out."

Her hand tingled with alarm as it held the message. She tried to return it. "Angus, I cannot let you take such a risk for me," she whispered. "If Duncan should find out you'd done this—"

His large hand closed around hers, making it impossible for her to release the message. "I've told ye before, lass, doona try to come between me and ma conscience." He raised his voice to a forced cheerfulness. "Now. Where arc the children? I'm ready to commence our lesson."

"Everyone but Baran is in the morning room. I'll send Nessa for him straightaway."

Someone who loved her?

Her stepbrother Hal?

There were no others, now.

The note fairly burned a hole in Catherine's pocket, but she managed to conceal the pounding of her heart and the barrage of questions that rose inside her.

Aunt Brigit bristled when she brought Angus into the morning room. True to her vow never to speak to the minister again, she marched back to the kitchen without a word while Catherine was explaining the purpose of his visit.

Catherine cupped Amber's cheek. "Dear, will you please fetch Cousin Angus some mulled cider?" As Amber left, she turned back to the minister. "Pray excuse me for a moment. I must attend to a few chores. I shall be back anon."

She forced herself to move slowly as she left the room, climbed the stairs, and retired to her room. Only when the door was shut and bolted did she dare to pull out the note and open it.

Papa's handwriting!

My precious one,
      So much to explain. Received word you were lost in the wreck, Charles spared.

Charles spared! Catherine's heart leapt, then promptly came crashing to earth. She reread the first words in confusion. But his other letter had said Charles was dead! She read on.

Have been secretly searching for you, but summoned home by Willa's sudden illness. Discovered evil afoot. Must meet with you, and soon. Take care no one follows.
Come to the church. I'll find you.
      Praising Almighty God for His mercy in delivering you,
      Your loving Mister Rob's A'ramble

Her heart caught to see the nickname after so many years. It had been their secret, so sacred to the two of them that they'd stopped using it when Charles was old enough to hear it. *Mister Rob's A'ramble*. A pulse of loss and love remembered welled inside her, making it hard to breathe.

Catherine reread the note three times, then stared at it,

her mind whirling. The words were plain enough, but they made no sense.

Why would he write first that Charles was dead, then turn around now to say he'd thought she was dead, instead? What evil had he discovered? And what about Willa's illness?

Only Papa had the answers, and he was in Annandale, hiding. She had to go to him. Now, before Duncan came back.

After changing into her riding boots, she fetched her gloves, scarf, and cloak. Then she hastened back downstairs.

Should she tell Aunt Brigit? Nay. That would only give the well-meaning woman time to try to stop her.

Catherine threw on her cloak and ducked into the foyer, praying Mouse could be easily found. As luck had it, she discovered him the first place she looked, at the stable.

"Mouse." For Mouse's sake, she made certain the other stable lads heard her instructions. "I've decided to pay a call on Sarah Maxwell. I may stop on the way home to take some supplies to Duncan. Gather two blankets, a jug of wine, some bread, and apples." What else might Papa need? "And cheese."

She handed him a saddlebag. "Put my saddle on the brown mare right away, then keep watch on the front door. When I come out, bring the horse to me without delay."

Mouse nodded, but his young face reflected concern.

Angus Maxwell had taken quite a risk in coming here alone. For Catherine to go back with him was rash, indeed. Yet Duncan hadn't forbidden her to leave the compound, probably because it hadn't occurred to him that she might do something so reckless. So Mouse was breaking no orders by helping her. "Remember, Mouse. I am mistress here."

He nodded, then went after the mare.

"Good." Catherine hurried back to the house. Breathless, she hung her cloak by the door, smoothed her hair, then glided back into the morning room as if nothing had transpired.

By early afternoon—against Aunt Brigit's frantic objections, and with Quinn and Rory along as unwelcome protection—she was halfway to Annandale, wishing Angus Maxwell could ride faster.

Up in the Maxwells' darkened guest room, Catherine sat in a chair by the narrow window, alert to every sound from downstairs. Knowing Quinn and Rory would never allow her to leave the house alone, she'd pleaded a headache and retired early. Now all she had to do was reach the church without getting caught. As soon as she heard Sarah begin to clear away the dishes, she planned to take advantage of the noise and sneak out the window.

Papa was out there watching and waiting. She could feel it.

She glanced over to the bed and worried again that the mounded covers looked skimpy, but there was no help for it.

Downstairs, chairs scraped away from the table, and conversation got louder.

It was time. A thrill of nervous energy propelled her into action. She stood in the chair and pushed open the narrow leaded-glass panel as far as it would go. Cold air flooded over her. Catherine carefully lowered her cloak to the slate roof, then set about climbing out the window. She managed to get her upper body through without event, but when she got to her hips, she stuck.

Goose feathers! Her blasted petticoats.

She wriggled back inside, closed the window, and listened. Kitchen clatter and after-dinner conversation rumbled up from beneath her. She hastily removed all her underskirts, rolled them up and added them to the "body" under the covers, then squeezed back out onto the slate roof, closing the window behind her.

It was freezing, but she scarcely noticed as she fastened her cape, then gained her balance on the roof.

Careful. One foothold at a time, she told herself. Check

to make certain the slate isn't loose or broken.

Every tiny crunch and scrape sounded loud as an avalanche, but step by step, she worked her way down and away from the common rooms to the lowest point of the roof. Divine providence smiled. She managed to get there safely, then drop to the ground with only a brief chuff as she landed.

Scrambling to her feet, she looked to the parlor window and was relieved to see the Maxwells chatting with Quinn and Rory by the fire. One thing about her Maxwell plaid, though: there was nothing inconspicuous about it. Even by the frail light from the parlor, the red background glowed like an ember in the darkness. So she climbed the stile and crossed to the far side of the hedge to creep toward the church.

A gust of wind sent dried leaves scuttling, and suddenly the darkness seemed ominous. Until that moment, she'd taken comfort from her unshakable impression that someone was watching her; now it turned sinister.

Catherine halted. "Papa?" she whispered, her throat suddenly dustier than an attic rafter.

No answer. Just the hurried rustle of dead leaves on the ground and the click of bare branches striking each other overhead.

Her confidence ebbed away, replaced by a growing sense of impending disaster. "Papa?" The word died on her lips.

A pulse of fear propelled her across the walkway and into the vestibule of the church. It was dark as pitch inside. "Papa?" she whispered into the gloom.

The empty church sucked up her voice like dried moss drank a raindrop.

Then a single word, almost a sob, came from near the altar. "Here."

"Papa." Catherine groped toward the blessed sound. They bumped into each other at the front pew. She collapsed into the familiar arms of the only father she had ever known. "Papa." She could not hold back her tears, and Robert Storey wept along with her.

He drew her close, his hands rubbing her arms and her back as if to reassure himself that she was real. "I knew something terrible was going to happen the minute I saw the *Dere*," he choked. "I wanted to take you back to River House, no matter what you said. But you were so insistent." He shook his head. "I should have forced you to come back with us. I never should have let you board that ship."

"Don't, Papa. Don't." He'd come for her. He still loved her. "What's done is done. You're here now. That's all that matters."

"And you're coming home with me." He drew her to the pew and sat down beside her. His arm around her shoulders, he stroked her hair the way he used to when she was a little girl.

A dark inner whisper intruded on her joy. *Too late*.

She could not undo what had been done, and part of her didn't want to. "No, Papa, I can't go back with you. I'm married now, to Duncan Maxwell, the Black Bastard of the Western March. My place is here."

"Married!" His voice echoed off the stone walls. "Mother of God! To a Scot? A bastard?"

"Shhh, Papa," Catherine pleaded in a whisper. "They'll hear us. There are guards inside the house. I don't know what they'd do if they caught you—"

"Guards?" he whispered. "Your husband holds you prisoner?"

"No, they're for my protection." She shook her head to clear it. Where to start? "Papa, about Charles—"

"A miracle, that both of you survived. A miracle."

"Charles is alive?" Catherine drew back to peer at his darkened silhouette.

"Aye, by the grace of Almighty God. The moment we heard of the wreck, I went north to search for you both. My friend George Salkeld lives near Carlisle, not far from the shipwreck. He took me in and provided a base for my search. Charles and I had hunted there. I knew if he was able, he'd somehow make it to the Salkelds', and I was right. It took him more than a week, but he managed to escape Scotland and find me."

Charles, alive. What did it mean?

Papa gave her a reassuring squeeze. "I know you and Charles have had your differences, but he insisted on going back into Scotland to search for your—" He cut himself short. "He was obsessed with finding at least some sign of you. Demanded that we look separately so we could cover more ground. He was fearless, almost possessed."

Charles? Catherine was skeptical, but immediately felt guilty for such an unworthy reaction. Perhaps her stepbrother's brush with death had changed him for the better.

A soft scrape from the vestibule caused her to freeze. "Sh." The admonition was scarcely more than a breath. Heart pounding, she gripped Robert Storey's hands and listened to the looming darkness, afraid Quinn or Rory might have discovered them.

Another gust of wind sent leaves against the windows, but she heard nothing more inside the church.

"Just the wind," her stepfather whispered after a long, tense interval.

Catherine did her best to calm the fear that had sprung full-blown inside her. "So you and Charles were searching for me."

"Until early September, when I was summoned home. Willa had fallen so ill with grief over losing you that the doctors feared for her sanity. I had to go back. Charles insisted on remaining behind to continue the search."

Why did she have such a bad feeling about this?

Robert Storey withdrew and bent his head into his hands. "Catherine, I'm so ashamed of what has happened. I hardly know how to tell you."

"What, Papa? About refusing to ransom me? I forgive you." She circled his shoulders. "But why did your letter say that Charles was dead?"

He sat erect. "I sent no letter until today." A confused pause followed. "Refused to ransom you? I never refused to ransom you. I thought you were dead. Charles said he'd seen the mast fall on you when the ship went aground, that your skull was crushed. We were searching for your body, Catherine."

"The mast?" Dread swirled up from her toes like a deadly fog. Why would Charles say such a thing? Unless . . .

The vivid impression of hands on her throat rose up inside her, then she felt herself falling into the sea.

Catherine sat there in shock as the cold air crystallized around her. Dear heaven, no. She'd known Charles resented her, was jealous of her, but—"The letter we received over your signature mentioned my will. Was it read?"

"Catherine, I told you, I sent no letter until today." His murmured denial was solid with truth. "There's no need to speak of wills now. You're alive. We've found each other. Somehow, we'll find a way out of this."

"Papa, this is important." Her low voice shook. "Was my will read?"

After a brief pause, he answered. "Aye."

"And what were the terms?"

"You know the terms. You had Charles write them out for you."

Charles, again. The darkness began to throb to the tempo of her heartbeat. "Tell me, Papa," she whispered numbly. "I have to know."

"You left River House to me and my heirs, free and clear." His concern was palpable. "Catherine, what's this all about?"

Catherine had never asked Charles to draft a will for her. But Willa knew where Catherine had left the real document, which granted everything to her stepfather on the condition that Hal take precedence over Charles to inherit.

The will that had been read was a fraud. Evil was afoot, indeed.

Catherine's mind fit the jagged pieces into an ugly picture that her heart fought to deny. In happier days, Willa had often entertained her with witty forgeries and caricatures. She and Charles must have counterfeited the will before Catherine had sailed.

And the letter from Papa. Another of Willa's forgeries?

"Papa, you started to tell me what happened . . ."

He exhaled heavily, then began in a low voice, "Every time I thought Willa was well enough for me to rejoin Charles, she relapsed. She'd taken to her bed again last Sunday, so I went to church alone. After the service, Pastor Braithwaite inquired about Charles and our search. Then he mentioned something about the message from Scotland. I told him he must be mistaken, that there had been no such message.

"The man went pale as paste. He gripped my shoulders and said he must see me alone, with no one else knowing, not even Willa. So that afternoon, I made an excuse and rode back to the church." A pained silence. "What he told me . . ."

Her stepfather's shoulders drooped. "Catherine, he told me of receiving your plea for help. Confessed to reading it before he delivered it to River House. I was in Carlisle then, so he'd given it to Willa. She promised to forward it immediately. He had no reason to doubt her." He took a shuddering breath. "But she never even mentioned it."

The truth sank home like a mighty stone. It was Willa who had suggested the position as Cousin Thelma's companion to Catherine. And Willa who had insisted Charles act as escort on the voyage. Now Catherine understood why: She was never meant to reach Cornwall alive. Her own family. Charles and Willa had plotted to do away with her. Planned it.

She relived that horrible moment on the ship yet again and knew it was Charles who had throttled her and thrown her overboard with superhuman strength. Quaking with revulsion, she shut it from her mind, focusing on her step-father's haggard confession.

Papa continued relating Willa's betrayal. "Pastor Braithwaite wondered when Willa announced confirmation of your death so soon after he delivered the message, but he supposed the rescue attempts had ended in disaster. It wasn't until I said there had been no message that he realized what had happened. The poor man was devastated." His voice broke. "He couldn't remember the name or location in the message, but he sent me to the minister who had delivered it to him." Her stepfather's anger and humiliation resonated in his next words. "I packed and left without seeing Willa. I could not bear to look on her. She—" He stopped, too choked by emotion to go on.

Catherine took his hand in hers and held it tightly. Poor Papa. She had been betrayed by her stepmother and brother, but Robert Storey bore the bitter shame and disillusionment of a beloved wife's treachery. And he knew only a fraction of the truth as yet.

Charles . . . How could she tell Papa? Should she tell him?

He recovered enough to go on in a harsh whisper. "It took me three days to find the minister who had delivered the message to England, but he referred me to Angus Maxwell and said I could trust him." His free hand stroked the tendrils at her temple. "I prayed every mile of the way from River House that I would find you safe and bring you back. And thanks be to God, here you are."

"Oh, Papa." She did not have to guess what Charles would have done if he had found her first.

A jarring flash of insight struck her. Had he found her already?

If Willa knew where she was, she was sure to have gotten word to Charles.

The attacks!

She had assumed they were aimed at Duncan. Everyone had. But assassins were not the reivers' way.

Her mind raced. Clearly, the attempts had been the

work of a skilled marksman. Charles couldn't hit a stag
at three paces. That could mean only one thing: Charles
or Willa must have hired someone to kill her!

Someone who'd been watching and waiting all these
weeks for her to leave the safety of Annanlea. Someone
who waylaid her along the road to Wat's.

When that attempt had failed, he'd followed them to
the race. But Catherine had been too closely guarded on
the way to the tower, and shielded from behind on the
platform. He'd had to wait until she was in the saddle
with Duncan to take his shots. And on the way home,
Wat's dozen men had prevented another attack.

It all made sense.

And now . . .

She gasped aloud. "Papa, you must leave here, quickly.
Charles and Willa have hired someone to kill me. If the
killer followed me here, your life is in danger."

Robert Storey went rigid. "Charles?"

"Oh, God. I hadn't meant to tell you. Not now. Not
this way."

He seized her hands. "Catherine, if you love me, do
not lie to me. Hold nothing back. You said Charles."

Tears of anguish escaped along with the hateful truth.
"Oh, Papa. Charles never saw the mast strike me. It was
all a lie. Someone on the ship throttled me and threw me
overboard before the wreck. Charles and Willa had forged
my will. And ever since Willa found out where I was,
someone has been trying to kill me. An assassin."

Her stepfather let out a quick breath like a man who
had just taken a bolt to the chest. "Charles. She's polluted
him with her poison."

"Please, Papa," she begged, "You must leave now.
Duncan will protect me. Go."

"I'll never leave you again, child," he declared, his
voice flat. "Come with me. I've brought an extra horse.
We can be back in England within days." He urged her
to her feet. "Regardless of what's happened, you do not
belong here. This is a wild and dangerous place."

"So is River House," she said harshly, snatching her hands from his. Home was no longer home. How could it be anything now but the place for which her own stepmother and stepbrother had tried to have her killed?

She could not go back, didn't want to. Too much had happened. Too much had changed. "My place is here now, Papa. Duncan has seven children. They're our children now. I love them, and they love me. My life isn't easy, but it has meaning. I'm needed, Papa."

"But an outlaw, a brigand? A *bastard*? Catherine, what sort of life is that? Her Majesty will order an annulment. You—"

"Duncan Maxwell is not a brigand, Papa." She forced her voice back to a tight whisper. "He's a decent man who has done the best he can to survive and protect his family. He does not exist by thievery. He's a merchant just like you, only someone stole all his salt, so he felt compelled to ransom me. But I knew you had no money to spare, so I refused to tell him who I was."

She had to make him understand. "After Willa got my note, she wrote back over your signature that Duncan could keep me."

Now it was Robert Storey's turn to gasp.

"The letter said Charles was dead. I thought you blamed me and refused to ransom me because of that. Suddenly, I had nowhere to go. No family. No home."

"Child, child." He groaned. "How could they do this to you? To both of us?"

"Duncan Maxwell may be a bastard, but he has never treated me with anything but honor. After the ransom was rejected, he could have done as he wished with me—cast me out; given me to one of his men; made me a slave; used my body."

"Dear God, Catherine—"

"But he did none of those things, Papa. He married me. Gave me a place of honor in his home. Gave me the children I had always wanted." Not to mention the comforts of the marriage bed.

"Catherine," he bit out. "Your ordeal has unhinged you." He grasped her upper arms, his voice terse. "You're coming with me, and there's an end to it."

She shook her head. "I'm not a child, Papa. I'm a woman grown, and a woman in full, at last." She softened her tone. "I love him, Papa." She laid her forehead to his. "River House is no longer my home. My place is at Annanlea."

Robert Storey froze. "Annanlea?" The whispered word had the sound of dry bones about it. "Did you say Annanlea?"

"Yes. Didn't Angus tell you?"

"He told me nothing," he shot back. "Just asked me questions, then said he would deliver my message." He recoiled. "You live at Annanlea? Your husband . . ."

What was happening? "It's been in my husband's family for generations."

"This bastard you have married . . ." His grip tightened on her upper arms. "How old is he?"

"He's thirty." She pried at his fingers. "Papa, you're hurting me."

Radiating shock, he released her abruptly and stepped backward toward the darkened altar. "Who are his people?" he demanded in a shaking voice. "Tell me of his people."

"I cannot tell you much," she said, frightened by the way he was acting. "His mother's father was Laird Kinnon Maxwell. All I know about his father is that he was English and abandoned Duncan's mother before he was born."

Robert Storey reacted as if he'd been bitten by a deadly viper.

Forgetting to whisper, Catherine moved toward him. "Papa, why are you acting this way? What's wrong?"

He continued to back away from her, almost stumbling on the step that led up to the altar. "His mother," he rasped out. "Was it Brigit? Please, God, let it be Brigit."

How did he know Aunt Brigit's name? "Brigit is his

aunt." Her sense of impending disaster bloomed afresh. "Duncan's mother was Gleana Maxwell."

"Was?" Her stepfather backed against the altar, then turned and dropped to his knees before it. "No. God, no."

Catherine stepped closer, then halted, afraid to touch him. "Papa, I don't understand. Tell me."

" 'Thy sins shall find thee out,' " he rasped. His gloved hands gripped the altar cloth. "Dear God. What have I done?"

Had this whole, horrible mess driven him mad? "Papa, you asked me for the truth. Now I ask the same of you. Tell me."

His head snapped up. "Have to get you out of here. Can't think about the rest." He launched to his feet with unnatural stiffness. "Come. Must get you back to England."

Behind them, the metallic whisper of a sword unsheathing sent a bolt of terror through her. "I'm afraid I canna be lettin' ye do that," a deep voice declared.

Duncan! Catherine spun around.

He advanced to the altar, an apparition of deeper black within the darkness.

"Duncan, don't hurt him. He's my stepfather, Robert Storey."

"Ah," Duncan said. "The loving stepfather who refused to ransom ye." He moved to the far end of the altar. "Let's have a look." Catherine heard him strike a flint, then saw him lift a glowing taper to light the altar candle.

"No! They might see us." She lunged for the candle, but Duncan caught her around the waist and held her fast. "The assassin was after me, not you," she said, struggling to free herself. "I can't explain it all now, but he may be out there this moment, ready to strike."

"What nonsense is this, Kate?" Duncan laid the tip of his sword to Robert Storey's throat. Her stepfather made no move to defend himself, just stared at Duncan as if he were seeing his own ghost.

"Shut the light," she insisted. "And lower your blade.

This is a church, man! Do you not fear God, drawing a blade on sacred ground?"

"I fear nothing, Kate," he said smoothly. "Ye've kent me long enough to be sure of that."

"And I've kent ye long enough to be sure you're not a fool, Duncan Maxwell," she argued. "I've told you, there's an assassin out there, probably aiming his crossbow right this very—"

"If an assassin had followed ye here," he said over her objections, "ye'd never have made it." He stepped back for a better look at Papa. "Quinn and Rory are outside keepin' watch now. There's nae assassin there."

There was steel in his voice when he spoke to Papa. "Still hurtin' her, I see. Nae enough, that ye broke her heart by denyin' her ransom."

At last, Robert Storey found his tongue. "I have been selfish in my life. Cowardly. Hurt those I loved," he said with agony on his face, his gaze locked to Duncan's. "Done much that is worthy of damnation. But I have loved Catherine as my own since the first time she climbed up into my lap. For all my sins, I have never denied her. I never shall."

Papa was the kindest of men, incapable of the things he'd accused himself of.

"Why are you here?" Duncan demanded.

"I came to take her home."

"We both heard what she said about that. Kate's home is with us now at Annanlea," he went on. "She doesna wish to leave."

"Have you given her the choice?" Papa countered.

Duncan paused. "Verra well." He searched her face. "What shall it be, Kate? England or Scotland? The choice is yours."

"Neither," she said, grateful for the choice—for both their sakes. "Hang Scotland. I choose you, Duncan Maxwell. And our family." The instant she said it, she knew it was right—the only right thing amidst the shambles of her life. Something deep inside her slipped into place, and she no longer feared for her future.

She turned to her stepfather. "Papa, I love you, and I believe you had nothing to do with what's happened." She tried again to wrest free of Duncan. "Let me go to him. Please." When his arm eased, she hurried toward her stepfather, shoving Duncan's blade aside.

"Go back to River House," she told Papa, trying to memorize every line in his beloved face. "I want you to have it. You've worked so hard for so long to keep me from losing it." Only his trading business had kept her from having to sell her jewels long ago to keep the place going. "Take it, Papa. Give Charles and Willa what they want." Her home was here, now, so she released the past, and gladly. "Witness, Duncan: I freely grant River House and all its goods and holdings to my stepfather." She faltered. "Maybe now Charles and Willa will be content, and you can heal, all of you. But watch over Hal, Papa. He needs your protection from the others."

"Catherine." Robert Storey's face was that of a broken man. "Forgive me, child. How could I have been so blind to what was happening?"

She embraced her father. "You loved them, Papa, believed in them. The sin was theirs, not yours."

They held each other for long seconds before Duncan said, "Kate, we must go back if we're to reach home before dawn."

Thank God. Duncan did not mean to take her stepfather hostage. She knew she should go before he changed his mind, but her arms wouldn't cooperate; they clung to Papa.

She had left him for good once before. How could she do it again?

He was the one who pulled away. "Go, then, precious one." He met Duncan's gaze without flinching. "I pray you're a better man than your father, sirrah. Be good to her."

Too emotional to react to the unexpected jab at Duncan's bastardry, Catherine took a long last look at Papa. "Goodbye, Rob's A-ramble."

"Rob's A-ramble?" Duncan repeated with deceptive softness.

"Just a nickname," she told him. Why had Duncan gone so still? "One nobody knows but the two of us."

He lifted the candle and peered at Robert Storey as if seeing him for the first time. When he set the candle down, his handsome features were dark with suppressed fury. "Not so secret," he said to Papa. "One other knew that name long before Catherine, didn't she?"

Papa closed his eyes in despair.

The hairs stood on the back of Catherine's neck. Duncan radiated hatred, all of it directed toward her stepfather. Something huge and terrible was happening. She stepped between the two men she loved most in the world, but Duncan shoved her roughly aside and raised his blade in challenge.

"So Robert Storey is your name," he said with deadly calm. "How many times I wondered. Dreamed of having you at the end of my blade." He whipped a taunting slash across her stepfather's doublet. "Arm yourself, Robert Storey. You're about to die."

"Duncan, no!" Dear God, she could see he truly meant to kill Papa! But why?

His back to the altar, Robert Storey spread his empty hands in a gesture of submission. "I cannot blame you for wanting to kill me, but I will not fight you. I've done you harm enough."

Harm enough? Papa had done Duncan harm?

Papa shot Catherine a look of infinite sadness, then looked back to Duncan. "Kill me if you must, but I fear Catherine will never forgive you."

"Stop this, both of you!" Catherine felt as if she'd been dropped into a nightmare. She moved again to intervene, but this time it was Papa who repelled her. "Stay out of this, Catherine. It has nothing to do with you."

A study in suppressed rage, Duncan paced before him in menace. "Defend yourself." He flicked a shallow cut up Robert Storey's cheek.

"Duncan," Catherine cried out. "Why are you doing this?" She looked to Papa. "Why?"

"Because I am his father," Robert Storey said with the bleakness of a thousand ages.

Catherine heard the words, but they didn't sink in.

"Aye, ma father, God curse him," Duncan spat out. The tip of his blade circled dangerously as he kept Papa trapped with his back to the altar. "Look at us, Kate. Our eyes. The color differs, but they're the same. Our mouths. The same. Our bodies. His is smaller, but the bones do not lie. This coward is ma father."

She saw it. "Dear heaven." That was why Duncan had seemed oddly familiar when she'd first seen him! The truth paralyzed her with shock. The two men she loved most in the world . . .

"Fight me, ye yellow-livered miscreant!" Duncan's voice was a tense monotone. "I demand it for the insult ye have done me and ma mother. Ye stole her innocence, then left her to suffer endless shame and scorn at the hands of even her own father." When Papa refused to respond, Duncan insulted him with an open-handed blow to his bloodied cheek. "Ye abandoned her—she, the kindest, gentlest, most loving of women. Broke her heart. Consigned me to life as a bastard half-breed, punished daily by my grandsire's contempt."

Why didn't Papa defend himself? He stood there, guilty, almost as if he welcomed Duncan's fury.

"I saw the pain of it in my mother's eyes until the day she died," Duncan went on. "Yet still she protected ye." He slashed another cut across Papa's doublet. "The only name she ever said was 'Rob's A-ramble.' A secret nickname, she told me, one only the two of ye kent."

Catherine watched the rage and frustration of a lifetime boil over in Duncan, compelling him toward a terrible retribution. She knew she should do something, yet feared her intervention might make things worse. Surely Duncan would not attack as long as Papa remained unarmed.

Dear God, show me how to stop this! she prayed. *Don't let Duncan kill Papa!*

"Fight me," Duncan ground out cold as ice. "Defend yourself." He struck another blow, knocking Papa to his knees.

"You are not a bastard," Robert Storey told him as he rose, his posture that of a broken man.

"Doona try to wheedle your way out of this with lies," Duncan snarled. "Answer for your debts." Another blow. "Arm yourself."

To Catherine's horror, Papa drew his sword. Terror propelled her to the doors of the church. "Help!" she cried out into the darkness. "Quinn! Rory! Help me stop him!"

Racing back inside, she saw Papa awkwardly defend himself against Duncan's lethal blade.

"You are not a bastard," he repeated as he deflected strike after strike.

She was halfway back to the front of the church when she heard the two guards run inside behind her. Thank God. Once they reached the aisle, though, the footfalls halted abruptly. She pivoted to see the brothers looking on in consternation. Clearly, their loyalty was to their master, so they were loath to interfere. "Rory, help me! Quinn!"

They regarded her with pained expressions, then looked away.

On her own, she felt a primal surge of energy unleash within her. She snatched up one of the tall, ornate wrought-iron candlesticks from beside the altar and swung it at Duncan. "Stop this! Now!" The four-foot long shaft bounced off his side, unfelt. With her next blow, though, Duncan caught the heavy iron shank in his left hand, wrenched it from her grasp, and hurled it halfway across the church. All the while, he hammered away with sword-strikes that Papa somehow managed to deflect.

"You are not a bastard," Papa repeated, louder this time.

Duncan answered only with the clash of steel.

"You are not a bastard, Duncan!" Papa roared, un-flinching. "I married your mother!"

But Duncan's rage had taken him past hearing, past seeing, past anything but killing. He attacked again and again like a brutal machine.

She could not watch helpless as her husband tried to slay the only father she had ever known. Torn, she searched for some way to end the conflict.

The candle! If she could blow it out, Papa could escape. She started for it, but despite Duncan's crazed state, his combat instincts were fully at work. He kept himself between her and the light.

"Duncan, I love you," she cried. "Do not do this. If you kill him, the poison will stay with you forever. For your own sake, let him go."

She might as well have been shouting at the waves to halt in their course.

Papa was no match for him. Inevitably, one of Duncan's lunges went home, piercing Robert Storey's side.

"Papa!" she shrieked, feeling the wound as if it were her own. She rushed to shield her father. Holding the crimson stain in his doublet, he spun away from his attacker.

Catherine put herself between them and faced Duncan without fear, her voice hoarse from shouting. "If you want to kill him, you'll have to kill me first!"

"Catherine, no," Papa said weakly. "Leave us." He tried to shove her aside, but the effort proved too much for him. He slumped against her back.

"Nay! I love you both." How badly was he injured? "I mean it, Duncan," she repeated. "You'll have to kill me first!"

His body vibrating with blood lust, Duncan gripped his sword with both hands and raised the blade for a murderous blow.

She fully expected him to bring it down and slay her, but she would not die silently. "Think of your children, Duncan! How will you tell them you've slain their Lady-kate?"

His blade faltered as a shudder wracked through him.

"What will they think of their father when you tell them you've murdered the mother they need so badly? And Bink." She deliberately used Duncan's pet name for Aunt Brigit. "How will she manage without me? She's weary, Duncan. Worn out from serving you and your family."

A flash of awareness crossed his features, but his blade hung poised as if opposing forces immobilized it. "The knave must die for what he's done." His grating words sounded as if they'd been wrenched from his gut.

Somewhere behind his fury was the decent, just man she had come to love and respect. She had to reach him. *Dear God, show me what to say!*

"Papa wronged you and your mother, Duncan. No one disputes that. But your mother loved him, protected him, even to the point of letting everyone think you were a bastard." She felt Papa slide down behind her, his body limp, but Catherine dared not turn to tend him. She took a step closer to Duncan. "Would your mother want you to do this?" Her voice eased to a calming tone. "Be honest. Look into your soul. Would she?"

The fire behind his eyes began to flicker. His face contorted. "Stand aside, Kate. He deserves to die for what he's done." At last, she saw the fury give way to torment.

She fixed her gaze to his, advancing with agonizing slowness. "Papa did a terrible thing to you. I know that. But the Robert Storey I know is one of the kindest, most decent men to grace God's earth. He's changed, Duncan. But I do not ask you to spare him because of that. I beg you to spare him for my sake. For our sake. I could not live with his death between us."

Duncan shook his head as if to shed himself of what she was saying, but still, the venom of his hatred held him captive.

Catherine risked a glance at Papa and saw he was unconscious. He could be dying. Dead already.

Nay. She refused to accept that.

Help, Lord. Please. I don't know what else to say.

A distant whisper breathed like a warm wind through her fear. *The jewels.*

The jewels? Why did that pop into her head?

In a flash of insight, she understood. She'd held them back, the only thing she had left that was truly hers. But now she could use them to draw Duncan's anger away from Papa.

"Duncan, I've lied to you," she said boldly. "I'm not poor. I have my mother's jewels. The two I gave Angus were not the only ones. I have more. Treasure, Duncan. Food for our people. Jewels!"

He blinked again, then finally seemed to see her. "Jewels?" He lowered his sword until it projected at her, but she wasn't afraid. If he'd been capable of killing her, he would have done it when she stepped between him and Papa.

Moving closer, she gently pushed the blade aside. "Aye, jewels enough to keep Annanlea for years." She watched a blessed sanity invade his expression.

Duncan quaked like a man coming out of a trance. "And ye kept them from me?" His bright blue eyes flashed, but there was rationality behind them now.

"My mother's jewels, husband. Thirteen emeralds, eleven rubies, eight large pearls, seven diamonds, and four sapphires. A fitting dowry."

"And ye kept it from me?" he fairly growled.

"Aye. But I've told you now. They're yours. Do with them as you will." At last, he dropped the tip of his sword. She wrapped her arms around his waist, her insides still quivering in terror.

Papa lay bleeding behind her, perhaps dying. He needed attention. "I'll have to cut them out of my shift, first," she said with a calmness she did not feel.

"The blasted shift!"

"Aye." She'd managed to ease the confrontation. What came next? Duncan still hated Papa, wanted him dead. She knew she would not be able to distract him for long. At the end of her wits, she decided on the truth. Her arms tightened around him. "Let me see to Papa, Duncan. Please. This doesn't have to be settled here and now." She drew back to meet his troubled gaze. "For me, Duncan. I beg you. Let me help him. His life is all I'll ever ask of you."

He tensed in her arms, his gaze locked on Papa. "Only for ye, Kate." Then he twisted free of her and strode toward the vestibule. He motioned with his sword to Quinn and Rory as he passed them. "Do as she wishes."

Relief paralyzed Catherine for several heartbeats before she brought herself up short and hastened to Papa. A broad crimson stain had soaked the right side of his doublet just above the waist. She knelt beside him, unable to hold back her tears. " 'Twill be all right, Papa. You'll see." He moaned and opened his eyes briefly, but only nodded. Catherine eased him onto his uninjured side and saw that the pool of blood beneath him was not mortal. "Quinn. Rory," she choked out. "Help me carry him to the house."

The two men advanced, their faces haggard. "Lady-kate," Quinn stammered, "we—That is, I—"

Too weary to address apologies, she dashed the tears from her eyes. "Just get him to the house, please. Gently." She bent and kissed Papa's eyes. "Hold on, Papa. Sarah and I will care for you."

Sarah and Angus! A sickening feeling bloomed in the pit of her stomach. Surely Duncan wouldn't have—"The Maxwells, Quinn. I fear what Duncan might—"

"We feared the same thing when he came in to get us," Quinn interjected, "but he did nae harm to his cousins." He scanned the candlelit church as they carried Papa toward the door. "This kirk has seen the last of Duncan Maxwell, though. Ye can count on that."

As they emerged from the church, Duncan barreled past them on Rogue, headed toward open country. Catherine reached out and called to him, but Rory shook his head. "Let 'im go, Ladykate. Best he rides it out."

Quinn seconded his brother. "Aye. I've seen him angry, but never like that. Trust me, ye doona want him hereabouts until he's settled down a bit."

They were almost to the house.

Rory exhaled heavily. "I'm that glad he didna slay yer stepfather."

Yet he had not helped her prevent it. Catherine's throat tightened. "Thank you, Rory." Would they be helping her now if they'd been there to hear that Robert Storey was Duncan's father, not hers?

Aye. They would, because Duncan had ordered them to.

A worried Sarah Maxwell met them at the door of the parsonage. "Dear heaven, child, what's happened? We heard ye shoutin', but these two reprobates had locked us in the larder." She held her lamp high and saw the blood on Papa's doublet and the trail that led down the stairs. "Oh, my. Angus! Bring ma surgical supplies." She motioned them inside. "Lay him on the settle." She glared at Quinn and Rory as they passed. "Ye two will answer to Almighty God for what's been done this night. As will Duncan Maxwell."

She hurried to put a supporting arm around Catherine. "Are ye all right, lass?"

"I'm unhurt," she managed. Physically, at least. But she was not certain her heart would ever be the same. Barring a miracle, this night would stand forever between her and Duncan. "Come. We must see to Papa."

Duncan rode as if the hounds of hell were after him. The road was smooth and wide, offering easy passage, so only concern for Rogue prompted him to slow at last. Panting, he slid to the verge and collapsed on a hummock of dried grass, his face to the clearing sky. He fought to empty his mind of everything that had happened, everything he had heard, but eventually, it all came back to him.

Kate's terror. And her courage.

Dear God, he'd come within a hairsbreadth of killing her.

Robert Storey's refusal to fight back. And his claim to have married Duncan's mother.

How could that be true? Surely he wouldn't have abandoned her if they were wed. And why wouldn't his mother have told Duncan he was not a bastard?

The mere possibility was enough to clamp his heart like a vise.

So many questions.

Kate clearly adored her stepfather. She was willing to give her life for him.

Even gravely wounded, Storey had tried to keep her from endangering herself on his behalf. How could Duncan reconcile that man to the looming monster he had always believed his father to be?

Nothing made sense anymore.

And Kate. The pain and fury in her eyes when she'd looked at him standing poised to strike her . . . He would never forget it. Could she? Would she even want to?

Hopeless. He loved a woman who loved a man he'd sworn to kill. How could they go on together with this huge and horrible thing between them?

Yet she had chosen to marry him, freely and resolutely. She'd even said she loved him. It was the one spark of light in this black, black night.

Duncan closed his eyes, glad for the permeating cold. He willed it to cool the fires that still ebbed and flared inside him.

Rogue snorted and shifted on his feet. "Walk on, Rogue," he commanded. Obediently, the stallion walked off some of his lather, but did not go far. The poor animal was probably half-dead after carrying Duncan all the way to Annan, then galloping halfway to—Duncan lifted his head and looked around—nowhere.

He let his pate drop back to the cold turf.

So many questions. He wanted answers. But getting them meant speaking to Robert Storey.

Duncan hadn't prayed from his heart for a long time, but his soul reached out in earnest. *Show me what to do. I care for Kate and doona wish to bring her pain. But Robert Storey deserves to die for what he's done to me—nae me. Ma mother.*

He lay there in the darkness beneath patches of stars, listening intently for an answer. Wanting to believe there would be one.

And when the answer came, it was his mother's voice that whispered deep inside him. *How could I regret the love that gave ye to me, the greatest blessing of ma life? I love ye both, Duncan. Search his heart, ma son, and ye will find me there.*

Her presence seemed so real, he could almost smell

her attar of roses, see the kindness in her gentle eyes. The peace that came with her loving face took the sword from his soul.

Duncan closed his eyes and did something he had not done since he was a very small child: He wept. For the father he'd never had. For the shame he and his mother had borne. For his grandsire's contempt. For the hardships Bink and his children had endured. And for what he'd almost done to Kate.

Catherine had fallen asleep sitting up beside Papa's cot in the parlor when the sound of slowly approaching hoof-beats roused her. Briefly disoriented, she sat erect for several seconds before reality caught up to her like a lowering cloud.

In the cold light of dawn, she lurched to her feet and hastened to the front window.

Duncan. Thank God. His jaw shadowed by dark growth, he walked Rogue toward the house.

Even from this distance, she could see that the fire had gone out of him. Overnight, he'd aged ten years. He looked bleak. Empty.

Part of Catherine wanted to rush out and embrace him, thanking him for sparing Papa's life. But another part of her remembered the black hatred in his expression when he'd towered over her with his sword. That part held back, wounded and afraid.

As always when she was afraid, she made herself use-ful, reviving the embers and adding wood, then leaning over Papa to sniff his bandage. Good. No stench of in-fection. And the bloodstain looked no larger. He was pale, but seemed to be sleeping naturally. She took the goblet beside him and pulled back his lip to drip watered wine against his gums. He swallowed.

The hoofbeats stopped, followed shortly by labored paces up the front stairs.

Catherine did not watch the door, afraid of what she would see. But when it swung open, she could no more keep her eyes from Duncan than lodestone could repel steel.

He ducked inside and stood, magnificent despite his windblown hair and haggard face. "Kate."

The weight of what had come between them was as palpable as a mighty wall, dividing them. They shared the same room, but might as well have been on opposite ends of the world. Was this how it would be, now?

He glanced down at Papa, his frown deepening. "Is he . . ."

"Time will tell. Sarah does not think you pierced his gut." She looked up into his eyes and saw the ghosts of a lifetime warring there. "I know I said I would ask nothing more than Papa's life of you, and I am grateful that you spared him. So grateful. But please, may I bring him home to Annanlea? Just until he's well enough to travel back to England." She faltered. "You need not see him. I'll tend him myself. And I'll still take care of my other responsibilities."

"He's so small," Duncan said, his voice hoarse. "I had always thought of him as a big man, a monster of evil." He shook his head. "He looks so . . . ordinary."

Catherine didn't respond, afraid she might stir up trouble or cause Duncan further pain. But she wanted to tell him that what Papa lacked in size, he made up in heart. And there was nothing ordinary about his kindness, his wisdom, his patience.

Duncan turned and headed for the stairs. "I'm going up for a long sleep. Rory is already on his way to Annanlea to fetch the carriage and more guards. Doona wake me until they arrive."

That meant Duncan had already decided to take Papa back with them. Catherine marveled, her gratitude and respect deepening. She wanted to hold him in her arms and comfort him for what he'd suffered because of Papa. "May I join you later?" she asked his retreating form.

His hand on the newel post, he paused. "Nae." Then he trudged up to the guest room.

Catherine felt his rejection like a sword-thrust to the chest.

Forced to choose between the father she loved and the husband who held her heart, she had chosen life for Papa. Now with a single word, Duncan had just told her the cost of that decision: the life they might have made together. The love they might have shared.

Taking her unconscious stepfather's hand, she laid her head beside his arm and wept in silence.

Chapter
TWENTY-TWO

Duncan rode into Annanlea to find Bink waiting on the doorstep beside a beaming Michael. It would be at least another hour before Kate arrived with Robert Storey, but he'd decided to give his aunt as much time as possible to adjust before they did. So he dismounted and went up to tell her, only peripherally aware that she and Michael seemed different somehow.

"Duncan." Worry deepened the lines around her eyes. "Where's the coach?"

"On its way."

"Oh, good." She brightened immediately. "I'm so glad ye're back. Michael and I . . . well, we sent the children to their rooms because we wanted to ask yer permission to—"

"Come inside, Bink." For once, he was glad his children were not waiting to greet him. "I've hard news to tell."

She went ashen. "Nae Kate. Please God, tell me she isna—"

"Kate is fine." He led the way into the parlor, then sank into one of the chairs opposite the settle.

Michael and Bink sat side by side facing him. "Let me have it straight, Duncan," his aunt instructed with characteristic stoicism.

"Kate went to Annandale to meet with her stepfather. I found the two of them at the church. The man professes that the letter we received was a forgery. Says Kate's stepmother intercepted her message, then plotted with her son to say Kate had died in the wreck so they could claim her inheritance."

Aunt Brigit's expression went slack with dismay. "Ach! Her own stepmother?" Anger sparked in her gray eyes. "Poor Kate. And her brother betrayed her, as well."

"Stepbrother," he corrected, leaning forward in his chair. "There's more. Much more. I still havena begun to sort out all that's afoot there." He met her gaze forthrightly. "But I learned one thing that caused the rest to pale: who her stepfather really is." Bitter denial made it almost impossible to say the words. But Bink had asked him to give it to her straight. He owed her that much, at least. "His name is Robert Storey, Bink, but Kate called him 'Rob's A-ramble.'"

"Nae." Eyes widening, she went rigid. "Surely a coincidence. He couldna be the same—"

"Aye. The same." He spit the truth out like a bite of rancid meat. "Ma father."

"The divil, ye say," Michael breathed, his arm tightening around Bink's narrow shoulders.

Bink stared into space, the anguish of the past three decades etched in her expression, but she said nothing.

What was there to say? The repercussions of this dreadful revelation went far deeper than words.

"He admitted it. I snapped. I fought him," he explained in bitter chunks. "He wouldna fight back, so I wounded him. But Kate interceded for his life." Duncan dropped his gaze to his hands clutched between his knees. He could not face Bink when he told her. "So I spared him."

Charged silence settled between them for long moments. Then Bink amazed him with, "I'm glad, Duncan." His gaze snapped to her to find her looking on him with infinite sadness. "I'm glad ye spared him, lad. Nae for him, but for ye—and Kate. He's the only father she's ever kent. Even after he refused to ransom her, she loved him still. 'Twas plain to see."

Was that supposed to comfort him? "He deserved to die for what he did to Mother. And me," he said, the poison rising in him.

"Gleana loved that man until her last breath. Why d'ye think she never told any of us his real name, nae even me? From the first, she thought only to protect him." Bink sighed as if something huge and tragic had finally shifted into its proper place at last. "She wouldna have wanted ye to bear the guilt of killin' yer own father, Duncan. I'm proud that ye didna."

She stood, "Come, Michael. Let's leave him alone with this." She always knew when he needed time to think.

Michael rose beside her, but made no move to leave. "Nae, Brigit. We had something to ask of Duncan, and we'll ask it." He took her hand and drew her to his side. "This changes nothing between us. And I willna let it interfere with our plans."

Duncan fully expected Bink to contradict Michael as usual, but she surprised him yet again. "As ye wish," she said with grateful admiration—perhaps even relief.

Michael colored, basking in the respect she granted him. He cleared his throat, then addressed Duncan. "I'm sorry fer yer trouble, Duncan, but as soon as Kate gets back and settled, we'd like the two of ye to stand up for us." He lifted his bearded chin. "Yer aunt's finally agreed to marry me, with yer permission. I want to tie the knot afore she changes her mind."

Bink countered with a halfhearted "Fie, auld man," whereupon Michael pulled her close to his side, the hunger in his expression that of a man a third his age.

Duncan's mind told him this was wonderful news, but his heart felt nothing. A thin smile was all he could manage. " 'Tis about time. I'll stand up for ye proudly." A twist of pain broke through his numbness. "But I canna speak for Kate."

"She will," Bink assured him, " 'Twas Kate who put the notion in ma head in the first place."

Duncan stood to embrace them both, holding on several heartbeats longer than propriety permitted. "I . . . Ye both deserve happiness."

"So do ye and Kate, Duncan," Bink said in a strangely thick voice. She took Michael's hand and left Duncan to his thoughts.

In the quiet vacuum following their departure, he sat

staring into space until the weight of silence became heavier than the guilt and pain he struggled to suppress. Then he unlocked the chest, took out his violin, and sought escape by the only means left to him: his music. But even there, he found no peace.

Much to Catherine's relief, Papa's wound stopped bleeding as soon as she had him safely bandaged and in bed. Secure that he was not in imminent danger, she left him with Nessa and hastened to the parlor. Nessa brought word that since Angus was keeping vigil with a dying parishioner, Duncan had been pressed into performing the ceremony. Even among the shattered remnants of her own hopes, Catherine was glad that Aunt Brigit and Michael were going to marry at last. The joy of that brought light into her own despair.

She found the bride and groom waiting at the hearth, surrounded by the children, who immediately sensed the tension between Catherine and their father. Abruptly, they fell silent amid anxious looks from her to Duncan and back.

Catherine did her best to focus on the glowing couple, but she could not keep her eyes from her husband. He stood there with the Book of Common Order in his hand, his eyes as dead as stones.

Without a word to her, he opened the book and read the same words Angus had read for their wedding only a few short weeks ago. Listening to them now, Catherine had to struggle to get through the ceremony without breaking down.

Immediately afterward, Duncan rode away without escort or explanation. He did not return for ten days—ten long, anxious days she passed with ceaseless work and prayer. Ten long, agonizing nights when she cried herself to sleep, then spent her dreams endlessly searching for Duncan.

*   *   *

The evening of his return from more than a week of fruitless searching, Duncan deliberately waited until Kate had tucked her father in for the evening before he entered the sickroom alone and closed the door behind him. He'd had a lot of time to think since he'd left. Now he meant to get the answers from his father that his soul demanded, no matter how painful those answers might be.

A single candle illuminated the room. Bink had said Storey was well on the mend, so it didn't surprise Duncan to find his father sitting up. The injury Duncan had inflicted had clearly taken its toll—Storey was gaunt and sallow—but he watched Duncan enter with an expression of anguished gratitude.

"I want the truth," Duncan said to the man with eyes, mouth, and shape so like his own.

"You deserve that, and much more," his father replied evenly. "I've prayed you would come back safe."

Duncan pulled a chair to within six feet of the bed, then turned its back and straddled it. "I'm listening."

"Aye." Storey stared unseeing into the middle distance. "I fell in love with your mother the first time I saw her. Your grandsire had brought her and Brigit to a fair in Dumfries where I had goods to trade." He shook his head, smiling at the memory. "What a contrast she and her sister were. Brigit sparked fire, but your mother glowed with a slow and gentle radiance that drew me like a spell. I couldn't take my eyes from Gleana."

It galled to hear him say her name as if he had the right.

Storey met his hostile gaze. "She caught me peering at her, and something passed between us. I shut my stall so I could follow her, hoping for a chance to find out who she was. Finally, she persuaded your grandsire to allow her and Brigit to tour the cathedral unescorted while he met with a merchant. I slipped inside and managed to steal a word."

It wasn't easy imagining his mother that way, so young

and impulsive. But she had loved this man. There was no denying that.

Storey's haggard face eased. "Brigit was irate, but Gleana begged her to leave us alone for a few moments in the pew. Your aunt adored your mother, as almost everyone did, so she went against her better judgment." He chuckled. "She didn't go far, though—just a few rows behind us, out of earshot." A shadow crossed his face. "She had cause to bitterly regret that later, I know."

Duncan felt torn as he listened. Part of him wanted to learn every detail, to understand why his mother and Robert Storey had done what they'd done. But the rest of him shrank from this man's version of the story. Yet it was the only version left, so he sat silent, ignoring the plea for understanding in his father's eyes.

" 'Twas dangerous," Robert Storey admitted, "but we met in secret many times after that. Brigit helped us only because she knew your mother loved me." He shook his head. "We were so young, so swept away by the attraction we felt." He sighed. "We both knew your grandsire would never have allowed us to wed. So we married in secret."

Another twist of pain penetrated Duncan's numbness. "Ye expect me to believe that?"

His father met his skepticism head-on. " 'Tis true. In the very church where you found me with Catherine. The minister was no more able to deny your mother than Brigit had been. He married us, with his wife as witness, and wrote it in the record."

Angus's predecessor. Duncan's mind engaged. "Then the entry would be there yet."

"Aye." His father nodded. "The date was October 12, 1559."

Why would this man make such a claim if it weren't true? The facts could be easily verified. But if the entry was there, why hadn't his mother told him? Confusion stirred Duncan's anger. "Why doesna anyone else ken this?"

"I can only surmise that your mother never told them."

"Surely the minister would have come forward when—"

"She must have begged his silence to protect me." Shame washed over his father. "I should never have left her behind, but I had almost no money. And I feared what my father might do." He looked down. "He was as harsh a man as your other grandsire. I knew my father did not love me, but I counted on his accepting my marriage when I presented it as a *fait accompli*." He made himself meet Duncan's gaze. "I was eighteen. Foolish. Selfish. Weak. Almost penniless. I planned to get the money from my father to return immediately and bring her home."

His eyes glazed. "We had only a few hours together before she had to go back to Annanlea. I did not know you had been conceived."

He faltered, and long seconds passed before he let out a pained sigh. "And I did not know until I got home that my father had betrothed me to another, a woman whose wealth would insure the success of our trading company. When I told him of my marriage, he flew into a rage. He held his cocked pistol to my head and threatened to pull the trigger if I didn't agree to go through with the betrothal."

Duncan heard the pain of that betrayal in his father's dry voice, but was not moved.

"He meant it," Storey went on. "Worse yet, I saw that part of him was hoping I would refuse so he'd have an excuse to kill me for what I'd done. That's all I was to him, you see, someone to be used for gain." He did not spare himself. "He detested my weakness, but used it to bend me to his will. So I gave away my soul; forsook honor, love, your mother—everything real and good in my life." He closed his eyes in anguish. " 'And the sins of the father shall be visited on the sons unto the fourth generation.' That is your legacy, Duncan. Abandonment. Betrayal."

Duncan refused to accept that. Not for his children. "Then the betrothal—"

"Was a fraud, and the marriage that followed."

"Kate's mother?"

"Nay." He stared out the window at the growing darkness. "My first wife lived for eight years, but we had no children. I saw that as God's punishment for what I'd done, yet I did my best to convince myself your mother was better off without me. She never wrote, so I prayed she had told no one and moved on in her life." His hands fisted in his lap. "If only I had known about you, everything would have been different. I never would have given in to Father, even if it had cost my life."

Easy to say, but by his own admission, he'd been weak and selfish then.

Struck by the futility of such conjecture, Duncan came back with, "If ye had and he'd killed ye, everything would have been the same, then, wouldn't it?"

"Aye." Storey's gaze came into focus. "Except I never would have known you. Hard as this is, Duncan, I'm grateful that we met. Perhaps the truth can lay the past to rest . . . for both of us."

Duncan doubted it. The sordid tale left him feeling a hundred years old. Such folly, on both his parents' part. It gave him no comfort to know he was not a bastard after all. He'd suffered the shame for a lifetime and survived. What good did it do now to know that stigma had been undeserved?

"And Kate's mother?" he challenged.

"I met her soon after my first wife died."

The coldness Duncan felt was audible in his words. "Ye were free. Ye didna try to find my mother then?"

Robert Storey sagged in shame. "By then I had convinced myself that contacting your mother would only open old wounds. 'Twas cowardly, I know, but the only way I could look myself in the mirror was to erase it from my mind." He gripped the covers. "Then I met Anne, Catherine's mother. She'd been widowed and needed a protector. And Catherine . . . such a frank, engaging child.

I loved them both at first sight. Saw them as a gift, a chance at atonement."

Loved on sight. God help the women Robert Storey "loved." "Ma mother was still alive, living in the shame ye brought on her," Duncan accused.

His father seemed to shrink. "Duncan, I cannot make up to you for what I've done. But in the past ten days, I've had time to think long and hard. I want to acknowledge you as my legal son. As soon as I return to England, I shall do so."

"As ye were going to acknowledge ma mother?" Duncan shot back.

"I deserve that," Storey said, "but this time, only death will stop me."

Had the man learned nothing from the havoc he'd wrought? Duncan rose, his anger barely in check. "Nae, sir, ye willna do it, for *I* will stop ye." He looked down on his father in contempt. "I've borne the shame of bastardry these thirty years. I wouldna visit it upon yer youngest, for Kate loves him as her own. That much I can do for her. I only regret that it will also benefit your other snake-in-the-hole of a son who tried to murder her." He pointed a finger at his father. "But your eldest shallna get away with what he's done. Ye may have escaped punishment for your sins, but he won't. Live with that, Robert Storey."

Pulse pounding, he left the man who had given him life to mull the consequences of his sin alone. His mood as black as the night sky, he stormed from the house and made for the peel. But even there with the cold wind purging him, he found no comfort.

He felt hollow. The truth had not put the past to rest. It had emptied him of what little he'd had left inside him.

He longed to find comfort in Kate's arms, but Robert Storey and Duncan's guilt stood between them like a two-edged blade.

Cold and bitter, he went for his violin, then made his

way to Michael's cottage, unoccupied now that the newlyweds lodged together in the main house.

'Twas as good a place as any to sleep alone.

Catherine lay in her bed for long hours before finally accepting that Duncan's return did not mean he'd come back
to her.

Perhaps it had been too much to hope for anyway. She
should have been content that he'd made it home safely.
Yet her soul and body ached for him. She even imagined
she heard the distant, mournful sounds of his violin in the
wind.

She could not even turn to God. She'd prayed so fervently for Duncan's safe return in the past ten days, and
God had granted her petitions. How could she presume to
ask for more?

She tried to console herself with the memory of the
joy they'd shared. No matter what happened now, nothing
could take that from her. And there were many blessings
left.

A useful life, she told herself.

An empty bed, her heart said back.

The next morning, Michael caught up with Duncan just
as he entered the stable for an early ride. "I didna wish
to disturb ye last night, but there's been news of the salt.
Who took it."

After all his months of obsessing, Duncan found it
ironic that Michael's announcement stirred not even a
spark of curiosity in him. He took Rogue's reins from the
groom and led the stallion into the chilly December dawn.

"Beelzebub's knees, man," Michael protested, following. "Ye doona seem to care."

"Nae." Duncan swung into the saddle, then looked
down on his mentor. "Now that Kate's jewels have redeemed us," he said more bitterly than he intended, "what
difference does it make who stole ma salt?"

Michael gripped Duncan's shin with enough force to

assure his attention. "It matters to Amber, Duncan. I ken ye've held back betrothin' her to Wat's lad until all this was settled. Well, now it can be. Wat had nothin' to do with the raid. 'Twas Johnstones. Their agent in Denmark sold off the whole lot of our salt only a week after it went missin'."

Stung by Michael's reference to Amber, Duncan snapped, "And why has it taken so long for ye to find this out?"

Scalded by the unworthy blame in Duncan's tone, Michael abruptly withdrew his hand. "The Danes kept the whole thing quiet. Part of the deal. But Johnstones bein' Johnstones, the knaves cheated those same buyers on a subsequent trade, so word got out." He glared up at Duncan. "Ma guess would be that the Danes were hopin' ye'd take revenge for the both of ye."

"Well, they hoped wrong," Duncan rumbled, his conscience stung by Michael's reminder of Amber's betrothal. "I shall write to Wat and settle the match for Amber. She'll be properly dowered. But as soon as that's done, I ride out again."

Michael sighed. "Where to this time?"

Duncan wished he knew. But until he could put the demons of his own and Kate's past to rest, he could not bear to stay here. "I doona ken. And I doona ken when I'll be back." He kicked Rogue to a gallop and made for open country, hoping he could outrun reality at least for a little while.

Three days after that, Catherine was helping Lucas with breakfast in the kitchen when Michael, his face grave, entered bearing in one hand a sealed letter with a cut through it, and an ornate silver dagger in the other.

She froze, recognizing the weapon immediately as one Papa had given Charles.

Michael proffered the message and the dagger. "Darby found these pinned outside the gate at dawn." His usually kind eyes were clouded with misgiving. " 'Tis addressed to ye."

The cold ache in the pit of Catherine's stomach escalated to a resurrected sense of impending doom. "Michael, I have nothing to do with this," she told him. "You must believe me."

She could see he didn't. "Have a care, Ladykate," he cautioned her. "Doona repay our trust wi' treachery."

"You are my family now," she said with absolute conviction. "I would never betray you."

He stood there in silence, clearly waiting for her to open the letter. But something inside her warned against facing the contents under his scrutiny.

"Pray, excuse me. I shall get to the bottom of this." She left the kitchen and hurried to her room.

Once there, she locked the door behind her, then with shaking hands laid the letter and the dagger onto the table. She sat beside them for long minutes before she mustered the courage to break the seal and open the message.

Rusty ink scribed the contents in Charles's familiar hand. Recognizing the color as that of blood, Catherine slammed her eyes shut and fought to quell the nausea that gripped her. A message written in blood. Was there to be no end to the horrors her stepbrother visited upon her?

Two deep breaths. Three. Four.

But no amount of delay would change what was, so she steeled herself and opened her eyes to read:

Sister,
I am being held by a notorious brigand, one Kinmont
Willie, who demands a ransom for my life, else he will
kill me when next the sun rises. Come alone and tell
no one, or he says he will slay the children one by
one, even if it takes ten years.

Not the children! Catherine's hands began to shake so hard she had to lay the letter to the table and brace herself to go on.

*Bring a ransom of a hundred pounds to the large elm
by the river at midnight. You will be told where to find
me. Catherine, I beg you, have mercy and comply.*

> *Your loving brother,*
> *Charles*

Loving brother, indeed.

Charles was one thing. He had sown the seeds of
treachery that might now be bearing bitter fruit. But Catherine could not risk the children. The threat was all too
plausible. She'd heard of Kinmont Willie. His ruthlessness was notorious, even among the reivers, and it was
common knowledge he bore no love for Duncan.

Rereading the note, she shuddered with revulsion.

Dared she risk it?

Dared she not?

Annanlea's guards were vigilant about keeping invad-
ers out, but escape from inside should be easy enough.
There was rope aplenty in the stable, and she knew just
where and when the lookouts made their rounds.

Could she trust this, though? Anything to do with
Charles was suspect. What if this was a trap, her stepbrother's way of luring her beyond the safety of Annanlea
so he could finish her off at last?

If only Duncan were here. But he wasn't. He'd told
Aunt Brigit not to look for him for at least a week.

Michael?

He would never let her go alone. Nor would Aunt Brigit. And Papa was still far too weak even to be told of
this latest threat.

Catherine sat slumped at the table, torn between her
love for the children and her suspicion of Charles. Ultimately love won out, as it always had with her.

Two emeralds would more than make the ransom, and
she would arm herself with a brace of Duncan's pistols.

The rest was in God's hands.

Catherine chose a deliberately indirect route to the river, keeping low along brush and hedge so no one could see her. She'd left as soon as it was well dark, wanting plenty of time to scout the meeting place in advance.

Getting down the barnekin hadn't been easy, but her gloves had taken the worst of the rope's punishment. In deference to speed and practicality, she'd worn her old clothes and shabby cape, leaving all but two of her jewels behind. Her sole task now was to avoid capture until she discovered what she'd gotten herself into.

Nervous, she checked again to make certain the emeralds were secure beside Charles's dagger, then readjusted the loaded pistols in her belt. She hadn't counted on the handguns' being so heavy, and wondered yet again if she'd have the strength to take a decent aim. But it was too late to worry about that now.

Heaven smiled, raising a stiff breeze that gusted toward her as she worked her way to the giant elm. But even with the wind to mask her progress, her every step sounded as loud to her as the clumping of some great bull.

She did not know what time it was when at last she found a discreet spot to lie in wait, but she judged it to be about ten. Adjusted to the moonless night, she peered at the dark masses by the river and strained for the slightest sound.

So she was caught completely unprepared when the cold muzzle of a pistol pressed into the flesh behind her ear. "Sister, dear. I knew you'd come."

Charles.

Catherine went rigid. She knew she should have been frightened, but all she felt was anger, not just for what

Charles had done to her, but for what he'd done to Papa. "So there is no Kinmont Willie."

"Oh, there is a Kinmont Willie," he said almost brightly. "He just hasn't anything to do with this." Charles always had loved to gloat.

Catherine listened to the night but discerned nothing besides her stepbrother and the nearby whicker of his horse. With exquisite care and slowness, she worked to cock the pistol beneath her cape, then ease it from behind her belt. "And your assassin, the archer?" she prodded, hoping he would tell her something she could use to end that threat.

"Oh, yes. Him." She did not have to see him to know he was smiling that arrogant, unpleasant sneer of his. "I'm afraid I had to kill him," he said as easily as he might have announced squashing a louse. "As your presence here attests, the man was incompetent. Yet he wanted me to pay him. Now I ask you, is that any way to do business?" He snorted. "He left me no choice. I couldn't very well let him live after he threatened to carry tales."

So that was why there had been no further attacks after the race.

A strong gust buffeted the underbrush around them, raising a swirl of dried leaves that sounded heavy with movement. Catherine froze. Was someone out there? But when the wind died, so did her hopes, for all fell silent.

Charles leaned in closer, his breath sending chills of disgust down the side of her neck. "The irony is, dear sister, that thanks to you, I've finally found something I'm good at. Something I love." An obscene kiss to her ear preceded his moist whisper. "Killing." He drew back, but only slightly. "And you were my first." A familiar petulance crept into his voice. "At least, you were supposed to be. I do not appreciate the trouble you've caused Mother and me by surviving that little swim."

She'd known he was selfish and cruel, but now she realized with growing panic that her stepbrother possessed no mechanism of conscience at all. Her only chance for survival lay in the hope that his greed outweighed his madness.

"I brought the ransom, Charles," she said, forcing a steadiness she did not feel into her voice. "Two of my mother's emeralds." Which both of them knew he could take from her after he'd killed her. "But there's more," she hastened to add. "Something that should make you very happy."

"Now what could you possibly offer, Catherine, that would make me happy, besides your death?"

"River House and all its holdings. What you and Willa have wanted all along."

He twisted the pistol's muzzle into her flesh. "A single shot," he purred, "and it's mine anyway."

"Nay, Charles." Now it was Catherine's turn to gloat. "Papa knows what you and Willa have done. All of it."

"I don't believe you." Alarmed, he grabbed her hair and jerked her head back. "He had no way to find you."

"Pastor Braithwaite read my note before he gave it to Willa. He told Papa where to find me." Heart pounding, she no longer feared he would pull the trigger right away. Charles was getting too much pleasure toying with her. If she was to escape with her life, she had to use that to her advantage. "Papa is safe inside Annanlea even now. And he's not the only one who knows the truth. So does my husband. And those who witnessed the signing of my new will. That too is safe inside Annanlea."

"Nay!" Charles snatched her roughly to her feet with the same strength he'd shown on the *Dere*. "You're lying!"

Catherine took advantage of the opportunity to bring the pistol beneath her cape to the ready, gripping it with both hands. But could she point it at her stepbrother and pull the trigger, even with her own life at stake? Praying she wouldn't have to find out, she faced him squarely. "There's no need for trouble between us any longer, Charles. Kill me, and River House goes directly to Hal." Sensing that any show of fear would only feed his madness, she let her anger warm the tremor from her voice. "Let me go, and I will sign River House and all its lands over to Papa," she lied. "That leaves you first in line to inherit."

He hesitated as the logic of her hastily concocted fiction sank in. Distracted at last, he lowered the hand holding his pistol. "Damn your scheming eyes, you daughter of a she-dog!" he shouted, his adolescent voice breaking. Furious, he stomped an erratic pattern in the dried grass, spewing curses as he went.

Catherine took great, gasping breaths, beginning to think her bluff might work.

But just when she allowed herself to hope she had succeeded, his steps quickened and his oaths grew louder and filthier, sharpened by an ominous note of hysteria. He was pushing himself over the edge, and that would leave her with only one way to stop him.

With shaking hands, she extended her pistol and brought it to bear on her brother. "Put down your weapon, Charles. You've won. River House will be yours, but you must let me go."

Snapping to brittle attention, he halted side-on to her with his pistol aimed rock steady toward her chest. "At this point, sister, River House seems far less appealing than killing you."

She saw the powder flash from his barrel, then the puff of smoke. What seemed like seconds passed before she heard the report and a painless impact flattened her with breath-stealing force, knocking her unfired weapon from her hands.

I commend my spirit into Your hands, oh Lord.

A harsh shout shattered the vacuum of silence that followed. "Over there!"

Duncan?

Catherine's spirit leapt with hope.

"Light the brands!" His voice again, closer.

Please God, let it be him!

The night exploded with riders, but Charles did not

even notice. Oblivious to everything but finishing her off, he scooped up her pistol, then stood at her feet, taking deadly aim by the light of the advancing torches.

She ordered her body to move, to get away, but it did not respond. She couldn't even catch her breath.

"Goodbye, Catherine," he sneered. "I've had enough of you."

"Duncan!" her heart cried out within her, anguished by the separation to come.

This time she heard the shot, but did not see the flash or smoke. Her eyes closed reflexively.

Strange. Again, she felt no pain, but now there wasn't even an impact.

Had God decided to grant her a peaceful passing?

Duncan, Duncan . . .

Then Charles fell atop her, slack-mouthed, releasing a white-hot stab of agony from her shoulder. A piercing scream passed her lips at last, but it wasn't born of pain; it erupted from the horror of her brother's dead weight atop her. She clenched her eyes shut and kept on screaming until her voice seized to a thready rasp.

Light flickered red through her closed lids. Pounding footsteps closed in from every side, but one sound stood out from all the rest. "Kate!"

Duncan! He'd found her.

Or had she gone as mad as Charles, only imagining what she wished was true?

Catherine struggled again in vain to call for her husband, but the weight of her brother's body made it impossible. Hateful warmth soaked through her clothes and rolled along her skin beneath like a deadly asp. Hers, or his? She could not tell.

Her skin felt clammy and her stomach roiled. Was this how it felt to die? Suddenly afraid, she wished Duncan's arms could be around her just once more. She shifted slightly, and Charles's face rolled against her cheek, the smell of his skin and open mouth obscenely familiar, shoving her to the edge of hysteria.

Abruptly, the grisly burden rolled off her, and Duncan knelt to catch her up into his arms. "Kate. Dear God. Speak to me."

Thanks be to God!

Catherine drank in his blessed, anguished face. She could die content now, safe in his arms.

Beside them, a grim Wat lifted his torch.

Duncan saw the blood that soaked Kate's clothes and staggered. He had witnessed far graver wounds, but none that struck him so deeply. Her lips shaped his name, but no sound came forth. She stared up at him with tear-filled eyes that were dull with pain and fear.

"Nae, Kate. Nae." He could not lose her. Realizing how much he loved her only now when she lay broken in his arms, Duncan crushed her to his aching heart.

"Ouch!" Pain would find a voice, it seemed, where none other could be summoned. "Gremlins and grind-stones, Duncan! My shoulder," she protested with vigor. "Are ye trying to finish me off?" Her strong complaint was the most blessed sound he had ever heard.

Wat barked a surprised laugh. "Ach. Listen to 'er, will ye?" He prodded Duncan. "Ease her back, lad, and let me take a look." The outlaw inspected her torso, then her shoulder. "One through the shoulder and out clean. Too high for the lung, God be praised."

Stepping back, Wat used his foot to roll Charles's body faceup. "Most of the blood is his, I'll marry. Ye laid one through his heart, Duncan."

Catherine buried her face onto the shelter of Duncan's chin with a spasmodic sob.

" 'Tis over, Kate. You're safe," he murmured hoarsely, his head tipped back in overwhelming relief. He would not have to live without her. That indeed would have been a curse. But now there was hope.

"She's fine, Duncan," Wat blustered. "Fine."

Her entire left side afire with pain, Catherine glared at him askance. "Speak for yourself, sirrah," she snapped. "This does not feel like fine to me!"

Grinning, the outlaw cocked a shaggy brow. "See there? Still spittin' vinegar. Just fine."

She saw the ghost of a smile flicker across Duncan's taut lips. After a deep, cleansing breath, he whistled Rogue to his side, then ordered, "Down."

Obediently, the stallion knelt and settled awkwardly to the ground.

Catherine curled into her husband's strong embrace. "Take me home, Duncan. Back to Annanlea."

"Aye." He managed to straddle Rogue without jostling her too much, but when the horse lurched to his feet, she could not suppress a moan of agony. It settled to a bearable ache once they were on their way at a cautious pace, but after only a few moments of relief, the heat and pain grew steadily stronger.

Duncan held her as if she were made of Venetian glass. "Faith, Catherine. When I saw ye lyin' there, covered in blood, ma own heart nigh unto burst with rage and grief. If only I'd gotten to him before he fired—"

"You were there when it mattered, Duncan," she forced out. Her shoulder was beginning to blaze, and every jolt threatened her self-control. "And not a second too soon."

He nuzzled his lips against her hair. "Another second, and I'd have lost ye." He made no effort to conceal the anguish in his voice. "Kate, I couldna have borne it."

Duncan cared for her! Despite her pain, Catherine felt a soothing swell of joy.

But his tender mood abruptly gave way to scolding. "What in God's good earth were ye doin' out there alone, Kate?" he demanded.

Catherine didn't feel much like talking, but she supposed she did owe him an explanation. "I was trying to protect the children. A ransom note threatened their lives unless I came alone. What choice did I have?"

"Did ye ken 'twas from Charles?"

"Yes, but he claimed Kinmont Willie held him hostage and would harm the children unless I ransomed him."

"Ye kent 'twas that double-dealin' stepbrother, yet still

ye went?" he chided. "Alone? Did ye *want* to die, then, Kate?"

"Nay." The pain was almost more than she could bear. She clutched at Duncan's sleeve with her uninjured hand. "Doona scold me, Duncan. I hurt."

"We'll have ye home anon, ma bonnie Catherine," he soothed, his blue eyes dark with worry when he met hers. "Aunt Brigit will have ye cleaned up and comfortable in no time."

"Then you shall play for me. Your music can chase the pain away."

"Aye, ma lass," he murmured, kissing her hair. "So it shall. And I'll play just for ye every night."

Catherine nodded and turned her face into his throat to hide her tears—tears of gratitude and tears of grief, pain, and remorse.

She shouldn't have gone out alone. If she'd only waited, Duncan might have safely apprehended Charles. Now her stepbrother was dead.

Dead. "Poor Papa," she murmured.

Duncan's body tensed, as did his voice. "The sins of the father bore bitter fruit in Charles."

"But not in Hal, Duncan." She drew back slightly, glad for the bracing night air. "Hal is Papa's, too, and he's strong and kind and good. Your half brother."

"And I suppose ye'll be wantin' me to meet this Hal someday."

"Yes." Catherine inhaled deeply, then gasped when it released a stabbing pain in her shoulder. "I know you'll like each other."

Duncan's arms tightened almost imperceptibly as he changed the subject. "Ye and your blasted plots," he grumbled. "Runnin' off into the night alone and getting' shot. There's na way around it this time, woman. I'll have to beat ye, of a certain."

"Ye and what army?" she retorted. Hurt though she was, Catherine had a few questions of her own. "Speaking of armies, how did you and Wat's army happen to be here?"

"We were trackin' your murderous brother. Where d'ye think I've been all this time?"

"How was I supposed to know? You did not vouchsafe to tell me," she retorted, almost overcome with pain and relief. "I thought you'd left because you couldn't stand to be around me after I tried to save Papa."

"Ah, Ladykate." Duncan shook his head. "How could I blame ye for that? Nae. What I couldna face was ma shame. I raised ma blade above ye to—"

Catherine pressed her fingers to his lips, silencing him. "You didn't do it. That's what matters. A lesser man would have given in to such rage, but you showed mercy. I'm proud of you for that."

He paused as the truth of her words sank in. "Ach, Kate. Doona ever risk yourself again," he rasped, his voice thick with emotion. "Can't ye tell I love ye, lass?"

Catherine did not trust her ears. "What did you say?"

"I love ye," he exclaimed, annoyed. "There. 'Tis said. Now doona try to make me say it again."

With that simple profession, all the broken pieces of Catherine's life shaped themselves into a picture of perfect provision. Suddenly she saw how everything had worked to bring them to this wondrous moment. Her troubles with Charles. The shipwreck. Duncan's stolen salt. His precious motherless children. Catherine's secret treasure. Their reluctant marriage. Her family's betrayal. Papa's dreadful reckoning. All of it.

He weaves perfection even from our sin, Angus had told her.

This was the miracle, the joy they had found in each other amid the careful pattern of chaos.

"I love you, too, Duncan Maxwell," Catherine said through her pain. "I love you, too."

"Good. Then 'tis settled. We'll have bairns of our own aplenty, Kate. And nae more of your plots."

"Bairns?" Her heart was so full, she could almost believe it.

"Aye, bairns," her husband murmured, his lips to the top of her head and his hand caressing her hair. "Or not. Either way, we'll wear ourselves out tryin'."

"I like the sound of that." The torches of Annanlea danced before them, its gates open wide with the promise of safe haven.

Catherine looked up into Duncan Maxwell's magnificent, resolute face and knew that it wouldn't matter whether they had children of their own or not. His boisterous, lively family was blessing enough to fill the years. And there would be more. Joy. And tumult. Adventures. And danger. Abundance. And loss. Happiness. And toil.

"There is one thing you can do for me, though," she said to him.

Duncan eyed her with healthy skepticism. "And what would that be?"

"You can be *my* hostage for a while, Duncan Maxwell," she said brazenly. "At least when we're alone together."

Duncan's laugh had the sound of happy release. "Aye, then, Ladykate. When we're alone, I shall be your hostage. For a while."

"I love you, Duncan Maxwell," she said again, reveling in the comfort it gave her even amid her pain.

"And I love ye, Catherine Maxwell," he murmured back. "There. I've said it. Now doona try to make me say it again."

Catherine smiled and snuggled deeper into his embrace. "Nay, sir. Remember, you are my hostage now. And so I bid ye say ye love me often, as long as 'tis true."

"Then ye shall hear it every day until ye die," he whispered, and Catherine closed her eyes, believing it with every resurrected fragment of her long-lost heart.

AUTHOR'S NOTE

America's Wild West would seem tame to the Elizabethan inhabitants of the Scottish and English border regions, called marches instead of counties at this time in history. Blood feuds, cattle rustling, savage raids, arson, kidnapping, treachery, blackmail, political corruption, and extortion were everyday components of border life. The border reivers, or Steel Bonnets as they were often called in the sixteenth century, made common practice of ransoming captured enemies for profit, a practical way to limit casualties in the endless tribal wars while generating goods or funds in an area with so little arable land.

Though most of the characters in this book are fictional, Auld Wat (Walter Scott) and his beautiful wife, Mary, really existed. Local legend and contemporary records provided the anecdotes about them I have included. Described as a Falstaffian character, Auld Wat was a direct ancestor of Sir Walter Scott, the famous romantic author of *Ivanhoe*. I just love tidbits like that, don't you?

*Determined to win back her family's castle,
she never planned on loving the enemy . . .*

Highland Princess

HAYWOOD SMITH

AWARD-WINNING AUTHOR OF *DANGEROUS GIFTS*

With her brothers imprisoned in their enemy's dungeons,
Princess Bera makes a daring bid to free them, disguising
herself to enter the enemy's lair—only to discover a dangerous and unexpected foe: a golden-haired knight of iron
and ice, so cold she cannot fathom how he heats her blood
to molten desire. Soon, passion will expose their deepest
secrets in a world where trust can be a double-edged
sword. And for Curran who is determined to win Bera's
heart, he must challenge a princess to her destiny . . . and
a love to its greatest battle.

"Smith delivers intelligent, sensitive historical
romance for readers who expect more from the
genre." —*Publishers Weekly*

AVAILABLE WHEREVER BOOKS ARE SOLD
FROM ST. MARTIN'S PAPERBACKS

Haywood Smith

"Haywood Smith delivers intelligent, sensitive historical romance for readers who expect more from the genre."
—*Publishers Weekly*

SHADOWS IN VELVET

Orphan Anne Marie must enter the gilded decadence of the French court as the bride of a mysterious nobleman, only to be shattered by a secret from his past that could embroil them both in a treacherous uprising...

SECRETS IN SATIN

Amid the turmoil of a dying monarch, newly widowed Elizabeth, Countess of Ravenwold, is forced by royal command to marry a man she has hardened her heart to—and is drawn into a dangerous game of intrigue and a passionate contest of wills.

AVAILABLE WHEREVER BOOKS ARE SOLD
FROM ST. MARTIN'S PAPERBACKS

Dangerous Gifts

HAYWOOD SMITH

AWARD-WINNING AUTHOR OF *DAMASK ROSE*

ENGLAND, 1097. Alone, penniless and desperate, Claire finds sanctuary with an aging village healer, Nonna. Claire's newfound peace is shattered when Palmer Freeman, Nonna's long-lost son, returns from the Crusades, bitter and broken in body and spirit—only to find a "wife" he never knew existed. Mistrustful and wary, Palmer and Claire agree to share the one place they both call home, as Nonna's illness draws them together in unexpected ways. But Claire's tragic past and Palmer's ceaseless torment threaten the love they most desire, until a bold act of courage offers love's greatest miracle—the gift of healing.

"Smith delivers intelligent, sensitive historical romance for readers who expect more from the genre."
—*Publishers Weekly*

"Haywood Smith always provides her fans with an exciting, extremely powerful historical romance."
—*Affaire de Coeur*

AVAILABLE WHEREVER BOOKS ARE SOLD
FROM ST. MARTIN'S PAPERBACKS

DG 1/01

ROSECLIFFE 3/00